FIELDS OF
FIRE

BY MARKO KLOOS

Frontlines

Terms of Enlistment

Lines of Departure

Angles of Attack

Chains of Command

Measures of Absolution (A Frontlines Kindle novella)

"Lucky Thirteen" (A Frontlines Kindle short story)

FIELDS OF
FIRE

MARKO KLOOS

47N♦RTH

Text copyright © 2017 by Marko Kloos
All rights reserved.

Published by 47North, Seattle

www.apub.com

Amazon, the Amazon logo, and 47North are trademarks of Amazon.com, Inc., or its affiliates.

ISBN-13: 9781503940710
ISBN-10: 1503940713

Cover design by Megan Haggerty

Cover illustrated by Maciej Rebisz

Printed in the United States of America

FIELDS OF
FIRE

CHAPTER 1

——— RUN, INTERRUPTED ———

The Lanky in my gun sights is gigantic, far bigger than any I've ever seen before. It fills the optic of my M-90's sight completely, even at zero magnification and even though I am still a few hundred meters away. It walks toward me unhurriedly, with slow steps that sound like artillery rounds exploding on the red soil. With every step, the Lanky's three-toed feet send up clouds of dust.

I aim the targeting reticle at the center of the Lanky's chest and squeeze the trigger, but it feels like the pull weight of it has increased a hundredfold. I press with all the force my finger can muster, but it moves backward with agonizing slowness. The Lanky in front of me, a hundred meters tall at least, takes another step that cuts the distance between us in half. Finally, the trigger on my M-90 clicks past the release point, and the shot breaks. Instead of the thundering boom and heavy recoil of my rifle's anti-Lanky rounds, the shot sounds muffled and feeble, and the rifle barely moves against my shoulder. The warhead flies out and hits the Lanky somewhere in the vast expanse of its upper torso, but I know the round is ineffective even before I see the little puff of the impact. I cycle the rifle's bolt manually to feed a new round and fire again, even though it's futile. I empty the magazine, one feeble round after the other. The Lanky doesn't seem to notice them. It's like I'm throwing pebbles against a mountainside.

Then the Lanky is right in front of me, towering into the gray sky, its wide cranial shield swinging from left to right as the creature turns its head. It swings one of its spindly arms and swats me aside casually and without effort. The world tumbles wildly in my helmet display as I am flung violently backwards.

I know this isn't reality because when I slam into the rock a few hundred meters away, the impact should have killed me instantly, crushed me like a bug on the polyplast windshield of a hydrobus, battle armor or not. Instead, I slide to the ground, fully awake and aware, and I feel no pain at all. My right hand still holds part of my rifle, but most of it is shattered. I throw away the piece of the gun I'm still holding and get to my feet.

The Lanky pays no further attention to me. It walks off to my left with huge, slow steps. As big as it is, it's moving away so fast that an ATV at full throttle would have a hard time catching up, even though the creature isn't moving in a particular rush. Following an urge, I run after the Lanky, not knowing what exactly I'll do to stop it once I catch up to it.

The Lanky walks away from me with long, thundering strides. In front of me, the rocky ridge I'm standing on slopes down and leads into a wide valley. The sky is the color of dirty steel, the soil the pale ochre of Mars dirt. I come to a stop at the edge of the ridge and take in the scenery below with astonishment. The Lanky, already a kilometer away, is striding toward a town, which is the inadequate name we gave to their settlement structures. The Lanky "towns" are vast, interconnected latticework edifices that look a lot like coral reefs, impossibly fragile looking for something built by such enormous beings. In front of me, the entire valley is filled with Lanky structures. They cover the Martian soil for square kilometer after square kilometer, as far as my helmet optics can see. In the open spaces between the hundreds—thousands—of Lanky shelters, I can see Lankies moving around, alone and in groups, many hundreds of them, more than I've ever seen together.

The Lanky that swept me aside continues down the slope toward the cluster of Lanky buildings. Halfway down the incline, it stops and turns around. The massive head swivels in my direction until it appears that the Lanky is looking right at me. We regard each other for a long moment. Then the creature lets out a wail that is deafening even from over a kilometer away. I've heard that wail, or versions of it, on the battlefield and in my dreams hundreds of times, and it's unsettling every time, as if it triggers some sort of instinctive response in the primitive parts of our human brains, the bits that make us scared when we're alone in the dark without a light nearby. The wail rolls over the landscape like an aural tsunami, washing over me and reverberating from the hillside behind me until it sounds like it comes from every direction at once. It goes on for what seems like a minute, then fades slowly and ends on a single note that sounds mournful, like a funeral dirge.

Down in the valley, the other Lankies take up the call and reply with their own alien voices, first hundreds and then thousands, maybe tens of thousands. I can feel their calls through the ground and the soles of my boots, and in the air all around, as if every air molecule in the atmosphere is moved by the sonic energy of this overwhelming alien chorus. It seems that everyone on this planet should be able to hear this cacophony, which sounds weirdly harmonious despite being made up of tens of thousands of discordant voices. The chorus goes on for a long time before it dies down slowly, one voice at a time.

The silence that follows is ominous and far more unnatural to my ears than what came before. I look up to the skies, dark gray and empty, and feel a slowly swelling dread seizing my heart. Then there's a new sound, faint in the wind but undeniably present and growing with every second, a sharp slicing sound that's just short of a whistle. Just like Lanky calls, I've heard this noise in the atmosphere before, and I know what it portends. I wasn't afraid when the Lanky slammed me aside on his way past me, or when tens of thousands of them started their unearthly wailing, but I am afraid now, scared to death of what I know is coming down through the atmosphere. I don't see the warheads, but I can feel their malevolent presence in the air and in my bones. The end of the world is coming, and there's nothing that can stop it, no shelter deep enough to hide in, no creature tall and strong enough to survive what is about to come.

In the last few moments before the detonation, there's a ripping sound in the air, small and dense objects displacing air as they streak toward the ground at hypersonic speed. Then the valley in front of me, all the Lankies and their elaborate latticework structures, disappears in a brilliantly, blindingly white flash, a new sun rising into existence right here in front of me on the surface of this planet. I feel the searing heat radiate out from the explosion instantly, and it's like standing right in front of the thrust nozzles of a fusion rocket. I should be incinerated already, reduced to my component atoms in a nanosecond, but my body holds together as the flash and heat from the nuclear explosion wash over me. I stay in one piece long enough for the sound and the shock wave of the multi-megaton nuclear burst to reach me up here on the plateau. It's impossibly loud, a world-ending crash, sound with so much physical force behind it that it might as well be a solid. But I can still hear and see, still feel the heart thundering in my chest, even as the shock wave lifts me off the ground, squeezes the air out of my lungs, and flings me into the air. I hit something solid with my head, and the sudden and unexpected sensation floods through me and yanks me out of the dream.

I wake up on the floor of the bedroom. The side of my head is throbbing with a dull ache. My heart is still hammering in my chest, and I roll onto my back and look at the ceiling for a minute or two until my heart rate has come down to a reasonable level. I'm wearing nothing but military-issue skivvies and an undershirt. The environmental controls in the building are turned off at night to save energy, and there's a cool fall breeze coming in through the filter screens in front of the open windows, but I can feel sweat trickling down my back. I check the chrono projection on the ceiling: 0438.

I get up slowly and without much enthusiasm. In the bed next to me, Halley is asleep. She's taking deep and regular breaths, so I know her dreams—if she has them—are a little less dramatic than mine. She has a med injector strapped to her arm that monitors her state and keeps her asleep with targeted injections. It's been over a month since we returned from the Leonidas system, and the bruises on her face and side still haven't fully faded.

The upstairs guest room at Chief Kopka's place is tiny, maybe half the size of the already-cramped quarters we shared on Luna in the year before the Leonidas mission, but it's down here on Earth in civilian country, not on a military installation. It's also only a fifteen-minute maglev ride away from Homeworld Defense Air Station Burlington, which is where Halley is going to rehab therapy every other day. She survived the ejection from her disintegrating drop ship, but the titanium clamshell capsule of the pilot-ejection pod closed prematurely and wrecked the left side of Halley's body pretty thoroughly. Her arm, leg, and hip were shattered, she suffered multiple internal injuries, and her skull now has titanium implanted in it. I know that she's still in a fair bit of pain, but I also know that the injuries don't hurt her half as much as having her flight status pulled. When it comes to shrugging off physical pain, my wife is the toughest person I know. I hate to see her hurt, but I'm more worried about what her idle status is doing to her head.

I walk over to the bathroom, close the door behind me, and turn on the water in the sink to splash my face. The water here in Vermont still tastes a little wrong to me. It's as clean as it can be—there's a pump in the basement of the property that pulls the drinking water right out of the water table in the ground below the town—but I've had reprocessed and filtered water all my life, first in the PRCs and then in the service, and my palate is still primed to it.

There's a window next to the sink, and I open it to let in more of the cool fall air. The street outside is quiet. There are no pedestrians or hydrocars out and about at this hour, and the upper-middle-class 'burber town of Liberty Falls completely lacks the nighttime soundtrack of the PRCs. The first time I slept down here, the lack of constant low-level background noise was so disconcerting to me that it took me half the night to fall asleep because I jumped at every little sound.

When I get back to the bed, Halley is awake. She is blinking at me sleepily, her head surrounded by a self-adjusting inflatable pillow. There's a big bruise running down the left side of her face from her hairline all the way to her jawline. It was black at first, then faded to blue green, and has now settled into an unhealthy-looking yellow and brown.

"Hey," I say. "Sorry if I woke you up."

"'S okay," Halley mumbles. She blinks up at the holographic time display on the ceiling. "Jeez. You going back to sleep?"

"I don't think so," I say. "Gonna go for a run."

"At this hour?"

"It's perfect. No civvies to avoid."

"Okay," Halley replies. "But you're on your own on that one."

The med injector on her arm lets out a soft beep. She reaches over with her right hand and pushes the override sensor that prevents the unit from putting her back to sleep with a dose of painkillers.

"Why are you up? Shit dreams?"

"Shit dreams," I confirm.

"You okay?"

"I'm fine," I say. "I'll go run a bit and clear my head."

"Okay." Halley looks at me with concern. "Be back for breakfast, or I'll call in the Rapid Reaction Force."

"Affirmative, ma'am."

———

The air outside is pleasantly cool and clean. It's late fall, and the nighttime temperatures have been dipping below freezing for a week or two now, but I like running in the cold air. I run down Liberty Falls' Main Street, past the shop fronts that are closed at this hour, exhaling little puffs of condensating breath with every step. I'm running in my camouflaged Combat Dress Uniform trousers and an undershirt, with a sidearm strapped to my belt and my personal data pad in the hip pocket. Technically, I'm supposed to carry my alert bag everywhere I go when I am not on duty, but it's hard to run with twenty-odd pounds of lightweight armor and automatic personal defense weapon slung over my shoulder.

I've always hated running, but somehow I've grown used to it—maybe even fond of it—in the last month, ever since we got back from Leonidas. It's what I do to clear my head when I can't sleep, when I want to be by myself for a while. As a side benefit, I'm also back to the weight I was before I took up the drill-instructor job at Orem for a year, where I got a little flabby on garrison chow.

As often as I have puffed up and down these streets, it's still a little surreal to be out here alone in the dark. In a PRC, this sort of thing would get me mugged or killed within ten minutes, but the 'burbers here in Liberty Falls are running a tidy, safe town. I usually see a police patrol out here on my run, and this night doesn't break the streak. When I'm just past the library in the center of town, a police hydrocar glides past me on the street. I glance over to see the cop giving me an appraising look. Then he raises his hand in greeting, and I wave back curtly. The police car continues down Main Street, the electric engine so quiet that I only hear the tires whispering on the asphalt.

Right behind the town hall, there's a road that veers off and goes up a hill. I've not yet made it up that half-kilometer incline without stopping for breath, but I get a little further each morning. Today I get more than halfway up the hill before my legs start getting heavy. This may just be the day I beat the hill and make it to the residential neighborhood at the top.

I'm three-quarters of the way up, winded but still in fighting shape, when my PDP chirps a message alert. It's the three-short, three-long, three-short pattern reserved for Priority One emergencies. I stop and catch my breath for a few moments. Then I fish the PDP out of my leg pocket while eyeing the crest of the hill, just a few hundred meters away, a few more minutes of huffing and puffing up a ten-degree slope.

Tomorrow, I guess.

The screen of my PDP shows only a short message, but the content serves to give me a healthy boost of adrenaline that makes my fatigue all but vanish.

"LANKY INCURSION IN PROGRESS—ALL OFF-DUTY PERSONNEL REPORT TO DESIGNATED RMAP AT ONCE— THIS IS NOT A DRILL."

RMAPs are the regional military assembly points, the closest bases with air/space fields to wherever we're spending our liberty or leave. For me and Halley, that's Homeworld Defense Air Station Burlington, fifteen minutes away. I slip my PDP back into my leg pocket and start running back down the hill.

Back at the chief's place, Halley is out of bed and half-dressed when I gallop up the stairs and into the guest bedroom above the restaurant. I peel off my sweat-soaked T-shirt and toss it aside, then grab a fresh one off the dresser.

"Breakfast will have to wait," I say.

"I got the alert," she says. "I'm coming, too."

"Like hell you are. You're in rehab and off flight status until the doc clears you."

"Try and stop me, *Lieutenant*," she says. "Would have had to go out to Burlington today anyway for the next physical-terrorism session. I might as well put on a flight suit just in case the shit hits the fan and they happen to have more birds than pilots on hand."

I know better than to argue about this with Halley, who is already zipping up her suit. I want her to return to bed and accept the reality that she's in no shape for a fight, that no wing commander is going to put her behind the controls of a drop ship as long as the military doc has her grounded. But I know that I don't have the right to make that call for her. So even though I don't want to, I take her shoulder holster from its place on the dresser and help her put it on. She winces a little when she threads her left arm through the harness, but then the holster is in place, and she's dressed and armed for battle for the first time since she came home to the solar system with me a month ago on a trauma cradle in the sick bay of NACS *Portsmouth*. She gives the holstered pistol under her arm a quick pat with her right hand.

"Feels good," she says.

"They haven't made an incursion in a month," I say. "I was hoping we wouldn't see another one of those things until Mars."

"Let's just hope it's a single ship and not their whole goddamn fleet," Halley replies. "It would suck having our shit jumped right before we pulled the trigger on our own offensive."

I grab my alert bag and sling it over my shoulder. Halley's bag is on the floor on her side of the bed, and I walk over and pick hers up as well.

"I guess we'll see in twenty minutes," I say. "Let's go. We can put on the hardshell and load the PDWs on the train."

When we step outside, we run into my mother and Chief Kopka, who have arrived to open the restaurant for the day. Mom looks alarmed when she sees us both coming out of the door with our gear bags and serious expressions.

"What's going on, Andrew?"

"Emergency alert," I reply. "We have to report to Burlington. There's a Lanky incursion."

"How many?" Chief Kopka asks.

"No idea. We just got the alert. Heading to the base to find out. You turn on the news and sit tight. Don't forget the lockbox in your office if things get hairy."

Chief Kopka nods, his expression as grim as ours. "Be careful out there, you two. And give 'em hell."

Mom hugs Halley, who winces a little but returns the hug. Then she hugs me, which she only accomplishes halfway because of all the extra bulk strapped to my body right now, fifty pounds of armor and gear.

"I know this is what you do. But don't mind if I hate it when you go off to fight."

"That's your right, Mom," I say. "Gotta go. We'll be back. But don't keep breakfast warm for us. We may be a while."

"I'll make you two a fresh breakfast whenever you get back. Any time of the day. Just get back here, please."

I don't say good-bye anymore when I leave. We walk off toward the train station without a parting ritual. It's better to act like you're just putting your own life on hold briefly to take care of some business, and you'll be picking up the threads you put aside once you get back, in a little while. If I gave a heartfelt good-bye every time I left, one that matched the real danger we faced, I'd have no emotions left.

On the maglev train, we just have enough time to put on our light armor kits and load our personal defense weapons, the short little submachine guns we carry in our alert bags to have something with a little more punch than a pistol. The train whisks us from Liberty Falls to Burlington in less than fifteen minutes—faster than usual because it's a military requisition running outside the regular schedule. We check and recheck each other's gear, even though there isn't much to fasten and calibrate compared to regular battle armor, but it's something for the hands and brain to do on autopilot, and it helps to fight the anxiety we both feel. Other than the first alert, there have been no further updates over MilNet, so our brains are coming up with a wide variety of possible scenarios, everything from a single Lanky ship to a full-scale assault by the Lanky fleet currently amassing around Mars. I remember my vivid dream from last night, and I hope it wasn't a ninety-six-hour glimpse into the future. I am not physically or mentally ready for that day yet.

HDAS Burlington has its own stop on the maglev line. We file out of the train along with the few dozen other corps members who answered the emergency call in the area. The security checkpoint at the base entrance outside the station is manned by half a dozen HD troopers in full battle armor, M-66 rifles at low ready. Halley and I check in to have our IDs scanned.

"A podhead officer," the lieutenant in charge of the checkpoint says when he sees my qualification ratings pop up on his screen. "Outstanding. We have a few platoons that need a drop-rated officer. Please report to the Bravo pad on the airfield; they'll assign you a bird."

"I'm going there, too," Halley says. "In case they need a pilot. I can fly anything in the inventory."

The officer of the guard scans her ID and hands it back to her. "Yes, ma'am. Sergeant Aponte, give these two officers a ride to Bravo pad, double-time."

"How many seed ships do we have incoming, Lieutenant?" Halley asks.

"None, ma'am." He looks from Halley to me and then down the line of troops checking in. "They're already here. They overran the joint base at Thule an hour ago. On Greenland. Came out of nowhere, right out of the ice."

CHAPTER 2

JOINT BASE THULE

Thirty thousand feet above Greenland's western coast, our drop-ship flight draws up in combat-descent formation, and we start our dive into a swirling vortex of ice and wind.

There's a storm above this part of the island, and from this altitude, it looks like the fury of winter made physical reality. The clouds are a steel-gray churning mass that extends from fifteen thousand feet all the way to the ground. When our drop-ship flight dips into the storm, the Hornets get instantly bounced around by the turbulent air currents. I've had many rough atmospheric entries in my podhead career, but as we careen toward the surface of Greenland in what feels like barely controlled flight, getting rattled like peas in a can, I can't recall ever having been in such violent weather before. But there are thirty junior enlisted SI and HD troopers sitting in the jump seats to either side and across the aisle from me, so I keep my face shield raised and do my best to appear unconcerned.

The tactical network is strangely quiet. I see our flight of four drop ships, a full company of troops, descending toward Joint Base Thule in the corkscrew pattern of a combat descent. There are more military flights in nearby airspace—two HD ground-attack birds coming in from the south, fifty klicks away and five thousand feet below us, and a flight of Eurocorps drop ships approaching from the interior of Greenland, still a hundred kilometers out and descending in Delta formation. But there's nothing coming from below, no tactical markers from the units that should be on and around the big joint air/space base we share with the Euros at Thule.

"Any word from the ground?" I send to the pilot.

"Negative," the HD lieutenant in the cockpit replies. "I got nothing. No comms, no active radar. AILS is out, too. This will be a fun approach in this swirly shit."

The outside camera views show nothing but blowing snow and ice. I have no directional or spatial references outside, and only my inner ear and the instrument feed from the cockpit provide the cues that we are still descending toward the surface at a twenty-degree nose-down pitch. Without a working AILS beam, the drop ship won't be able to make an automated landing on the pad at Thule, and only the pilot's skill will determine whether we make it down in one piece or become a smoking crater in the ice in a few minutes. The pilot in the cockpit isn't Halley—they wouldn't let her take charge of an HD bird—and I'm simultaneously very relieved and distraught that my wife is sitting this drop out on the flight pad at HDAS Burlington.

"Where the hell did they come from?" one of the platoon's sergeants asks on the command channel over the general comms chatter.

"The pod that crashed last month," I offer. "We chased it down and hosed the Lanky that climbed out. Pod went in the ice. There must have been a bunch more in that thing."

"They survived in the ice for a whole frickin' *month*?"

"That's what it looks like right now, Sergeant," I say.

I remember the drop from last month—the cataclysmic impact of the hull fragment, the seedpod we found on the ice a short while later, the Lanky that climbed out of the wreckage and into our gunfire, and the terrible noise when the ice gave way. The seedpod slid into a crevice in the ice that was too deep for the high-powered searchlights on the Wasp to illuminate all the way to the bottom. The Euro military took over shortly afterward, and they sanitized the crash site, but from the look of things, I'd say they failed to thoroughly check for surviving Lankies. Maybe there's no way to check for life under an ice sheet that's a kilometer thick. We've fought these things for half a decade now, and every time we go up against them, they still confound us and make us change our tactics.

"Outside air temperature is negative eighty-three Celsius," the drop ship's crew chief announces. "Negative twenty-nine on the ground, with ninety-knot winds. May want to check your heating units, or it'll be a short deployment."

I've traded the light armor kit from my alert bag for a loaner HD armor from the drop ship's armory. Greenland's environment is as unforgiving as they come on Earth, especially in early winter. My light armor has no heating elements in it, and stepping out of the drop ship in a winter storm with nothing but light laminate shell would have me turning into a combat-ineffective popsicle inside of five minutes. I toggle the test function for the heating system in my loaner armor, and a few moments later, I feel the heat from the built-in thermal elements radiate inward.

"Fuckin' Greenland," the platoon sergeant grumbles. "I thought those things didn't like the cold."

"They don't," I say. "Doesn't mean they can't survive in it, apparently. Check squads for readiness. And nobody better chamber a round until we're on the ground and clear of the bird."

"Copy that, Lieutenant. You're the expert."

The ship lurches violently to the right, then pitches down, then up again, a bouncing cork in churning rapids. Without our seat harnesses, the platoon in the hold would be flying all over the place right now. The hull of the Hornet creaks under the stress, and I find myself wondering just how much atmospheric stress these old and tired birds can endure before metal fatigue and physics see us raining out of the sky over Greenland in a loose cloud of debris.

"Visibility on the ground is going to be shit, and Lankies don't show on thermal," I tell the platoon sergeant and my squad leaders. "Once we're off the tail ramp, we form an extended firing line. Fifty meters' space between each trooper. That way we at least have TacLink share of visuals beyond our individual lines of sight. Anything comes out of the storm, you light it up without delay. This will be a short-range fight, so stay alert. And keep active transmissions to a minimum. They can sense those."

The squad leaders click back their acknowledgments one by one. The crew in the hold of the Hornet looks tense but determined. These aren't the green kids who dropped into Greenland with me almost two months ago. They're almost all HD troopers, not the battle-hardened platoon of SI space apes I'd rather have with me right now, but none of them look like they are just out of Basic, and quite a few are seasoned enlisted and NCOs who look and act like they've seen plenty of combat drops before. The new doctrine for Lanky incursions emphasizes a rapid response: go in with what you have and hit them as soon as you can, instead of wasting time waiting for just the right force composition. Everyone in the North American Commonwealth Defense Corps gets training on anti-Lanky weaponry now because everyone may end up facing them at any time.

"Showtime in three," the pilot announces. "Passing through three thousand feet. Lotta thermal signatures below."

My suit's computer shows us a few kilometers outside Joint Base Thule, the sprawling military facility we operate in cooperation with the European Union's defense force. Thule has a large drop-ship airfield and two five-thousand-meter runways that will accommodate anything with wings in the NAC arsenal. I check the sensor feeds from the drop ship's nose and see nothing but swirling snow on the optical feed. The thermal sensors show a different story. Up ahead, there are dozens of large and small fires burning in the spot where the base is hugging the northwestern coastline of Greenland.

"Make a low pass before you drop us," I send to the cockpit.

"For whatever good it'll do," the pilot replies. "Visibility is zero-zero out there."

I turn off the visual feed from the outboard cameras because they don't do anything but give me vertigo and anxiety right now. Without any visual references out there, no sky or horizon, I can't tell whether we're oriented right side up or upside down, and my inner ear is trying to convince me that it's the latter. So I focus on the world right in front of my nose again, the drop-ship cargo hold packed with thirty-six troopers under my charge.

"Sixty seconds," the pilot calls out. The red light above the tail ramp starts blinking. All around me, troopers are doing last-minute checks of their equipment.

"Firing line," I call out over the platoon channel. "Fifty-meter spacing. Weapons free as soon as your boots are on the ground. Something large moves in front of you, shoot it a lot."

I check the local TacLink for the other platoons in the air with us. They are descending slightly behind us on our portside, half a kilometer astern and poised to set down half a klick to our north. The Eurocorps drop ships are still fifty kilometers out, ten minutes or more of flight time. Right now, it's us and whoever else is left on the ground at Thule base. I toggle into the local defense channel.

"Thule base personnel on the ground, this is HD flight Burlington One-Five. We are about to go skids down at the midpoint of runway oh-eight Tango with a full platoon of infantry. Anyone down there, uplink your TacLink data and sit tight."

The TacLink transmitters in our suits are designed to connect to other suit computers in range and join the ad hoc network of whatever NAC units are on the ground, so there's no time delay in sharing information in the heat of battle. As we descend toward the runway at

Thule, there are worryingly few updates popping up small bubbles of awareness in the gray haze that is the tactical picture on my computer's data overlay.

"Got a visual on multiple fires," the pilot says.

I check the optical feed and see blots of orange through the swirling white mess outside—half a dozen large fires at least. My computer uses the visuals and does a quick overlay with the tactical map. The largest orange glow is coming from the refueling facilities next to the large drop-ship landing-pad cluster beyond the runway. But it looks like the Lankies didn't limit themselves to breaking the fuel infrastructure. If my computer's navigational bearings are correct, they've also wrecked the main barracks building and the fusion reactor that powers the whole facility. *Of course they went for the reactor. They always do.*

"Give me a count on silver bullets," I send to my squad leaders.

"Three," the reply comes back.

That's it? I want to say out loud but don't. The silver bullet, the troops' nickname for the new anti-Lanky round for the MARS launchers, is a scaled-up version of the new gas-filled rifle round, with ten times the amount of explosive gas and a much sturdier penetrator needle. They are expensive and have a very limited shelf life, and most of the production is going to the stocks of the Mars invasion fleet, so I should be glad we have any on this boat at all.

"Put one on each flank and one in the center," I say. "And try not to miss with those."

"Copy that," the platoon sergeant replies, and I can almost hear his eye-roll. *Shit-hot second louie from Fleet, thinking we HD grunts don't know how to do our fucking jobs.*

The drop ship's tail ramp starts opening right before the skids touch the icy runway, and an arctic blast of air cuts through the cargo hold like an invisible blade. Outside, the storm is in full swing, an environment as inhospitable as the worst, barely terraformed moons I've seen out in the settled part of the galaxy. I don't know why we as a species insist on living in places where the weather can kill you almost as quickly and just as surely as a Lanky or an enemy fléchette round.

"Off the boat!" the platoon sergeant shouts when the tail ramp touches down on the snowy runway with a muffled thump. "First Squad left. Second center. Third right. Haul ass!"

The HD troopers file out of the ship, weapons at the ready. I'm in the back of the bus, so I have to follow the grunts out of the boat. I unbuckle my seat harness, grab my M-90 out of its holding clamp, and follow the last few troopers down the ramp at a run. At the bottom of the ramp, I work the charging handle of my rifle and chamber a fifteen-millimeter anti-Lanky round.

Outside, my line of sight is maybe thirty meters in the driving snow that is swirling all around the drop ship. My computer overlays my visor display with all the available TacLink information. The company is deploying in a widely spaced firing line as the drop ship behind us roars off into the sky again to provide for support from above. There are blue silhouettes to my left and right—troopers I can't see with the naked eye but whose position is known to my suit's computer, which talks to everyone else's over our short-range tactical network.

"Move out toward the complex," I order, and mark the nearby building clusters on the tactical map. "And go thermal. You won't see Lankies that way, but you'll spot people."

I toggle through my own helmet's visual overlays until I have thermal vision, warm colors of orange and red pinpointing heat sources in the featureless white mess before us.

"One-Five Actual, I can't see shit up here except for you guys," the pilot sends from above, where my computer shows a three-dimensional representation of the drop ship hovering two hundred feet over our heads.

"Movement left," one of the troopers calls out, and a fresh surge of adrenaline floods my already-wired system.

I can feel the Lanky through the soles of my boots before I can see it. They're not nearly as heavy as we first thought, but they still weigh several hundred tons, and when one walks around nearby, the tremors generated by its feet hitting the ground give its presence away to anyone in a quarter-kilometer radius. These tremors are harsh and quick—a Lanky on the run.

On our left flank, something huge and white materializes out of the snow squall. The MARS gunner on the end of our firing line swings his launcher around, but the Lanky is too close and too fast. It swings a spindly arm and sweeps it across the ground right where the MARS gunner has just brought his weapon to bear. It knocks him away, and he disappears in a spray of snow and ice, flung into the storm by something thirty times his size and a thousand times his weight. The MARS launcher and the priceless silver bullet, a third of our anti-Lanky rocket stock, disappear with the unlucky TA trooper in a blink.

I don't need to shout orders to re-form the line to the left and open fire. Several M-90s blast their gas-filled projectiles at the silhouette of the Lanky even before the cloud of snow from the impact settles. The Lanky takes two, three, then four rifle rounds to its torso, a target that's almost impossible to miss at this range. It stumbles and staggers forward with an earsplitting wail. I fire my own rifle at it, pulling the trigger until the magazine is empty and the bolt locks back. The cannons on the drop ship above our heads open up with a long and noisy burst, and shell casings fall out of the sky like steel rain. The Lanky tries to right itself, and it almost makes it back to its feet despite the hail of shells peppering its body and kicking up little geysers of ice all around it. Then a MARS launcher booms behind me. The angry firefly glow of the rocket streaks toward the Lanky at the speed of sound. It hits the creature dead center in the torso and explodes with a dull, wet-sounding thump. The Lanky's loud wail turns into a drawn-out gurgling that sounds disturbingly like a human's death rattle as it falls forward into the snow.

"Burlington One-Five, cease fire!" I shout into the air-support circuit. "One down. Save your shells."

"Copy that."

The gunfire from above ceases. According to my computer's chrono,
the entire engagement took less than twenty seconds from the moment
the Lanky appeared out of the snow squall, but I am out of breath and
winded as if I had fought all morning.

"We'll get stomped out here in the open," the platoon sergeant
sends. "One silver bullet left. Range that short, the rifles aren't stopping
'em fast enough."

"Head for the hangars over there, double-time," I order. "We'll use
the space between the hangar as shelter and work our way out from
there."

The platoon dashes for the relative safety of the aircraft shelters,
which are over a hundred meters away. As we run across the frozen
concrete of the tarmac, I try to pay attention to the telltale vibrations of
the ground under my boots that will announce the approach of another
Lanky. I'm used to fighting them at a distance, where I can see them
and take advantage of the reach of our weapons. Stumbling around in
a blizzard with unseen Lankies prowling nearby makes me feel like I'm
back to being very small prey. I change the magazine in my rifle at a run
and release the bolt on a fresh cartridge. Overhead, the roar from the
drop ship's engines shifts as the Hornet keeps pace with us and covers
us from above.

"Local defense, local defense, any units on this channel, please
respond," I send, trying not to pant into my helmet mike.

"Burlington One-Five, copy. This is Lieutenant Selbe, Homeworld
Defense."

"What's your location, Lieutenant? I don't have you on TacLink."

"We're in the shelter below the control center. They wiped out the
guard platoon. Half the guys down here aren't even in armor."

"How the fuck did they let themselves get jumped by a bunch of twenty-meter critters?" the platoon sergeant with me wants to know over the platoon comms. We are filing into the space between two concrete hangar domes, and I hunker down next to one of the hangars, mindful to keep an eye on my surroundings.

"Would you expect Lankies out here?" I reply. "They were sitting at morning chow in the middle of a fucking winter storm. On the frozen ass end of Earth."

On the TacLink screen, the control center looks to be another two hundred meters away from the hangars, on the other side of the airfield's big VTOL landing pad for drop ships.

"Sit tight," I tell the HD lieutenant. "We have a company on the ground, and more are inbound. Did you get a head count on the Lankies?"

"Negative. They showed up and started taking apart the complex right when the storm picked up. Best guess from TacLink is maybe a dozen."

"Fucking awesome," I murmur without transmitting. Hunting down a dozen Lankies in this mess with just infantry and without stand-off air support is a near-suicidal task.

"Burlington Actual, come in," I send to the captain in charge of the company on the top-level command channel.

"One-Five Actual, this is Burlington Actual, go ahead."

"We're between the hangars on the other side of the VTOL pad. One of those shits jumped us as soon as we got off the boat. We dropped him, but we already have a KIA. Suggest we hunker down for a minute and wait for the Eurocorps grunts to get here. If we attempt to link up in this shit, we'll get stomped."

"I have no issue with that assessment," the captain says. According to TacLink, he's south of the control center by the ammo bunkers. "We're just a hundred meters from the control center, so I'll take First

Squad over there and secure the perimeter. You sit tight and link up with Second and Third Squads once the Euros get here."

"Copy that," I reply. Then I switch over to the squad channel.

"We're waiting for the Euros," I tell the squad. "Our guys are in the shelter. No point rushing to get killed."

The platoon sergeant makes a sound that has distinctly dissatisfied undertones.

I check the TacLink screen and decrease the scale to check on the incoming drop-ship flight from the east. They are thirty kilometers out and descending toward the airfield in combat formation, five minutes out at their current speed. From the west, the direction of the North American coastline, there are now half a dozen different formations of drop ships and attack birds inbound, but as far away as they still are, they might as well be on the moon right now.

"Uh-oh," the platoon sergeant says. Under our feet, the ground is trembling again in familiar pulse-like low-frequency tremors. The sounds are coming from the eastern end of the concrete canyon between the hangars where we're sheltering.

"Contact east," I send to the squad. "Get the silver bullet up, and stay away from the front of the hangars."

"It's like they knew to go for it in the storm," one of the platoon's squad leaders says. "Like they knew we weren't going to have air support."

"So maybe they did. They have spaceships and terraformers. Just 'cause we can't talk to them doesn't mean they're dumb animals," the platoon sergeant replies.

"They build *cities*," I contribute. "They're not just dumb animals."

"*Ants* build cities. Doesn't mean they can plan assaults."

The computer does its best to estimate the location of the unseen Lanky stomping across the drop-ship landing pad on the other side of the hangar. The map updates with a lozenge-shaped area of contact—enough for us to know roughly where the bastard is, but not accurate enough to call down air support. One of the squads has formed a firing line across the alley between the hangars, weapons at the ready, but the Lanky doesn't do us the favor of trying to squeeze into the tight space and make itself an easy target for our platoon's concentrated firepower. Instead, the tremors grow more faint as it moves off into the storm.

I run up to the firing line formed by First Squad.

"Friendly passing through," I announce. "Check those muzzles."

"Watch yourself, sir," the squad leader warns. "Those things can move fast."

"Don't I know it."

I dash to the corner of the hangar, carbine at the ready. Behind me, there's a whole platoon with weapons trained in my direction, and if the Lanky shows up unexpectedly at the mouth of our little alley, things will get sporty in a hurry.

Just as I reach the corner of the building, the wind slacks off noticeably. For a few moments, the snow squall in front of me lifts just enough for visibility to increase past the few dozen meters it has been since we got off the drop ship. Ahead and to my right, I can just barely see a huge silhouette in the snowstorm, its back turned to me, walking toward the main control building with long and unhurried steps.

"Burlington Actual, one's coming your way!" I shout into the command circuit. "He's approaching the north side of the building. One-Five, do you see him on TacLink?"

"I got him," the pilot sends, satisfaction in his voice. "Guns hot."

Above us, the drop ship's cannons thunder. A bright streak of tracers slices through the swirling white mess and races out toward the Lanky. I make a right turn and run toward the Lanky on the drop-ship pad, to make sure I keep him in sight and feed the drop ship overhead visual targeting data. I have to dodge and weave through chunks of debris lying on the concrete, and when I glance to my right, I see that the heavy laminate-steel doors of the hangar are torn to shreds. The aircraft inside, half a dozen ground-attack birds and Hornet drop ships, are twisted and mangled wrecks, smashed into scrap and scattered all over the hangar floor.

The burst of fire from the drop ship slams into the back of the Lanky and sends it tumbling forward. It crashes into the snow-covered concrete with a loud wail, limbs flailing.

"On target!" I shout to the pilot. "Keep it up."

Our drop-ship pilot does just that. Another burst hammers into the Lanky just as it tries to get back on its feet. When it crashes to the ground again, it stops moving. Our pilot rakes the Lanky with a third burst just to be on the safe side.

"Another one down," I send on the company channel.

"The Euros are coming in from vector one-one-zero," the captain announces. "Twenty klicks. You want to sit tight until they have boots on the ground, your call."

I gauge the situation and think for a few seconds.

"Sarge, move the squads around the corner and into the hangar for cover," I send to the platoon sergeant. "Stick to the back wall."

The platoon sergeant sends back a wordless acknowledgment. On the TacLink map on my helmet display, the icons representing my platoon's troopers start moving and re-forming as the squads follow my order and redeploy into the hangar behind me. The hardened shelter is a big dome of reinforced concrete, apparently too tough even for the Lankies to demolish, and any threats coming at the platoon will have to come through the front doors, a predictable vector.

The storm slacks off a little more. The drop-ship landing pad is a large square of a hundred by a hundred meters, and I can see the hangars on the far side through the diminishing squall. The doors of the shelters on the other side look like they received the same treatment as the one on the hangar where my platoon is now sheltering, but there is no Lanky in evidence. I can't even feel one walking around nearby, sense no familiar ground tremors that mean one of the twenty-meter behemoths is on the move within a quarter kilometer. I conclude they've either left this part of the base, or they've learned to walk around on tiptoes. A few years ago, I would have laughed off the second possibility, but the spindly bastards have shown an unsettling ability to adapt to our tactics and environments.

"One-Niner, this is Actual," the company commander sends. "We are on the sublevel by the shelter. Got fire teams on the building corners, so mind your backstop if you have to open up."

"Copy, Actual. Drop-ship pad is clear. No hostiles evident on the pad or in the hangars. If there are any left, they've moved off," I respond.

"One-Five, what's the view like from above?" the captain asks our drop ship's pilot.

"Actual, I see precisely zip. No activity. Gonna check out the northern end of the runway and the radar facility."

"Hook a bit east, and make a low pass over the power plant, too."

"Copy," the pilot replies. I already know what he's going to find there. Wherever the Lankies attack one of our settlements, they go for the fusion plants first and smash them to rubble. I don't know if there's something about the emissions they don't like—which is the common theory—or if they've figured out that most of our tech is powered by the fusion bottles in those buildings and that we can't last long without heat and lights and water pumps.

"Plant's on fire," the pilot sends a few moments later. "What's left of it, anyway. No contacts."

"The hell did they run off to?" I wonder aloud.

"Maybe we got 'em all," the pilot offers.

"Negative. HD guy said it was maybe a dozen. We only dropped two so far."

"What do they usually do out on the colonies?"

"They wreck our shit and kill our settlers, and then they stick around," I reply. "Hit-and-run isn't their battle plan. They're nearby."

The awareness bubbles on TacLink grow and shift around over the next few minutes, the four platoons on the ground changing positions and moving carefully through the ruined base to flush out the Lankies, who have made the very best of the lousy weather. I don't want to think of them as intelligent and wily, because that would be profoundly unfair considering the huge physical advantage they have over us already. But as our company methodically reclaims the base meter by meter without running into any Lankies, I can't shake the unsettling feeling in the back of my head that we've been had. We are on our own turf, on the planet we've evolved on, in weather and terrain we've adapted to for tens of thousands of years, and we once again have to react to Lanky initiative, change our tactics to adapt to theirs. Dance to their music.

"NAC forces, this is Eurocorps. Do you copy?" I hear over the local defense channel. The voice has a strong Scandinavian accent. I fall back to my combat-controller mode and address the hail while scanning TacNet for the new arrivals. An eight-ship flight of atmospheric drop ships is descending into the airspace over Thule in a double-V formation.

"Eurocorps units, this is NAC Homeworld Defense," I reply. "We are on the ground with a company of infantry. We have platoons on the ground at the drop-ship landing pad, in the ops center, and at the south end of the airfield. Two confirmed LHOs are down. There are more that are unaccounted for, so watch yourselves. Visibility down here is under a hundred meters. You won't see the bastards until they're almost on top of you."

"NAC, understood. We will land on the drop-ship pad and at the north end of the runway. Check your weapons, and hold your fire."

I hear the Euro ships long before I can see the first one, but the sounds have a muffled quality to them in the swirling snowstorm overhead. The new engine noises have an unfamiliar pitch. A minute or so after I hear the Euros overhead, the first Eurocorps drop ship descends out of the storm, does a 180-degree turn to face the open area to our north, and then sets down on the concrete landing pad in front of the hangar where my platoon has taken cover. In size, the Eurocorps drop ships are bigger than Wasps or Hornets, but not as large as Dragonflies. They look sleeker than our ships, less angular and utilitarian, and infinitely more elegant than the SRA's martial-looking Akula-class drop ships. Unlike both NAC and SRA drop ships, the Eurocorps ships have a modular cargo-hold arrangement. The entire back and bottom of the hull from the wing roots back is a detachable module that can be swapped out depending on mission requirements. The ships that now descend out of the storm one by one and go skids down on the landing pad have troop-transport modules attached. Their tail ramps drop onto the concrete surface of the pad, and Eurocorps soldiers in battle armor start pouring out of the holds. They immediately deploy in quick 360-degree cover formations around their ships. I wave at the nearest of the Euros facing the hangar, and the soldier looking at me lowers his rifle and gives me a curt wave back. I leave cover and trot to the front of the hangar, my carbine at low ready.

The Euro troopers are wearing battle armor that's almost dainty looking compared to our bulky NAC kit. Their helmets are streamlined, without a single hard angle on them, and they look like they're about two-thirds the size of ours. The soldier I'm approaching raises his hand in a brief greeting and then flips open the visor of his helmet. The camo pattern on his armor is a blotchy mélange of black, reddish brown, and light and dark green tones that looks like someone kicked over a few buckets of earth-tone paints. The only signets on the armor that stand out are the Danish flag on one arm, and the rank insignia on his chest—two five-pointed stars, first lieutenant rank.

"Lieutenant Grayson, NAC Fleet!" I shout my introduction over the noise of the drop ships nearby.

"Lieutenant Hansen, Danish army," he replies. "Eurocorps."

I give the Danish lieutenant a quick rundown of the situation. Our TacLink battlefield-data network doesn't interface with the Euros, and every time I have to lay out with my words what would take five seconds to display via helmet-visor screen, I marvel at the ability of precomputerized armies to communicate efficiently at all.

"We will expand the perimeter," Lieutenant Hansen says when I am finished sketching the rough situational picture for him. "Cover east and west with two platoons each."

"You'll need a bit more than that in this weather," I caution.

Lieutenant Hansen smiles curtly and nods at the second wave of drop ships landing on the pad behind him.

"We brought more," he says. "Don't worry. We know this place well."

The modules underneath the second flight of Eurocorps ships look different from the troop haulers, less tall but slightly wider, and I have an idea what's inside even before they have lowered their ramps. I hear the whining of powerful turbines over the din of the drop-ship engines, and an armored vehicle rolls out of the cargo module of the nearest drop ship and makes a hard left turn. It's a six-wheeled vehicle, smaller than our mules, but no less efficient looking. The tires are big, knobby, honeycomb, run-flat units that look like they're made for deep snow. As I watch, the vehicle's driver turns on the exterior lights, which are blinding enough at this range to make my helmet shut its visor and turn on the eye-protection filter. A gun mount unfolds itself from its transport position on the mule's roof and snaps into place. It's a mean-looking three-barreled rotary cannon that's half the length of its host vehicle. The other three drop ships discharge their own mules one by one before roaring back into the sky. The platoon of cannon-armed mules rolls up the landing pad to the north. Then two swing to the west, and the other pair to the east, cannons swiveling on their roofs as the sensor packages on the mules look for targets in the frigid storm.

"We'll meet up with our other platoons at the ops center and do a sweep south," I tell the Danish lieutenant, who nods and turns around to follow his troops, who have formed up into squads and are trotting up the landing pad in the tracks left in the snow by the Eurocorps mules.

"Actual, One-Five Actual," I send to the company commander. "The Euros are on the ground. They brought armor and are sweeping the west and east approaches. Request permission to join Fourth Platoon and set up a perimeter to the south with First and Fourth."

"One-Five Actual, go ahead. We're coming topside, too. Civvies and wing-wipers are staying down here in the shelter until we know we are clear. Meet up at the southwest corner of the ops center in five."

"On the way," I reply. Then I switch back to my platoon channel. "Sarge, we are heading for the ops center to link up with Fourth Platoon. Let's move it out."

We leave the shelter of the hangar and venture back out onto the landing pad. As we walk toward the ops center, a hundred meters to our south, we pass the massive body of the dead Lanky our drop-ship pilot killed. I notice that most of the troopers alter their paths a little to increase the space between themselves and the Lanky, which looks menacing even in death. The massive head is turned in our direction, and even though Lankies have no eyes, it feels like it's studying us as we pass by. The toothless mouth is slightly ajar. Once again the shape of the skull and the way the lower and upper jaws of the Lanky come together in a vaguely birdlike fashion remind me a little of Earth dinosaurs. The mouth is a good three or four meters wide, and I briefly wonder what it would feel like if one of these things scooped me up and decided to test the hardness of my armor with the edges of those massive jaws. Then I shake the thought off and concentrate on my TacLink screen again.

South of the ops center, we see evidence of Lanky activity everywhere. There are deep footprints left by huge three-toed feet, which even the steadily falling heavy snow hasn't filled in yet. The auxiliary refueling station at the south end of the airfield is smashed to rubble, twisted metal strewn over half an acre. But the creatures who wrecked the base so thoroughly are nowhere to be seen. Their footprints disappear in the white mess to our south and east, and I don't have the sense of adventure to want to track them down on foot and maybe stumble into an ambush a few kilometers from the nearest hard cover. Thankfully, the HD captain in charge of the company shares my assessment.

"No point chasing after them on foot," he says. "Let the Euros roll their armor. They can cover ground much more quickly anyway. Secure the perimeter for the reinforcements and wait until this goddamn shit weather clears."

"You heard the man," the platoon sergeant sends to the squads, obvious relief in his voice. "Back to the ops center, people. And stay sharp, in case they decide to come back and finish the job."

An hour later, the joint base is as busy as it probably hasn't been in years. Our HD company and the Euros are no longer the only boots on the ground. Three more companies have joined us from the NAC mainland—two HD and one SI—and half an armored Eurocorps battalion is now widening the perimeter around the wrecked base. The storm has subsided to merely annoying levels, and visibility is now a hundred meters or more. The drop ships are still flying around on instruments only. By coincidence or cunning, the Lankies picked the perfect time and weather to attack the base while we couldn't make use of our sensors or offensive air power.

"We are heading back for showers and chow as soon as the next HD company gets here to relieve us," the captain announces to the platoon leaders. We are keeping an eye on the base's southern perimeter, and one of our platoons is picking through the rubble of the damaged ops center with what's left of the garrison platoon to make sure we didn't overlook any injured or trapped survivors.

I relay the information to my platoon, where it is received with unanimous relief. The wind has slacked off, the storm is dying down, but the outside air temperature is still minus thirty degrees, and the heaters in our suits are working overtime. I always knew the Lankies were incredibly resilient, but if they were able to survive this environment without support for months, they're even hardier than we thought.

A few minutes later, I hear the captain's voice again, this time on a private channel.

"Lieutenant Grayson, you're pod-qualified, right? You've fought these things before?"

"Yes, sir," I reply. "Three hundred drops, give or take."

"The Euros just found something in the ice twenty klicks north. They're asking for our SI company. I'm going to send Lieutenant Thiede your way to take over First Platoon. Meet up with the SI company at the drop-ship pad in five, and report to their CO."

"Copy that, sir," I send back, surprised. "On my way."

I pass the news on to the platoon sergeant and check my gear. Then I trot back toward the ops center and the landing pad beyond it. Some of my platoon's troopers exchange curious looks.

The disappointment I feel at the postponed return to a hot shower and warm food is overshadowed by the new dread in the pit of my stomach. What the hell did the Euros stumble across in the ice that made them call for all the Spaceborne Infantry and podheads in the area?

But as I slog my way through the snow that reaches almost up to my knees, I find that I have a pretty good idea.

Next time I'm out for a morning run, I'm leaving the PDP at home by accident, I decide on the spot.

CHAPTER 3

—— HUNTING A BEAR IN WINTER ——

Twenty kilometers to the north of Thule base, the scene looks like some sort of international military jamboree. There are drop ships from the NAC's Fleet Arm and Homeworld Defense, Danish Eurocorps ships and armored vehicles, and personnel in battle armor with at least five different camouflage patterns. The airspace is almost as crowded as the ground. When I step off the ramp of the drop ship with the SI platoon, there are several flights of NAC and Eurocorps drop ships circling overhead, all with air-to-ground ordnance visible on the external racks. The weather up here is less of a mess than the storm around Joint Base Thule. The clouds overhead are the color of molten metal, but it's not snowing, and I can see further than my voice will carry.

"Delta Company, hustle," the company commander sends. "The area of interest is two hundred meters to the northeast."

The "area of interest" is very obvious even without the visual overlay the company commander puts on our helmet visors. This is the part of Greenland where the ice sheet meets the rocky hills and mountains along the coast, and there are lots of ravines and valleys in the ice and the rock, clefts and canyons that look cold and dangerous and entirely inhospitable. The motley assembly of international forces is gathered on a frozen glacial riverbed, runoff from the nearby glacier making its way to the ocean just a kilometer or two to our west, and kept in icy stasis by the cold winter weather. Up on the northern side of the frozen river, there are wide fissures in the slope that makes up the bank of the ice river, and half a dozen armored vehicles are lined up in front of one of them, gun mounts trained on the gap in the rock.

We make our way up the icy slope. By the time we reach the top of the incline, I am winded, a reminder that I am not yet back in my usual fighting shape after that year of garrison duty shepherding trainees at NACRD Orem. The fissures in the rock wall are a hundred meters away. The ground in front of them is sharply inclined, like a ramp made of ice, and there are many imprints from large three-toed feet on the surface snow.

"Guess we know where they went," the platoon sergeant says.

"Where's the fleet guy?" someone in the group up ahead says, and I trot over to the motley gaggle of NAC and Eurocorps troops gathered between the armored vehicles.

"Lieutenant Grayson," I introduce myself to the highest-ranking officer I see, a major from HD. There's a captain from the Eurocorps standing with him, a tall guy with an Icelandic flag on his armor. "I'm the fleet guy."

"Captain Clary says you've done a shitload of drops against these things," the major says.

"Yes, sir. A few hundred. I'm a combat controller."

"Ever seen anything like this before?" he says, and points a thumb over his shoulder at the icy ramp carved out of the glacier surface. The dark crevice in the rock beyond looks forbidding and hostile.

"No, sir," I say. "They usually build their structures on the surface. I've never seen them go underground. Never seen them in this kind of weather, either."

"We have at least half a dozen separate sets of tracks going into that. The mules are keeping a lid on the perimeter out here, but we need to find out what's in there. Grab an SI platoon and find me a way down for the armor, and we'll smoke the fuckers out."

I look at the gap in the rock again. It's maybe twenty meters tall and less than five meters wide. It's hard to believe something the size of a Lanky could have squeezed through there. I don't feel terrifically enthusiastic about descending into that rocky funnel after them, not even with a platoon of SI at my back. But I'm the only podhead with Lanky experience on the ground right now, and it seems I just got nominated for the job.

"What about drones? Got any RQ units on one of the drop ships? We could send those down there without risking grunts."

"Those aren't standard kit on HD drop ships, and we can't wait for a stocked SI boat to show up. Just poke your head in, and give me some footage for the armor guys. No heroics."

"Can do, sir," I reply, and snap a salute that's way more confident than I feel.

———————

"MARS launchers, one per fire team," I say to the platoon's squad leaders as we gear up on the plateau, trading fléchette rifles for M-90 anti-Lanky rifles. "Silver bullets in the launchers, as many as you can grab from the mules and the drop ships. No thermobarics, unless you want to have a thousand tons of rock and ice come down on us."

"We're going in there with hand weapons only?" one of the sergeants asks.

"We gotta make sure the mules can fit through there," I reply. "We poke around a bit and then send in the armor. I have no interest in sticking out my neck for the Euros today, Sarge."

"Copy that," the sergeant replies.

With all that firepower lined up on the glacier behind us and patrolling overhead, it seems idiotic to go after the Lankies with unsupported infantry again, the squishiest and least powerful weapons system in the arsenal. But the Lankies went where the mules and drop ships can't reach them, and so we gear up and start making our way down the glacier slope to the rock crevice in widely spaced formation, lots of room between squads and lots of MARS launchers at the ready. I take three steps on the sheer ice before the cleats on my armor's boot soles deploy automatically. Even with the triangular spikes of the automatic cleats providing extra traction, I only barely manage not to fall on my ass ungracefully every ten meters. With the fifty pounds of gear strapped to me, I'd probably slide all the way into the rock crevice below us without stopping again.

The slope down to the rock crevice is a hundred meters long. I am with First Squad, which reaches the gap in the rock first. Behind us, Second Squad moves up to join us while Third and Fourth Squads cover our advance with their MARS launchers from halfway up the ramp.

"They won't show on thermal or infrared, not even in the ice," I send to my platoon. "Helmet lights, max lumens. You'll only spot them visually, so make the beam as long as you can."

Just in front of the rock crevice, the icy ramp makes a hard right turn and dips down at an even steeper angle. This is the seam between the ice of the glacier and the rock walls of the riverbed, and the ramp bends at a sixty-degree angle and follows the course of the rock wall. Ten meters past the threshold where the ramp turns into an ice tunnel, there's a sharp drop-off.

"Will you look at that shit," the sergeant next to me says.

In front of us, the ice tunnel's floor drops a good five meters, continues for another ten, and then drops again. The pattern repeats itself as far as our helmet lights reach into the darkness. I turn on my night vision to see half a dozen steps carved into the ice, a staircase made for creatures ten times our height.

"Son of a bitch," I say.

"Ain't no way we're gonna roll armor in there."

"No, there ain't," I agree. "Mules won't make that drop."

I toggle over to the company command circuit.

"Major, the armor is a no-go."

"Yeah, I see the footage," the HD major replies. "How in the hell did they manage that?"

"Not a clue. I've never seen anything like this. Didn't even know they could do angles."

I turn in a circle to give the major a good view of our surroundings through the telemetry link from my helmet camera. We are twenty meters beyond the right-angle turn in the ramp. To the left of us is the sheer rock wall of the riverbed. To the right is the ice of the glacier, and in front of us is the monstrous staircase the Lankies have managed to carve out of the ice sheet, descending into the darkness like a monument from a long-lost culture. There's nothing moving in the darkness at the edge of our lights, and it's quiet except for the wind whistling through the crevice.

"Are they *that* smart?" I wonder aloud, more to myself than anyone else.

"What do you mean, Lieutenant?"

"Well," I say. Then I turn around and point to where the ramp makes a sharp right turn as it meets the rock wall.

"The drop ships and the attack birds can't just shoot ordnance down into the hole," I say. "It'll just splash against the rock and close the entrance. And we can't send armor down because they made a big staircase. It's like they know our weapons and built their hidey-hole accordingly."

"Goddamn," the major says. "It's bunker-building 101. Angle the exits and deny straight shots. You think?"

"Shit, I hope not." I step up to the edge of the first step and look down. The five-meter drop is just enough to make it impossible for armor to crawl down to the next level without flipping end over end, and it's too much for infantry to climb down easily without mechanical assistance.

"See if you can recon a little further down that tunnel, Lieutenant."

"Copy that, sir," I say. "We're going to need some help to get down there. Winch cables from the mules. Have them clip a few together. We'll need about two hundred meters."

"I'll send the word," the major replies.

"You really want to climb down there, sir?" the platoon sergeant asks me over private comms.

"You got any other hot plans today, Sarge?" I ask, and he chuckles.

"I can think of a few things I'd rather do with my day than climb into a dark tunnel after a shitload of Lankies," he replies. "Sir."

"No, I'm right there with you."

"But we're going in there anyway."

I look down into the tunnel, past the giant staircase, as far as my helmet light can illuminate the darkness. Nothing is stirring down there, but I know that won't be the case for long once we climb down those huge stairs.

"Yep," I say. "We're going in there anyway."

———

Ten minutes later, two steel tow cables are running from the back ends of the mules down the hundred-meter slope and into the tunnel we're standing in. We'll all be able to rappel down the Lanky staircase in a hurry, but getting back up will take quite a bit longer.

"I'm going ahead with First Squad," I tell the platoon sergeant. "Second follows us down as soon as we're in overwatch position. One squad moves, two squads cover, until we're all the way down."

"We have about a hundred meters line of sight down there. Won't be a lot of time to engage if they come out in force."

"If they come, they'll come one at a time, and they'll be on all fours. Tunnel's not big enough for them to stand up or go side by side."

"Let's get this done with, then," the sergeant says, and I grunt agreement.

I rappel down to the step below with First Squad, a quick and adrenaline-accelerated deployment that only takes ten or fifteen seconds. As soon as my boots hit the ice of the step below, I disengage from the rappel line and pick up my slung rifle again. The SI private who dropped down on the cable next to mine has a MARS launcher on his back, which he shoulders and readies. We move forward to the edge of the step and aim our weapons down the tunnel as the rest of the squad follows us down in three-second intervals, as fast as gravity will let them slide down the cable. The ledge behind us is five meters tall, high enough that we won't be able to get back up the step without the steel cables from the mules. I can't suppress the feeling that we just took the first step into a mousetrap.

We repeat the process, leapfrogging squads down the slope until we're all at the bottom of the staircase except for Fourth Squad, which is keeping an overwatch from the last ledge. The tunnel we're in measures maybe ten meters between its rough and irregular walls, and the ceiling is at least that high. It's not enough to let a Lanky stand up on its hind legs down here, but it's enough to make me feel acutely aware of how much bigger and heavier they are, and how puny a single human form looks in front of a Lanky. *We finally have ourselves a bug war, and it turns out that we're the bugs*, I hear someone from my past in my memory.

"Delta Actual, are you seeing this?" I send to the company commander. When the reply comes, it's riddled with static noise.

"Comms are two by five, Lieutenant. Data link keeps cutting out, too."

"We're not that far down yet. We are at the bottom of the stairs and have eyes on the next hundred meters down here. Suggest you send a few guys down the slope and around the bend after us so we can relay data and comms off their suits. We'll let you know if something comes our way."

"Copy that. Advance, but be careful."

"Captain says to be careful," I relay to the platoon sergeant, who shakes his head and chuckles.

"I was in the business of *careful*, I'd be back at base folding laundry in the supply group," he says.

Sixty or seventy meters into the tunnel, we finally see something other than darkness at the end of our low-light vision displays. The tunnel seems to terminate in a dead end up ahead, but as we draw closer, we see that it's merely the elbow of another almost-right-angle bend in the tunnel.

"Another turn." I annotate the image from my helmet cam for the captain, who is watching our progress from the back of one of the mules. We are running our comms through suit relays, a line-of-sight chain of SI and HD troopers stationed on the slope and in the mouth of the tunnel.

"If that thing turns a few more times like that, we'll have to leave half the platoon behind for relay," my platoon sergeant says.

"If the thing turns a few more times like that, we're heading back to the surface."

I check my tactical display, which is almost worthless down here in the dark tunnel. There's an entire platoon lined up behind me in pairs with three-meter intervals between them, thirty-odd troopers stretched out over almost a hundred meters. As a platoon-wide firing line on an open field, we could bring three dozen weapons to bear on any charging Lanky, but down here we'll be lucky to get clean shots with the first few pairs of troopers. The Lankies couldn't have designed a better way to negate almost all our advantages. The further we progress into the dark tunnel, the louder the paranoid little voice in my head tells me to get out and let the Euros roll some nukes into this place instead.

"Sarge, go back down the line and bring up the rear with Third Squad," I tell the platoon sergeant. "If shit goes down up front, I need you at the back to expedite the pullout. Tell Fourth Squad to keep their launchers hot and the winches ready. We may have to exfil in a hurry."

"Copy that," the platoon sergeant replies, not quite able to suppress the relief in his voice. "Don't be gunning for a Medal of Honor today, Lieutenant."

"I don't have the slightest use for one of those, Sarge." I gesture back the way we came. "Hoof it and guard the rear, or take point. Your choice."

"Hoofing it, sir," he says. He nods at me and turns around, then trots back the way we came. The troopers he passes look at him with thinly concealed envy. First Squad's leader, a corporal whose face behind the shield of his helmet doesn't look a day older than twenty, moves up to take the platoon sergeant's slot.

"If we have movement in the tunnel up ahead, I want all three MARS launchers ready to put rounds downrange," I tell First Squad. "They'll come at us headfirst, so try to shoot past the cranial shield. That thing is tough as armor plating."

There's another straight stretch of tunnel past the bend. It pitches down into the ice a few degrees, a steady descent toward the bottom of the glacier, which may still be hundreds of meters below us as far as I know. It's cold and quiet down here except for the crunching of our cleated boots on the uneven surface of the tunnel.

"It's getting warmer down here," someone behind me says.

I check the temperature readout on my display and find that the trooper is right. The outside air temperature was negative thirty degrees, but down here it's only a few degrees below zero. The environmental system in my suit tells me that the CO_2 concentration in the air has increased by almost a full percent. Lankies like their air warm and humid and loaded with carbon dioxide. Whatever they did down there, they didn't just dig a fancy hole in the ground; they found a way to do some very localized terraforming in the most hostile environment our planet has to offer.

If a thousand of these things manage to make footfall instead of just a dozen or so, we are utterly fucked, I think, and shudder at the memory of just how close we came last year to exactly that sort of scenario.

The next tunnel segment is several hundred meters long. It curves ever so slightly to the right, and the floor still slopes downward. We are still walking on ice, not rock, and I wonder just how thick the ice sheet on this glacier can be so close to the rocky coastline.

Somewhere ahead in the darkness beyond our lights, a low rumbling noise drifts out of the deep, a sound like boulders slowly rolling down a gravel slope.

I stop and raise my hand.

"*Hold,*" I say over the platoon channel. "MARS launchers up front. Mind your fields of fire, everyone."

"Squads, go four and four," the platoon sergeant orders. "Tunnel's wide enough. When we have contact, first rank kneels, second shoots over the first."

Behind me, the squads reshuffle their formation as ordered. With eight rifles to bear on a Lanky at the same time, we should be able to drop it in time. There are still a good hundred meters of mostly straight tunnel in front of us, and any Lanky coming up the tunnel will have to crawl on all fours.

The rumbling noise in the tunnel ahead of us ebbs away slowly, until the dark beyond our lights is as eerily silent as before.

"Well, that was ominous," the platoon sergeant comments dryly.

We wait, weapons aimed into the darkness, expecting to see the Lanky that made the noise to come charging up the tunnel. As scary as they are in close combat, I'd almost prefer to have one of those things to shoot at instead of sneaking around in the dark down here and jumping at every noise.

"They need to shit or get off the pot," my platoon sergeant says, agreeing with my thoughts. "Smashed a whole base to rubble, and now they want to play hide-and-seek."

"Be careful what you wish for, Sarge," I say. The targeting lasers from our M-90 rifles paint green streaks on the uneven ice walls of the tunnel, but there is nothing for our ballistic computers to lock on to.

To my right, there's a new noise, a faint scraping sound. I see nothing but tunnel wall in the cone of light from my helmet lamp, but the sound is very close. I rapidly cycle through all the sensor modes: night vision, thermal, infrared. When I reach the microwave mode, the one we call the heartbeat sensor, my heart skips a full beat or two. Something is moving behind the ice of the tunnel wall, something large and indistinct, only visible to my helmet sensor because of the vibration of the air molecules it displaces while moving. It's huge, and it's right next to us, much closer than it ought to be unless the tunnel wall to our right is just a few meters thick at most.

I realize what is about to happen, and I have to fight every instinct in my body to not drop my gear and run, run, run back the way we came before the trap snaps shut.

I whirl around and open the all-platoon channel.

"Back!" I yell. "Get back!"

The scraping sound to my right turns into a creaking rumble, and I know it's already too late, that we are right in the middle of the mouse-trap that's snapping shut right now, a trap I've led everyone into like a careless idiot.

The troopers don't need encouragement to follow my order, with everyone's nerves on edge already. The MARS gunners lower their weapons and turn around to follow First Squad's riflemen, who are already a few dozen meters back up the tunnel's slope. To my left, long fissures appear in the wall of the tunnel with cracks that sound like rifle shots.

I make it five or six steps back up the tunnel when the wall of ice to my left explodes and fills all the space around me in the blink of an eye. There's no more up or down or sideways. I am swept off my feet and lose my grip on the rifle, which is torn from my hands. It feels like someone just parked an entire drop ship on top of me, crushing weight pushing in from all directions. Without my hardshell armor, I know I'd be pulped beef already, but even with the protection of my armor, I feel like I'm being squeezed in a giant vise. The helmet visor's display stops working abruptly, and all I see in front of me is darkness as my helmet light goes out as well. I want to scream into the platoon circuit, tell my troops to get out, get back to the surface, but I can barely get enough air into my lungs to keep breathing. Just a few seconds have passed since I spotted the movement beyond the tunnel wall with the microwave sensor of my helmet. I don't even have time to be scared. Instead, I just feel a wild sense of frustration, anger at myself for letting the Lankies get the better of me on our home turf. Nearby, so close that it sounds like it's just a few meters from my head, a Lanky wails its unearthly cry, but it sounds muffled through the ice, merely painful to the eardrums instead of completely unbearable.

I try to move my arms and legs, but I am fixed to the spot by all the ice bearing down on me, and whatever breath I can force into my lungs isn't enough to cover the new exertion, and I fade out of consciousness before I even have time to get scared again.

CHAPTER 4

──── UNDER THE ICE ────

I don't recall waking up. I don't even recall being unconscious. All I know is that I am on my feet again, and that the crushing weight squeezing me from all sides is gone. I take a few ambling steps before my legs give out and I sink to my knees. My whole body hurts, and there's a stabbing pain in my chest whenever I force air into my lungs.

I cycle through the sensor modes on my helmet one by one until I am back at the green-tinged night-vision mode. I'm in the tunnel that just exploded onto us and almost crushed the life out of me. Behind me, the tunnel is filled with a huge pile of ice and rock. My display is flickering in and out of life every few seconds, and every time it goes dark momentarily, I can't see anything in front of me at all. I try to turn on the high-powered light on the side of the helmet, but it stays dark when I toggle the control switch. My armor just took a horrible beating from the tons of ice that came down on my platoon, but the laminate hardshell saved me from being crushed like a ration box in a garbage compactor. It's deathly quiet again. My TacLink screen is off-line, and I have no idea who is dead or alive in the huge pile of frozen rubble blocking the tunnel behind me.

It takes me a while to work up the stamina to get back to my feet again. I lost my rifle in the collapse of the tunnel wall, the only thing in my possession that can harm a Lanky. I walk over to the pile of ice and try to dig for it, but most of the pieces are too large and heavy for me to move by myself. I am alone in the dark, injured, with no contact to the rest of my platoon, and no way to defend myself if I run into a Lanky down here. There's a pistol in my thigh holster, but the handgun's small-caliber fléchettes are as useless against a Lanky's tough hide as spitballs. Still, it's the only weapon I have left other than my combat knife, so I pull the pistol from its holster and make sure I have a full magazine and a round in the chamber.

I take a deep breath. The sudden stinging pain lancing through my chest brings me to my knees again, and I cower on the ground and try to breathe in shallow breaths without losing consciousness again. Thankfully, the armor's automated med kit still works. I can feel the stab of a needle at the base of my neck, and a few moments later, the pain in my chest fades as the pain meds enter my bloodstream.

With the way back closed off by tons of rock and ice, my only two options are to sit tight and hope for rescue, or press on and look for another way out on my own. I don't want to wait on my knees for a Lanky to show up and finish me off. I stand up again carefully and start down the tunnel once more, pistol in hand.

Every channel on comms is silent: squad, platoon, company, even the local defense channel. I don't even hear the static of a carrier wave. The headset in my helmet is completely dead, and I conclude that the comms unit in my suit is busted. My armor no longer fits me properly— several of the hardshell segments are dented and pushed inward, where they press against my cushioned underarmor suit uncomfortably.

I make my way down the tunnel slowly, careful to make as little noise as possible. I want to broadcast a call for help on my radio just in case the transmitter still has life in it, but I know that the Lankies can sense radiation sources, and the very last thing I want to do right now is to draw the attention of one while walking around in busted armor with only a puny sidearm for self-defense.

Another fifty meters from the spot where we got ambushed and buried, the tunnel curves to the left slightly. Beyond the bend, the floor of the tunnel, which has been at an incline since we entered it from the surface, evens out into a flat stretch. I can see rock poking through the ice of the tunnel walls and floor in various spots. I don't know how deep I am beneath the glacier, but knowing that I probably have a million tons of ice over my head doesn't help my anxiety levels. I'm alone in the dark with the Lankies, and I'm more afraid than I've ever been in my life because I am practically unarmed and have nowhere to run.

I work my way around the bend and into the flat stretch of tunnel slowly and carefully. The tunnel at the bottom gradually widens to at least three or four times the width of the sections where we descended with the platoon. Down here, the armor groups could roll two or three mules side by side with some room to spare. The size of this tunnel makes me feel puny, all alone in the dark and holding a little peashooter of a gun.

Up ahead in the darkness somewhere, that low rumbling noise starts again, closer and more ominous than before. I keep my pistol trained on the far end of the tunnel. If a Lanky shows up and spots me, I have seconds to live, but I want to be spending them emptying my magazines at it instead of cowering or screaming.

The rumbling noise fades away as it did before. I eye the tunnel walls to my right and left, but there's no scraping sound, nothing to indicate there's a Lanky waiting to bury me under a few tons of ice again. I move over to one side of the tunnel as quickly and quietly as I can. The tunnel walls are uneven and have bumps and protrusions, and I may be able to hide behind one of them if a Lanky decides to come this way.

The tunnel ends in a wide mouth that opens into darkness. It is easily twenty meters across and just as tall. My night vision can't yet pierce the dark space beyond it, so I move toward it carefully even though it's the last thing I feel like doing right now.

When I reach the tunnel mouth, I finally discover just what the Lankies have been doing with their time in the Greenland ice.

The space beyond the mouth I am standing in is roughly circular and so vast that it looks like the entrance of a cathedral. The ceiling is at least fifty meters high, and the whole space is a hundred meters across or more. A solitary structure stands in the middle of this giant room like a huge pillar. I have seen something like it many times before, albeit at a much bigger scale. It's a smooth, white, bone-like shaft that looks like a tree stripped of its bark. The Lanky terraformers on the colonies they took over look a lot like this, only they are many hundreds of meters tall and ten times as big around. The air down here is so warm and moist that I have to keep wiping condensation off the outside of my helmet's visor and the lens of the night-vision sensor. My environmental readout tells me the precise temperature: 33.4 degrees Celsius. The CO_2 warning below the temperature readout informs me that the carbon dioxide concentration is over 10 percent, more than enough to turn me unconscious quickly if I removed my helmet or raised the visor.

Near the middle of the room, two Lankies are moving, their backs turned to me. They are near the spire in the center, one walking around the left of it, the other around the right. They don't seem to be in a particular hurry. I crouch near a rock crevice by the mouth of the tunnel and watch the Lankies as they walk away from me and toward the far corner of this huge underground dome. My night-vision gear doesn't reproduce colors accurately—everything is in shades of green and black—but the walls of this cavern don't just look like plain ice to me. They have a dark sheen to them that looks almost metallic. The walls of the cavern have tall, narrow recesses that are fifteen or twenty meters tall.

I hope my suit camera is still recording to storage, I think, amazed at the sight in front of me. No human beings before me except maybe some unlucky bastards on Mars have ever seen what I am witnessing here.

Almost every one of the dozen nooks in the cavern wall holds a Lanky. The nooks are less high than the creatures inside, and the Lankies are crouched and curled up in a sort of weird upright embryonic position. Whatever the Lankies do for rest—sleep, stasis, hibernation, whatnot—the ones curled up in these crevices are doing just that. They are completely still and unmoving. As I watch, one of the awake Lankies walks over to an empty nook and starts lowering itself into it. The soldier part of my brain, the part that's way more pissed than scared right now, starts thinking up ways to put death into those tight recesses in the ice. The overpressure from a thermobaric MARS warhead would be devastating in such tight quarters. We could probably take out all these resting Lankies with a single squad of MARS-armed fire teams. Eight rockets, two seconds, and we would rack up the fastest infantry kill streak on Lankies ever achieved on the battlefield. But I don't have a MARS launcher, or a squad to back me up. All I have is a pistol, and I'm not sure the Lankies would even feel the tiny fléchette darts. Right now, I'd pull the trigger on a thermobaric rocket with grim pleasure, even if I knew for sure it would bring down the entire glacier on us.

The last Lanky on its feet does not go for one of the empty nooks. Instead, it keeps walking around the terraforming pillar in the center of the cavern. I move back into the rock crevice when the Lanky faces my way, but it doesn't make any move toward the cave entrance where I'm hiding. It just keeps walking around the center of the cavern slowly, swinging its head from side to side occasionally as it goes.

Somewhere in the darkness behind me, I hear a human voice. Then there's a little squelch on my helmet's headset, and I hear a choppy transmission.

"First Platoon," the voice sounds. "First Platoon, anyone. This is Alpha One-Three, PFC Cameron. Anyone, do you copy?" The transmission ends with a strained-sounding cough.

In the cavern in front of me, the Lanky pauses its slow and steady walk and swings its head around until it feels like it's looking right at me. I get up and dash back into the tunnel, heart pounding.

Up ahead, there's a fork in the tunnel I don't remember passing earlier. In the fork to the right, I can see the flicker of a light dancing on the walls of the tunnel. Behind me, heavy footsteps announce the Lanky striding across the cavern toward me. I take the right-hand branch of the tunnel and dash toward that flickering helmet light as fast as my hurting legs will carry me. At the last moment, I remember to turn on my own helmet light so I don't get shot by a panicked private with a twitchy trigger finger. Even with this precaution, I find myself staring at the twin muzzles of an M-80 rifle when I sprint around the tunnel bend and see the lone trooper in the middle of the tunnel thirty meters in front of me.

"Hold your fire!" I yell at the top of my lungs. For a dreadful moment, the green targeting laser from the private's rifle flashes across my chest armor before PFC Cameron points the weapon away from me.

"Turn off your comms!" I shout at PFC Cameron, who is staring at me with wide eyes through the translucent visor of his helmet. "Turn them off! They can sense the radiation!"

Behind me, there's a loud, low scraping sound in the tunnel. If the Lanky is following us, it's less than a hundred meters away, and it has sealed the exit like a big ugly cork in a bottle. There's nowhere left to run or hide.

"He's on my six!" I shout to PFC Cameron. "Shoot the bastard when he comes around the bend."

PFC Cameron looks like his knees are about to buckle, but he nods and aims his rifle past me into the dark tunnel. He's carrying an M-80, the oldest of the three anti-LHO rifles in the arsenal. Two barrels, only two shots before a slow reload that's easy to fumble under stress.

I look at the pile of ice rubble blocking the tunnel and barring our way out. The tunnel is filled almost solidly with ice chunks of all sizes, but near the top of the sloping pile, my helmet light dips into a little bit of shadow.

Behind me, something huge is coming up the tunnel, making scraping noises that sound like small earthquakes. I look up the rubble slope again and start climbing the pile. The noises in the tunnel spur me on in a way no drill instructor ever managed.

"Up here!" I yell to PFC Cameron, but he doesn't seem to hear me. He's staring down the tunnel, where the Lanky sounds close enough to be just behind the split in the corridor fifty meters away.

Maybe it's too big to make the bend now, I think. Please, let it be too big to make the bend. But I already know it's wishful thinking—they came through here before, and even if it can't make it past the rubble, it can get to us.

"Cameron!" I shout. I'm halfway up the slope of the rubble pile by now, three meters up. Cameron's helmet light keeps shining the other way, toward the danger.

I pause my climb and stare at the huge Lanky head that appears just at the edge of PFC Cameron's helmet light. The way the creature is stooped, it has to be crawling on all fours. The skull with its cranial shield at the back takes up most of the space in the tunnel. As I watch, transfixed, the Lanky reaches out with a front limb and grasps a section of tunnel floor to pull itself forward. Its toothless maw is slightly open. There are no eyes in its massive skull, but I still have the feeling that the Lanky is looking right at us.

"Cameron, move!" I yell. Finally, Cameron tears his eyes away from the monstrosity working its way toward us. He looks up the rubble slope, and our eyes meet briefly. I gesture up the slope and make the "double-time" hand sign for emphasis.

Behind us, the Lanky wails.

Without my helmet's electronics, all I have to block out the noise is the physical insulation of my helmet liner. Down here, in this confined space, the noise is so powerfully, infernally loud that it feels like an artillery shell just exploded next to us.

Below me, Private Cameron turns and aims his rifle. I can see that he's firing one of his barrels, because I can see the enormous muzzle flash of the propellant and the recoil making the heavy weapon buck in his grip, but I can't hear the shot at all. The round from Cameron's rifle hits the Lanky right in the center of its skull and shatters against the cranial shield's base in a puff of fragments.

"Shoot low!" I scream. "Aim for the torso! Aim past the head!"

I can't even hear myself. It feels like my ears have been filled with concrete, and a high-pitched, ringing whistle is the only sound I hear.

The Lanky moves forward again with a lurch. Cameron fires his second round. I tear my attention away from the uneven fight and resume my hasty climb with greatly renewed urgency. I know that we are both as good as dead, and the only hope I have lies in the tiny space between the rubble pile and the ceiling of the tunnel.

I scale the last meter or two faster than I've ever climbed anything before in my life. At the top, I see that there's maybe half a meter of air between the rubble pile and the tunnel ceiling—more in some spots, much less in others. I turn around once more and see PFC Cameron frantically trying to reload his rifle. He almost manages to get another round into the barrels when the Lanky reaches out as if to pull itself forward again. One huge four-fingered hand scoops up Cameron in an almost-casual motion and flings him backward into the darkness of the tunnel behind the Lanky. If he is screaming as the Lanky seizes him, I can't hear it, and I'm glad for my deafness for a moment.

I climb up into the low gap at the top of the ice-rubble heap that buried my platoon and crawl into the gap as quickly as my hurting body will let me. I don't want to waste time by looking back and counting down the seconds to my death if the Lanky catches up and digs me out of the pile. Without my armor, I would be dead right now instead of just badly hurt, but right now I wish I didn't have it on, because the space I have found up here is claustrophobically small, and I just barely fit into it, constrained by the inflexible volume of the hardshell segments wrapping around my torso. I crawl into the crevice headfirst, pushing forward with cleated boots, meter by meter, away from the thing in the tunnel behind me.

I can't hear the Lanky tearing into the rubble pile, but I can feel it. The ice under my body shifts suddenly, tossing me to the left half a meter and half burying me in another pile of loose ice. I struggle free and continue my frantic crawl forward. The pile gets another massive jolt from behind me. This time the movement flings me forward and into a depression in the pile. The ice chunks sweep me forward in a cold, hard, unrelenting wave. I struggle to keep myself upright, to not lose track of up and down again.

I crawl across the top of the ever-shifting rubble pile for what seems like hours. Every few minutes, I feel the jolt of whatever the Lanky is doing to the ice pile behind me. But as large and strong as they are, I'm glad to see that even a Lanky can't just casually clear hundreds of tons of ice out of the tunnel quickly, that even these overwhelmingly powerful creatures have physical limitations. I'm sweat drenched and out of breath, but I continue my crawl, not daring to pause and maybe end up sharing PFC Cameron's fate because I stopped to catch my breath one too many times. More than once, the gap between rubble and tunnel ceiling all but disappears, and I have to dig chunks of ice rubble out of the way, convinced every time that I am now well and truly stuck. I've long since stopped feeling the pain in my chest and limbs, and my hearing is still gone except for that high-pitched noise that won't go away.

When I reach the far end of the rubble pile, the slope of the ice mound is so steep that I fall down the incline headfirst before I can stop my sudden slide. A series of bumps flips me sideways, and I roll down the rest of the way, limbs flailing. The impact with the tunnel floor at the bottom of the slope knocks what little air I have left right out of me. For a few moments, all I can do is lie on my back in the dark and gasp for air. Then a loud, scraping rumble from the ice pile behind me forcefully reminds me that there's a Lanky on the other side working to close the distance between us. I get to my feet again and stumble up the tunnel.

The pitch of the tunnel floor is much more steep than I remember. I have to pause and catch my breath every few dozen steps. From the way my chest is hurting every time I take a deep breath, I suspect I cracked a rib or three.

When I round the next bend in the tunnel, there are helmet lights up ahead, and surprised voices. There's a steel cable snaking down the middle of the corridor, and I trip over it, stumble, and fall ungracefully. When I hit the ground, the pain in my side flares up again and makes me gasp for breath. Then there are voices around me, and I feel several sets of hands grabbing my arms and the drag loops on my armor.

"Careful now. Pick him up, easy. Are you okay, sir? Lieutenant?"

I shake my head and hold up my hand. Then I nod back the way I came.

"Lanky on my ass. He's trying to dig through that ice pile. First Platoon?"

"Third and Fourth Squads made it back out. You're all we've seen from First and Second, sir. What the hell happened?"

I look at the speaker, an SI NCO with staff-sergeant rank stripes on his armor.

"They ambushed us. Set a trap. Made the tunnel walls collapse."

"Son of a bitch." The staff sergeant gestures to a few of the SI troopers behind us and points down the tunnel.

"Get a pair of MARS launchers pointing around that bend and covering the tunnel. Possible incoming. Anything looks or sounds funny, you come running right back here. We are grabbing the lieutenant and clearing out for now."

"I have data in my suit," I say. "I need to get back to Company. I saw what they have on the other side."

"Get the lieutenant out of here," the staff sergeant says to the troopers helping me up. "If you have a Lanky on your tail, let it grab you guys first if you have to. But make sure the lieutenant gets back to the mules. *Go.*"

———————————

I emerge back into the daylight five minutes later with an SI trooper propping me up on each side and a whole squad shielding us to the rear. When I am out of the tunnel and back on the icy slope of the glacial river, the sky is overcast, but everything is still bright enough to hurt my eyes. I open the face shield of my helmet and breathe in the fresh Greenland winter air, even though it's so cold that now my lungs hurt as well.

Up on the top of the slope, the military presence has at least doubled since we descended into the tunnel. Over by the command mules still lined up in a firing line of four abreast, I see the platoon sergeant of our ill-fated recon platoon, standing in the middle of a cluster of SI troopers, presumably Third and Fourth Squads. They see me and rush to assist the SI troopers propping me up on both sides. With the heating element of my suit off-line, the residual heat isn't quite enough to keep me warm in the cold wind up here, and I start to shiver involuntarily.

"The lieutenant needs a medevac," the corporal on my left side announces. "He's banged up pretty badly."

"Never mind that right now," I say. "Sarge, I need to go see the CO and plug my suit in. My TacLink is down."

"Make way, shitheads," the platoon sergeant addresses the troops between us and the command mule. The crowd parts to let us through. From one of the other mules, the HD major in command and the Icelandic Eurocorps captain come trotting over to meet us at the back of the command mule.

"Pull the guys out," I say to the major. "The Lankies have figured out how traps work. We won't do much good down there with just infantry."

"It's all we have right now," the major replies. "Can't get armor down there, as you've found out."

I pull off my helmet and toss it aside. When it hits the ground, I see dents and scrapes in the formerly smooth surface of the alloy.

"Get me a data plug, and hook this armor up to the console," I say. "I was down past the ambush, down where they built their shelter. If the suit was recording, you'll have another way."

CHAPTER 5

UNFRIENDLY TRAFFIC

I'm injured, and my suit needs to be within a meter of the tactical console's data jack, so they let me have the seat right in front of the mule's main command console. The major and the Eurocorps captain are standing to either side of me, and there are half a dozen other officers watching from the open rear hatch of the mule. I hardlink my suit and initiate the download from the console, hoping that the central processing unit and the memory modules of my armor survived whatever smashed the TacLink transmitters and half the sensor suite.

The display above the command console pops into life and shows three separate feeds. One is the recording from my helmet cam, one shows my vital signs and environmental data, and the last is a positional marker overlaid on a map of the area. The feed begins in the drop ship right before the landing, and I scrub the timeline in fast-forward through the relatively uneventful parts. When we start descending down into the tunnel and my helmet vision turns green with the image-intensification filter, I slow the footage down to normal speed. On the small monitor above the console, the tunnel looks much more narrow than it did in reality.

The attending officers watch the next ten minutes of footage, the recording that chronicles my platoon's descent toward disaster. I can't quite remember how long we were in the tunnel before the trap snapped shut, but I recognize the long, straight passage of tunnel about five seconds before the footage goes all chaotic. I switch my filter to the heartbeat detector and spot movement behind the wall of the tunnel. There's a loud cracking sound, and the view from my helmet camera pans to the right. My helmet light shines on a long, wide crack in the tunnel wall, and just before the wall explodes toward us, it seems to bow out, and the crack widens. Then the footage gets jumbled as I get pushed around and turned upside down. The Icelandic captain watching the footage next to me lets out what has to be a quiet curse in his own language.

"Son of a bitch," I concur quietly. In just one moment, two full squads are wiped off the roster, buried under hundreds of tons of ice, and a few moments after the rumbling subsides, there's nothing but heavy silence on the sound feed.

For the next fifteen minutes, the camera view shows only darkness. I scrub through the black screen footage at fast-forward, amazed at the time I was buried under the ice rubble. It's a surreal experience to watch myself digging out of the ice and breaking free on the far side. The filter switches back to night vision, and the field of view starts bobbing slowly as Andrew from an hour ago starts his short trek down to the mouth of the tunnel. I remember that my helmet display was flickering on and off at the time, but the footage on the memory module of my armor is uninterrupted.

"Here it comes," I say.

When the camera's field of view pans over the interior of the Lanky cave, everyone in attendance reacts with gasps or muttered curses. The Icelandic captain and the HD major move their faces closer to the screen to make out more detail. I move the chair back on its sliding mount to give them some space. I don't need to look at the footage any more closely. They watch, with fascination and repulsion on their faces, as the Lanky curls up into the recess on the cavern wall and the other one continues its slow walk around the miniature terraformers in the middle of the huge room.

Andrew from an hour ago is looking around in the cave for less than a minute before the audio feed picks up Private Cameron's call in the tunnel. The camera view shakes and whirls around.

"Hang on. Replay that. The last twenty seconds," the HD major says. I oblige, happy to be able to delay seeing the footage of Cameron and me trying to get away from the Lanky. I stop the stream and go back to the moment I have eyes on the Lankies and the entirety of the cavern.

"Stop it right there," the major says. "Freeze frame, at thirty-seven minutes, fifteen seconds."

I freeze the feed at the ordered time coordinate. Past Me is looking at the central terraforming spire where it meets the ceiling, a good fifty meters above.

"Cross-check the coordinates, and compare it to the map," the Icelandic captain says in his strongly accented English.

I let the map display take up the whole screen. If my suit was tracking true through dozens of meters of solid ice, my little blue position dot on the overlay map is smack in the middle of the frozen glacial river, almost at the point where it comes off the main glacier, half a kilometer upstream from where we are standing.

"How high do you think that cave ceiling is?" the HD major asks.

"Fifty meters, give or take ten," I reply, and the Icelandic captain nods in agreement.

I reset the screen to quadrant view and zoom in on the location data in the lower right corner. My little blue dot is in a spot seventy-one meters below the surface of the glacial river, plus or minus half a meter.

"That spot right there," the major says, and points at the ceiling of the cave where the terraformer spire meets it and branches out like an upside-down tree sprouting roots.

"That spot," I repeat. "There's only twenty meters of ice over their heads."

"Exactly." The major smiles grimly at the screen.

"We would need half a day to drill through that much solid ice," the Eurocorps captain says. "And they will probably hear us and leave. Or ambush from somewhere else."

"I'm not saying we drill through," the major says.

"You'd have a hard time getting through twenty meters of ice even with a kinetic strike from orbit," I say. "It may collapse the ceiling. If we're lucky."

"We need to turn that cave into a smoking hole in the ground, and we need to do it quickly and decisively," the major says. "We lollygag around, they'll just redeploy. God knows how many more tunnels they've prepared down there."

He turns to the Icelandic captain.

"Captain Haraldsson, I suggest you get on the line with your Eurocorps chain of command and get authorization for us to deploy nukes. I want to shift the nearest nuclear-capable NAC unit in orbit and put a five-kiloton bunker buster on top of that cave as soon as they can get a firing solution."

The Eurocorps captain looks visibly shocked. "This is Danish territory. I do not think they will let you deploy nuclear weapons on their ground."

The major shakes his head slowly. "Run the request by them. Tell them they can either send a few battalions of infantry to smoke these things out, or they can give us the green light for a single strike. Send the footage from Lieutenant Grayson's armor along with your request. And do let them know that if they pick option one, it may take a few days. We just lost a platoon in the span of three seconds. Want to bet how many of your Sirius guys are going to walk out of there in the end? And if the Lankies disperse, God knows where they'll pop out of the ice again."

The captain looks from the major to me, then back to the major. Then he shrugs. "I will convey your request," he finally says, reluctantly. "Stand by."

He turns and walks out of the back of the mule. When his boots are on the ice, he falls into a brisk trot and heads over to the nearby Eurocorps command vehicles.

"Call our grunts back out of the tunnels," the major orders. "We get the green light, we're gonna have to un-ass the AO in a mighty hurry. Have the mules keep the perimeter. And get me regional command. They'll shit a brick when they get the request. Might as well give them time to find a crapper and get situated."

I laugh out loud and immediately regret it when a sharp pain lances through my side. I wince and lean forward in my seat. The major looks at me with concern.

"And get a medic over here to look at the lieutenant. He's coughing up blood."

The medics take me to the rear, which out on this glacier means a second echelon of armored vehicles that cover the back slope of the frozen river. They take off my armor and have me lie down on a diagnostic stretcher in the back of a medical mule. I prop up my head just enough to keep watching the scene on the glacier out of the open tail hatch of the mule.

"Two broken ribs," the medic, a burly staff sergeant, pronounces after checking the full-body scanner. "You have a concussion, too, and a bunch of bruises and cuts. We'll have to send you to Great Lakes to get the ribs fixed. Can't do it in the field."

"I'll go to the med unit at Burlington," I say. "It's closer to home."

"Up to you," the medic replies. "Won't take more than a day anyway. We'll fly you out there once we get a clear Hornet."

"Don't bother taking up a whole bird just for one clumsy-ass lieutenant," I say. "I'll ride back with the rest of the company when we pack up here."

"You sure? We may be here a while."

"I can deal with it, Sergeant."

"Copy that, sir." The medical sergeant exchanges a look with his corporal assistant that tells me he thinks I'm a dumbass for not taking the ticket to Great Lakes, where the medical facilities are ten times better than the little medical unit at HDAS Burlington, which is mostly equipped to handle nosebleeds and hangnails.

I let the medics stick dermal patches to my cuts and bruises and try to keep my breaths shallow. While they are busy dressing my minor scrapes, I keep a watch toward the top of the slope, where the frontline row of mules is guarding the perimeter in front of the Lanky tunnel entrance.

Ten or fifteen minutes in, there's a burst of activity by the tunnel, troops coming up the slope in a rush and climbing into the backs of the waiting mules. One by one, the mules close their rear hatches and head up the slope toward the glacier. From the front of our mule, I hear some garbled comms chatter. Then the intercom crackles to life.

"We are moving to meet the Hornets for exfil," the driver says. "Hang on in the back."

The tail ramp closes, and the driver puts the mule into motion before the ramp is closed all the way. Without any visual reference, I can't tell where we're going, but we're definitely moving up the slope fast, the mule's engine whistling its characteristic high-pitched whining noise at full throttle.

I guess they got their authorization, I think. The thought of a nuke being aimed at the spot of ground I'm currently passing in a lightly armored vehicle should alarm me more than it does. I've been in the same grid-square neighborhood with thermonuclear detonations dozens of times, even if those were on newly unpopulated colonies instead of

Earth. I try to remember whether the combat use of nukes on the territory of a friendly alliance is a violation of the Svalbard Accords, but then I find that I really don't give a shit. A dozen Lankies in that sort of fortified setting can take out whatever we can send into the tunnels after them, and we can't afford to let them get away and regroup, or next time it will be a city instead of an air base, thousands of civvies dead instead of a dozen security troops. If I could launch that nuke myself, I'd do it with a cheer.

We've been driving over bumpy terrain for fifteen minutes when the mule comes to a halt, and the tail ramp opens again. The medics make moves to carry me outside on the mobile stretcher but relent when I wave them off and sit up with a grimace. Instead, they prop me up on each side, and we walk down the tail ramp together. Almost immediately, the cold bite of the Greenland air makes me feel like I just stepped into a walk-in freezer.

We're on the featureless, flat ice of the glacier. Behind us, the mules have all pulled up in a row to unload troops. In front of us, there's a line of Eurocorps and NAC drop ships, half a dozen of them, with engines running and position lights blinking. The cold air out here smells like exhaust fumes.

"Pick a bird, and grab a seat," the order comes over the command channel and echoes across the ice from the external speakers of the mules. "Don't worry about unit composition or nationality. We are all going to the same place."

The medics help me up the ramp and strap me into one of the jump seats. It feels utterly strange to be sitting in a drop ship without armor or a rifle. All around me, the seats start filling up with a mix of HD, SI, and Eurocorps personnel.

"You okay sitting for a bit, Lieutenant?" the medic asks me when he checks my harness straps.

"I'll be fine," I reply. "Thanks for patching the leaks."

"Don't mention it."

The two medics take seats to either side of me.

"Buckle up, boys and girls," the pilot says over the intercom in a British accent. "We are leaving before the unfriendly traffic arrives. Nuclear fire mission inbound in seven minutes."

With every seat in the drop ship full of anxious-looking troops of various nationalities, the tail ramp rises and locks into place, and the bird lifts off with what feels like maximum power. They'll only use a small tactical warhead, and we are ten kilometers or more from ground zero, but I can understand why the Eurocorps pilots want to get distance between themselves and the impending bang in a hurry. Unlike the fleet and the SI, the terrestrial forces have no experience with nukes, especially the Euros. They consider themselves more civilized for it, but the rest of the world was glad for the NAC and SRA stockpiles of fission warheads when we needed a few thousand of them to fuel the Orion missiles that have kept the Lankies away from Earth for over a year. Turns out Lankies don't respect civilized war-fighting methods in the least.

The nuke hits seven minutes later, while we're in formation heading out to sea, forty thousand feet above the show. The Eurocorps birds have small windows, and almost every soldier in the cargo hold tries to get a glimpse of the sun-bright fireball that blooms on the ground off to our starboard side. It's just a five-kiloton bunker buster, one of the smallest warheads in the arsenal, but I have to admit that it makes for a spectacular display—first the hardened warhead streaking through the atmosphere at hypersonic speed, trailing glowing plasma like a comet, and then the fission detonation itself, a bright little ball of star fire that grows larger every second until it roils into the polar air and darkens with the cooling debris it sucked up from the ground. Belowground detonations are dirty as hell, and this part of Greenland will be pegging radiation alerts for a while. The mushroom from the nuke is tiny compared to some of the multi-megaton stuff I've seen, but it's sufficiently awe inspiring to the Euros and the green HD troopers in the hold. Instead of following suit and gawking at the mushroom cloud, I close my eyes, but open them again quickly when I see the image of Private Cameron's terrified face behind his helmet visor as the Lanky grabs him and flings him into the darkness like a foul-tempered toddler chucking a toy. If he was still alive somehow, he just died in a microsecond, his brain evaporated by a million-degree fireball along with the rest of his body before it could process the nerve impulses from his skin.

I fixate on the unfamiliar geometry of the Eurocorps drop ship's interior and start counting weld lines and rivets, even though I am suddenly tired enough that I'm sure I'd fall asleep within seconds of closing my eyes.

What a thoroughly fucked-up morning.

CHAPTER 6

BANGED UP

"This is a change," Halley says when she walks into the hospital room. "Usually I'm the banged-up one on the stretcher."

"Next time," I say, and sit up in my bed with a wince. "We'll take turns."

"You have a few to catch up on. How are you feeling?"

"All right, I guess. Better than half the platoon."

"What the hell happened?"

I swing my legs over the edge of the bed and put a hand over the bandage wrapped around my rib cage. The broken ribs are back together, but I know from experience that I'll be sore for a week from the fusing job.

"They were waiting for us," I tell Halley. "Built a nice ambush for us to wander into. And I led the platoon right into it, like a fucking idiot."

Halley takes my face into both hands and kisses me gingerly. Then she sits down on the bed next to me.

"I offered to pilot one of the spare HD birds, but they wouldn't let me. So I had to wait it out on the tarmac at Burlington. Listened to the command channel throughout the whole thing. That was torture, not being able to jump in and help out."

"Once we scraped them off the airfield at Thule, they went into their hideout," I say. "They dug in, right on the glacier, in the friggin' ice. Tunneled into it like it was dirt. Couldn't reach them with armor or airpower, so I took in a platoon to scout."

"They should have sent remotes in there instead of risking that many grunts," Halley says.

I shake my head. "I had the same thought. But we barely had comms down in the tunnels. And that was with guys acting as relays at every bend. We couldn't get telemetry on the remotes. Trust me, I would have gladly sent the drones instead."

"So what happened?" Halley asks gently.

"I think they built the trap right into their little hideout from the start. The tunnel was just wide enough for them to crawl through. By the time we were in with the whole platoon, we were two abreast and strung out. I had them space the fire teams out so we'd have room to bring our guns to bear to the front. When I figured out what was going on, we were spread out over a hundred meters of tunnel."

I reach for the plastic water cup on my bed's nightstand and take a long sip. Then I offer the cup to Halley. She shakes her head curtly.

"They had a second tunnel right next to the one we were in. I picked up something on the heartbeat scanner, but we didn't have time to clear out. Motherfucker brought down the whole tunnel wall. Buried two squads in the ice. The only reason I made it out at all was because I was leading from the front."

"Jesus," Halley mutters. "Lankies setting fucking traps for us now."

"That's not even the part that scares me the most."

I describe to Halley what happened after I dug myself out of the ice—the Lanky lair, Private Cameron alerting the nearby Lanky with his radio transmissions, my narrow escape, the orbital nuclear strike.

"I think they knew exactly how we would respond. They knew how our weapons worked. Our capabilities. Our tactics. They built that little hideout just right. Couldn't roll armor, couldn't call in air strikes, couldn't even use comms without stringing out half the platoon to play mobile relays. And then—*pow*. Springing that trap right when we were most vulnerable."

"Could have been coincidence. Dumb luck on their part."

"That's an awful lot of dumb luck, don't you think?"

"Yeah, I know." She shrugs and shakes her head slowly. "It's just more comforting than thinking they're that smart. Not when we're about to go head to head against a few thousand of those things on Mars in a few weeks."

I think of the footage we saw on *Indy*'s cameras when we did the high-speed flyby of Mars a little over a year ago on the way back to Earth. I've never seen more Lanky settlements in one place. We saw dozens of Lanky towns down there, and that was thirteen months ago. If they've kept up their pace, there'll be twice as many towns on the surface of Mars now. Our usual plan of attack would be to nuke their settlements from orbit to spare us the casualties a ground assault would cost. If the Lankies on Mars anticipate our tactics the same way those ten or twelve interlopers on Greenland did, there aren't enough troops among all the armies of Earth to take the planet away from them again.

Behind Halley, a medical NCO enters the room. He has a PDP in one hand and a meal tray in the other.

"How are you feeling, Lieutenant?" he asks.

"Little sore, but I'll be fine," I reply. "Are my CDUs out of decon yet, or can you scrounge me up a loaner set?"

The medical sergeant puts the meal tray down on my nightstand. "In a hurry to leave? With two ribs repaired, we ought to keep you here twenty-four hours."

"Call the on-duty doc and get me clearance to go, please. I'll be fine," I repeat. "I'm only twenty minutes away. Pretty sure the captain here can drag me back in if I start bleeding from the eyes or something."

The sergeant looks like he wants to argue but then seems to change his mind after glancing at Halley, who is frowning. He consults his PDP and shrugs.

"I'll see what the doc says. Your CDUs should be out of decon by now. Why don't you eat lunch while I track them down for you?"

"Thank you, Sergeant," I say curtly. The medical sergeant nods and leaves the room.

"Wouldn't hurt you to stay until tomorrow morning," Halley says. "I have my final PT appointment at 0900 anyway. Doc said I'll be put on flight status if I pass the tire-kicking tomorrow. I could come fetch you after."

"I don't sleep worth a shit in medical centers," I say.

Halley inspects the meal tray on the nightstand. "You sure you want to pass on these delicacies?"

She picks up the fork on the tray and pokes the decidedly grayish-looking pile of mashed potatoes and the soymeat patty next to it.

"God, remember what the food was like when we joined? Real beef. Mash from real potatoes, with cream and garlic. Not this reconstituted powdered shit. Fresh veggies."

"Pastries," I add. "Doughnuts. Fresh fruit."

"Those were the golden days," Halley says. "Remember how we used to smuggle desserts back into the platoon bay to eat after lights-out?"

"Yeah. And the DIs knew about it all along. We ate the whole stash the night before graduation, remember?"

"Easier times," Halley says with a smile. "At least back then we only had to worry about getting caught fooling around in the showers at night."

I smile at the memory, which feels like it's from an earlier life, lived by earlier versions of ourselves, cocky kids who didn't know anything but thought they had the universe by the balls. Seven years ago, we were raw recruits, the military chow was the best food you could get in the NAC, we had over a hundred colonies, and there were three million settlers on Mars. A little more than half a decade later, we choke down the same shit as everyone else, all our colonies are gone or cut off from Earth, Mars is a graveyard with lethal CO_2 concentrations in the atmosphere, and we're dancing on the razor's edge of global apocalypse. Nobody in the military talks about retirement options anymore.

"I get flashbacks to Great Lakes Medical every time I stay in a med unit," I say.

"You mean, after Detroit?"

I nod. "I think it's the smell. Disinfectant and whatever else these places always smell like. I can't stand it. No wonder hospital food tastes like shit."

"Well, then." Halley puts down the fork she has been using to prod the soymeat. "Let's get you out of here as soon as the corporal comes back with your shit. Maybe Chief Kopka can whip up something made from ingredients that haven't already been digested by someone else before."

Twenty minutes later, we are walking out of Homeworld Defense Air Station Burlington and over to the maglev station. The weather outside is much sunnier than my mood. It's a crisp and cold day, and the air here in Vermont smells even cleaner than usual. My side hurts like someone has been working it over with a meat tenderizer for a few hours, and the straps of my alert pack rub uncomfortably, but I don't mind the discomfort. At least I am still alive to feel it. Somewhere on

Greenland, there are twenty troopers who aren't feeling anything anymore because they've been reduced to their component molecules by the nuclear warhead we fired at the Lanky lair.

"This feels so strange," I say to Halley as we make our way across the station plaza, weaving through civilians on the way home from work, upper-middle-class 'burbers heading back to their safe little manufactured refuges along the Green Mountain maglev line.

"What does?" Halley asks.

"This part-time soldiering. Going to battle in the morning, and then being out in the civvie world in the afternoon. After Detroit, they didn't even let us out of the squad bay without a psych eval. I was shooting at Lankies on Greenland a few hours ago, for fuck's sake. Now I'm walking around in a public-transit station with an automatic weapon on my back."

"I don't know," Halley replies. She looks up into the sky, which is showing patches of blue peeking through the cloud cover, and squints at the sun. "I don't mind it so much. On Luna, I spent months between classroom, hangar, and quarters. I didn't get to see anyone who wasn't wearing a uniform."

She looks around at the civvies heading into the station with us. "This is not so bad. It kind of helps remind me why we're risking our necks. And I get to feel the sun on my face every now and then."

You fly a drop ship, I want to reply. *You don't go into dark tunnels after monsters.* But I immediately feel bad about the thought popping into my head, because I know it's not fair. Halley isn't a grunt, but she has taken more risks than most grunts I know, and her life in the service is every bit as dangerous as mine. She saved my platoon from getting wiped out a month ago on Arcadia when she broke stealth and shot down the renegade Shrike that was about to blow us out of the sky. We lost three of our four priceless Blackfly drop ships, and Halley got mauled badly while ejecting from her ship. Half the Blackfly crews on the Arcadia mission died in that place. Their casualty rate was much higher than that of our SI grunts, and I have no right to quantify her occupational risks. We all face death every day in different ways. Even the civvies rushing off to their homes all around us do. In a lot of ways, they have it worse. All they can do is to rely on us to stop the monsters. I realized a while ago that I still wear the uniform because I want to have a little bit of control over my fate. Sitting down here on Earth and looking to the sky in fearful anticipation whenever something strange happens, with no way to fight back—that's a trade I wasn't willing to make.

We walk into the station, scan our military IDs, and wait on the platform for the maglev that will take us back to Liberty Falls. We're not the only military personnel on the platform, but the others—three HD troopers and a fleet sailor—are junior enlisted, and they keep a respectful distance from us, if only to not get close enough to have to salute us. The civilians standing nearby give us glances and nod respectfully when we catch their gazes.

The maglev train glides into the station almost silently. The maglev cars are clean and in good repair, unlike the shitty trains of the public-transit systems in the PRCs. There's even some generic synth-pop playing softly from the overhead speakers, and the announcements to stand clear of the doors sound like a polite request rather than a near command. Halley and I find an empty row, stash our alert bags, and sink into the comfortably upholstered seats. I want to take a nap, but the ride out to Liberty Falls only takes fifteen minutes, and there's no time to get situated and fall asleep. Instead, I lean my head against the window and look out at the scenery.

"What's on your mind?" Halley asks. I glance at her reflection in the polyplast window and see that she is watching me.

"Why do you ask?"

"You look like you're chewing on something," she says.

I shake my head. "When that Lanky tunnel collapsed, I thought I was done breathing fresh air. All dark, helmet sensors knocked out, no weapon except the dumb little pistol. And knowing there are Lankies nearby. I've never been so fucking scared in my life. It's like the train is coming for you, and you are standing in a tunnel and can't get off the tracks."

"I have no trouble believing that," Halley says.

"But that wasn't the worst of it."

I tell her about Private Cameron, the poor bastard who dug himself out of the rubble just after I did and who drew the attention of the Lanky by turning on his comms again and calling for help. It was a dumb mistake, but he was a green trooper, barely out of boot, and combat against Lankies is the most unforgiving proving ground there is.

Halley listens to my account with a serious expression on her face. "You think you should have done more."

"There wasn't a damn thing else I could have done. You know those pistols don't punch through Lanky skin. But yeah. I climbed up the rubble pile and got away while that green kid tried to hold the line."

"He did what he was trained to do. You should send his DI a gift basket or something. Because that green kid did his job."

"I know. Still won't help me not to see the replay in my dreams."

I look out the window again, where the sky is starting to get dark. The stretch of maglev track from Burlington to Liberty Falls runs through forested mountains, more trees in a kilometer or two than a PRC resident sees in a lifetime.

"I have a bad feeling about Mars," I continue. "A really bad feeling. I think we are about to bite off way more than we can chew. Nobody's going to come back from there."

Halley shrugs. "We almost died on *Versailles* together when all of this started. Then we went off to war for six years. How often did we almost get killed in those six years? You, on the ground with your pod-heads, and me, in my cockpit? You know how many drops I did where we lost a bird or a whole flight?"

"Probably as many as I did where we lost podheads," I say.

"Precisely. And then Earth, a few months back. And Leonidas. And a dozen other scrapes we've each had where we figured we'd just not worry the other too much with the nasty details. And don't even deny that you've kept some shit from me over the years. Because I sure as hell kept some from you."

"One day, our luck's going to run out," I say.

"Maybe it will. But so what? You want to turn in your tags and resign your commission? Stay down here in 'Burberville until the nerve-gas pods come raining down?"

I snort and shake my head. "Not likely."

"You've got a bad feeling about Mars," she says. "Well, no shit. We're about to throw every last thing we have against more Lankies than we've ever fought before." She leans her head against my shoulder and exhales. "I feel the same way. But honestly, it feels like we've been on borrowed time ever since *Versailles*. I don't want to die just yet. But if I have to die, I want to have my hands on throttle and stick, and my finger on the launch button." She plants a kiss on my cheek and puts her head on my shoulder again. "Besides, Mars is not your biggest worry right this second."

"What do you mean?"

"We all get staggered leave before Mars. I'm on a medical chit right now anyway. I told my parents we'd come see them before the deployment. To clean the slate."

I let out an involuntary groan. "You have *got* to be kidding me."

"Not even slightly," Halley murmurs with a little smile. "We've gone to see them *once* since we got married. We need to go again and settle our affairs with them before Mars. In case we don't come back."

I groan again, the forlorn sound of a man who has just been told he will face a firing squad at dawn. "Until just now, I've never actually wished for an emergency-deployment alert."

She chuckles softly. "You've faced Lankies in battle a hundred times. You can face my parents again."

"I'd rather be in a drop ship on the way to the surface of Mars right now," I say, and I'm only half joking.

CHAPTER 7

——— 'BURBER THEME PARK ———

Before the Exodus and the first Lanky incursion a year ago, you could hopscotch your way across the continent on the maglev network by taking various regional lines to their hubs. Between the metroplexes, the maglev does four hundred kilometers per hour, so it was a reasonably efficient way to travel long distances. Since the Exodus, however, the network is fractured and fucked all to hell. There's a crescent of what we now call dark territory, areas burned down in the riots or out of the control of the NAC government, where police were driven out, Lazarus Brigades haven't moved in yet to restore a semblance of order, and the remaining HD battalions don't dare to tread there. The swath of dark territory cuts right across the midsection of the country and then curves down through much of the southeastern NAC. The trains now stop short of entering dark territory, because there's no security, and nobody in their right mind wants to go into the massive conglomeration of out-of-control PRCs anyway.

Luckily, the dark territory cuts the northern maglev routes off from the southern ones, and Halley's parents live on the other side of it. Unluckily, they live in San Antonio, which is still under full NAC control because it is the southern military hub of the NAC Defense Corps. It's the site of one of our recruit depots, and it hosts Joint Base Lackland, the biggest air/space facility in the southern NAC. That means it's not hard at all to get there by military air transport. So three days after the mess on Greenland, Halley and I leapfrog our way south on a succession of military shuttle flights, to visit her parents in their safe little enclave.

"I feel like a crate of combat rations," Halley half shouts to me when the transport shuttle lurches in rough air for what feels like the fiftieth time since we left HDAS Norfolk on our third hop toward San Antonio.

"Doubt it," I reply. "Combat rations can't get queasy. You look a little green. Are you sure you're a pilot?"

"It's like driving," she says. "I'm fine when I'm behind the stick. Put me in the back, and I get motion sickness. Especially in these flying dump trucks."

We can hitch rides on military transports as a perk of our status, but that perk comes with a few snags. The shuttle fleet is mostly cargo haulers, so if you don't have one of the personnel movers going where you want to go—which is going to be most of the time—you ride in the windowless cargo hold, strapped into a ratty sling seat next to a few tons of priority military freight. It's faster than the maglev trains, but that's about the only good thing about this ride. If we could have taken the train to San Antonio, I would have preferred that mode—both for comfort and the fact that it would have taken another day before I have to put up with Halley's parents again.

The shuttle lurches again, more violently than before. My stomach does a little backflip. I don't ever regret having lunch at Chief Kopka's place, but right now I wish I hadn't had the maple pudding for dessert. When I tell Halley this, she laughs.

"I can't see how anyone could have turned that down. He had *real* maple syrup. I hadn't had any in years."

"My first time," I say, and try to ignore the roiling feeling in my midsection. "I swear to you, if we crash into a dark PRC, I'll give you no end of shit for this."

The PDP in my pocket buzzes to notify me of an incoming message. I pry it out of the pocket of my CDU trousers with a feeling of dread. Halley reaches for her pocket at the same moment, so I know her PDP buzzed at the same moment as mine.

"Shit," I say. "Here goes."

I turn on the screen and read the message I just received. It's not a priority alert ordering us to report to the nearest regional military assembly point. I read the brief text, two paragraphs in total, and the relief I feel mixes with irritation. I hold the screen out to Halley so she can read it.

"I don't believe this shit. Of all the priorities."

Halley looks at my screen and then shoots me hers. She got an identical message, with just a few words differing from the one on my screen. Both messages are from NAC Fleet Command. Both are boilerplate notifications. Halley and I manage to curse at precisely the same time.

Our messages notify us that we have been awarded decorations for valor for our actions on Arcadia. The only difference in the messages is the award name: mine is a Silver Star; Halley's is a Distinguished Flying Cross. According to the documentation, both were put in by the CO of the ground operation: Major Khaled Masoud, fleet Special Operations Command.

"It's only been a month," Halley says. "Why the hell would they ram this through so quickly?"

I erase the message from my inbox and stuff my PDP back into its pocket. "Fuck *that*."

"You can't turn it down. It's already part of our personnel files."

Once upon a time, they used to do award ceremonies—they'd have the highest ranking officer of your battalion or division pin the medal onto your CDU blouse. Since the Lanky business kicked off, medals get awarded through the computer system, and nobody bothers sending out physical medals anymore. If Halley and I wanted the actual tin, we could pick it up at the supply unit on base, same way you'd get a new pair of boots or a clean set of sheets. They'd check our personnel files in the system to verify and hand them over without any pomp or ceremony.

"I'm not adding that star to the ribbon," I say. "Didn't do a thing to earn it."

"That's bullshit, Andrew, and you know it. Don't talk out of your ass."

I want to tell her how many people my platoon lost in the assault I ordered, but she already knows. I want to tell her that the mission would have failed without Major Masoud and his SEALs pulling the trigger on their nuclear surprise for the renegade leadership, but she knows that, too. I can't argue that she didn't earn her second DFC—her flying saved the lives of two platoons, after all—but I refuse to accept a reward for losing a third of my platoon. I don't want to look at the star on that ribbon and be reminded of the unlucky private that was blown apart by an autocannon burst five meters in front of me. Or Lieutenant Dorian, who saved our asses as our drop-ship pilot several times before that Shrike shot him out of the sky, just a few minutes before the surrender of the renegade garrison.

"He knows I hate his fucking guts," I say. "Why would he put me in for a valor award?"

"Maybe because he thinks you earned it," she says. "Maybe because he wanted to give the brass some motivational items for the fleet news. Maybe both. Who cares?"

I decide to drop the subject, but the whole thing has made me cranky. Getting a Silver Star should be a momentous occasion in a military career. It shouldn't feel like I just got used by Major Masoud once again for his own ends.

"I hope I see him on the ride to Mars, so I can tell him to stick it up his ass," I say.

We descend into Lackland an uncomfortable hour later. When the ramp of the shuttle opens, it lets in a gust of warm air that smells like aviation fuel. Halley and I unbuckle our harnesses and gather our gear bags. I've never been more glad to get off a military craft.

"You want to get lunch here on base before we head out into the city?" Halley asks.

It's midafternoon, and we haven't eaten since we left Liberty Falls this morning, but the motion sickness has killed my appetite comprehensively, and I shake my head.

"I'll come if you want to grab something."

"Nah," Halley says. "It's just going to be shit chow anyway. Let's go see the folks. I'm pretty sure they're planning to feed us good food tonight."

"Last meals are usually pretty good," I say.

Joint Base Lackland is a sprawling facility on the outskirts of San Antonio. It houses an HD air base, four battalions, a fleet spaceport, and half a dozen training commands, including one of the four NAC Defense Corps Recruit Depots. It takes us almost an hour just to get from the airfield to the main transport hub on the base, and the place is as busy as Gateway Station when half a dozen capital ships dock there at the same time.

The train ride into the city is uncomfortable. The train cars are in good shape and clean, but they are packed with people at this time of the day, and Halley and I have to stand at the back of one of the cars with our alert bags and luggage between our legs. The people streaming into the city after work on the base are half troops in uniform, half civvies, and a good portion of those civvies look like military personnel who have changed into civilian garb. Most of the troops in our car are junior enlisted, with a few sergeants here and there, and a first lieutenant sitting two rows in front of us. Ordinarily, the officer ranks on our shoulders serve to create a little respect bubble, but the train is so packed that there's no space for that courtesy, and we stand shoulder to shoulder with privates and corporals who studiously avoid looking at the officers among them.

Halley's parents live in the 'burbs in San Antonio's northeast, and Joint Base Lackland is in the southwest of the city, so the ride takes almost another hour of frequent stops and the constant shuffling of passengers onto and off the train, Halley and I swaying in the human current like trapped driftwood. By the time we reach the station for Olmos Park, I am tired and even more cranky than I would normally be at the prospect of a stay at the in-laws' place.

"Too many people," Halley grumbles as we drag our stuff off the train and make our way up the escalator to the surface part of the station. "That was worse than chow time in the mess hall on a frigate."

Out here, the ratio of civvies to uniformed military personnel is considerably higher than out at Lackland. There are very few people in camouflage in the crowd of well-dressed civvies. The station is clean and well lit, and I can even smell some deodorizing aerosol in the air. Olmos Park is an upscale suburb, and the station looks nothing like the public transport hubs in a PRC. Instead of vendor stalls, there are shops and restaurants with glass fronts. The floor is made of granite tiles, and the walls are clad in decorative stucco. Even the windows are glass and have decorative elements, something that wouldn't last three minutes in a PRC transit station before getting smashed into a thousand pretty shards.

"I feel a little out of place here," I tell Halley.

"Welcome to the club," she says. "I've been feeling out of place here since I was twelve."

We walk through the concourse and out of the transit station into bright sunshine. I notice that there is barely a security presence here—a few civilian cops with sidearms and stun sticks are standing by the door, and there's a pair of police hydrocars parked outside in front of the station, but I see no HD troops in armor, no automatic weapons, no helmets. The civvie cops give us curt nods as we walk by with our alert packs, which contain more firepower each than the little gaggle of cops carries among them in total. San Antonio needs no riot cops, because San Antonio gets no riots. Its status as a military hub and a defense-industry center means it's a secure enclave, separate from the Dallas and Houston metroplexes nearby. There are no PRCs dominating the city skyline. Transportation into San Antonio is screened and controlled, and no penniless PRC rat would ever get within twenty kilometers of the outer ring of suburbs. There's a whole swath of Old Texas that's dark territory now, but San Antonio is as firmly in 'burber hands as it was before the Exodus. If the end of the world is around the corner, you wouldn't be able to tell from going into San Antonio.

"Here we go," Halley murmurs when she spots her father on the plaza in front of the transit station. He spots us roughly at the same time and waves.

It's very obvious which parent Halley takes after when it comes to looks. She's tall like her father, their hair and eyes are the same color, and she has inherited his nose and cheekbones. Halley's dad is a good-looking guy, trim and lean in the carefully sculpted manner of a 'burber with access to decent health care and exercise equipment. You could put a 'burber and a PRC hood rat in a lineup next to each other without clothes on, and you'd be able to tell from fifty meters away who belongs where. And Halley's father is the stereotypical upper-middle-class 'burber, right down to the even teeth and the tan. He waves at us again as we cross the transit plaza toward him. Then he pulls an electronic key fob out of his pocket and casually points it over his shoulder.

"Hello, you two," he says to us. He gives Halley a hug and extends his hand to me. "How was the ride down?"

"Not bad," I say, and shake his hand.

"Terrible," Halley says simultaneously.

"Well, you made it," he says. "It takes a lot longer now to get up north. I have to go up to Bethesda twice a year and hate it every time."

Behind him, a sleek and shiny hydrocar rolls up to the curb and chirps its proximity alert. Halley's dad nods toward our bags and then toward the car that is now automatically opening its doors and trunk lid for us.

"Well, load up your stuff. At least the last leg of your trip is going to be comfortable."

We leave the city center behind and head into the suburbs on smooth and well-maintained streets. Halley's parents live in one of the nicer parts of town, but the other ones we see as we're gliding through them aren't exactly shabby, either. Houses with front yards, plenty of personal transportation, neat shopping squares with food stores that have no lines in front of them. Halley's dad lets the computer drive the car almost the whole way, only taking manual control once when we enter a highway that has a secured access ramp. We have to slow down in front of the barriers that block the ramp. Then a little transponder module high up on the car's windshield lets out a friendly chirping sound and flashes a green light, and the barriers in front of us retract into the ground. We cruise through the access gate at low speed, and as soon as we've passed the barrier, it shoots back up behind us, far faster than it had receded. The highway we're on now has only light traffic on it, and the walls on either side of the roadway are ten meters tall and topped with security wire.

"Little job perk," Halley's dad says to me when he notices that I am looking up at the top of the barrier that delineates the side of the highway. "I get to take the express lane whenever I need to."

It's hot in San Antonio, but even though the roof cupola of the hydrocar is a big bubble of transparent polyplast, it's cool and pleasant in here. Invisible air vents are gently blowing cool air into the passenger compartment, and the roof automatically darkens to filter out the sunlight when it's beating onto the car directly. It's the most comfortable and luxurious way I've ever traveled.

With the hydrocar gliding along at 150 kilometers an hour, we are in the Olmos Park suburb in less than fifteen minutes, half the time it took us to get out to the city center by public transportation. We exit the highway through yet another secured ramp, and then we are in the upscale neighborhood where Halley grew up.

Halley's parents live on a quiet street lined with trees. All the houses are obscenely large by PRC standards, single-family dwellings as big as the two-story units back in Boston that housed eight parties. All the houses in this neighborhood are spaced apart generously, and each lot has a big front lawn. This is where the top layer of the middle class lives, the people who work upper-echelon jobs for defense contractors or the colonial administration and who have never been within ten kilometers of a PRC their entire lives. Real food, bought with real money. Hydrocars in every driveway, expensive air filtration and climate systems humming next to every house, and lawns that have real, bio-engineered grass on them. Even the trees are real. It looks even more manufactured than Liberty Falls, like a set from a Networks show. Just a few hundred kilometers away, there's a metroplex with a dozen PRCs ringing it, and the space allocated to a single family in this suburb would be enough for a ten-story Category Three housing unit for five hundred people.

When we pull up to the house, there are a dozen hydrocars parked in the driveway and along the curb of the street.

"Dad," Halley says in a slightly pleading tone of voice. "Don't tell me that you're having a party tonight."

"Just a small dinner with a few friends," her father says.

"We just got here. We're wearing fatigues, and we're all sweaty. We're not really dressed for a dinner party. And I wouldn't be in the mood for one even if I wasn't in rumpled cammies."

"It's no big deal, honey. It's not a formal thing. Your mom just invited a few people over for drinks, that's all."

"You know it's never that simple," Halley says. Then she looks at me and rolls her eyes with a sigh.

Halley and I walk up to the house while her father parks the car in the garage. I know that the house has very good security and surveillance systems, and that Halley's mother was aware of our arrival the moment we got within fifty meters of their front door, but she still lets us wait a good twenty seconds after Halley rings the doorbell before her face appears on the security screen next to the door. She smiles and unlocks the door, which glides open and lets out a gust of cool air.

"Diana," she greets her daughter. Halley makes a little grimace at hearing the first name she never uses. They exchange a stiff-armed, awkward hug that looks like both of them are performing the act for the first time. Then Halley's mother looks at me and gives me the same not-quite-genuine smile she flashed at the security screen.

"Andrew," she says. There's an awkward moment when we both try to figure out whether to shake hands or hug, but then she seems to have decided to err on the side of gregariousness and upgrade me to a hug, which she gives me in the same stiff-armed way she hugged her daughter. "It's so good to see you. Both of you."

"It's good to see you, too," I say.

"Well, come in," her mother says. "You must be tired from carrying those packs around all day." She eyes the sidearms in the leg holsters

Halley and I are wearing. "I really wish you'd not bring those into the house, though."

"Regulations, Mother," Halley replies.

"We are required to be armed at all times when we are off base," I supply. "In case there's a Lanky incursion. And for personal safety. Lots of riots these days."

"There are no riots here, Andrew. The nearest welfare city is hundreds of kilometers away. And this city is perfectly safe, with all the police and military around."

"No, it's not," Halley says. "Not from orbital incursion. Another seed ship comes close to Earth and starts spewing out pods, you could have a dozen Lankies on this street in twenty minutes."

Halley's mother looks uncomfortable at this flatly stated fact. Then she shakes her head as if she's trying to shoo away a fly.

"Well, who am I to argue with military regulations," she says in an airy tone.

The house is air-conditioned and quiet except for the muted din of low conversations from the dining room. The floors are covered in synthetic laminate that looks just like wood—not even Halley's parents would be able to afford real wooden floors—and the place looks more like a suburban lifestyle museum than a dwelling. Maybe it's the years I've spent in military berthing, or my childhood in the PRC, but the living space Halley's parents have for just two people seems wastefully excessive. The house is so big that you could subdivide it and turn it into half a dozen PRC apartments at least. There's a big entrance foyer, a living room bigger than my mother's old two-bedroom unit, a kitchen full of gleaming appliances and shiny gray countertops, and three separate bedrooms. They even have two bathrooms, both with showers, and both more spacious than an officer berth on a warship. This is only the third time I've set foot into this house, and I'm even more appalled by all this waste of space than on my previous visits.

"I had the guest bedroom made up for you," Halley's mother says. She leads us over to the door and slides it open. "The dresser is empty, if you want to unpack your things, but it doesn't look like you brought much. Why don't you freshen up a bit and then come say hi to everyone before dinner?"

We drop our alert bags in the guest bedroom and unpack the little weekend bags we brought while Halley's mother wanders off toward the living room to tend to her guests again. Neither of us brought civvie clothes—I haven't even worn any nonissued clothing in over a year, and I'm pretty sure Halley doesn't even own anything but CDUs and flight suits anymore. Halley takes her PDW out of her alert bag, removes the magazine, checks the chamber, and aims the weapon at the floor while peering into the electronic sight on top of the gun. Then she smacks the bolt release of the little submachine gun with her palm, to let the bolt ride home in the noisiest and most mechanical-sounding manner. She looks at me and smirks.

"I want to wear this thing slung in front of my chest when we sit down for dinner," she says. "Next time I'll bring an M-95 and lean that meter-and-a-half-tall son of a bitch against the kitchen counter while we eat."

"Why stop there? I'm sure I can get a MARS launcher out of the armory," I reply with a grin, which she returns.

She stows her PDW back in the alert bag and fastens the stickythread strips that hold the weapon in the bag firmly.

"On the other hand, this may be our last visit," she says. "That would be the only good thing about buying it on Mars."

There are a bunch of people in the dining room when Halley and I make our entrance, and all heads turn toward us. I sense Halley stiffen when she recognizes someone in the group, but they're all people I've never met before.

"Everyone, you know Diana," Halley's mom says to the group. "And this is her husband, Andrew."

She introduces me to everyone separately. The guests are two couples about the age of Halley's parents and just as clean cut and well dressed, and a younger guy who looks to be in his late twenties. He's handsome in the same regularly and carefully maintained way as Halley's father, and I know he can smell the PRC on me the second we shake hands even though I left Boston for good over seven years ago.

"Andrew, this is Kenneth Harris. He went to school with Diana," Halley's mother says. "Ken, this is Andrew Grayson. He's Diana's husband. He's an officer, too."

"I've heard a lot about you," Ken says.

"I've not heard a word about you," I counter.

He smiles at me, exposing the typical straight and white teeth all 'burbers can afford. "Well, Diana and I go back quite a bit. We were together in school, before she went and joined the military."

I exchange a look with Halley, who looks a little hot under the collar already. She sits down at the table, and her mom directs me to the chair to the left of her. Ken sits down in the chair on the other side of Halley, who almost but not quite flinches when she realizes how her mother has arranged the seating order.

"Hands off your sidearm," I murmur, and she lets out a soft chuckle, but we both know that I am only mostly joking.

The dinner is a strange and awkward affair. Halley's mom introduces us to the other couples at the table and tells them about our history together, our jobs in the military, and our contributions in the Battle of Earth last year. The 'burber friends make appropriate noises of wonder and appreciation, but it's all as forced as a recruiting commercial on the Networks. She also gets so much of our job descriptions incorrect that we find ourselves taking over her explanations and bending them back into something resembling reality.

"Well, I'm not a military person," she says when we've corrected our job descriptions for the audience at the table. "I've never been a fan of guns."

"They came in pretty handy last year when the Lankies made planetfall," Halley says. "Worked better than strongly worded petitions."

Guns are what keep your little paradise from getting overrun by half a million pissed-off welfare rats, I think, but I'm too polite to toss that out in front of the dinner crowd. Instead, I just look around in the dining room and imagine what a bunch of soy-fed, hardened PRC gang members would do to this air-conditioned place and its immaculate floors, inhabited by people who look down on the soldiers and cops that keep this place safe from the unwashed masses. *Is this what we fought for all these years? So these squeaky-clean, stuck-up suburbanites can keep thinking of us as something necessary but embarrassing, like the ugly guard dog you keep in the basement when visitors stop by?*

The family friends at the dinner table are pleasant and polite, but the difference between them and people like me has never been clearer to me until now. Their outlooks and experiences are so different from mine that we may as well be separate species. They mean well, and I know they don't want to sound like they're talking down to us, but they are. We progress through a dinner of salad and grilled fish, and every minute of awkward and cautious conversation feels like an hour. I notice that Halley's mother tries to steer Halley and Ken toward talking about their time in school together, attempts that Halley shoots down curtly and abruptly.

For dessert, Halley's mother serves up fresh fruit with a side of real cream, a decadence worthy of Chief Kopka's restaurant. Halley and I enjoy the slices of melon and the grapes and strawberries carefully one by one.

"We haven't had any fresh fruit in the fleet since last year," I say, and the statement is met with polite interest around the table.

"So the quality of the military meals has gone down?" Ken says next to Halley. "That's a shame. I thought that was part of your contracts."

"Not the food," Halley says. "That was always understood to be a perk. But it wasn't set in stone. We have less to go around now, and the priorities are with the Orions and the new battleships."

"Yes, we have spent a great deal of time on those missiles," Halley's father says. "The Russians and the Chinese even sent over teams for collaboration, if you can believe that. They have good ideas, but they have this crowbar approach to hardware."

"They have that approach to battle, too," I say. "But they know their stuff. I've worked with a few of their people."

"Everything's changing so quickly now. We used to fight the SRA; now we're designing weapons with them. And the military is letting in way more people than they did before. When you two joined, it was much more selective. That's part of the reason you don't get fresh fruit anymore. Same budget, just more mouths to feed."

"I'm okay with eating soy if it means we get more bodies into uniform," I say. "Against the Lankies, we need everyone willing and able to hold a rifle." I can't help but give Ken a pointed glance, who looks fit and healthy sitting next to Halley.

"It's not for everyone," Ken replies. "I mean, I have the utmost respect for what you do up there, but it's not something I'm cut out for. I'm better with the theory than with the practice."

"You're better with the talk than with the action," Halley says matter-of-factly, and I can see her mother flinching a little.

Ken smiles at her and shrugs. "Look, there's a need for both. Thinkers and doers. Don't think less of those of us who choose computers and blueprints over attack ships and rifles."

"A lot of people don't get that choice," she replies. "Be glad that you don't have to risk battle for a shot at some fresh honeydew melon." She pushes the dessert plate away from her and gets up.

"Excuse me for a bit. I think I need some fresh air. It's getting a bit stuffy in here."

My wife stays gone for the rest of the dinner, leaving me to pick up the conversational slack for her. Halley's mom looks visibly steamed over her daughter's absence. Her dad just looks a little sheepish and embarrassed, and I know this isn't the first time he's had to be a spectator when Halley and her mother lock horns over something. There's a good reason we don't go down to San Antonio more often, and why I dread it when we do.

Halley's parents see their guests out an hour after the meal, when feet start shuffling under the table with boredom and we run out of polite conversation subjects. Ken, Halley's old school friend, gives me a firm good-bye handshake as we exchange the usual courtesy phrases, but it seems that his interest in the whole evening went out the front door with Halley when she left. As soon as she sees the guests out of the driveway, Halley's mother disappears upstairs, and I am left to make strained and awkward conversation in the living room with her dad, who wants to pretend that nothing's wrong with the evening at all.

Halley returns half an hour later. Her father answers the doorbell, and she strides right past him and into the living room. Then she puts a hand on my shoulder and kisses me on the cheek.

"Sorry about that," she says. "I shouldn't have left you with that pack of morons."

"It's okay," I say.

"I needed to walk off some anger."

"Did it work?"

"Not completely," she replies.

Behind Halley, her mother walks into the living room, with a facial expression as if she had just bitten into a freshly cut lime.

"Diana," she says. "That was very much the *height* of rudeness."

"I concur," Halley says, her voice dropping to the same temperature as the refrigerated air coming from the AC vents on the walls. "You are absolutely the rudest bitch I've ever known."

"*Honey*," her father says in an imploring tone. Halley holds up a finger to interrupt him, her eyes never leaving the face of her mother, who looks like she's just been doused with cold water.

"How dare y—" she begins, and Halley cuts her off harshly.

"How dare *you*," she says. "How fucking dare you indeed. We come home to see you two because we are about to ship out to Mars, and you throw a goddamn social event without telling us." She looks at me and then back at her mother, barely suppressed fury in her eyes. "You invite the guy I dated in college, seat him right next to me, and then bitch passive-aggressively for two solid hours about how much you think our jobs suck, and how uncouth all this soldiering business is. You disrespect my husband and his background while he's sitting right in front of you, trying to play nice for your idiot friends."

Her mother looks like she wants to say something but can't think of anything cutting enough to use for a retort. Maybe she's intimidated by Halley, who projects an air of contained fury and danger without moving from her spot. Instead, she just glares at Halley, but I notice the little sidelong glances she's giving me and her husband, as if she's hoping one of us will rein Halley in.

"We are in the corps," Halley continues. "That's what we have chosen to do. You think that's not a respectable career choice. You're having your goddamn dinner parties and your social-status bullshit games while poor kids from the PRCs are dying by the fucking thousands to keep your ass safe from the Lankies, and you think they're vulgar trash. I've seen plenty of those kids die for you. And any one of them is worth twenty of you."

Halley's mom makes a strangled sort of noise in her throat, and her cheeks flush with anger. Her father takes two steps toward Halley, hands outstretched, and Halley glares at him. Her dad stops in his tracks.

"Don't touch me without permission."

"Honey," he says. "I was just going to—"

"I know," she says. "But I don't want you to. You've been cleaning up the fallout from her shitty games for too long. I'm not going to let you get her out of this one."

"This is my house," her mom says slowly, enunciating every word very clearly. "How dare you talk to us both that way."

"Oh, I dare," Halley says. "I should have dared years ago." She glances at her father again. "But I didn't want to break Dad's heart. You don't have one to break." Then she looks at me. "Would you mind getting our stuff, Andrew? I think it's best if we leave now."

"You don't have to leave," her father says. "Please."

"I think that's a grand idea," Halley's mother says. "Now that you've told us what you really think of us. Your parents. The people who raised you. Gave you all these opportunities."

"And that *burns* you, doesn't it? That I took all those opportunities and turned them into a uniform? That I'm not married to Kenneth and working a nice nine-to-five somewhere nearby so you can keep meddling with our lives? That I married someone from the PRCs instead?"

Halley looks back at me again, and her expression softens. Her dad is standing off to the side, looking from her to his wife and giving me the impression that he'd love for the ground to open up and swallow him right about now. I've never seen another person look so awkwardly uncomfortable and helpless.

"We're going to leave now," she says to her mother. "You'll never have to put up with me again. We're probably going to die on Mars in a few weeks. But even if we don't, I don't want to see you anymore."

Halley smiles back at me, a sad but affectionate little smile, and I return it almost reflexively.

"If we come back, I want to start a family with Andrew. I know I said I'll never want kids, but I think I've changed my mind. If we make it back from Mars, I think I want to work on that with him. I want to make sure I have a piece of him to continue on, because I hate the thought of him being gone from the world for good."

She looks at her mother again, who seems to be out of good retorts.

"If I get pregnant before we finish our service, I'll have the embryo frozen until I make it out of the corps alive. If we both die in the service, I'll have it destroyed. I'll run naked through a Category Five PRC waving commissary vouchers before I let you get your hands on that child and fuck it up like you tried to fuck me up. I'm done with you for good."

Halley's dad looks like he's about to break into tears. Her mom just stands there, with a stony expression, jaw muscles clenching visibly, but Halley pays her no more attention. Instead, she turns to her father.

"Dad, you can give us a ride to the transit station if you want. If not, we'll walk. No big deal. But we are leaving for Lackland. We'll stay on base in the Transient Personnel Unit and get a ride back north tomorrow morning."

Her father elects to drive us back to the transit station. Neither Halley nor I say good-bye to her mother, who disappears upstairs anyway while we get our gear bags and put them by the front door.

When we pull up to the transit plaza, Halley's dad starts crying quietly. She puts a hand on his arm and leaves it there for a few moments.

"I meant it, Dad. I don't want to see her again. But you can still message me through MilNet if you want."

"Don't blame me for her," he says. "Your mother has never been an easy woman to live with."

"I don't blame you totally," Halley says. "She's a hard woman to stand up to. But when you stand by while she's trying to fuck with my marriage, you're not helping, either."

She leans over and kisses him on the cheek.

"Good-bye, Dad. I'll keep you posted if I can. Maybe you can visit us up in Vermont after it's all over. But come by yourself, because she's not welcome."

When her dad's hydrocar disappears in the distance, Halley lets out a long, shaky breath, as if she had just relieved herself of a terrible burden. I want to make a quip about how the day has improved, something to break the tension and share some levity, but I don't feel that it's appropriate right now. In any case, Halley preempts me. With her father's car finally out of sight, she hugs me firmly and breaks into tears. And for a few minutes, I do the only thing I can do right now. I hold my wife and let her come to terms with what happened.

"Thank you," I tell her when she has dried her eyes on the sleeves of her uniform.

"Can't promise I'll always take your side on everything," she says, and kisses me. "But I can promise you that I'll stand with you every time. Against anyone."

We sort ourselves out and shoulder our bags to go back into the transit station for the ride back to Joint Base Lackland. The TPU quarters we'll share tonight will be far less luxurious than the guest bedroom back at the house we just left, but I know I'll be sleeping infinitely better tonight despite the hard and narrow military cots and the crummy chow waiting for us there.

CHAPTER 8

——— FINAL DAYS ———

It's strange to think of any place on Earth as *home* again after all this time moving around for the corps, but I've come to think of Liberty Falls that way, even if it is a middle-class enclave and nothing like my old neighborhood. I don't feel shame anymore for enjoying the 'burber amenities—real trees, grass, decent food, and safe streets. It's the very tail end of fall, and the nights are cold, but the air is clean, and I know there will be snow any day now.

Halley and I are sitting in a booth in Chief Kopka's restaurant, drinking coffee and sharing some pancakes for breakfast, when our PDPs buzz with incoming message alerts at the same time again.

After having the damn things in your pocket constantly for over half a decade, you are attuned to them beyond the different vibration and sound patterns for critical or routine alerts. The haptic engines in the PDPs can only vary the strength of the vibration and its length, but every troop will swear that some alerts feel weightier than others. Halley has been moved back to active duty and flight status since we got back from San Antonio, so whatever is going on right now will draw in both of us.

Halley and I look at each other as we take our PDPs out of our pockets.

"Deployment orders," she says.

"Probably just admin shit," I counter. "Change of menus at the chow hall."

"You wish." She smiles and turns on her device, and I follow suit. We both look at our incoming messages for a few moments.

"Deployment orders," I concede.

I am ordered to report to Joint Base Coronado for predeployment fitting of a new bug suit, after which I am to report to a new command: SOCOM Task Force Red.

"What the fuck is SOCOM Task Force Red?" Halley says when I show her the text on my screen. I scroll through the message until I find the deployment location.

"Embarked on NACS *Phalanx*," I read. "One of the Hammerhead space control cans."

"Pod drop," Halley says matter-of-factly, and I nod.

She flips her PDP around so I can read her orders. She has to report to Assault Transport Squadron Five on NACS *Pollux* (CV-2153) to take command of the squadron's Alpha Flight. ATS-5 and *Pollux* are part of Task Force Purple, whatever that is.

"Looks like we won't be riding to Mars in the same bus," Halley says.

"Nope."

I don't dispute her determination of our deployment target, even though the orders make no mention of it. We all know where we're about to go and what we are about to fight.

We both look at our screens for a few moments without saying anything. Then Halley puts her PDP facedown on the table and picks up her coffee mug.

"That's in three days. I suppose we don't have to rush breakfast."

In a way, it's freeing to know our date and time of deployment precisely, to be able to count down our remaining time on Earth to the hour and minute without having to anticipate the alert buzz of the electronic leashes in our trouser pockets.

The Lazarus Brigades are now semiofficial ancillaries of the corps, but they're not so tightly integrated that I can reach Sergeant Fallon easily via MilNet. We do, however, have backdoor channels for exchanging updates, and I send my old squad leader a status update to let her know when we're going to Mars even though I'm sure that Lazarus's intelligence network is already aware of the news. Sergeant Fallon sends me a message back a few hours later through the shadow account we set up just for communications between us.

>Better you than me. I'd tell you to be careful, but you're in the business of seeking out shit to stir. Good luck to you and your wife, and God help the Lankies. See you on the other side.

All my best,

Briana

I wish I could get Sergeant Fallon to serve under me again, but she's not qualified to do pod drops, and I doubt that a division of SI could pry her out of her PRC and get her to go back into space. And in all honesty, I'm glad she'll get to sit this one out.

On the day after we receive the deployment orders, we do something we've never done before in our time here in Vermont. The chief packs us some food for lunch, and we go for a hike up into the mountains that surround Liberty Falls. Neither Halley nor I feel like carrying twenty kilos of extra kit up and down the hills, so we decide to piss on the regulations and leave our alert bags locked up in Chief Kopka's office along with our PDPs. It's a crisp, cold day, and the otherwise well-groomed hiking trail is covered in dry brown leaves, remnants of the gorgeous fall we never got to experience because we were 150 light-years from the Green Mountains a month and a half ago when all the colors turned. We are wearing our CDU cammies and weather shells and only carry sidearms and a bag with our lunch and water. I can tell the hike strains Halley much more than it would have before she got injured, but I know that she wants to prove to herself that she is up to the challenge despite not being healed up completely yet. If she can't hike a small hill on Earth in ideal conditions, she'll have no chance if she gets shot down on Mars and has to make an escape through much worse terrain.

"Will you look at this view," Halley says when we reach the top of the trail two hours later. We're at the top of a tall ridge, and Liberty Falls is nestled in the valley below, a few kilometers away.

"Bet you it was something else back in October," I say. The deciduous trees here in the mountains have shed their leaves, and the hills are brown and gray. I've learned a lot about trees in the last year or two, coming down here regularly.

"It's still something else. Just listen."

"I don't hear anything."

"Precisely," Halley says.

The town below is quiet. No noise makes it up to where we are standing, where the trees are swaying and rustling softly in the cold wind. I am once again struck by the difference between small-town 'burber life and the PRCs. The residence clusters just swallow the landscape, blanket it and take it over. Liberty Falls, manufactured and manicured as it is, just kind of nestles in the valley, molding itself to the shape of the landscape. None of the buildings in the town are taller than four or five floors. There's a stream running through the town, and the water is glittering in the rays of the sun that's poking through the holes in the cloud coverage. The solar-cell pavements of the residential neighborhoods have almost the same color as the river water, muted tones of dark green and blue.

I sit down on a fallen tree trunk nearby, and Halley joins me. The walk up was just strenuous enough for both of us to break a sweat despite the low temperature. We enjoy the view in silence as we catch our breath again.

"Feels weird," I say. "I don't think I've ever been out in the field without a rifle and a pack."

"We're not in the field," Halley says. "We're in nature."

"Never heard of it. That's what this is? Nature?"

"Smart-ass." She looks up into the sun poking through the clouds and closes her eyes. "Remember Arcadia? All those trees. You never saw it from the air the way I did from the cockpit. Lakes. Forests. Grassland. Like a little Earth, only without all the people."

"I remember," I say. "And then we set off a nuke on it."

"We didn't. The SEALs did. Major Masoud. And we'd be dead if he hadn't lit up that terraformer."

"Yeah, I know. Still seems like a shit thing to do, though. Four settlements on that rock, and one of them is now irradiated."

"They can be glad he didn't just hit the trigger on all of them. We can build more towns. Lots of space left on that moon."

The Arcadia mission is still gnawing on my mind. As a small-unit covert action, it was one of the most successful ones in NAC military history, mostly thanks to Major Masoud's planning and ruthlessness. We lost thirty troops and three advanced black-ops drop ships, but we seized an entire colony moon and half a million tons of top-of-the-line fighting ships. More importantly, the success of the mission restored a sense of justice among much of the NAC population. The new government—made up largely of veterans—gained a lot of goodwill and respect for hauling the renegade former NAC president and his entire circle of conspirators back to Earth in the brig of a supercarrier. It showed the people that the old elite was still subject to our laws, and that we will go 150 light-years and fight our own to drag them back to Earth if they betray us. But most of the thirty troops who died fell in the final assault on the admin complex in Arcadia City, and that mission was my initiative. I have tried to take Sergeant Fallon's advice about not second-guessing myself, but that sentiment is hard to reconcile with the rows of body bags that rode home with us on *Portsmouth*.

"What are we going to do after we get back?" Halley asks me. "Do we come back here? Live the 'burber life?"

"Well, we sure as shit aren't going to be anywhere near your folks," I say. "Not after last week."

Halley makes a little grimace at the mention of her parents. Then she looks back at the valley and the tidy little town tucked away in it.

"I suppose this isn't the worst of places to put down roots," she says. "If we're going to come back from Mars, that is."

"We will," I say.

"Oh?" Halley smiles and blinks into the sun again. "You got strategic intel you're not sharing? We're about to assault a colony world with thousands of Lankies on it. A dozen or more seed ships in orbit. And we're going into battle with whatever was left in the scrapyard."

"Well, there's a few stars in the lineup. Thanks to Major Masoud. As much as I hate to give that little bastard praise for anything."

"You think that'll make a difference?"

"No," I say. "Not the extra ships. Although they'll be nice to have."

I open the lunch bag Chief Kopka packed for us and go through the contents. There are sandwiches with turkey and cheddar—real stuff, not the soy shit they use in military mid-rats—and two thermal cups of soup. I pop the lid on one to check the contents. It's potato soup, thick enough to make a spoon stand up in it.

"That smells good," Halley says.

I hand her the container and a spoon from the bag and get another one out for myself.

"We'll win because it'll be all of *us* against all of *them*," I say. "The Russians, the Chinese, the Euros, the Africans, the South Americans, and us. And nothing but Lankies on the receiving end. No bullshit skirmish over some clump of dirt somewhere past the Thirty. No traitors. No questions about who needs shooting and why."

"Going all in," Halley says. "There's beauty in that." She looks at me quizzically. "You're looking forward to that fight, aren't you?"

"What?" I laugh. "Who the fuck looks forward to *combat*? Other than psychopaths. Or maybe Sergeant Fallon."

"Come on, now. I know you. You were a bit of a mess before Arcadia. So tense I could practically hear the humming coming from your nerve strands. And now you're all calm about Mars. Projecting a win, even."

I shake my head. "I'm not calm about it. And I'm sure as hell not looking forward to it."

"What is it, then?"

"I'm looking forward to finally being done with it," I say. "One way or the other. It's been hanging over our heads for over a year now."

"One way or the other," Halley repeats.

We eat in silence for a little while. Halley finishes her soup and methodically scrapes out the little thermal container with her spoon to get every last bit of it.

"Buying it on Mars isn't my worst fear," she says. "I don't want to check out just yet, but I'm not afraid of it."

"Then what *is* your worst fear?" I ask.

"Coming back without you," she says. Then she pops the lid back onto the soup container and puts it back in the bag. I am not used to Halley getting sentimental or mushy on me, and I'm still trying to decide how to respond when she stands up and shoulders our lunch bag.

"Come on," she says. "Let's see if we can make the top of the next hill before we eat those sandwiches. We'll be cooped up in a spaceship before too long. Might as well stretch our legs while we can."

"Might as well," I agree.

We pack up our little bit of gear and shoulder our packs again. I carefully watch Halley when she puts on her pack and notice that she grimaces a little bit when she slips the straps onto her shoulders, but she looks back at me with determination and nods toward the path.

"After you, Lieutenant."

"That first part is downhill," I say. "Speed march, six minutes per kilometer. Let me know when you can't hack it anymore."

She grins at this open challenge, as I knew she would.

"The day I tap out of a speed march with a light pack is the day I'll start folding your laundry for you, Andrew."

"Oh *ho*," I say. "An *incentive*. Let's go then, Captain."

I turn and start trotting down the path, and Halley follows me, a renewed spring in her step. The path to the next little peak only goes on for two kilometers, but right now I wish it would stretch for a thousand.

When you're embarked on a carrier and heading out for deployment to some backwater colony, and your ship is doing what seems like an interminably long transit to the Alcubierre node, three days seem like an eternity. But here in Vermont, with the knowledge of our impending separation, three days seem like no time at all. We go out into the hills during the days because it's quiet and there are few other people, and because we won't be able to see sky and trees again for quite a while. In the evenings, we spend time with my mother and Chief Kopka, having dinner and talking about the things we'll do after Mars, more to keep my mother's spirit up than ours. We spend the nights together, of course, upstairs in the chief's guest bedroom, just the two of us, uninterrupted time without any 1MC announcements or alerts blaring outside our door. In all my time with Halley since we got married on *Regulus* last year, the three days before our deployment are the most peaceful ones I've had since I joined the military.

On the morning of our departure, we wake up early and have breakfast downstairs in the still-dark restaurant while the chief and my mother are conducting their preopening business, making coffee and preparing the menu's breakfast items. They're a bit more sparse and a lot more expensive than they used to be the first time I came to this restaurant, but the food is still way beyond anything the military serves, better even than the good stuff we got to eat when I first signed up. We have coffee, scrambled eggs, and bacon, and the chief made us a tall stack of pancakes and decanted some of his diminishing maple syrup reserve. I want to drag this breakfast out forever, but time advances with no regard for my sentiment. We usually clear out and vacate the table before the chief opens his restaurant at seven o'clock so we don't take up space for paying guests, and we stick to that routine today as well, but not before polishing off the entire stack of pancakes.

It's just getting light outside when we step out, carrying our alert bags and dressed in freshly laundered CDU fatigues. It's a Friday morning, and the November air is cold and smells like impending snow. The chief and my mother follow us outside to see us off to the train station for our fifteen-minute ride to Burlington, where we will take separate shuttles to get to our next commands. Halley's ship is docked at Gateway. I have to hop across the country to get to Coronado on the West Coast before I can come up to Gateway as well. By the time I get there, Halley's carrier will have already left for the assembly point.

"Godspeed," Chief Kopka says, and shakes our hands firmly. "Give 'em hell. And watch your six."

"Affirmative, Chief," I reply. "Thanks for everything. Keep the heat on for us in the guest bedroom. We'll be back before you know it."

"I sincerely hope so. Wish I could go up there with you and stand my post again for a bit."

"They'll need you down here if things go to hell on Mars," I say.

"If you all don't come back, there won't be much I can do here."

"If we don't come back, you close up shop, load all the food into your truck, and head north until you run out of continent," Halley tells the chief. "You stay away from the big cities. The Brigades won't be able to keep a lid on the pot if it all goes south. The Lankies don't like cold places too much."

I know that the chief is well aware of the fact that the Lankies' first order of business during settlement is to scrape any humans off the planet with their nerve-gas pods. If they show up in orbit, they'll drop those on the cities from up high. Then they'll land their settler pods and start building terraformers to increase the CO_2 content in the atmosphere to levels that are lethal for humans. If we lose the battle, and the Lankies show up uncontested, there will be no place on the planet remote enough where we can escape. But my mother is standing here with us to see us off, and nobody wants to hear that death is inevitable if our dice roll comes up short. So the chief just nods, and we go on pretending that it won't be the end of all things if this mission fails.

"I know you hate it," I tell my mother. Mom wipes a tear from her cheek and hugs me tightly, or as much as she can while I'm carrying twenty kilos of kit.

"I know you have to do this," she says. "I know what's at stake. And I'm proud of you for what you're doing. But yes, I hate every damn minute of it when you're gone. Mother's prerogative."

"I can't argue with that, Mom." I kiss her on the top of her head—she seems so small now—and return her hug. I look at Chief Kopka over the top of Mom's head, and he nods. I know that if things don't go well for us, he'll take care of my mother until the last, and I know that he'll do what needs to be done to spare them both a drawn-out, agonizing death at the hands of the Lankies. In any case, she'll be much better off here with the chief than she would have been in the PRC, which will turn into the ninth circle of hell once the Lankies show up in force.

Mom hugs Halley, too, every bit as fiercely as she hugged me, and maybe even a few moments longer.

"Come back, the both of you," she says. "Do what you have to, and come home. You two have a life to live when this is all over."

We make the short walk to the train station in the cold morning air, in no particular hurry to get where we are going. We have to report to our new posts by the end of the day, and we'll easily get there long before the deadline, even if we wait until noon to hop our flights.

As we walk up to the main entrance of the maglev station, a few snowflakes fall from the sky. They descend leisurely, buffeted by the cold morning wind. I look up at the gray sky and see more flakes drifting down, a first harbinger of the winter that's about to come. I came to Liberty Falls for the first time on a winter day almost two years ago, and I'll always see it in my mind with a blanket of clean snow covering the lawns and sidewalks, sparkling in the streetlights, making the town look like a relic from a long-gone time to someone from the PRCs. Maybe this isn't reality—it certainly isn't for any of the people I grew up with. But is it so bad to want to live like this instead of living out life in a stack of concrete boxes a hundred floors high?

Halley tries to chase down a snowflake with her tongue but misses. She catches the flake with the back of her hand instead and watches it melt on her warm skin. Then she looks over at me and smiles coyly, like I've just caught her doing something childish.

"Four weeks until Christmas," she says. "Let's not miss it. It's my favorite time of the year down here."

I don't know what exactly it is about this moment that suddenly makes my heart hurt, and the pain I feel is far worse than the physical wounds I've collected in the service, because I know that there are no trauma packs for it. And I know that if I come back here without Halley, I'll be broken in ways that no military surgeon will be able to fix.

The fifteen-minute train ride to Burlington feels like no time at all.

After so many years of separate deployments, Halley and I have a lot of practice saying good-bye. We both have dangerous jobs, so it makes no sense for this good-bye to feel any different, but it does. We check in at the gate together and climb into the same bus for the ride to the airfield. Ten minutes later, we're in front of the air station's ops center, where we will split up to catch our respective rides—hers straight up into orbit to Gateway, and mine to the other coast.

Halley kisses me and fixes the stand-up collar of my CDU fatigues, even though I know it needs no fixing.

"This is it," she says. "The Big One. Are you nervous?"

"No," I lie.

"Me, neither," she lies right back.

"We'll still be able to talk on MilNet. Unless they black out near-field comms, which they won't. At least not until we're out of the assembly area and well on the way to Mars."

"So write," she says. "Maybe we'll even have the bandwidth for video."

"Thank you for standing up for me back in San Antonio. Against your folks, I mean."

Halley pulls me close for another kiss, ignoring the gaggle of enlisted personnel milling around nearby who are eyeing the two Fleet officers playing kissy-face.

"You are my folks now. They're my parents, but you're my husband. I'll always take your side. Without blinking. Never doubt that."

"Wouldn't dream of it," I say.

"I love you," she says. "I always will, even when I'm back to being stardust." Then she kisses me one more time and shoulders her alert bag.

"Let's get this over with. Do your thing, and come back in one piece. You heard your mom. We have a life to live. And those spindly fucks are standing in the way of that."

"Yes, ma'am," I say.

I watch her as she walks out to the shuttle pad to catch her ride into orbit. My wife, the only constant thing in my life since I joined the military, and probably the best drop-ship pilot in the fleet. She has always known her course, and she has never failed to steer it. We've had the talk about death many times over the years. Not once did she say that she was scared of dying, and not once did I fail to feel gratitude for someone like her wanting to share her life with me. If I get nothing else in this life, I got that at least, and it's enough.

"Let's get this over with," I repeat. Then I pick up my own alert bag and walk over to the atmospheric shuttle pad to board my own ride.

CHAPTER 9

GETTING THE BAND BACK TOGETHER

When we first encountered the Lankies, our military bureaucracy kicked R & D into high gear to come up with weapons and gear to fight the new threat. In typical bureaucratic fashion, even high gear took a few years to produce the first usable prototypes, and the new stuff was hit or miss. But one thing they definitely got right from the start was the new anti-Lanky battle armor. In the supply chain and in official documentation, it's called the HEBA: hostile environment battle armor. The troops—those lucky enough to get issued one—call it the bug suit.

When I got my last bug suit, it took six days to get me fitted for one. The bug suits aren't off-the-rack items. They have to be tailored to the user. In the almost five years since I got my suit, they've stream-lined the fitting process down to a day. It's still a day of mostly standing around while laser sensors map out every square millimeter of your body, but it beats the laborious hand-measured fitting process from half a decade ago. On Friday, six hours after I say good-bye to Halley at Burlington, I report to Joint Base Coronado, the main Fleet base on the West Coast and home to the fleet's Special Operations Command. I spend the whole Saturday getting laser-measured and hooked up to various diagnostic systems, and the fitted suit is ready for me by Sunday afternoon.

"That took no time at all," I say to the supply specialist when I put on the suit for the postfitting testing and calibration. "Last time they didn't have the suit ready for a week."

"What happened to it?" the tech asks.

"Burned up with *Manitoba* at Sirius A."

"Wow. You were there? Not too many guys came back from that one."

"No, they didn't," I say.

"Yeah, we have way more suits than people who are qualified to wear them," the tech says. "We fitted more this week than we did all year, but you're only number seven."

"I feel special."

"Hell, they should let us give you a spare suit while you're here. Just in case this one burns up, too."

I chuckle without much humor. "If this suit burns up, I don't think I'll be needing a spare."

On Sunday evening, I get onto a shuttle to Gateway Station, where my next command is docked right now. It's obvious that a big operation is about to kick off—the shuttle is full to the last seat with passengers bound for orbit, and when I step out of the shuttle and onto the station an hour later, Gateway is as busy as I've ever seen it. The main concourse is crammed with throngs of uniformed personnel streaming in both directions. I can't help but notice how green most of them are. I see lots of junior enlisted, privates and PFCs and corporals, and damn few sergeants or officers. This is the last batch of trainees we ran through the cycle just before Mars. I wonder how many former recruits from boot-camp platoon 1526 are somewhere in the crowd, rushing off to their assigned commands, nervous enough to throw up. Depending on their occupational specialties, many of them had just enough time to squeak through tech school in time to be part of this offensive.

It takes half an hour at a brisk jog to traverse Gateway's main concourse from one end to the other when the station isn't packed to the bulkheads. Overcrowded as the concourse is right now, it takes me over an hour of drifting with the crowds until I reach the part of the station where my new command is docked. It's in the capital-ship section of Gateway, and the big screen next to the airlock displays the ship's name and hull number, along with other information.

"NACS PHALANX CA-761," it reads. "CO: COL YAMIN, S."

I remember *Phalanx*. She's one of the most advanced ships in the fleet, a heavy space control cruiser with enough firepower to take on an SRA task force by itself. She was also one of the ships the renegades stole and shuttled to the Leonidas system, to safeguard their little paradise with the best hardware the fleet had left. When the former NAC leadership on Arcadia surrendered, we reclaimed almost every ship from the stolen task force to pad our roster for the Mars assault. When we left the system, all they had left at their orbital anchorage was an older frigate for patrol duties. *Phalanx* and the rest of the renegade fleet rejoined the NAC forces in the solar system a week later. The ships are still mostly run by the renegade crews because we don't have the manpower to replace all those well-trained specialists, but everybody who wasn't part of the Exodus is keeping a close eye on everybody who was.

The airlock is guarded by two SI troopers, a private and a sergeant. The private looks like he just got out of SI training last week, but the sergeant seems to have been around the block a time or two. Her name tape says "BULL, S.," and she wears a no-nonsense expression to go with the sidearm on her belt. The drop badge above her left breast pocket is stitched in silver thread—more than twenty drops, less than fifty. I dig out my PDP and show her my orders. She scans it and verifies the data on her own PDP.

"You're looking for Delta Deck, sir," she says. "Section Forty-Seven, Grunt Country. Have you been on a Hammerhead before?"

"A few times," I say.

"We have the near-field network activated. Just follow your PDP's directions."

"Will do. Thank you, Sergeant."

I step through the hatch, across the docking collar, and onto NACS *Phalanx*. My PDP's haptic engine bumps my palm gently to direct me down the passageway ahead. *Phalanx* is as modern as Fleet ships come, and the ship's nonslip passageway liner looks almost pristine, not worn down to the laminate deck like the ones on long-serving units. Everything looks like the ship just came out of the builder's dock last year, and for all I know, that may be the case. It's only when I get deeper into the ship, following my PDP's directions down ladders and along fore-and-aft passageways, that I see some signs of prior battle damage, expertly but obviously patched holes and faint scorch marks on bulkheads and decks. I've seen such damage before, and I conclude that *Phalanx* has come too close to Lanky seed ships or proximity mines before.

Every major warship in the fleet has a Grunt Country, the berthing section reserved for the ship's Spaceborne Infantry or SOCOM contingent. Frigates can carry a platoon; destroyers and light cruisers carry two. A Hammerhead space control cruiser is built for supporting planetary assaults, so it can carry a full company, and their Grunt Country makes up a fairly big chunk of real estate in the aft end of the ship. On *Phalanx*, it occupies two sections on either side of a passageway close to the main fore-and-aft "expressway" in this part of the hull. I consult my PDP for the location of the administrative section and step into the module where the command element is housed.

There's no name tag on the hatch of my new commanding officer's space, just a sign that says "CO SOCOM DET"—commanding officer, special operations command detachment. The hatch is halfway open, and I knock on the doorframe.

"Come in," a familiar voice says.

I push the hatch open all the way and see Major Masoud, the man who led the mission to Arcadia a month and a half ago, the man who put a gun to the collective head of the old NAC leadership and won us the battle. He's sitting behind his desk, typing on a data pad.

"Lieutenant Grayson, reporting as ordered, sir," I say, and salute, the traditional gesture indicating a respect that I don't really feel for the major since his stunt on Arcadia. I know he considered me and my troops expendable back then, and I have no reason to believe that his attitude has changed.

Major Masoud looks up from his data pad and nods. "Come in, Lieutenant. Have a seat."

I do as ordered and sit down in the chair in front of Major Masoud's desk. He's wearing Fleet fatigues, with the sleeves rolled up so smoothly and tightly that I'd probably need a magnifying glass to spot any wrinkles.

"Welcome to SOCOM Task Force Red," Major Masoud says. He smiles a wry little smile. "Incidentally, there are exactly as many letters in that name as there are members in it."

I count the letters up in my head. "Seventeen," I say.

Major Masoud nods. "And we're lucky to even have that number."

"So what are we doing, sir?" *With a measly seventeen troops*, I don't add.

"The mission briefing will take place after the task force has assembled. But you will be performing in your main MOS for the assault, if that is your main concern. You'll be our unit's combat controller."

"Copy that, sir. Anything else you can share before the official mission briefing?"

Major Masoud gives me a thin-lipped smile. "If I told you that I don't know much more than you do, would you believe me?"

"No, sir," I say. "Not after Leonidas."

He looks at me for a moment, still smiling. "I suppose I can't blame you."

He picks up his data pad again and taps the screen a few times. "We're going to Mars. That's no big secret. And SOCOM will be first in the dirt, as usual. That's about all. The details are just garnish at this point, aren't they?"

"Yes, sir. But they're still nice to know."

A month and a half ago, when he stepped off the drop ship after the surrender of the renegade colony at Arcadia, I could have shot this stocky little bastard on the spot. He used my platoon as bait to lead the garrison on a wild-goose chase while his SEAL teams stuck nuclear demolition charges to half the terraformers on that moon. In the time since the mission, I've had enough time to reflect and realize that he did the absolute best with what he had, and that our final body count was an exceedingly cheap price to pay for what we got out of the mission. But I'll never forget the fact that he used my troops as a diversion without letting us in on the plan. Thirty dead, and if Halley hadn't been exceedingly lucky, I would be a widower right now. Professionally, I have to admire this crafty, ruthless bastard. Personally, I can't help but hate him.

"I'll share what I can when we are under way," Major Masoud says. "*Phalanx* is departing for the fleet assembly point in thirteen hours. I suggest you get settled and meet your teammates. Take care of any last-minute comms business. We'll be cruising under EMCON once we're under way."

"Yes, sir." I get up, salute, and turn to walk out of Major Masoud's little office again.

"And Lieutenant?"

I turn around again. "Yes, sir?"

"It's good to have you on the team. And I say that without reservation."

"Thank you, sir," I say, mildly surprised.

Joining a new command always reminds me a little bit of those awkward first days of class in a new school, when you have to get used to your environment and get a feel for the social flow of the place at the same time. But the Special Operations community was small enough even before we lost three-quarters of SOCOM, so I expect to see at least a few familiar faces on *Phalanx*, and I am not disappointed.

I step into the mission-personnel berth with my kit bag to one of the strangest sights I've seen on a fleet warship. The berthing area looks a lot like the module for my platoon on *Portsmouth*—four staterooms on either side of the entry hatch, a larger assembly space beyond, and group berths on the far side of that. In the assembly space, there's enough room for four foldout tables and benches to form booths, and there are a dozen troops sitting at those tables and engrossed in conversation. Five of them are wearing the distinctive mottled camo pattern of SRA marines. The SRA trooper closest to the door has his back turned to me, but he turns around when the SI troopers on the other side of the table spot me and pause their conversation. Dmitry Chistyakov, senior sergeant of the SRA marines, raises a hand in a casual greeting, as if he had just spotted me across the room in a bar on New Svalbard.

"Andrew," he says. "Is good to see you. Come and sit." He nods at an empty section of bench across the table from him.

"Gentlemen," I say to the NAC troopers at the table with Dmitry. They nod at me, and I slide into the booth next to them. One is an SI lieutenant, and the other is a fleet master sergeant. The lieutenant has the black beret of the SI's Force Recon arm tucked underneath his rank sleeve, and the master sergeant is a Spaceborne Rescueman. All around us, the conversations in the room pick up again.

"Do you know this character?" the Force Recon lieutenant asks, and nods at Dmitry.

"You could say that," I say. "We've dropped together, in Fomalhaut. He knows his stuff."

Just a little over a year ago, it would have been almost unthinkable to see an SRA trooper on a Commonwealth warship in any place but the brig. Seeing not one, but five of them here in the troop berth without handcuffs or armed NAC guards standing next to them is still a crazy thing to see. And if it seems crazy to me, with all my exposure to the SRA troops during our joint mission in Fomalhaut, I can't imagine just how bizarre the sight must be to the NAC troops who weren't there with us.

"What's the word from upstairs, Lieutenant?" the Spaceborne Rescueman asks.

"We're going to war, I think," I reply, and the other troops at the table chuckle. "Seriously, I haven't heard much," I tell the master sergeant. "Our CO isn't the chatty type. We're leaving for the assembly point in thirteen hours. That's about all I know."

The master sergeant looks around in the room and shrugs. "Doesn't take much intel to figure out what we're going to do," he says. "Podheads, the lot of us."

"First into the LZ," I agree. "How long has it been since your last pod drop?"

"Year and a half, not counting training drops. You?"

"Same. It's all been taxi rides ever since." I look over at the SRA trooper sitting next to Dmitry, who follows the conversation with a politely neutral expression. "Who's your colleague, Dmitry?"

Dmitry points at the trooper next to him. "*Mládshiy Leytenánt* Bondarenko," he says. "Leader of Alliance reconnaissance squad. And at other table is Sergeant Gerasimov, Sergeant Dragomirova, and *Mládshiy Serzhánt* Anokhin."

At the other table, the SRA troopers he names raise their hands in greeting one by one when they hear their names. Sergeant Dragomirova, who has long dark hair that's tightly pulled back and secured in a pony-tail, flicks a little salute with the cup in her hand. Then they resume their conversations with the NAC troops at their tables.

"Is good squad," Dmitry says. "Good fighters. Have killed many Lankies together. I drop with them a few times before."

Considering the newness of the situation, and the fact that until a year ago, we were still in a shooting war with the SRA, the atmosphere in the personnel berth is downright low-key. It helps that the berths and common areas of a warship aren't terrifically spacious and don't lend themselves to keeping one's distance. And I do notice that the SRA troopers and their NAC counterparts sit across the tables from each other and don't mingle on the same benches. But overall, the SI troopers seem to be rather laid-back about having their former enemies in their midst. With the assault against the Lankies imminent, it seems that old animosities aren't all that important anymore. We will fight those things together, just like we did at Fomalhaut, and we will live or die together.

"You learn any Russian, Andrew?" Dmitry asks. "You have year to learn."

"*Da, nemnogo,*" I reply. *Yes, a little.* Dmitry rewards this with a smile and a nod.

"You spend time well since last year," he says. "No longer squishy around middle."

"How's Maksim?" I ask. Dmitry smiles again, clearly pleased that I remembered the name of his spouse.

"Still big. Little less dumb. Maybe you will meet him on Mars. Eight hundred seventy-sixth Desant Battalion, on carrier *Rossiya*." I see the shadow of a sorrowful frown on his face as he mentions the unit of his husband, and I know exactly what he's feeling right now. Both our spouses are riding out to this battle as well, but in different units and embarked on different ships, and barring an extremely unlikely coincidence, our paths on the battlefield won't cross. We will see them after the battle, or never again.

"You ever drop in an NAC bio-pod before?"

"Yes," Dmitry says. "In simulator. Is not so hard. Pod does all the flying. You are just bullet in big gun."

"That's pretty much it in a nutshell," I say, and look over my shoulder at the rest of the troopers in the common space. The berthing module is designed to hold a whole platoon, forty personnel, and we're not even half that number.

"Three fire teams, a pair of combat controllers, and a medic," I say. "That better be a really small LZ, or we'll be stretched mighty thin."

The hatch of the berthing module opens, and I look to see who's arriving. For just a moment, I have the wild, irrational hope that Halley is going to walk into the room unexpectedly, just like she did on *Portsmouth*. But the newcomer isn't my wife. It's a soldier in Eurocorps camo, and he has a fleet sergeant in tow. The Eurocorps trooper is a wiry guy with an ultrashort buzz cut. He wears a blue Euro flag on one sleeve, the black-red-gold German flag on the other, and lieutenant-rank insignia on the front of his camo tunic.

"Sirs," the fleet sergeant behind him says. "This is Lieutenant Stahl. He's this ship's Eurocorps liaison."

"Germans, Russians, North Americans," I say to the table in a low voice. "It's like a little United Nations in here all of a sudden."

"Not like United Nations," Dmitry says. "We are not, how do you say, debate club? We are better at shooting things a lot, I think."

"That's the *only* thing we're good at," I correct.

There aren't many private spots on a warship, not even one the size of *Phalanx*, but after a few years in the fleet, you figure out where the quiet corners on each type of ship are located. *Phalanx* is a Hammerhead cruiser, halfway between a destroyer and an assault carrier in size, and she has a little astrogation deck in her dorsal hull, a small polyplast bubble on top of the armor, accessible through a narrow ladder. It's a long climb through two decks' worth of laminate armor plating, so it's not occupied very often. But when I go up there to compose a few messages to Halley and my mother while looking at the stars, there's someone else sitting in one of the observation chairs already.

"Excuse me, ma'am," I say when I see the rank insignia on the sleeves of the occupant's uniform. "I didn't know you were up here."

Colonel Yamin, *Phalanx*'s commanding officer, nods at the row of empty chairs in front of her.

"No intrusion, Lieutenant. This is a crew space, after all. Come and sit. I was just about to leave anyway."

I finish climbing out of the ladder well and walk over to one of the chairs to sit down.

So far, I've only known the skipper as a disembodied voice on the 1MC. The woman in the standard Fleet uniform sitting in the chair across from mine has long dark hair, green eyes, and a vaguely sad and pensive air about her. She reminds me a little bit of Halley, only with another ten years of combat and hard choices etched into her face.

"You're one of the SOCOM guys," she says.

"Yes, ma'am. Combat controller. First ones down, last ones up."

She looks at the ring on my right hand and nods toward it. "Podhead's not a great job for a married man."

"She doesn't mind. She's a drop-ship jock. At least we both have our asses on the line at the same time."

"How long have you been doing this?"

"Five years in this specialty. Married for a little over a year. We got married on *Regulus* right before the Lanky incursion last year." I smile at the memory. "She had the skipper marry us while the ship was in condition Zebra and getting ready for battle."

"Sounds like she has her priorities straight," Colonel Yamin says with a little smile.

I look at the stars outside the ten-meter polyplast bubble of the observatory. "I've been in the fleet almost seven years. I feel like I ought to be able to identify constellations by sight. But I still can't tell most of them apart."

"They drill that into you in cap-ship officer school," Colonel Yamin says. "Like we're ever going to stand up here with a sextant and navigate a thirty-thousand-ton cruiser by eyeballs."

"Yeah, well, I'm not even a real officer. Limited duty. Got promoted last year, right before the Leonidas mission."

I remember half a second too late that *Phalanx* was one of the ships stolen by the renegade NAC government, part of the fleet reclaimed by nuclear blackmail.

"How long have you had *Phalanx*?" I ask.

"Two and a half years. I took command six months before the Lankies kicked us off Mars." She gives me a sad little smile. "Yes, Lieutenant, I am one of *those* people. The ones who tucked tail and ran."

"I'm sure you had your reasons, ma'am," I say, careful to sound neutral. A little over a month ago, this woman was with the group that tried to kill us while we tried to kill them right back. All the ship commanders are still in charge of their units, but the ones who went with the renegade government have suspicious eyes on them at all times, and there's still talk about a court-martial for them after Mars if any make it back alive.

"Everyone has reasons for what they do," she replies. "Sometimes they're even good ones. If there's one thing I learned from it all, it's that I am in no position to judge someone else's."

"We fought," I say. "When you were all gone, and the Lankies came calling. We fought with what you left us. Frigates, corvettes, all the old shit you didn't take. We stopped them, but you have no idea what it cost us."

She looks at me, and I can see anger welling up behind those green eyes. Then she sighs and shakes her head slightly. "When the Lankies took Mars, we were docked in orbit," she says. "Getting ready to make the run back to Earth, for refits and crew R & R. Half the crew was planetside. My XO got killed on the surface, rescuing settlers. I sent this ship out to save shuttles and lifeboats. Lots of lifeboats. We gave them everything we had, which is a lot. You know the firepower of a Hammerhead. They shrugged it off like we were throwing pebbles."

She speaks softly, recounting her memories as if retelling a dream.

"Of the crew I had left, I lost two hundred when the Lankies hit us. We patched her up and limped back to Earth. The ship was unable to fight, barely able to run. And then we passed the counterattack going the other way."

She closes her eyes and tilts her head back.

"My little brother was on one of the ships in the counterattack. I told them it was no good. Told them they'd be running themselves against a wall for nothing. They went anyway because they had to. And my brother didn't come back."

I don't say anything, and the silence between us stretches out for a few moments.

"I would have turned the ship around if I had been able to fight with them. But I had four hundred crew left who didn't need to die for nothing. So we went home, and instead of coming home with Darius,

I got to give my father a flag folded into a triangle. We didn't even have a burial capsule to drape it over, because his ship was lost with all hands above Mars. So don't tell me I don't know what it cost you. We all paid dearly. Those who left, and those who didn't."

"I wouldn't have left with them," I say. "I wouldn't have left everyone behind."

"You say that now," she says, and looks at me evenly, without anger. "Your wife is in the fleet. My parents and my kids were not. They let me take my kids, but not my mom and dad. I left my parents behind to save my kids."

I don't have a snappy response for that, so I just look at the field of stars above our heads. I try to imagine what I would do if I had to make a choice between Halley or Mom, choose one of them to come to safety with me and leave the other one to near-certain death.

Colonel Yamin takes a slow, long breath, exhales, and gets out of her chair. Then she tugs on the front of her uniform to smooth it out.

"I should get back to CIC and leave you to your business. As you were."

She walks over to the ladder well and swings one foot over the threshold.

"Don't be so sure of your judgment. *You ran, we stayed, you're wrong, we're right.* I hope you never have to make that kind of choice. But if you ever do, maybe you'll remember this. Nobody's ever the bad guy in their own mind, Lieutenant. Sometimes you just have to pick between two bad choices and decide which one is a little less awful than the other. The one that'll let you sleep a tiny bit better at night."

She nods at me and starts her climb back into *Phalanx*'s hull, leaving me alone with my thoughts underneath the star-studded blackness of space.

CHAPTER 10

— FLEET ASSEMBLY POINT ECHO —

Phalanx leaves the dock at Gateway precisely at 0700 hours on Monday morning. It's November, and I don't know whether it's overcast down in Liberty Falls right now, but it feels overcast here in this ship even though there's nothing but black above and behind us. I got out of my bunk at the last watch change an hour ago, and I'm returning from the officer mess and a sparse meal of scrambled eggs and coffee when the overhead announcement system trills.

"All hands, this is Colonel Yamin. I just gave the order to clear the docking collar and secure all airlocks. In a few minutes, we will disconnect the service umbilicals and cut loose from Gateway for our run to the fleet assembly area."

Phalanx's commander pauses for a few seconds before she continues her address.

"You all know what we are about to do, and where we are about to go. I've ordered the CIC watch to put the video feed from *Phalanx*'s main camera array onto every viewscreen on the ship. Take a moment, and look at the feed if you can."

I turn on the little viewscreen in my stateroom. It shows a slice of Earth below *Phalanx* and Gateway in ultrahigh resolution. Most of the continent below us is covered in clouds, but I can make out part of the North American coastline, the familiar shape of the northern East Coast. It's a perfect shot if you wanted to include a promo image of Earth in some sort of intergalactic travel guide—the blue-and-white planet, teeming with life and activity, and the thin sliver of atmosphere separating all that life from the vastness of space. You only realize how thin that atmospheric layer really is once you get to see it from this vantage point. The horizon in the distance goes from white to light blue, then to star-studded dark blue in the space of just a few degrees of view angle. My physics teacher used to say that the atmospheric layer is as thin as the condensation on the peel of an orange when you breathe on it. Even the moon is cooperating for the beauty shot—it's up above the horizon just above the atmospheric transition layer, so close and clear that I can make out the network of structures on Luna City and its surroundings.

"This is what we are going to defend," *Phalanx*'s commander continues. "This is where we started crawling out of the mud a hundred millennia ago. This is where we built our cities and made our histories. This is where our friends and families are, everything we hold dear. This is what's going to be taken from us if we don't beat the Lankies back here and now. We stand and fight, or we fade into the black forever."

I look at the slice of Earth visible on the camera feed, so vast when you're this close to it, and yet so small when you consider how much nothingness is all around us just in the solar system, never mind the rest of the universe. On a cosmic scale, our species and its history are utterly irrelevant, probably just one sentient life-form among millions. But I'm not ready to let it all disappear into the void just yet.

"So we stand, and so we fight," the skipper says. "Stand to and man your posts. We will return when we've done our jobs, and that little blue orb will still be home. I'll be damned if I let those bastards kick us off. All hands, prepare for departure."

The announcement ends, and I am left to think about the skipper's words as I sit alone in my stateroom, looking at the screen in front of me, where Earth keeps on rotating slowly in space. I've left Gateway on combat deployments so many times that I thought I was inoculated against the feeling I have right now, the premonition that I'm seeing my home planet for the last time. I see myself on the surface of Mars again, thousands of Lankies in front of me, and then nuclear fireballs, a dream that may be on the way to becoming reality.

Half an hour later, as we coast away from Gateway at the low speed prescribed for orbital maneuvers, the skipper's voice comes over the 1MC again. I look up from my PDP and the message I am typing out to Halley.

"All hands, check the viewscreens."

Colonel Yamin says nothing else, and I look over at the screen in my stateroom again. The camera angle no longer shows Earth. It's trained on the section of orbit between Gateway and Independence Stations. There is a lot of orbital traffic between us and there—civvie freighters, orbital shuttles, corvettes, and patrol boats from smaller countries. Every one of the dozens of ships in sight has its exterior lights on, and they're all blinking in synchronicity, a coordinated farewell to the departing warships on the way into battle. I've been feeling glum all morning, but the sight of this unexpected gesture from the people who can't go off to battle with us suddenly makes me feel glad to be up here. Billions of people on the planet and thousands of personnel here in orbit have no choice but to sit this fight out and wait anxiously to see if they get to live on. I get to have a hand in the outcome of the battle. As small as my contribution may be in the end, I get to add my weight to our side of the scale, and that's more than almost everyone else gets.

>We are under way. See you at the assembly point. I love you.

I send the message off to Halley, taking the opportunity while we're still in range of the relay on Gateway. Underway, ship-to-ship traffic will be limited to mission essentials, and the near-field comms only work between ships if they are within a few kilometers of each other.

Her reply comes back a few minutes later.

>Pollux is leaving the dock in 45 minutes. I love you too. See you when it's over. Good hunting.

The screen in my stateroom reverts back to its normal condition, a display of general ship information—course, speed, position, ship-wide announcements. One quadrant of the screen is taken up by the feed from the tactical plot in CIC, a three-dimensional representation of the space around the ship. I reach over and flick the tactical display so it takes up the entire screen. Gateway is already a few thousand kilometers behind us as *Phalanx* is accelerating to full military power and pulling away from the anchorage. We are part of a long line of blue and green lozenge-shaped icons, each representing an NAC or allied ship, each labeled with hull number and name. We're not even at the fleet assembly point yet, but the space around *Phalanx* already contains more warships than I've seen in one spot since the run back from Fomalhaut. There's something exhilarating about seeing that much combat power in motion, for once tackling the threat with a plan and a realistic chance instead of just throwing hardware against a wall to see it shatter.

When forty-five minutes since my exchange with Halley have passed, I check the display again for her ship, NACS *Pollux*, but we are too far ahead in the queue by now, and the awareness bubble of the

CIC's situational display isn't large enough to track the carrier. Still, I know that she's behind me somewhere, a few thousand kilometers astern from *Phalanx* and heading the same way.

We spend the day squaring away kit and eating meals in our respective facilities—the mess hall for the enlisted, and the officer wardroom for the junior officers among us: Lieutenant Bondarenko from the SRA marines, Lieutenant Perkins of the SI's Force Recon team, Lieutenant Stahl from Eurocorps, and me. All the officers on the embarked SOCOM team are from different service arms and wearing four different camo patterns. When dinnertime comes around and we still don't have orders or a schedule from our commanding officers, we all end up around the same table in the officer wardroom for lack of something else to do.

Lieutenant Bondarenko isn't as gregarious as Dmitry, and his English isn't half as good, so he stays mostly quiet, but he seems to like the officer chow just fine because he finishes off two plates. Lieutenant Perkins from SI is a year younger than I am but has almost as many combat drops and the typical cocky Force Recon devil-may-care attitude. The Eurocorps lieutenant is fluent in English but speaks with a heavy German accent. We exchange pleasantries and speculate about the upcoming landing on Mars.

"It'll be the largest spaceborne assault in history," Lieutenant Perkins says. "I've heard we're dropping a whole division in the first wave, another with the second."

"You think we scraped together enough troops for several divisions?" I say.

"You don't think so?"

"I've done nothing but run boot-camp cycles for the last year to fill the roster. Two whole divisions? That's four brigades. Sixteen battalions.

Before we lost Mars, the whole SI was just three divisions. But with the SRA and the Europeans kicking in, who knows?"

"They will tell us soon enough," the German lieutenant says. "I know that Eurocorps has sent one regiment."

"Every bit counts," I say, feeling slightly disappointed. One regiment means two battalions of troops—not nothing, but thirteen hundred troops are a mere sliver of the total Eurocorps manpower. But then I remind myself that the Eurocorps troops are mostly geared for peacekeeping on Earth, not space warfare, and that the regiment they're sending probably constitutes most or all of their space-trained troops.

Counting heads in this room, however, does not make me feel overly confident just yet. The SOCOM team assembled on this ship is pitifully small for spearheading a landing in what is supposed to be the biggest spaceborne invasion ever. But right now there's nothing to do but to wait for our mission parameters, so we can find out just how much we'll have to stretch the four podhead teams in this berth.

For once, command updates us on our prospective fate without much undue delay. Ten hours after we leave Gateway, *Phalanx* turns and burns for our scheduled deceleration. Twenty hours out of Gateway, we coast into a section of space that's crowded with more warships than I've ever seen away from an anchorage together. The safety distance between each ship is five kilometers, and ships are bunched into little groups for as far as the hundred-kilometer tactical display in CIC can render units. I try to get a rough count of ship markers on the situational display in my stateroom but have to give up after three dozen, and I know that there are at least twenty more ships inbound from Earth in the queue behind us. Two-thirds of the markers are NAC or SRA units, and the last third is made up of units from just about every other spacefaring alliance on Earth: South America, Africa, Oceania, European Union. It looks like we weren't the only ones mobilizing our reserve fleets and refurbishing scrapyard candidates.

"Now hear this," comes over the ship's 1MC. "This is Colonel Yamin. We have arrived at Fleet Assembly Point Echo. This is our jump-off point for the offensive. We will take our assigned place in the battle formation and prepare to commence combat operations. From this point on, be ready for battle, because the next combat-stations alert means there are Lankies in the neighborhood and we're about to send live warheads downrange. From now until we return to Gateway, there will be no more drills. Every alarm will be real."

Until we return to Gateway, I think. The station is old and worn-out and a pain in the ass to navigate on a busy day, but I find myself hoping that the optimism of *Phalanx*'s skipper isn't misplaced, and that I get to curse out the idiot who designed the station at some point again in the near future as I walk Gateway's scuffed and dirty corridors.

For lack of something better to do at the moment, I watch the display from CIC for a while. The mass of icons slowly moves on the situational globe as *Phalanx* maneuvers through the assembly area to whatever holding spot they assigned to us. I see that all the groupings of units are truly multinational and interalliance—SRA ships mingling with NAC ones, and Euro or African Commonwealth ships here and there. The capital ships are all NAC or SRA because no other spacefaring nation needs heavy units for extrasolar deployments. They have corvettes, light patrol boats, supply ships, and the occasional frigate or destroyer, all the space fleet needed for policing solar-system outposts and mining nodes. Right now, all those support units are welcome padding for our invasion fleet.

I tear myself loose from the icon ballet on my screen when the comms unit buzzes. I manage to pick up the receiver before the second buzz.

"SOCOM detachment, Lieutenant Grayson."

"Lieutenant, Major Masoud. Report to briefing room Delta-505 at 0800. All hands, not just the officers. Bring everyone."

"Aye, sir," I acknowledge.

I hang up the receiver and get up to bring the word to the rest of the short SOCOM platoon milling around in the berth outside. Whatever our part in this offensive, we are starting now, and we are doing it with what's on the board.

The briefing room in Grunt Country is more than big enough for the entire usual troop detachment of a Hammerhead cruiser, which is a full company. With the SOCOM detachment numbering little more than a squad, we have plenty of elbow room even with everyone present. When I walk in, Dmitry and his SRA comrades are already sitting in the first row, and I file into the row behind them to sit down at the far end. One by one, the rest of the detachment files in and takes seats in the first three rows: the Eurocorps lieutenant, the two Force Recon teams, and the Spaceborne Rescueman.

Major Masoud walks through the hatch at 0759. The Spaceborne Rescue master sergeant, who is sitting in the spot closest to the hatch, gets to his feet and shouts "Attention on deck!" before we can sort out the formality of rank seniority among us lieutenants. We all get up and stand to attention, even the SRA troopers.

"As you were," the major says. "Take your seats."

We sit down again and watch as he strides to the front of the briefing room and turns on the holoscreen that takes up the front bulkhead. He dims the lights in the room with a tap on the screen of the data pad in his hand. The holoscreen behind him displays a slowly rotating seal of the ship: NACS *Phalanx* CA-761.

"Good morning. Now that we are in the assembly area, I am cleared to brief you on what we are about to do. The name of this operation is Invictus."

The image behind him changes from the ship seal to a shot of Mars. It's not a still image, but rather a high-resolution surveillance feed. It's clearly from the vantage point of an NAC warship because the corners of the feed show the familiar readouts of an optical-sensor array.

"It's not a big secret that this is our target," Major Masoud says. "That feed, by the way, is twelve hours old."

We exchange glances and look back at the feed, and there's some low murmuring in the room. Even considering the maximum magnification of our best optical arrays, the ship that took the footage must be suicidally close to Mars. There are at least half a dozen Lanky seed ships evident against the red-and-white background of the Martian planetary surface and its cloud cover.

"Who's on station out there, sir?" I ask.

"NACS *Cincinnati*," Major Masoud replies. "They have been observing the target zone for the last two weeks undetected."

Cincinnati is the sister ship of NACS *Indianapolis*, the ship that Colonel Campbell flew into an approaching Lanky seed ship last year during the first incursion, enabling the dregs of Earth's fleets to defeat the incursion and buying us the time to finish construction on the Orions and the battleships. With the destruction of *Indy*, *Cincinnati* is the last surviving member of her line, the newly designed orbital combat ship. The OCS is a small stealth unit designed for surveillance and orbital patrol. If *Cincy* has been keeping eyes on the Lankies for us all this time, she's probably the most valuable ship left in the fleet despite her low tonnage and light armament.

"Situation," the major continues, in his typical curt manner. "We are at Fleet Assembly Point Echo as part of the Multinational Joint Task Group. Mars is held by a sizable presence of Lankies, including twelve seed ships in orbit and several thousand Lankies in various settlement clusters on the surface. There are eight known emergency shelters with human survivors in need of relief and evacuation. In less than twelve hours, we will have completed our predeployment refueling, and we will depart for Mars in our assigned combat formation, Task Force Red.

"The mission of the Joint Task Group is the destruction of the Lanky fleet in orbit around Mars, the landing of combat troops on the surface, the evacuation of survivors from the still-active emergency shelters, and the elimination of the Lanky threat on Mars."

"That's all?" one of the SI Force Recon guys behind me whispers to the SI trooper next to him.

"Execution," Major Masoud says. "The battle plan has six phases. It will be the longest and most complex spaceborne battle plan we've ever executed. Because we can no longer afford mass casualties, each of the phases are designed to allow aborting the rest of the plan and evacuation and retreat of remaining troops if the phase fails catastrophically."

Major Masoud taps his screen, and the almost-live feed of Mars behind him is replaced with a graphic of a tactical plot.

"In Phase One, the Joint Task Group will engage the Lankies above Mars and destroy them. For that purpose, we are taking along almost the entire remaining stock of Orion missiles. They will be towed by the support ships and fired at maximum range. The target data will come from NACS *Cincinnati*, which will remain on station throughout and update targeting solutions. The Lankies have been able to sneak up on us many times. This time we are doing the sneaking up, and this time they won't be able to disappear in the black unseen."

From the SRA troops in front of me, I hear the muted computer-translated Russian coming through the earpieces of the translator units the fleet has provided our new allies. I know that Dmitry doesn't really need one, but he is wearing an earpiece anyway and follows the major's briefing with a serious face. Just a minute into the briefing, the major has already checked off several objectives that are so great in their scope as military achievements that I feel stunned at the magnitude of the task ahead of us.

"Once the Orion salvo has destroyed the bulk of the Lanky fleet, two battleships, *Arkhangelsk* and *Agincourt*, will advance and engage any surviving seed ships in close combat."

Behind the major, the display shows a bunch of little starship icons firing a few dozen missiles at the orange lozenge shapes representing Lanky seed ships. Most of the orange icons blink out of existence when the Orion volley arrives. Then two of the friendly icons, one blue and one green, close the distance and wipe the few remaining orange icons from the map.

"Phase Two is where the SOCOM teams come in, so pay close attention," Major Masoud continues with a wry little smile. "The cruisers will advance behind the battleships and deploy their embarked SOCOM pathfinder teams via bio-pod to the designated landing zones on the surface of Mars. There are eight landing zones, each color-coded to the task force assigned to assault it. Our landing zone, as you may be able to guess, is Red Beach. You will land, deploy, secure the perimeter, and then get to work feeding targeting data to the cruisers overhead. You will prepare the landing zone for the follow-up forces by directing orbital bombardment and close-air support."

This part of the plan is the most conventional thing I've heard so far. It's what we are trained to do, of course, and exactly the sort of mission we've been craving. But the preconditions for us to even launch down to the landing zone are insanely ambitious considering our military prowess against the Lankies up to this point.

"In Phase Three, the carriers and their escorts will advance. The cruisers will make holes in the Lanky minefields and then resupply their magazines on the fly from the munition ships. The carriers will then launch their infantry contingents. Each landing zone has one carrier task force assigned to it. The assault will land in two waves—one in

Phase Three, one in Phase Four. Each wave will land a full regiment into each landing zone, for a total commitment of four divisions of infantry."

"Whoa," I say involuntarily, and most of the troops in the room echo that sentiment in some form. We have never landed four divisions of troops in a single operation—the entire Spaceborne Infantry arm only had three divisions at full strength before the Lankies cut us down to size. In just two waves, we will land over twenty thousand combat troops on the surface. In the Earth-based wars of the twentieth and twenty-first centuries, twenty thousand troops were a nonremarkable concentration of force on the strategic scale of their respective conflicts. For the space-based colonial infantry engagements we're geared and trained to fight, four divisions are an overwhelming logistical and tactical challenge to move and coordinate.

"Phase Four will be the landing of the second wave, securing of the landing beaches and their expansion, and the rescue of the surviving personnel on Mars from their holdout shelters. Once the survivors are evacuated and the beaches secured, we move on to Phase Five, which will be the expansion and linking of the invasion beaches.

"Finally, in Phase Six we will mop up the remaining Lanky resistance and eliminate their strongholds and infrastructure via aerial and orbital bombardment. Once the mop-up is complete, we will evacuate the bulk of our combat forces and leave the remaining cleanup business to an orbital garrison force."

Everything I just heard is so bold in scope that it ought to be ludicrous. But nobody around me is laughing or even chuckling. All the troops are listening to Major Masoud's briefing with dead-serious faces.

"In a moment, I will go over Phase Two in detail because that is our main bread and butter," Major Masoud says. "Questions or comments so far?"

For a moment, nobody says anything. Then Dmitry clears his throat, and every pair of eyes in the room looks at him.

"Is grand plan," he says. "Plan that great, can only be two outcomes. Will be best success in all of history, or complete disaster."

Major Masoud looks at the SRA sergeant for a few seconds and then nods. "I agree, Senior Sergeant. We will succeed completely, or fail completely. I don't have to tell any of you what is going to happen if we limp home defeated, with a few broken ships and a handful of troops. So let's go through the briefing for Phase Two and do our part to make sure that it does not come to that."

The in-depth briefing for Phase Two lasts another hour and a half. Not only is this operation by far the boldest we've ever planned, but even the SOCOM tasks are completely out of the ordinary. Because we didn't have the time to integrate all the communications networks between the two alliances, we will have integrated units from top to bottom. Each task force has a mix of SRA and NAC ships, each infantry brigade has both NAC and SRA regiments in it, and our SOCOM teams are dropping with mixed personnel as well. For us, that means our two SI Force Recon teams will be joined by an SRA team, and I am dropping into battle teamed up with Dmitry. Our job is to direct the close-air support and orbital strikes, and having a combat controller from each alliance in the same landing zone means that we'll be able to talk to whatever unit is overhead, whether it's an SRA or an NAC bird. We are taking decades of established doctrines and habits, and we are throwing them right out the window, winging it as we go.

"Jump-off time is within the next twelve hours," Major Masoud says when we've gone through all the briefing points thoroughly and nobody has any more questions or comments. "If the assault makes it to Phase Two, we will be fully committed, whether or not the rest of the task group moves on to Phase Three and beyond. If things go wrong once the pods are on the ground, there will be no return. But that should be nothing new to any of you."

He looks at the assembled ragtag group of podheads, sixteen of us from three different alliances and four different services. Major Masoud has always looked hard and craggy, but it seems to me that he has aged a few years since I saw him last on Arcadia, a little less than two months ago. He reaches for his data pad and turns off the screen behind him.

"There will be no drills until we suit up," he says. "Use the time at your discretion. It may be the last quiet time you get. Dismissed."

The SI troopers and the Spaceborne Rescueman get up and leave the briefing room, talking among themselves as they walk out. After a few moments, Dmitry and his four SRA comrades follow suit, exchanging words in Russian that's beyond my limited vocabulary. I get out of my seat and walk up to Major Masoud, who is shutting down the briefing console.

"Something on your mind, Lieutenant?" he asks when he turns and sees me standing in front of his little podium.

"Are you dropping with us, sir?"

"That's a negative." His expression looks almost pained for just a second. "I am the senior SOCOM officer in Task Force Red. Once you are all on the surface, I'll be coordinating your efforts with those of the other teams from *Phalanx*'s CIC."

"On Arcadia, you told me we'd see each other on Mars," I say.

"Yes, I know. And I requested to drop with the team. But the general staff had other ideas. Trust me, Lieutenant, there's nothing I'd rather do than to launch with the Phase Two pathfinders."

"Is that so?"

"That is so, Lieutenant. And you know it's true, because you'd make the same pick if you had a choice." He powers down the console and picks up his data pad. "No podhead will choose to die in a CIC, looking at a holotable instead of side by side with his comrades on the ground. That's a punishment, not a privilege. Whatever you may think of me,

Lieutenant Grayson, I know that you don't consider me a chickenshit console jockey."

I have to grin despite the anger I still feel at Major Masoud over Arcadia. "No, sir. You're a ruthless bastard, but you're not a chickenshit console jockey."

He looks at me with that unreadable, frosty expression of his, and I briefly wonder whether I'll get to spend the time to launch in the brig for insubordination.

"I can live with that assessment," he says. Then he nods toward the briefing room hatch. "Catch up with your team and enjoy what time we have left, Lieutenant. I hear that the Russians may have brought some liquid refreshments along. I also have it on good authority that nobody in this Fleet is going to enforce the dry-ship rules for the next few days. *Dismissed*," he says again, in a tone that tells me I've used up my one free chit to speak my mind.

"Aye-aye, sir," I say. Sometimes you just have to know when not to press your luck.

CHAPTER 11

PHASE ONE

"General quarters, general quarters. All hands, man your combat stations. Set material condition Zebra throughout the ship. This is not a drill."

When the general-quarters alert sounds over the 1MC, I'm already in my underarmor ballistic liner, which I put on after getting out of my bunk in full anticipation of our imminent deployment. Now I step over to my gear locker and start the ritual of putting on my HEBA suit. The task is made a little more difficult this morning because I haven't put on a bug suit in a hurry in almost two years, and because I have a pretty fierce hangover from the night before. The Russians brought their personal kit bags over from their carrier, but those bags weren't filled with personal gear. Instead, they each brought half a dozen bottles of what they call "engineering vodka," and the entire SOCOM detachment took the liberty to sample the stuff over the last few days of transit. At one point last night, Major Masoud stuck his head into the SOCOM compartment, but instead of chewing us out for drinking alcohol on a fleet ship in flagrant violation of the regs, he stepped in and had a liberally sized sample as well.

I don't have a picture of Halley taped to my locker to touch before going into battle like a fighter pilot in some old Network show. I don't even bother to get my PDP out to send her a message. She's in Task Force Purple, too far away in this assembly area to get near-field comms, and she wouldn't have time to read it because she's probably gearing up for her own general-quarters alert right now. But I know she's thinking of me right now, just as I am thinking of her, without any totems needed to remind us of each other.

I step out of my stateroom and walk over to the common area, where most of the SOCOM detachment are already assembled in their respective battle suits. It's still strange to see the angular SRA hardshell with its mottled camo pattern mixed in with the Fleet and SRA camo patterns. For the last half decade, I only ever got to see people wearing that armor through the targeting optic of my rifle. Dmitry looks over at me and says something to the SRA troops next to him, and they chuckle.

"I know, I know," I say when I've closed the gap. "Big imperialist insect."

"No, no. Is fine armor. Makes you look like fierce, strong warrior. Very fearsome."

"Just wait until we're on the ground," I say, resisting the temptation to demonstrate the polychromatic-camouflage feature right here in the berthing area. The bug suits used to be highly restricted—we weren't even supposed to take them along on missions against SRA settlements so they couldn't capture one and try to reverse engineer it—so Dmitry and his comrades have no idea what this superexpensive piece of butt-ugly attire can do on the battlefield.

Of the ten NAC personnel in the group, I'm the only one in a HEBA suit. The Spaceborne Rescue sergeant is wearing standard Fleet battle armor, and the two SI Force Recon teams are in their own branch's hardshell. The Euro lieutenant sticks out almost as much as the SRA troops. His armor looks lighter and more flexible than either the SRA or NAC suits, and his helmet almost looks dainty next to the big, faceted things the SRA marines have tucked under their arms.

Behind us, the hatch to the berthing module opens, and Major Masoud steps into the room. He is wearing armor and carrying a helmet as well.

"*Attention on deck!*" I shout, and everyone snaps to.

Major Masoud nods curtly. "As you were," he says. He looks over the small group of SOCOM specialists and Alliance personnel and smiles his thin-lipped smile. "I wish I had ten times as many troops for this. But I know you will do. Weapons issue and suit check at the armory at 0800. Then it's off to Pod Country. If anyone needs to make final arrangements or send any last messages, now is the time."

We gather at the armory to take on our weapons and ammunition load-out for the mission. I'm surprised to see that *Phalanx*'s armory has SRA weapons on the racks, because when Dmitry and the SRA team step up to the window, they receive their own standard rifles, not our M-90 or M-95 heavy anti-Lanky weapons. The Sino-Russian guns have a lot in common with ours—we took some design and function cues off their rifles when we designed our own—but the ammo isn't interchangeable, and I figured they'd issue them our guns to keep resupply simple.

When it's my turn at the window, I take a pistol out of habit, even though the tiny little fléchettes from the M109 service handgun are useless against Lankies. Then I receive an M-95 autoloading rifle that looks so new that it probably still has factory grease in the action. I plug the rifle into my suit and let the computer in the gun talk to the one in my armor. There's a calibrating target on the far bulkhead in the armory, and we all take turns sighting in our weapons. My helmet visor displays the targeting reticle of the rifle on the calibrating target and reads the output from the laser mounted parallel to the barrel, and it takes just a few seconds for the armor's data unit to calculate the ballistic trajectory from this specific weapon seamlessly from point-blank range to a thousand meters, adjusted for Mars gravity and atmosphere.

We are just finished with the weapons issue and filling up our magazine pouches when the 1MC comes to life overhead again.

"All hands, this is Colonel Yamin. Listen up."

We all interrupt our activities to pay attention to *Phalanx*'s skipper.

"We have reached the forward edge of the battle area with Task Force Red. Mars isn't far, we have the first Lanky targets in our Orion missile envelope, and we will be in combat soon. This is not the first time this ship has gone up against the Lankies, which is not something that many Fleet units can claim. I have the utmost faith that this ship and her crew will complete her assigned mission, and that *Phalanx* will bring us home when this is all over."

Colonel Yamin pauses for a moment, and the area in front of the armory is as quiet as can be except for the soft, delayed translation I can hear from the earpieces of the SRA team.

"I have been ordered to share a message before we go into battle. As of this moment, every ship in this task group is playing a similar announcement from the leader of its alliance or commonwealth. All hands, stand by for the president of the North American Commonwealth."

There's another short pause on the 1MC, and then a new voice comes on, one I've heard before both in Network news footage and in person, on the hangar deck of NACS *Regulus* during Colonel Campbell's posthumous Medal of Honor ceremony a few months ago. It's the voice of a woman speaking with a faint southern drawl that reminds me of most of the pilots I've ever known.

"Men and women of the Commonwealth Defense Corps, and members of our allied forces," she says. "I'm not very good at profound speeches. I am an old fighter pilot, and our communications tended toward brevity unless we got drunk in the O Club together after missions. But I would not be a very good president if I did not see you off with the best wishes of the rest of us, those who have no choice but to wait for the outcome of a battle that depends entirely on you all.

"Sitting here in this office, knowing what you are about to face and not being able to be up there with you is the hardest thing I've had to do since taking this job. There's very little I wouldn't give for a shot at a seat in a Shrike cockpit right now, sitting in the docking clamp and waiting to take the fight to the enemy. And make no mistake: you, all of you, regardless of the nationality patch on your armor, are fighting the true enemy. You are going into battle against the worst threat we as a species have ever faced, the threat we should have been preparing for all these years instead of killing each other. You are about to fight the most important battle in the history of the planet, and you are going to bring us back from the brink of extermination.

"Be assured that everybody looking to the stars tonight wishes you strength, courage, and skill in battle. I join them in this even though I know that you already have all those things in abundance. It's an honor and a privilege to be your commander in chief, and I know that you will do us all proud.

"And as an attack-bird jock, let me add just one more thing. If this is the day you get to claim that seat at the table in Valhalla, make sure you arrive there with your magazine pouches and ammo racks empty, and a pile of dead Lankies behind you. Good hunting."

We don't break out into wild cheers like the ragtag resistance forces in some corny military movie on the Networks. Instead, we just grin at each other, and some of the troops nod approvingly.

"Top shit, that speech," the Spaceborne Rescueman says next to me, and continues filling his magazine pouches.

"We make it back, she has *my* vote," I say.

In almost two years of garrison duty and standard drop-ship deployments, I had almost forgotten just how small a ballistic bio-pod actually is. The thing itself is fairly large on the outside, but a lot of that size is shielding and barrel sabot. The pod has an irregular surface to mimic a natural piece of celestial debris, but it needs to be launched from the ordnance tube of a cruiser, so there's a sabot liner wrapped around the pod that separates from the pod as soon as it's out of the launch tube. The walls of the pod are also pretty thick, to survive the thermal stress of atmospheric entry, so the actual passenger compartment is much smaller than the overall size of the pod would suggest. Whenever I step up to an open bio-pod right before deployment, I am uncomfortably reminded of their resemblance to coffins.

Pod Country is the part of the ship where the mission pods are prepared and loaded before a launch. It's a small section right behind the magazine control for the ship's ordnance autoloader, which hoists munition into the launch tubes on demand. Cruisers like *Phalanx* have a set of dorsal launch tubes for nuclear missiles, but those are permanently loaded. The ship-to-ship and ship-to-surface launch tubes are in the center of the ship and face forward and out, and the space-warfare officer in CIC can select any of the ship's half dozen different missile types to be loaded automatically. For this mission, the sixteen missile tubes on *Phalanx* will spit out a full salvo of bio-pods, each with one of us inside.

We load our gear into the bio-pods and secure it. On a drop ship, there's more room for kit, but on a pod launch, all I can take along is the rifle I just picked up, my combat-controller deck, and a very small kit bag with a few spare power cells for the deck. Everything else I need is already attached to my armor or integrated in it. When I am done securing my gear in the pod, the ship's pod rigger steps up and double-checks all the fasteners and the load balancing.

"Good to go, Lieutenant," he says when he is done with his check. "Good luck, and Godspeed."

My pod is the first in line on the portside. Right behind me, Dmitry is finished loading his own gear, and the pod rigger checks his work as well, to make sure nothing is loose or likely to throw the pod off-balance on its trajectory. We are lined up with eight pods on both port and starboard sides, and all the Russians are with me in the port-side queue. Bringing up the rear on the portside are the Spaceborne Rescue sergeant and the Eurocorps liaison. The starboard row of pods is taken up entirely by the two teams of SI Force Recon.

I walk toward the back of Pod Country and claim one of the jump seats on the bulkhead. We don't climb into the pods until the last possible moment before the launch because we don't want to start depleting the oxygen in the suits earlier than necessary, so we get to ride out the time until the green light back here, in rather closer proximity than back in the berthing module. One by one, my fellow podhead comrades finish their checks and come back to join me at the rear bulkhead. It occurs to me that I've never dropped with any of the troopers in this group except for Dmitry. I wish I had some of my old friends here—Philbrick, Humphrey, Nez, or Macfee, my fellow combat controller who is still listed as MIA since the disaster at Sirius Ad even though there's very little doubt that everyone we left behind in that place is now dead. But the only familiar face on this drop isn't a longtime SI or fleet friend; it's a Russian combat controller who was my enemy not too long ago.

"Now hear this: Orion launch in T-minus thirty," the 1MC sounds. "Phase One begins in thirty minutes. Stand by on pods."

I put on my helmet and activate the data monocle. Then I turn on my suit's tactical computer and let it do its electronic handshake with *Phalanx*'s neural network. As a combat controller, I have elevated access to the ship's tactical systems, enough to at least get a view of the picture in the neighborhood around the ship. It's not strictly against the regs to use that access while I am still on the ship, but it's not exactly encouraged, either. But I hate being situationally blind and having nothing to look at but the autoloader hatches on the bulkhead while the battle is about to start, so I let my suit computer finish its connection and bring up the tactical plot from the holotable in CIC.

Phalanx is at the head of a formation of six ships. In the middle of the formation is NACS *Polaris*, one of our few remaining supercarriers and the obvious centerpiece of our task force. Flying in close protective formation off her starboard is the SRA cruiser *Kirov*. On her portside, the Eurocorps frigate *Westfalen* is keeping pace, and trading slightly behind the carrier is the SRA destroyer *Yinchuan*. Bringing up the rear is a familiar hull number: AOE-1, NACS *Portsmouth*, the large fleet supply ship that served as our mobile base during the Leonidas mission almost two months ago. I turn on an external camera feed off *Polaris's* stern and see that *Portsmouth* is still wearing the rough and pebbly black paint job she received in the SOCOM yard before we set out on our covert mission to reclaim Arcadia. As a strike force, this is as much combat power as I've seen put together since the joint-fleet evacuation of New Svalbard, and it's almost unbelievable at this point that there are seven more task forces of roughly similar composition moving toward Mars with us.

With nothing better to do than to wait for the green light, I watch the plot, our little cluster of blue and green icons creeping closer to Mars every minute. The tactical officer in CIC cycles through the magnification scale every few minutes to give the skipper updates on the big picture. The task group is split neatly into task forces, all waiting their turn in the battle order, spread across five hundred kilometers of space in all directions. It's a mind-blowing display of combat power, but I remember *Indy's* desperate run around Mars last year, and the amount of capital-ship wrecks that were floating in space as we zoomed by at full throttle, Lankies on our tail. For a force of this magnitude, the comms are eerily silent. I don't hear any of the usual chatter that goes with maneuvering a task group of this size. The Lankies can sense active radiation, and the fleet has been cruising under EMCON Bravo—strictly limited transmissions—since we left the assembly point.

"Orion launch in T-minus fifteen. Stand by for final FO targeting update."

FO, the forward observer, is NACS *Cincinnati*, on station a few tens of thousands of kilometers ahead, a black hole in space. *Cincinnati* has been using its powerful optical arrays to keep tabs on the Lanky seed ships near Mars. The Orions need a while to get up to Lanky-killing fractional light-speed velocity, so we need to fire them from much further out than the task force can spot the Lankies on passive arrays, but with *Cincinnati* feeding us updated targeting data, it will be like aiming a rifle at a target just out of arm's reach. And for the first time ever, we are ambushing them, initiating the attack instead of reacting to theirs.

The update from *Cincinnati* comes in a minute or two later, and the tactical display updates with the current position of every Lanky ship between us and Mars. My heart skips a beat when I see the orange icons representing seed ships all popping up at once on the long-range situational display. We are far out of their weapon range, but seeing the color orange on a tactical plot will give me anxiety for the rest of my life, even if we win this battle and I get to live to 110.

The ships towing the Orion missiles are at the front of our formation, in a staggered wall that's five abreast and five deep. One by one, the towing ships detach their missiles and launcher units and turn to reverse course. Once the Orions light their engines, they'll start squirting nuclear charges out of their tail ends and detonating them against their ablative pusher plates at the rate of one per second, and no skipper wants to stick around when hundred-kiloton nuclear warheads are about to go off in the neighborhood. The Orions are dangerous, crude, and unwieldy, too large to fit on any ships, and a threat to anything smaller than a planetoid in their path if they miss their targets. But they are the only shot we have at pulling off that crucial first volley, to take out as many seed ships as we can in one single strike before they are aware of our presence and start dispersing.

"Orion launch in T-minus five. All units, clear the backblast area. Level-one radiation protocol in effect."

On the tactical display, each Lanky seed ship in range has two target markers on it. We are about to fire two Orions at each seed ship, to account for misses and weapon malfunctions. I look at the trajectories and see that a lot of them are going to come dangerously close to Mars if they miss. I try to do the math in my head to imagine what a ten-thousand-ton block of pykrete will do on the planet's surface if it hits at a few thousand kilometers per second, and decide that I'd rather not think about that right now. This is our one shot, and if we miss, Mars is lost to us forever anyway.

Out in space a few hundred kilometers in front of our task group, fourteen dual Orion launchers train themselves on to their target bearings with little bursts from their maneuvering thrusters. Each of the missiles attached to the launch modules are as long as a capital ship, heavy sledgehammers to crack open the seed ships that are impervious to any other weapon we've ever thrown at them.

"Orion launch in T-minus two. Switching Orion batteries to network control. Birds free."

Someone in CIC has decided that the entire crew should be kept in the loop for this event, and puts the audio chatter from CIC on the general-announcement system. The skipper isn't commenting on the launch at all, but we all know what we're about to do. We are smacking the hornet's nest with the biggest stick we have, and if we fail to kill the Lanky fleet in one swipe, the survivors will come swarming for us. I should be scared way more than I am right now. For some reason, knowing that we're striking the first blow for a change makes me feel more excited and impatient than afraid.

"Orion launch in T-minus thirty seconds. Twenty-eight. Twenty-seven . . ."

I look over at the other members of my team. Most of them are looking at the forward bulkhead like there's a holoscreen mounted on it that shows a championship game in progress. Dmitry sees me looking at him and gives me a fleeting grin and a thumbs-up, but I can tell that even the usually unflappable Russian is as nervous as the rest of us. If the missiles do their job, we'll be in the pods and bound for Mars in thirty minutes. If they don't, we'll either die on this ship today or be witness to the end of civilization soon. Either way, once the Orions launch, it's completely out of our hands.

"Ten seconds. Nine. Eight. Seven. Six . . ."

I take a deep, shaky breath and concentrate on my tactical display again, because it's the only thing I can do.

"Three. Two. One. Launch."

On the plot, two dozen blue V-shaped icons representing antiship missiles pop into existence at the front of our battle line. I check the optical feed for a camera that's trained on at least some of the launchers. At this distance, I can't make out much detail, but I can clearly see the two massive Orions slowly floating away from the dual launcher. Then there's a flare like a tiny sun that washes out the optical feed despite the automatic brightness filters.

"Birds away, birds away," the tactical officer says over the 1MC. "Separation and launch on Orion 82 through 86, 88 through 92, and 94 through 106. Launch failure on Orion 87 and Orion 93. Repeat, we have two misfires."

The Orions accelerate so quickly that the line of icons is on the plot one second, and gone the next. The nuclear charges that go off behind them every second pump most of their energy into the pusher plates and fling the missiles forward at acceleration rates that would puree a human crew even with an anti-grav system active.

"Fifteen minutes to intercept," CIC announces. "Battleships are moving into linebacker position."

The two icons representing the huge battleships, one lozenge shape blue and the other green, accelerate through the center of our formation to follow the Orions at flank speed. They're much slower than the missiles, but they aren't meant to catch up with them. The battleships are there to mop up any seed ships that survive the Orion volley before they can threaten the invasion fleet. I watch the two icons, labeled "AGINCOURT" and "ARKHANGELSK," making their way past the clusters of task-force groups in a staggered formation, twenty kilometers between them. I still don't know what the precise nature of their armament is, but I know that *Aggie* and *Archie*, as the fleet nicknamed them about ten seconds after their official commissioning, both carry immense high-energy-particle pulse cannons mounted on their center-lines. I've seen that weapon system at the fleet's testing range when they used it to blow up a bunch of target hulks, and the close-range punch of those ships is absolutely devastating. But they're very short ranged, which means that the battleships have to get close enough to the seed ships to be in their weapon range as well, and from what I saw at the target range a month and a half ago, the bugs are nowhere near ironed out.

Next to me, Dmitry gets up and stretches his back, then his arms and shoulders. "Waiting is not thing I like," he says. "For food, maybe. For doctor of teeth. But not for fight."

"I'm right there with you," I reply.

Dmitry reaches into the personal document pocket of his armor and pulls out a plastic pouch. Then he opens it and takes out a picture. I recognize it as the one he showed me last year on our trip back to Earth on the *Indianapolis*—it's his husband, Maksim, a broad-faced, smiling guy in an SRA marine uniform, lizard-pattern camo and an undershirt with blue and white stripes. He looks at the picture for a little while and then kisses the first two fingers of his right glove and touches it gently. I feel vaguely like a voyeur watching him, but Dmitry doesn't seem to mind. He looks over at me and holds up the picture before stowing it in his document pouch again.

"Your wife, the pilot. Halley. She is good woman."

"She is," I agree.

"When battle is over, maybe we sit down and have drink together. You, me, Maksim, Halley. Drink much vodka, tell many war stories, maybe even some true ones."

"Let's do that," I say. "But it won't take much for you to drink me under the table, I think."

"Is not competition," he says. "Is for friendship, and remembering. Maybe forgetting, too."

He smiles wryly.

I look at this Russian marine, this friendly, earnest, and competent man, and think of all the dangers we've shared even though we've only known each other briefly. I may have faced him in battle before on some colony moon somewhere. He may have killed some of my friends, and I may have killed some of his. I am once again struck by how much alike we are—how similar the grunts on both sides really are—and I know that when this battle is over, I don't want to go on fighting him and his friends over dumb shit that could be settled at a table in one evening by half a dozen grunts from each side and a few bottles of booze between them.

CHAPTER 12

—— **KICKING THE DOOR OFF** ——
THE HINGES

The next fifteen minutes are the slowest ones of my life. The CIC's holotable displays the tactical map at strategic scale to show both the task group and the Lanky fleet, as well as the two dozen blue V symbols that are racing from our cluster of blue and green icons to their cluster of orange ones. Far out in front of us, so close to the Lanky fleet that the icons almost touch at this scale, is the lone little blue icon that says "CINCINNATI OCS-2" next to it. *Cincinnati* is still in her forward-observer position, running under stealth, tracking all the Lankies optically and relaying the target data back to the task group, which in turn feeds the information to the Orions. So far, we have only fired Orion missiles at Lanky seed ships that were approaching Earth at high velocity, and those shots were much more difficult than this volley at slow-patrolling Lanky ships that are practically stationary to an Orion moving at one-twentieth of light speed.

All those beatings we got from you bastards over the last few years, I think. *Let's see how you like getting sucker-punched back.*

On the tactical screen, the blue Vs are rushing toward the orange lozenges. The scale of the display means that the situational orb is half a million kilometers across, but the Orions are chewing up the distance between us and the Lankies like nothing I've ever seen moving through space, and their nuclear-propulsion charges are still accelerating them after they're way past the halfway point. Fifteen minutes of remaining flight time turn to ten, then five, then two.

"One minute to intercept," CIC announces.

With every second that passes, I expect the orange icons at the far range of our awareness bubble to scatter and rapidly change course, detecting the incoming Orions and throwing off our final targeting fixes. But however the Lankies perceive the space around their ships, sensing missiles coming toward them at fifteen thousand kilometers per second, which is what the Orions are up to in the last minute of their targeting run, doesn't seem to be within their abilities. The Lanky seed ships continue their leisurely patrol pattern, unaware of the kinetic energy coming their way.

"Flight One impact in ten seconds. Nine. Eight. Seven. Six. Five."

It takes all the self-control I have to stay in my seat and not jump up and pace the deck.

"Three. Two. One. *Impact*."

The two dozen blue V icons merge with the cluster of orange lozenges in quick succession. Then the tactical display stops updating the icon positions.

"*Cincinnati* has lost visual. FO is reporting multiple high-energy impacts. Stand by for poststrike assessment."

Several minutes pass as the sensor suites on *Cincinnati* and the leading ships in our battle line seek to reestablish a picture of the tactical situation. The kinetic warheads are just big blocks of pykrete, ice mixed with wood pulp, harder than concrete and much less brittle than pure ice, but they release all their energy on impact, billions of joules.

"Getting a new fix from the FO now," the tactical officer in CIC says.

On the plot, the blue missile icons are gone, and so are most of the orange seed-ship icons. Three missile icons are at the very far limit of the plot, streaking toward Mars.

"Multiple impacts," the tactical officer announces, in a voice that sounds first amazed and then jubilant. "FO reports impacts on ten bogeys. Multiple hull breaches. Visual feed incoming."

I waste no time tapping into the camera feed from *Cincinnati* that arrives just a minute later. The space in near-Mars orbit is littered with Lanky ships that are clearly mortally wounded. Several have their entire front thirds missing and are streaming chunks of hull as they careen through space with an obvious lack of controlled propulsion. Two of the Lanky ships are torn in half, the segments drifting away from each other slowly at this magnification, with clouds of smaller hull debris between them.

"We have high-yield impacts on Mars," someone else in CIC says. "Three misses on bogeys. One went by the planet and burned up in the upper atmosphere. Two impacted the surface near the equator, five hundred fifty klicks apart. Megaton-class thermal bloom."

"Ouch," someone in my group says next to me. Three of the priceless Orions missed their targets, and two of them smacked into Mars at almost full speed, barely slowed down by the atmospheric friction upon entry. I find myself hoping fervently that the errant Orions took out a Lanky settlement or two instead of landing right on top of a bunker with human survivors in it.

"Two more misses," the audio from CIC continues. "Orion 90 and 99 went wide and failed to impact. Self-destruct in one hundred seventeen minutes."

The two Orions that missed their assigned targets continue on their trajectory past Mars and off into the deep space beyond, each having used up hundreds of the world's remaining low-yield nuclear warheads for no gain. But most of the rest have done their jobs. There are a few minutes of tension and controlled confusion in CIC as the sensors from the task-group ships and the far-off *Cincinnati* attempt to sort out the optical, thermal, and radiation clutter in the section of space where we just unleashed planetoid-killing amounts of kinetic energy. Then the feed from *Cincinnati* burns through the noise, and the tactical display updates itself.

"Splash *ten*," the tactical officer says, and he makes no effort to conceal the glee in his voice. "We have ten confirmed seed-ship kills."

All around me, rousing cheers go up—not just in the Pod Country compartment, but also in the neighboring sections, so loud that they're audible through the bulkheads. In the space of one second, we have destroyed more Lankies—both ships and individual creatures—than in the entire war against them so far.

"Knock knock, motherfuckers!" our Spaceborne Rescue sergeant shouts, and pumps his fist.

"Battleships are advancing to grid Delta Five-Seven for intercept," the tactical officer in CIC narrates. I see the two battleships accelerating toward their assigned intercept coordinates on the plot, burning their fusion engines at flank-speed setting.

"Contact," CIC warns. "We have two bogies incoming from bearing zero-two-zero relative by negative zero-one-three, and zero-three-five relative by positive three-zero. Designate Lima-11 and Lima-12. FO reports they have a visual on both Lanky seed ships."

The two remaining seed ships are on the move, but it's clear they don't know what they're hunting. They move away from Mars, accelerating as they're going, and changing course slightly every few minutes. *Cincinnati* is much closer to them than the rest of the fleet, and the little OCS is keeping the two Lankies in her sights relentlessly, feeding precise targeting data back to the rest of the task group. By herself, she has no hope of fighting those two behemoths, but the battleships do, and thanks to *Cincy* they can plot perfect intercept trajectories.

Neither the battleships nor the Lanky seed ships move at anything near the insane acceleration the Orions pulled earlier. The blue icons on the tactical display creep across the situational-awareness sphere, closing the distance minute by minute. I keep scanning the edges of the display for more Lanky ships, expecting to see a cluster of orange icons to come out of nowhere and head for the task group to close the trap they surely laid for us. But the display remains empty except for the tight cluster of blue icons in the center, the two orange lozenges at the far edge of the scale, and the two symbols representing our battleships halfway between. They have the acceleration advantage over the Lankies, and they have the guidance telemetry from *Cincinnati*. In the past, we got jumped in every engagement because we could never see the Lanky seed ships coming until they were already almost in weapon range. This time, the tables are turned. It's clear from their course on the plot that the surviving seed ships don't know where we are, or that two of our battleships are closing in to intercept them.

Agincourt leads the battleship formation, five hundred kilometers ahead of her sister ship, and she reaches firing position first.

"Lima-12 crossing laterally from bearing two-nine-zero, speed six hundred meters per second and accelerating. Range to target twelve thousand kilometers. *Agincourt* is signaling they have a firing solution."

"*Agincourt*, weapons free, weapons free. Light the bastard up," the command comes in the background of the audio feed from CIC.

"Copy weapons free," the reply from *Agincourt* comes, equally muffled and tinny. "Reactor to pulse afterburner. Range ten thousand kilometers. Alpha mount, fifteen-shot burst, fire for effect."

At the last second, the Lanky seed ship seems to have sensed that someone else is in their neighborhood. On the tactical plot, Lima-12 starts changing its bearing toward the incoming battleships. But the course correction is too little and too late, and the particle cannon's charge has virtually no travel time at what is almost point-blank range.

"Firing Alpha in three. Two. One. Fire."

I switch to the visual feed from *Cincinnati* just in time to see the bloom from the particle cannon's impact on the Lanky's hull. *Cincinnati* is fifty thousand kilometers from the event, but her cameras are so good that I can clearly make out the oblong, organic shape of the seed ship against the blackness of the space behind it. Then the image washes out in a brilliant white flash. When the brightness subsides enough for me to make out anything again, the point in space where a Lanky seed ship just moved across the camera's field of view at hundreds of meters per second is just an expanding cloud of superheated gas.

"Target destroyed," the tactical officer half shouts in CIC, and a cheer goes up again.

"Holy mother of fuck," I murmur into my helmet. The particle cannon mount on *Agincourt* just turned a three-kilometer seed ship with a hull twenty meters thick into a loose conglomeration of atoms with a second and a half of burst fire.

"Would maybe be good idea to make many more battleships like that," Dmitry says with a broad grin.

On the plot, *Agincourt* breaks off its attack run to avoid the plasma cloud by swinging the nose of the ship to port. The particle cannon is a short-range weapon, and at *Agincourt's* current speed, it takes only a few seconds to cover the ten thousand kilometers that are the outer edge of the cannon's effective range.

"Bogey Lima-11 is changing course to intercept," someone else in CIC warns. "Aspect change from bearing zero-two-zero relative to zero-four-five. They're going for *Agincourt*."

Whether the Lanky ships communicate with each other or the second Lanky simply could not miss the massive energy release that wiped out its companion, our presence is no longer a surprise. Contact Lima-11, the second surviving Lanky seed ship, comes around and heads for *Agincourt*, which is now swinging around to counter-burn its fusion engines and arrest the momentum that will carry it clean past Mars and into deep space otherwise.

"*Agincourt*, you have incoming, bearing two-six-six by positive three-five."

"Alpha mount is off-line," *Agincourt* sends back. "Repeat, we have lost function on the particle cannon. Unmasking rail gun batteries."

I'm reminded of the test-firing a few months back, when *Agincourt* lost all power after firing the main gun once. The particle cannons they built into *Aggie* and *Archie* are insanely powerful, but brand-new technology, mounted in experimental and uncompleted ships. At least *Aggie* still has her engines, but her rail guns won't do her much good against the incoming Lanky.

With the counter-burning maneuver, *Agincourt's* acceleration advantage over the remaining Lanky disappears. The seed ship closes to thirty thousand kilometers, then twenty thousand, homing in on the battleship like a shark that has smelled blood in the water.

"*Arkhangelsk* has a firing solution on bogey Lima-11." The tactical officer on the SRA battleship sends his own updates in excellent English that has just the barest trace of a Chinese accent.

The second battleship is coming in at flank speed to close the distance for an intercept before *Agincourt* gets overtaken by the Lanky. I can see just by looking at the plot that this is going to get ugly. The particle pulse cannons on the battleships are insanely powerful, but their short range means that the battleships have to be almost in knife-fighting range, tactically speaking. *Agincourt* had no time to counter-burn at the end of her attack run, so she had no choice but to move into range of the second Lanky seed ship, and *Arkhangelsk* is about to do the very same thing by necessity to save her sister ship.

"Hold fire, *Arkhangelsk*. *Agincourt* is too close to the bogey."

The range between the seed ship and *Agincourt* is now down to five thousand kilometers and shrinking with every second. *Agincourt* is at full burn again to reverse her earlier course, and the seed ship just has to keep accelerating to catch the battleship from astern with her metaphorical pants down.

Eleven seed ships destroyed, and we may still lose this right here, I think. If the last seed ship on the plot manages to destroy or disable the battleships, it will be able to carve through the entire task group like an axe through a soy patty.

On the plot, *Arkhangelsk* is changing course to get a clean shot at the seed ship. The camera feed from *Cincinnati* frames both the seed ship and *Agincourt* hurtling through space on a near-parallel course. *Agincourt's* stern is aglow with the fusion flare of her engines burning at full output.

"Incoming ordnance," *Agincourt* sends. "Taking fire from the bogey."

I can't hear anything on the channel for a few seconds, and the camera resolution from *Cincy* is not good enough at this distance to see the clouds of penetrator rods shooting out from the flank of the seed ship and hurtling through the space between the two ships, or the impact blooms on the battleship, but I know they are getting peppered with superhard quills right now that can go completely through the hull of any capital ship in the task group. *Agincourt* and her sister are built to withstand this sort of kinetic attack, but they've obviously never been tested in battle until today. When *Agincourt* sends again, there are warning klaxons in the background of the transmission.

"We took multiple direct hits on the hull. Penetrations in three sections, but the armor plating kept most of it out. Propulsion unaffected. Alpha mount is still off-line. If *Arkhangelsk* has the shot, let her take it."

"Lanky is changing course again," the tactical officer cautions. "They're closing the distance. I think they are going for a ramming kill."

The Lanky seed ship, millions of tons in motion, will do to *Agincourt* what the battleship did to the other seed ship just a few minutes ago if the ships collide at their current speed. Armor plating or not, *Agincourt* will get smashed like an egg on a sidewalk.

"Ready to fire," *Arkhangelsk* sends. "*Agincourt*, change course to relative zero by negative zero-nine-zero on my mark. We will fire a three-shot burst from the Alpha mount."

"Copy course change to relative zero by negative nine-zero on your mark. Call it. And try not to miss," *Agincourt's* tactical officer replies.

I see what *Arkhangelsk* is trying to do. They want to scrape the Lanky seed ship off *Agincourt's* back with a short burst that may not have the energy output to kill the Lanky outright, so *Agincourt* has a chance to clear the impact range without getting caught in the energy release. We are now calling tactical shots on the fly with weapons we've never used outside the gunnery range, with hundreds or thousands of lives riding on a guess.

"Reactor to pulse afterburner. Range twelve thousand kilometers. Target is locked. *Agincourt*, break away in three, two, one, *mark*."

Agincourt's helmsman lights off the dorsal-bow thrusters, and the ship ducks away from the Lanky behind it and goes through a ninety-degree rotation along its lateral axis far faster than I would have expected a ship of her size to be able to move. The angle of separation to the Lanky seed ship widens momentarily, and then the Lanky ship starts dipping its bow end to follow the battleship. On the plot, both icons are almost on top of each other. On the camera feed from *Cincinnati*, I can see that there are no more than ten kilometers of space between the ships.

"Alpha mount, three-round burst. Fire."

The particle beam coming from *Arkhangelsk's* main armament isn't visible in space, but its effects on the seed ship are, and dramatically so. The short burst *Arkhangelsk* just fired doesn't blot the seed ship out of space instantly like *Agincourt* did with her own target, but there's a blinding flash of thermal radiation that once again triggers the filter on the camera lens, and the sudden and instant energy release shears the Lanky in half somewhere around the front third of its hull. The two parts of the Lanky ship continue their forward momentum, trailing streams of superheated plasma, huge chunks breaking away from both pieces of the broken hull. Some of the wreckage parts slam into *Agincourt's* hull and bounce off the dorsal armor plating of the ship, but one piece of superheated hull fragment finds its way to the battleship's stern and into *Agincourt's* fusion-rocket engine pods. I see the bright plumes from her engines go out almost instantly. The Lanky, clearly broken, continues on the trajectory it had started when it tried to match the battleship's evasive maneuver, but it's clear that the seed ship is out of control. It yaws around its own lateral axis and then flips stern over bow, inert mass carried by its own momentum.

"Target disabled," *Arkhangelsk* sends. "Alpha mount is recharging."

"All units, *Agincourt*. We have lost main propulsion. Heavy impact damage to the fusion-rocket array. Reactors are safe, but we are coasting ballistic."

Agincourt was counter-burning to negate the acceleration from her attack run when the Lanky intercepted her, but the burn wasn't nearly enough to reverse her course. She's drifting stern first, still moving at over a thousand meters per second, and the projected trajectory on the plot will carry her clear past Mars and into deep space. With a broken propulsion system, she'll travel at that speed indefinitely, and there's not a tug in the combined fleet that can catch up to a 150,000-ton warship going more than a kilometer per second and stop its momentum. The skipper of *Agincourt* really has only one choice if he wants to save his crew, and it doesn't take him long to exercise it.

"All units, *Agincourt*. We are abandoning ship. I repeat, we are abandoning ship and releasing pods. Godspeed, and come collect us when you can. *Agincourt* Actual out."

"Goddammit!" I shout into my helmet. *Agincourt* and *Arkhangelsk* did their jobs precisely as designed, and yet we've just lost an irreplaceable piece of hardware, one of only two ships in the entire fleet that can take on a Lanky head to head and destroy it. But there's no other call to make for the skipper, and I'd do the same in his place. If they stay on the ship and then fail to repair the fusion engines, they'll be out of reach of the rest of the fleet within hours, and then they'll just coast through space until everyone on board starves or suffocates. Maybe they can catch up to the battleship after we've won Mars, and maybe there'll be a way to repair or salvage her, but the crew needs to get off the ship while they're still in range of friendly forces that can pluck the escape pods out of space.

"Alpha mount, ten-round burst, fire for effect."

Arkhangelsk's commander is leaving nothing to chance. The Lanky seed ship, clearly broken and now only a little more than half the size it was just a few minutes ago, disappears both from the plot and *Cincinnati*'s camera feed. On the plot, its icon merely winks out of existence. On the camera image, the broken seed ship disintegrates in a brilliant flash, leaving nothing behind but a glowing cloud of atomic debris that expands into a sphere and then begins to dissipate.

"Target destroyed," *Arkhangelsk* reports.

For a heartbeat, the world seems to come to a standstill. Then another cheer goes up, and this one doesn't just come from the neighboring compartments of this ship, but also over the fleet's tactical command channel. On my screen, there are no orange icons remaining, just our cluster of blue lozenge shapes, and nothing between us and Mars but empty space. The sucker punch worked beyond my most cheerful expectations. In just a little under an hour of combat, we have wiped out the entire fleet of Lanky ships guarding Mars. There may be more out there, patrolling the Alcubierre nodes or prowling deep space, just like last year during *Indy*'s stealth run back to Earth. But wherever they are, they won't keep us from landing our troops. Right now, the door to Mars isn't just open—we took a running jump and kicked it right off the hinges.

"All units, all units. The beaches are clear. Repeat: the beaches are clear. Initiate Phase Two. Execute Battle Plan Quebec."

Overhead, the ascending two-tone trill of an all-ship announcement from the bridge cuts through the radio chatter and ends our courtesy narration of the unfolding battle.

"Now hear this: all hands, seal your suits. I repeat: all hands, seal your suits. We are advancing toward the Lanky minefield. All bio-pod personnel, prepare for launch."

Up ahead on the forward bulkhead, the readiness light changes from red to green. I get out of my sling seat, grateful for the opportunity to stretch my legs again briefly before having to wedge myself into the tight bio-pod.

"That's us," I say to Dmitry. "Remember, just like in the simulator. The pod flies itself."

"Too much sitting in chair," Dmitry says, and stretches with a groan. "But I do not think we will be bored again very soon."

We do a last-minute armor check and walk over to our pods. The pod riggers help us into the tight containers and strap us in with quick and practiced movements. The rigger working on my pod connects my suit to the life-support system and the data bus and gives me a curt thumbs-up, which I return.

"Give 'em hell, sir," he says, and I nod.

The pod doesn't have a hatch, because it would be a weak point for superheated plasma to enter during the atmospheric descent. Instead, the top third of the pod is a separate part that gets lowered by a mechanical arm and then sealed into place with titanium bolts from the outside. Until I pull the handle for the explosive separation charges once I am on the ground, I am sealed into the pod as if it's a natural chunk of space rock. It's a supremely claustrophobic setup, but I'll take the discomfort for a little while if it decreases the likelihood of burning up in the planetary atmosphere or getting shot out of space by a Lanky mine. The most unnerving part during a pod launch is that my fate is totally out of my hands and dependent on the ballistics computer of the dorsal missile tubes.

I turn on my helmet's data display again and cycle through all the systems to make sure I don't have a last-second malfunction. Going through the checklist again gives me something to do while waiting to be loaded into the cruiser's launcher magazine like a piece of ordnance. Some guys claim they can take naps in their pods throughout the launch process, but I know they're full of shit. Getting fired at a planet is an unnatural act, one that tends to remind one of the fragility of the human body and the many ways it can break irreparably. I've not done a proper pod launch in over a year, but I find that I didn't miss this feeling in the least.

When the lid of the pod closes on top of me, it has an air of finality to it. The fleet just pulled off the biggest surprise victory in our military history, but we don't have the time to celebrate or even reflect on what just happened. For us podheads, the battle hasn't even begun, and the hard part is still ahead.

The pod is airtight, and the hull is so thick that I can't hear the warning klaxon in the pod bay, but I can feel the bump and the upward and forward motion as the loading arm of the rotary launcher picks up my pod and feeds it into one of the chambers.

One last drop, I think. *Let me make it down to the deck just one more time. If I'm going to die today, let it be on the surface with a gun in my hands.* But I know that the gunnery computer can't hear my thoughts, and it wouldn't give a shit even if it could.

CHAPTER 13

PODS AWAY

Early on in my podhead career, I used to keep my situational displays up and running whenever I dropped in a pod. After the third or fourth drop, I switched to running dark, all screens turned off, because I didn't want to know when I'd be passing through the Lanky minefield. I didn't want to see death coming if I ended up colliding with a mine or triggering its quills. For over two hundred drops, I rode down into the atmosphere blind and deaf, with only the buffeting from atmospheric entry signaling that I had once again made the gauntlet.

For this drop, I don't want to be unaware.

When *Phalanx* launches my pod out of its dorsal missile tube and toward Mars, my suit's visor display is on, the abstract tactical map that shows my trajectory and the space around me side by side with the feed from the camera in the nose of the bio-pod. *Phalanx* launches our pods at the very edge of her range, to keep far away from the Lanky minefield surrounding the planet, and I have plenty of time to reflect on the rashness of my decision to switch career tracks five years ago. The northern Martian hemisphere takes up most of my forward field of view, red and orange and white, swirling clouds over an ochre landscape. Even from the vantage point of the pod's crummy fixed-magnification camera lens, the panorama is breathtaking and terrifying at the same time. There's nothing like a pod launch, your body hurtling through space in a shell barely big enough to keep the vacuum out, to make you understand just how insignificantly small a single person really is.

The Lanky minefield surrounding Mars is much more dense than any I've ever seen around an occupied colony world. I know that the mathematical probability of my pod hitting a mine is very small considering the precision of the cruiser's ballistic computer, but like on every other launch I've ever done, the stakes bother me much more than the odds. There are thousands of the irregularly shaped proximity mines out here in this pod's camera field of view, each maybe twenty meters in diameter and loaded with lethal quill-shaped penetrator rods. My pod streaks through the minefield at hundreds of meters per second, and for the first time since my first few pod drops, I am very aware of the fact that I am tickling the surface of a spring-loaded trap with a hair-trigger release.

A few tense minutes later, my pod has cleared the orbital minefield. I take a long breath and unclench my fists. This phase of the entry is the calm between two stretches of white-knuckled terror, because the atmospheric entry that's about to follow is as unnerving as the minefield in its own way. If there's a defect in the pod's surface, some unseen crack or unsealed gap, the hot gases from the atmospheric friction will enter it and start burning through the pod, and then I'll burn up in the atmosphere. If I make it close to the ground and the mechanism for the descent chute fails, I'll hit the Martian soil at a few hundred meters per second and get ground into paste. But at the same time, this is the most exhilarating, death-defying ride in the universe, and nothing will make you feel more alive than climbing out of a pod after a successful descent.

When I enter the top layers of the Mars atmosphere, the truly blind portion of the descent begins, helmet screen or not. As I arc down toward the planet's surface at the precisely calculated angle computed by *Phalanx*'s artillery hardware, the pod is surrounded by a shroud of superheated plasma. I've seen the effect in a drop-ship cockpit a few times, and the incandescent, glowing plasma streaming past the cockpit windows is so bright that it blocks out everything else. In a pod, you don't see anything at all except for sun-bright flares from the little nose-mounted camera lens.

The blind part of the descent takes another fifteen minutes. When I see the pale-blue Mars horizon and the swirling cloud cover of the planet again, my anxiety should lessen, but it doesn't. The planet is shrouded in heavy clouds, the hallmark of a world that has been terraformed by the Lankies for a while. They like it warm and humid, and once they set up shop, their terraformers are amazingly efficient. The pod has no active sensors, so I'm slicking through the cloud cover almost blindly, with only the passive thermal vision and the useless view from the forward camera array to see where I am going. If *Phalanx*'s aim was true, I'll be somewhere near the middle of Red Beach, on the outskirts of Olympus City. If their aim was off by a few dozen kilometers—something that's rare, but not out of the question—I may end up coming down right in the middle of a Lanky settlement or somewhere else I definitely don't want to be right now.

Luckily, *Phalanx*'s gunnery was on the mark. When my pod breaks through the cloud cover, I am less than five thousand feet above the ground. Behind me, there's a muffled bang as the explosive charges blow the lid off the compartment for the drogue chute, and the triple parachute deploys behind the pod. Below the nose of the pod, I see the familiar geometry of human settlements—streets and buildings, lots of right angles, the boxy shapes of colonial housing units and power stations. Mars was the closest thing to Earth before the Lankies came and took it over, and Olympus City had more than half a million people living in it.

I bring up the tactical display again and let the computer figure out where I am. The Lankies destroyed every one of our satellites in orbit, so the computer looks at the topography underneath the pod's camera lens and compares it to the stored map data for Mars instead of getting a satellite fix. Three seconds later, the pod's CPU concludes that I am right at the edge of the landing zone designated Red Beach, halfway between Olympus City's center and our objective, the huge spaceport on its outskirts. The cannon cockers on *Phalanx* only missed their bull's-eye by two or three kilometers, which isn't bad considering they took the shot from a fast-moving platform tens of thousands of kilometers away.

The pod is descending through three thousand feet when I spot the first Lankies in the camera's field of vision. They're so large that they're obvious even from this altitude. Two of them are walking together, one behind the other, across the Mars plains, kicking up puffs of orange-red dust with every step. Another solitary Lanky is making its way down a street almost directly below the pod, stepping over piles of rubble and destroyed vehicles. The computer says I am descending into the campus of Sagan University, the main college in Olympus City and home to what used to be a cluster of research laboratories. Now there's barely a building down there that hasn't been at least partially destroyed, and the streets are littered with debris and hydrocar wrecks.

The pod descends through two thousand, then one thousand meters. The nearby Lanky is walking away from the projected landing site, but it's still too close for comfort, just two hundred meters at the most. The pods don't have radios or radar, so I have no idea where the other pods in my launch group are descending in the area, and I have no way to warn them anyway until I am on the ground and out of my pod.

Just before it hits the ground, my pod clips the corner of a building, and I get jarred so hard that I nearly bite my own tongue. Despite the triple canopy of the drogue chute, the descent speed of the pod is still anything but gentle. The pod hits the pavement of the street in front of the building and slides a good twenty meters before the computer cuts the drogue-chute lines, and I hit something solid and come to a sudden stop. With the nearby Lanky in mind, I waste no time pulling the release lever for the pod's lid, and the explosive charges blow out the locking bolts and eject the lid, which lifts half a meter off the rest of the pod and tumbles onto the street.

The air outside is typical Lanky atmosphere, warm and humid, gray skies the color of dirty concrete. I hit the quick-release latch on my harness and climb out of the pod, then release the clamp for my weapon and lift it out of its holder. I chamber a round and turn around to get my bearings. The building behind me is six floors high and may have been a sleek and elegant office tower when it was whole, but now most of the huge glass panes on the front of it are shattered, and a quarter of the structure is twisted rubble. My bio-pod came to rest with its nose against the burned-out hulk of a hydrocar with police markings. More car wrecks are littering the road, some turned over, some smashed flat, others charred black from hydrogen fires or explosions.

Nearby, I hear the familiar sound of thundering footsteps. They echo along the street, and the vibrations make some of the loose rubble on the sidewalk move a little. A hundred meters to my north, I see the familiar cranial ridge of a Lanky head towering over the roofline of some nearby buildings, and it's heading my way.

I run for the entrance of the partially destroyed office building behind me and turn on my polychromatic camouflage at the same time. But as ruined as the top half of the building is, the security lock at the entrance is closed, a double-layer polyplast sliding door secured by a roll-down security barrier made from titanium-alloy mesh. I would need a MARS launcher to blow the door open, and I didn't bring one and wouldn't have the time to use it anyway. I turn left and run along the front of the building, away from the approaching Lanky, looking for a way in. The Lanky appears in the street behind me, half a block away, just as I reach the corner of the building and skid around it to find some cover. The polychromatic armor has worked well against the Lankies so far, but I've never had one come closer to me than a hundred meters, and I don't want to be the test case to see if the electric camo can fool them at very short range.

The space next to the building is a service alley. Fifty meters ahead, I can see a ramp that leads down into the office building's lower levels—a parking garage or emergency shelter. I sprint the distance and run down the ramp, very mindful of the vibrations of the concrete under my feet heralding the approaching Lanky on the other side of the building. But the vehicle-sized opening at the bottom of the ramp is sealed with another security barrier, and I crash into it with a curse.

Behind me, at the corner I just turned, the Lanky steps into sight and then stops at the mouth of the service alley. Its head swings around, first left, then right. Lankies look nothing like dogs, but the way this one is moving reminds me of a hound trying to catch a scent. I duck behind the retention wall of the vehicle ramp and make myself as small as possible. To my own helmet optics, I'm just a vaguely concrete-textured outline, but we know precisely fuck all about how the Lankies sense their environment, even after having dissected a few dozen back on Earth, so for all I know I could be as obvious to the fucking thing as a clown at a funeral. I check the loading status of my rifle again. If the Lanky decides to check out this alley and come any closer, I'll have to see if one magazine of gas rounds is enough to stop one of those things in just fifty meters.

The Lanky turns the corner and takes one step into the alley. I know I have about three seconds to decide whether to keep running or stand and fight. I know I can't outrun the thing if it has spotted me, so I slowly bring my rifle to bear over the lip of the retaining wall and aim the reticle square at the center of the Lanky's spindly body.

The Lanky takes another step into the alley. Their strides are so long that he's already a quarter of the way to the spot where I'm hiding. I tighten my finger on the trigger and take up the slack.

Five rounds, and then I'll run my ass off if he's not down, I tell myself.

Behind the Lanky, a rolling cavalcade of gunshots thunders. The echoes roll up the alley and bounce back from the nearby buildings. The Lanky shrieks its earsplitting, piercing wail and stumbles forward, then starts to turn around. Its cranial shield clips one side of the building to my left and sends chunks of polyplast and twisted steel raining into the alley between us. I put my targeting reticle right in the middle of the Lanky's mass and pull the trigger once, twice, three times. The heavy gas rounds hit the Lanky in the side and tear big holes into it, the gas mixture from the rounds igniting inside the body and blowing chunks out of its tough skin from the inside. Whoever is firing at the Lanky from the other side lets loose another fusillade of half a dozen rounds at least. The Lanky wails again and falls onto its side, blocking almost the entire alley with its massive bulk. The head hits the concrete not ten meters from where I am crouching, and the impact knocks me off my feet and sends me sprawling on my ass. I get up again and aim my M-95 at the Lanky, but the head blocks my shot at the rest of its body, and I know better than to shoot at a cranial plate I've seen deflect autocannon rounds. But the Lanky's wail dies, and then the creature stops moving. I take my finger off the trigger and exhale sharply.

Up at the mouth of the alley, behind the now-lifeless form of the Lanky, a group of troopers in SRA battle armor appears. One of them gives me a two-fingered little wave, and I know it's Dmitry. He trots up the alley past the dead Lanky and ejects an empty case out of his rifle on the move. The brass case clatters onto the concrete with a metallic ringing sound, and Dmitry pulls a fresh round from his harness and reloads his gun before the empty shell case stops rolling.

Behind him, two of the SRA marines and the Eurocorps lieutenant bring up the rear of the little group. The German lieutenant looks at the fallen Lanky with awe, and I notice that he keeps as far away from the body as he can in the tight confines of the alley. I remind myself that the Euros have had very little exposure to the Lankies, and that this is probably the first time he's ever seen one close up.

"You can turn off magic invisible armor now, I think," Dmitry says over squad comms. I toggle the polychrome camouflage off, and my armor becomes matte black again instead of reflecting the background.

"Where's the rest of your guys?" I ask.

"Leytenánt Bondarenko is one kilometer further in city," he says. "Pod dropped on top of very tall building. Sergeant Anokhin is close, two blocks that way." Dmitry gestures behind us with a gloved hand.

"Thanks for the backup," I say. "Figures that my pod lands practically right in front of one of those things."

"Is no problem," Dmitry says. "Will be first kill of many today, I think." He holds out his hand to help me up, and I get to my feet. "Come. We go meet Lieutenant Bondarenko. He is in good place for looking around."

In the distance, we can hear the slow thrum-thrum of Lanky footsteps. They're far off, probably several blocks away, but they sound like they're heading our way. Maybe the gunshots got the attention of the nearby pair of Lankies, but the shrieking of the one we killed just now probably didn't help to keep our entrance stealthy, either.

I check my suit's vitals: oxygen 93 percent, power cell 97 percent, all functions in the green, no damage.

"Higher ground sounds good right now," I say, but then remember the Lanky crawling up the atrium of a PRC building in Detroit a year ago. "Just bear in mind that these bastards can climb pretty well."

As we trot off toward Lieutenant Bondarenko's position, Dmitry looks back at the dead Lanky sprawled out in the alley, five meters of cranial shield blocking most of the thoroughfare like a wall made from bone.

"Is shame we cannot take head with us. You know, as souvenir."

"You want me to take a picture with you in front of the head instead?" I ask with a grin, and Dmitry grins back.

"Head would look much better on wall of Alliance carrier flight deck than little picture. I could trade to chief engineering officer for many bottles of vodka."

———————————

The Lankies in the area are definitely stirred up and alert. We leapfrog across intersections and along streets littered with broken vehicles and building debris, and take cover whenever a Lanky walks past within a block of our route. Every once in a while, we spot the familiar empty oblong husks of Lanky nerve-gas containers, which are the size of hydrocars. The Lankies followed their usual protocol when they took over Mars—gas the population from orbit, move in and mop up the remnants, then set up the terraformers. They got to skip their usual step of seeking out our own terraforming stations and smashing them to rubble, because Mars had been colonized for decades, and all the terraformers have long been deactivated and converted to fusion plants. But as much destruction as we see here on the streets of Olympus City, I see very few dead bodies. Some are still in vehicles, decomposed and desiccated after a year in the humid and CO_2-heavy atmosphere. More bodies are in the buildings we cut through for cover and concealment. But out on the streets, there aren't many bodies when there should be thousands of corpses out here, civilian casualties or troops who died trying to fight off the invaders. It's eerie to be in a city devoid of people, dead or alive.

Lieutenant Bondarenko, the leader of the SRA marine squad, saved himself a twenty-story climb by pure accident. His pod landed on the roof of a residence tower. When we get to the top of the building after climbing twenty flights of stairs in the darkness, we see that his free ride to the top of the tower almost came with an express elevator down to street level. His pod is right at the edge of the roof, a meter or two away from tipping over the side and tumbling onto the plaza eighty meters below. His drogue chute, having already collapsed, would have been no help at all. Judging by how pale the SRA lieutenant still looks, I can tell he knows very well how close he just came to splattering on the asphalt like a bug on a windshield.

Up here on the roof and no longer dodging Lankies in the streets for a bit, we can finally get our comms gear into action. I break out my admin deck and send a burst message to our C2 center on *Phalanx*.

>Red Team One infil success. Commencing approach to Red Beach.

The reply comes via encrypted burst just a few minutes later.

>Task Force Red standing by for target coordinates. Good hunting.

The SI Force Recon team from the starboard launch tubes landed at the other end of the drop zone. Our target, the huge air and spaceport outside Olympus City, is four kilometers to our northeast and three kilometers to their northwest. I fire up the platoon channel and contact the SI group.

"Red Team Two, this is Red Team One. You guys all make it down in one piece?"

"That's affirmative," Lieutenant Perkins replies. "We had some hostiles near the drop zone, but we managed to avoid them. Take it the gunfire earlier was from you."

"Yeah, we had to drop one. Now they're stirred up."

"Can't be helped. Let's get the data link going. Can't see how it can hurt at this point anyway."

I turn on my TacLink, and almost immediately I see the icons for the eight SI troopers on my tactical map, five klicks almost directly to our east.

"We're legging it to grid Echo One-Eight and get eyeballs on target from the south end," Lieutenant Perkins sends.

"Copy that," I reply. "I'm going to use the high ground for overwatch and then move up to grid Delta One-Five and go in from the northwest. We'll meet in the middle when the LZ is clear."

"Let's get to it," Lieutenant Perkins says. "We got a whole brigade up there waiting for us to roll out the welcome mat."

"Don't get stomped," I send. "Grayson out."

From up here on the roof, I have a good view of a large swath of Olympus City. Every time I spot a Lanky in the streets below, my tactical computer marks its position with an orange icon and shares the information with everyone else on our TacLink node. I spend a few minutes marking Lankies and mentally mapping out a way over to the spaceport. Four kilometers to our east, there are half a dozen runways and drop-ship landing pads that need to be cleared for our first and second assault waves to land. I can see that the hardened shelters on the military side of the spaceport are still standing. Designed to survive a near miss from a tactical nuke, they were either too hard for the Lankies to demolish, or they didn't want to bother with the spacecraft shelters once they had cleaned out the people. I wonder just how much ammunition, ordnance, and fuel is still safely sheltered in those concrete domes, waiting to be put to good use by our SI regiments. It's precisely that fuel and ammo, and those largely undamaged facilities, that make the spaceport the most important landing zone on this hemisphere. Other cities on Mars have airports and space facilities, but the one here right by the capital is the largest military base outside Earth.

"Look at that," Lieutenant Stahl says. He's standing by the edge of the roof and looking north. I walk over to where he's standing and follow his gaze.

There's a Lanky settlement well north of Olympus City, out in the plains a good thirty kilometers away. I switch my optics to maximum magnification. The strange, reef-like latticework structures the Lankies built look just like I remember them from my last drops onto conquered colonies. On the plains between the Lanky structure and the outskirts of Olympus City, dozens of Lankies have gathered. But they aren't advancing toward us or the airfield. Instead, they are looking at the sky. I shift my view upward and cycle through all the filters until I spot what they are looking at.

"What is that up there?" the Eurocorps lieutenant asks.

I let the suit computer track the object in the sky that is just now breaking through the cloud cover and streaking across the horizon in a steeply descending arc. Then I dial up the magnification again until I recognize what it is.

"It's one of theirs," I say. "One of the seed ships we destroyed. Or part of it, anyway."

The piece of wreckage is trailing flames and smoke, smearing a wispy arc across the dirty gray sky. Then it disappears from view behind the Alba Mons mountain range on the northern horizon. The trail of smoke remains for a little while until the winds begin to disperse it.

"Take a good look at it, motherfuckers," I say to the Lankies gathered on the plain. "That's a bad omen for you."

Then I get out my admin deck and draw a box around the map grid where two or three dozen Lankies are still looking to the skies.

"*Phalanx*, Tailpipe Red One. Fire mission," I send on the tactical channel. "Kinetic strike, target reference point Alpha One. Twenty-plus hostiles. There are no friendlies within twenty klicks of the TRP."

"Tailpipe Red One, copy. Fire mission, TRP Alpha One," *Phalanx* sends back. Right now, the cruiser is orienting one of her dorsal rail gun mounts toward the target reference point coordinates I uploaded. We are strictly limited on nuclear-fire missions because we used most of the warheads in existence for the Orions, but kinetic warheads are cheap, and we have plenty of them.

"Firing Delta mount. Three-round burst, shots out."

I close the admin deck again, warn the SI team to expect fireworks in the distance soon, and keep watching the Lankies, who are in no particular hurry to be somewhere else right now, even though they must know that something out of the ordinary is happening. The rail gun shots from *Phalanx* are much faster than the pods in which we arrived because they don't have a living payload. The kinetic warheads streaking through the atmosphere are too far away for me to hear the sound they make as they slice through the air when they arrive.

The Russians and the Eurocorps lieutenant holler in surprise and amazement when the three kinetic rounds from *Phalanx* hit their target a few minutes later. The geysers of Mars dirt that follow the impacts reach hundreds of meters into the sky. The thunderclap from the impacts reaches our helmet audio feeds a minute and a half later, and the echo rolls through the streets of the city below, a sound like a giant clearing its throat. It'll take an hour or more for all the dust to settle, but I already know that the Lankies within a quarter kilometer of the impact points are no longer cohesive organisms. Tough as they are, they still have to obey the laws of physics, and while the rail guns are useless against the seed ships, they will make mincemeat out of their passengers once they are outside their protective shells.

"Let's catch up to the SI boys," I suggest. "We have a spaceport to clear for the drop ships."

"Cannot let marines sit on asses up in space all day," Dmitry agrees.

"Yeah, that's what the fleet is for," Lieutenant Perkins contributes via squad comms.

"Hey," I grumble. "Watch it, ground pounder."

CHAPTER 14

—————— RED BEACH ——————

For once, the size of the Lankies works in our favor in battle. Here in the confines of Olympus City, they are obvious, easy to predict and avoid, and not very nimble. We make our way east through the empty streets, using alleys and buildings as cover, hiding whenever a Lanky passes nearby, and cutting through buildings as much as we can to stay out of sight. There are fewer of them prowling the city than I would have predicted, maybe fifteen or twenty at the most. Still, the dash-and-hide march across the rubble-strewn city takes us a good hour before we have the spaceport in sight. The SI troopers have beaten us—their tactical symbols are already in position on the south side of the spaceport, and more and more orange Lanky symbols pop up on our TacLink screen as the SI Force Recon guys spot them. The spaceport is huge, with a civilian and a military part, four runways for atmospheric landings, and a sprawling administrative complex. Our combined force of sixteen troopers would be hopelessly inadequate if we had to secure the whole place, but that's not our task. We are here to give the big guns something to aim at. We pick the highest structure in the immediate neighborhood, an eight-story building that's only lightly damaged, and climb up to the top floor. From up here, Dmitry and I have a good view of much of the spaceport, and the SRA squad is pulling security on the roof edge, keeping an eye out for Lankies in all directions.

"We have eyes on roughly twenty at the south end. They're all over the tarmac between the hard shelters," Lieutenant Perkins reports from his position a kilometer to our southeast. "Make that twenty-three confirmed."

My TacLink updates accordingly, and I study the map. "That's right near one of the refueling nodes. If we call in kinetics and they crack an underground tank, the place will go sky high."

"How do you propose we get them out of there?" Lieutenant Perkins asks.

"I don't know. You feel like running out onto runway zero-five and blowing a few raspberries in their direction?"

The SI lieutenant laughs. "Not if we can avoid it."

The Lankies between the hangars are out of the effective range of our weapons, so we can't start picking them off with gas rounds, but there are too many of them anyway, and we don't have the ammo to drop twenty or thirty of them. We need to get them off the spot that has a few hundred thousand liters of aviation fuel under it. As satisfying as it would be to see the whole group disappear in a huge fireball, losing all the fuel would be a major setback for the landing force. With the installation relatively intact, they can refuel and rearm the drop ships without having to get back to the carrier.

"We need to get them to move so the fleet can drop kinetics on their heads," I tell Dmitry. "Any ideas?"

Dmitry ponders my question for a few moments. "Make them come to us? Get closer, shoot. When they come to us, we move. Take new position, shoot again."

"That'll get them off the pad and into the city. But then we're in the way of the kinetic strike."

"Make them go other way, then. Out to runway."

Give them something to chase, I think. *What's good for getting a Lanky's attention?*

177

I have a sudden flashback to the graduation exercise of my last boot-camp flight a few months ago, when I let them defend a simulated ter-raforming station against a Lanky assault. Some of the more adventurous recruits commandeered an ATV and distracted several Lankies from the ter-raformer. The Lankies were computer generated, but we know they react to anything that makes mechanical noise or puts out radiation. I have a trans-mitter in my armor that can put out thousands of watts of radio energy, but I don't want to test my sprinting abilities against twenty Lankies, and we don't have any ATVs around to outrun them once they come chasing us.

I step over to the edge of the roof and look down at the street below, where a bunch of cars are cluttering the roadway. Some are burned out, others smashed, but there are quite a few that still look operable.

"Any of you people know how to chip-jack a car?" I ask.

"What is 'chip-jack'?" Dmitry asks.

"Disable the security chip in the computer console and steal the car," I reply.

He grins and looks at his SRA comrades. Then he says something in Russian, and Sergeants Anokhin and Dragomirova laugh.

"You want to steal car, we go steal car."

———————————

There's no shortage of vehicles out on the street in this neighborhood. The burned-out hulk of a hydrobus blocks the street diagonally, and several other cars are wedged up against it. From the burn marks, it looks like they rammed into each other and all burned up in the same hydrogen fire. But there are some cars in parking nooks on the other side of the street that mostly look undamaged.

"The hydrocars are no good," I say. "They've been standing around for a year. The fuel cells will be broken down by now. Look for an EV."

We fan out and check every vehicle in the row, keeping an ear out for the footsteps of approaching Lankies. Near the corner of the block,

Sergeant Dragomirova looks into a little commuter car and shouts something in Russian. We trot over to her position.

"Figures," I say. "The only all-electric around, and it's the size of a gym locker."

Dmitry tries the door and finds it locked. Then he takes out the combat knife he wears strapped to his leg armor, taps the laminate panels on the frame next to the car door for a few moments, and puts the tip of his knife against a spot ten centimeters from the edge of the door. He smacks the pommel of his knife hard with his palm, and the blade pops through the laminate of the car body. There's a sharp, short hissing sound, and when Dmitry pulls on the handle again, the door opens without resistance.

"Main pressure cylinder for environmental control," he says. "Controls door locks, too."

"Good to know," I say. "For the next time I want to jack a ride."

Dmitry calls Sergeant Anokhin over, who climbs into the driver's seat and taps the center console screen. It comes to life with the logo of the car manufacturer. Sergeant Anokhin uses his own knife to work loose the bezel of the control screen and pulls the whole thing out of the console. Thirty seconds later, I hear the hum of an electric engine, and the car's running lights turn on. Sergeant Anokhin tosses the control screen out the driver-side window, and it clatters onto the asphalt of the parking nook. Then he gets back out of the car. Dmitry pops his head into the passenger compartment and looks around.

"Battery is fifteen percent," he says. "You want to go fast, you will not drive for very long."

"It'll have to do," I say. "We're not going far in this anyway."

We work out a battle plan on the fly. Dmitry is going to go back up to his eighth-floor vantage point and spot targets with Sergeant Gerasimov. Lieutenant Bondarenko and Sergeant Anokhin will provide cover, and

Sergeant Dragomirova will join me and drive the comically small electric car we just hot-wired.

"We'll get within rifle range, I'll pop off a few rounds, and turn my suit to maximum transmitting output so they get nice and pissed off," I say. "We'll drive out onto the runway and see how many of them come after us. If there are any left over on the landing pads, you go with your original idea. Put rounds into them from this end so they'll come looking for you, and get the hell off that roof and to an alternate OP. When the Lankies are out in the open, you call down the thunder from *Kirov*. We hook around the north end of the base and find cover over there, and then we have eyes on the place from both ends."

"What if little car breaks when you are in middle of runway?" Dmitry asks.

"Then we're fucked," I say, and Dmitry grins. "Let's get to it. And I really hope that your artillery is accurate. We won't be too far ahead of the Lankies."

"Is Russian artillery," he says. "Mostly hits right target. *Mostly.*"

———

The vehicle is built for two passengers riding tandem, one behind the other, but it's not designed to accommodate armored troops and their weapons. Luckily, Sergeant Dragomirova is fairly small even in her angular battle armor, so we both fit. Dmitry and I pop the rear window out of the car and throw it aside so I have clearance to fire my rifle out the back. Then the Russians trot back to the building we just left a little while ago to resume their observation posts. I send an update to the SI troopers on the south end of the base and let them know what we are about to do.

"We're going to move up toward the hangars as soon as you start your run," Lieutenant Perkins says. "Just for the record, that's some crazy-ass shit. But good luck."

"We just got here by letting them shoot us out of missile tubes," I reply. "And we're fighting five-hundred-ton creatures with hand weapons. There's no part of this that's sane."

———————————

Sergeant Dragomirova speaks just a few words of English, but Dmitry translates the plan for her so I won't have to rely on the accuracy of my suit's interpreter software in the heat of battle. She takes her spot in the driver's seat and places her rifle across her lap. The Russian anti-Lanky rifle is a bit longer than our models, and the muzzle end and about thirty centimeters of barrel are sticking out the right-side window.

I sit in the backseat, which can swivel to face rearward, and rest my own rifle on the frame of the rear window.

"Tell me you are talking to your arty guys, Dmitry," I send on the squad channel.

"Yes. All good. They will shoot when I say to shoot."

"They better. If I get stomped flat, you're the only one with a direct line to the gods."

"So drive faster than Lankies."

"Brilliant idea," I reply. "I'll give that a shot. Keep us in sight, and stay on the radio. Grayson out."

I check the chamber of my rifle and make sure there's a fifteen-millimeter gas-filled round ready to ruin some Lanky's morning. Then I turn to Sergeant Dragomirova and pat the back of her headrest.

"Let's go," I say.

She puts the car in drive, and we start down the street and toward the spaceport a quarter kilometer away.

Both of us have our tactical screens up on the visors of our helmets, and we can see all the information from the respective TacLink feeds of our allies. Sergeant Dragomirova races the electric car through the city streets at breakneck speed. She's able to avoid streets and intersections with Lankies in them because the spotted ones show up on our map overlay complete with movement vectors. We make it to the perimeter fence of the base, which is torn down in many spots. Sergeant Dragomirova slows down for a hard left turn and steers our ride through one of the gaps in the fence. Then she floors it again, and we're headed for the VTOL pad of the base, driving up to the dragons to tickle their tails and run away.

We're a hundred meters from the VTOL pad when I spot the first Lankies. They're much taller than the surrounding buildings and almost as tall as the hardened concrete domes of the big spacecraft shelters nearby. I turn my suit's transmitter up to full power, which is enough radio energy to send messages to the waiting ships in orbit. If the Lankies are really sensitive to radiation, I just turned on a superbright flashlight in a dark basement.

"Come on, you bastards!" I shout. "Over here."

Behind me, Sergeant Dragomirova turns on the little car's entertainment system, which starts blaring a K-pop tune. She turns the volume all the way up, and the music is so loud in the confines of the car that my helmet reduces the incoming volume by three-quarters to preserve my hearing. I don't speak Korean, so I don't understand the lyrics, but the tune is pretty catchy, with lots of bass beat.

Our combined efforts to get the Lankies' attention has the desired effect almost at once. I don't know whether it's the radio energy from my suit or the K-pop or both, but the nearest Lankies turn and start walking our way. Even when they're not in a hurry, they can outrun a human easily with their five-meter strides, and when they are agitated, they can move much more quickly than their size would suggest. The first Lanky comes off the VTOL pad in a brisk walk that turns into a trot. Sergeant Dragomirova whips the electric car around and floors the accelerator. We race away from the VTOL pad and over to the open space of the triple runways. The tarmac is strewn with debris and destroyed vehicles, and the SRA sergeant has to do a slalom to avoid wreckage and concrete chunks.

The car is fast, but the Lanky isn't much slower, and it doesn't slow down for obstacles. Instead, it steps right over them. Behind the first one, four more have decided to give chase to our loud little car. I let my suit update the target data for the rest of the squad. Then I bring my rifle to bear and switch the fire-control system to computer control. With my finger on the trigger, the suit's ballistic computer takes over. I center my helmet reticle on the closest Lanky, now eighty meters away and closing the distance, and point the muzzle of the gun in the same direction. The computer waits until the barrel of the gun lines up with the intended target, and then the gun adds its thundering report to the noise of the pop tune blasting from the car's speakers. For a human, an eighty-meter hit on a moving target from a weaving and dodging platform would be a one-in-a-hundred shot, but for the computer, it's a trivial matter. The round hits the Lanky in the upper chest, and the explosive gas payload blows a head-sized hole out of its thick hide. The Lanky collapses midstride and crashes into the wreckage of a fuel bowser, and the impact is so loud that it drowns out the pop music from the car momentarily. The Lankies behind the first one keep following, undeterred, but I notice that they're loosening up their formation a little, fanning out past the fallen body of the one I just dropped.

"You have five behind you," Lieutenant Perkins says over the squad channel. "Whatever you do, don't fucking stop. They're too far for us to engage."

"Four more coming," Dmitry announces. "From between hangars, trying to cut you off. Turn right and go faster."

I turn to my right and see the four Lankies Dmitry announced, emerging at a fast clip from the space between the nearby hangars. I yell to Sergeant Dragomirova and point over to the newcomers, and she kills the entertainment system and silences the K-pop tunes warbling from the speakers at a hundred decibels. Then she steers to the right, away from both Lanky groups. We race across the runways on a diagonal course. With fewer wrecks and bits of debris out here in the open,

Sergeant Dragomirova can go full throttle, and we're up to a hundred kilometers per hour and still accelerating by the time we're across the third runway. I shoot the rest of the magazine at the Lankies trying to catch up to us to keep them pissed off.

"Now would be a great time to shoot some arty at these things," I send to Dmitry.

"I sent request. Go over this point in twenty-five seconds; then go straight another ten seconds and make turn to three hundred degrees," he says, and marks a spot on the map a kilometer ahead. Then he gives instructions in Russian to Sergeant Dragomirova, and she sends back a terse acknowledgment.

Somewhere out in high orbit past the Lanky minefield, a Russian cruiser is aiming its ventral rail gun battery at Dmitry's target reference point right now and letting fly with whatever their gunnery department deemed appropriate for a squad-sized group of Lankies out in the open. It's not a comforting thought at all, even though I know that Dmitry knows what he's doing. But kinetic projectiles don't distinguish between friend and foe, and an aiming error of a tenth of a degree can make a shot miss by hundreds of meters at this range. We race ahead of the group of Lankies, who are now keenly interested in the little electric car kicking up a rooster tail of red Mars dirt by the side of the runway. I eject the empty magazine from my rifle and insert a full one from one of the ammo pouches on my armor. The anti-Lanky rounds are so large that the magazines are way too cumbersome for something that only holds five measly rounds. Two quick engagements, and I've already gone through a quarter of my ammunition. And if we don't clear this space for the main landing force soon, there won't be any resupply.

Sergeant Dragomirova has to kill a few seconds to reach the spot marked by Dmitry at exactly the right time, so she slows the car down and whips it around in a circle before looping back to our old heading. That maneuver reduces our distance to the nearest Lanky from over two hundred meters to less than a hundred. The two groups of Lankies are converging on our position, and I have a good idea why Dmitry directed us the way he did.

"Mark," Dmitry says. "Now ten seconds ahead, full speed. Next mark, turn to three hundred degrees. *Chetrie, tri, dva, odin,* mark."

Sergeant Dragomirova turns the wheel and whips the nose of the car to the left. The electric engine is running at full output, and I don't want to check how much battery life is left in this thing. If it dies on us in the middle of this wide-open stretch of dirt, the Lankies will only be a brief worry before the air strike gets here. I've called lots of ordnance down into my neighborhood, but I've never had any called down practically right on top of my head.

"Seven seconds," Dmitry says, and now there's urgency in his voice. "Go faster."

I shout at Sergeant Dragomirova, who is yelling at Dmitry into her helmet's headset, and the leading Lanky outside, now two hundred meters away again, lets out a screeching wail that sounds pissed off and frustrated at the same time.

Not having any fun, eh? Join the fucking club, I think.

This time, I can hear the whistling sound from the kinetic rounds overhead. It's a sharp, shrill sound, like a knife blade hacking through sheet metal.

The kinetic warheads from the Russian cruiser smack into the dirt by the side of the runway where the Lankies are following us in an untidy gaggle. They hit the ground in half-second intervals, each pounding like giant sledgehammers. For just a second, I am convinced that the Russians have elected to use tactical nukes. Sergeant Dragomirova is aiming the car at a gap between two hangars, and we've almost reached it when the impacts bounce us off the ground and fling the car into the air like we're a ration can that someone kicked down an alley. I hear a low explosion in the car, and then I see only white and dirty red in front of my eyes. The car rolls over, then again, and again. We were close enough to the hangars that I expect the world to end any second now, that we'll get crushed against the concrete wall of a spacecraft shelter. But then the car rolls one last time and comes to a stop. The dashboard display still works, but it's blinking a red "LOW BATTERY" warning among a host of error messages, and the whining from the electrical drivetrain ceases. The little stolen car has driven its last meter. I move my arms and legs, but it feels like I'm moving through syrup instead of air. The whole inside of the vehicle is filled with foam from the crash safety dispensers installed in the civilian car. It's meant to keep the occupants of a vehicle from suffering impact injuries, and I very much appreciate that safety feature right now, but it makes it a lot harder to get out of the car quickly to get to cover. I guess the designers never had "getting chased by Lankies" or "narrowly getting missed by an orbital strike" on their list of possible safety hazards. I can't see Sergeant Dragomirova, but I know she's still alive as well, because she's cursing up a storm in Russian as she, too, is trying to free herself from the embrace of the rapidly solidifying safety foam.

When I've finally freed myself from the wreck of the electric car, I can't see anything outside but red dust. I cycle through my helmet's sensor modes until I reach the microwave mode that warned me of the presence of the Lankies in the tunnels on Greenland. All around us, rocks and dirt are raining down. I can barely see my hands in front of my face, microwave mode or not, and I sure as hell wouldn't notice a Lanky in this mess even if it walked right up to me.

Behind me, Sergeant Dragomirova struggles free from the overturned car and gives the wreck a last kick. We're both covered in dust and the residue from the safety foam that probably saved our lives just now, because the car looks like it went three rounds with a battlecruiser in a head-on collision contest. My rifle is gone, but the sergeant still has hers. She checks the action of her rifle, points toward our west, and yells something my way in Russian.

"*That way is cover,*" my computer translates for me. I give her a thumbs-up, look around on the ground for my rifle, and then decide to write it off as a loss. If that M-95 is the only thing I'll lose today, I'll come out well ahead. I turn toward Sergeant Dragomirova again, who is already trotting off to the west, toward the row of spacecraft shelters we were trying to reach right before the kinetic rounds hit. I can't see them in this mess, but my computer's map says they're seventy meters away, so I trust the silicon and follow my SRA companion.

It's good to see that even the Lankies have limits to their physical strength. The spacecraft shelters are all still standing, domed structures made out of reinforced concrete several meters thick. But the heavy roll-away doors that sealed off their fronts are gone, torn off their tracks and scattered all over the tarmac in front of the shelters just like at Joint Base Thule back on Earth. Sergeant Dragomirova and I make our way into the nearest hangar for cover and gape at the destruction inside. This particular hangar had half a dozen civilian interplanetary passenger ships in it, and they're all thoroughly wrecked, smashed into each other and reduced to component parts by the Lankies. The whole hangar floor is littered with twisted and mangled bits of steel and alloy. There are scorch marks and charred wreckage bits from long-extinguished fires, and the presence of several fuel trucks tells me that they were in the middle of fueling the birds in the hangars for a rapid evac when the Lankies landed. But just like in the streets of Olympus City, I see almost no human remains here. If they got jumped while trying to get the ships ready for takeoff, there should be dozens or hundreds of dead crew and service personnel out here among the wrecks, but I can't see a single body out in the open.

"That was too fucking close, Dmitry," I send over the squad channel to let him know we're still drawing breath, in case he's not watching our icons on the tactical screen.

"Was not *too* close," he says. "If too close, you would be dead both."

I bite back a cranky reply—can't argue with the Russian's logic, after all—and look back at the open end of the hangar, where the red Mars dirt is still raining down everywhere.

"Got eyes on the bad guys?"

"No more bad guys," Dmitry says. "Not on landing pad. And cannot see too good out by runway, but no movement so far."

"I concur," Lieutenant Perkins sends from the south. "That strike wiped out half the map grid. Gotta hand it to the Russians: that was dead-on. Couldn't have done it better with a guided shell and a laser to ride it in. We are advancing toward your position."

I check my tactical map. "Copy that. You guys take up station at the south end and secure the VTOL pad and the refueling stations. We are moving north to get eyes past the northern end of the runway. Let's secure this bitch so we can call down the grunts."

"Let's," Lieutenant Perkins concurs.

By the time the dust from the kinetic strike settles, Sergeant Dragomirova and I are already half a kilometer north of the impact points. I don't have to turn around and lay eyes on the area where the Lankies got caught out in the open by three kinetic rounds from *Kirov* to know the result of the strike. The airfield has three main runways, each five kilometers long to accommodate even the heaviest interplanetary shuttles and freighters, and one of them is now out of commission because one of the Russian kinetic rounds tore a twenty-meter crater into it. But we still have two runways undamaged, and the refueling stations are all intact as well. Lieutenant Perkins's two fire teams take up perimeter guard around the VTOL pad and its subterranean fuel tanks to guard them from the Lankies that are still milling around in the city streets.

The main air/space-traffic-control tower for the Olympus City spaceport sits on a little hill on the north end of the base. The radar installation and fusion reactor a hundred meters away are little more than rubble, but the control tower is only slightly damaged. Sergeant Dragomirova and I break open a door and make our way up the emergency staircase of the tower.

The main control room at the top of the tower is empty, and other than the fact that half the windows in the place are shattered, things here look mostly intact, like someone could just turn the power back on and start directing inbound traffic again if the base radar down the hill wasn't all wrecked to shit. We're fifty meters above ground level, higher up than even Dmitry and his squad on their rooftop to the south of the base. The view from up here is excellent, and I can see far to the north, where the Martian plains extend underneath a gray and cloudy sky. And what I see in the distance makes me wish for a hole to crawl into.

"We have incoming from the south," Lieutenant Perkins sends. Five orange icons pop up on my tactical map beyond the south end of the base, close to where Dmitry's squad is providing overwatch for the SI guys.

"Uh-huh," I say, preoccupied with the view from the north-facing windows of the control tower. "We've got incoming from the north, too."

"How many?" Lieutenant Perkins asks.

In the distance, eight kilometers away according to my computer, the biggest group of Lankies I've ever seen together in one place is coming across the plains toward Olympus City and the spaceport. The only thing I can think of is Gateway Station on a busy day, when there are so many people moving on the central concourse that the crowd moves like a stream.

"Every last fucking one of them, I think."

CHAPTER 15

——— RODS FROM THE GODS ———

I don't even bother mourning the loss of my rifle, or the fact that only two of us are up here on the north end of the field instead of the entire team. What's coming down from the plains is beyond our ability to stop with hand weapons. Depending on how they're positioned in orbit relative to our location, it may even be beyond the fleet's ability to handle.

"*Phalanx*, Tailpipe Red One. Priority fire mission. Sending TRP data uplink now."

It takes a few seconds for the signal to travel up to *Phalanx*, and then a few seconds more for the tactical officer in CIC to process what he's seeing on his display. The plain to the north of Olympus City is a sea of orange icons, hundreds of Lankies in motion, flowing in our general direction at twenty kilometers per hour.

"I read your uplink," the tactical officer says, and I admire the professionalism that keeps the incredulity in his voice to a very slight note. "Call the ordnance, Tailpipe Red One. You are in the clear for a nuclear strike."

I think about it for a moment. That many Lankies out in the open are a tempting target for a hundred-kiloton warhead. The whole group would be gone in a flash, but then the follow-up troops would have to deal with the fallout and the radiation. And I know that *Phalanx* has a pitifully low number of nuclear warheads on board. The battle has just begun, and we have no clue what else they may throw at us once the first wave is on the ground. If I have them start using nukes right now, we may all regret it later.

"Negative on nukes," I say. "They're bunched up enough for kinetics. But we'll need a lot of them."

God, I wish we had some close-air support already, I think. The Shrike pilots would have a party with that many Lankies out in the open and with no orbital support of their own.

"Give us a time-on-target strike," I continue. "All the rail gun barrels you can bring to bear. Make it a hundred rounds. Saturate grid Romeo Alpha Nine-Seven as they pass through it, in"— I check my TacLink screen and do a quick calculation—"eight minutes, thirty seconds. I will call in follow-ups as needed."

Rail gun projectiles are cheap, and the task force carries plenty of them, but a hundred rounds will make a big dent in our supply. The tactical officer on the other end of the link does not argue the need. He can read a plot, and he knows just as well as I do that if a few hundred Lankies overrun the spaceport and the city, Red Beach is going to be a no-go for landing troops.

"TOT strike, eight minutes, thirty seconds. Clock's ticking," he sends. "Can't promise a hundred rounds, but it'll be close enough to make no difference for those things. Keep your heads down."

"Oh, that's pretty much assured," I reply. "Tailpipe Red One out."

I relay the information to the rest of the team. Down to our south, there's the sporadic booming from big anti-Lanky rifles as the SI fire teams engage the first Lankies coming out of the city and onto the spaceport from the south. Compared to what's coming toward us from the north, it's a trivial number of Lankies, but we're only sixteen troops, and we're spread out across three positions and as many kilometers of ground.

The next eight minutes are agonizingly long. Sergeant Dragomirova and I are keeping tabs on the Lankies coming in from the north, and that's all we can do. I can't leave my observation post and go to help out the teams in the south, and I wouldn't be much good to them even if I did, because I lost my rifle. So I watch the plot and listen to the exchanges on the squad channel as my teammates fight off half a dozen Lankies three kilometers to my south. They're too close for Dmitry to call in a kinetic strike, so the Russians decide to add their fire to the SI squad's defense and pick off Lankies from the rooftops. One by one, the orange icons blink out of existence on the tactical plot. Five minutes into the fight, and four of the Lankies are dead, the last one felled just fifty meters short of the edge of the landing pad. Two more have decided that discretion is the better part of valor, and they've retreated from the coordinated rifle fire of the SI teams. I've never seen Lankies act on a sense of self-preservation until now.

"Two running away," Dmitry says from his rooftop vantage point. "We go chase, or stay in position?"

"Sit tight," I reply. "Kinetic strike is incoming in two and a half minutes. Stay in cover in case they have a flier or two."

"We just used up half our ammo load," Lieutenant Perkins warns. "If they make another push from the south, we may not be able to stop them again."

"Cavalry will be here soon," I say, and hope that it's true.

———

The kinetic warheads from the task force arrive right on time, down to the second. The rounds from the first salvo, a dozen warheads or more, smack into the advancing Lankies simultaneously. Five kilometers north of the spaceport, a square kilometer of Martian soil erupts into dirt and rock geysers a thousand feet high. Then the next salvo hits, and the next, so many individual warheads that I lose count of the impacts. I've seen nuclear detonations, and they're terrifying to see from close range, but this strike somehow seems more cataclysmic than even a nuke. The kinetic rounds keep smashing into the plain, one after the other, like blows from a giant sledgehammer, a pissed-off god working the planetary surface over with a vengeance. I've never felt any pity for the Lankies we've killed over the years, but witnessing this barrage, I come closer than ever before to working up a tiny bit of it. Fifteen seconds after we see the first impacts, the sound of the barrage pulverizing Mars rock reaches our position and rolls over us, and it's the scariest, most ominous thunder I've ever heard.

"*Bozhe moi,*" Sergeant Dragomirova says next to me.

"Rods from the gods," I say.

There's a reason why the treaty that prohibits the use of weapons of mass destruction against each other's territory in space explicitly includes kinetic weapons, and why we fight out our colonial battles with small-scale infantry actions instead of pelting each other with tungsten warheads from orbit. Once you start unleashing this much cheap and easy-to-deploy destructive power, it's hard to stuff that genie back into the bottle. Against the Lankies, however, anything goes. We have no treaties with them, and they have no reservations about gassing our colonies like nuisance ant hives, so we're free to give it back to them in spades whenever we can.

Without their seed ships keeping our cruisers away, the Lankies out in the open have no way to escape this death and destruction raining down on their heads. This is payback time, vengeance for all the fellow soldiers and sailors they've killed, for five years of hardship and fear and uncertainty. Still, it's hard not to feel just the slightest bit of sorrow at the sight of this utter devastation. These are living, sentient beings, and if they have emotions at all, they must feel fear at getting killed from the sky by something they can neither see nor fight back against.

When the steady drumroll of impacts ceases a few minutes later, there's a dust-and-debris cloud ten kilometers across on the plains north of the base. Five minutes pass, then ten, but I don't see any movement other than billowing dirt.

"*Phalanx*, Tailpipe Red One. On target. Stand by for poststrike assessment and follow-ups."

"Standing by for poststrike and follow-up," *Phalanx*'s tactical officer confirms.

"That was something else," Lieutenant Perkins says on the squad channel. "Never seen anything like it."

"Neither have I," I reply.

———————

Fifteen minutes later, the dust from the kinetic strikes has settled enough for a visual poststrike assessment of the target area. I scan the plains for signs of Lankies, and my professional evaluation is that ten map grids of the Martian surface just got fucked all to hell several times over. There are Lankies on the very edge of my optics range, beyond the patch of ground the fleet just plowed with millions of joules of kinetic energy, but the closest one is ten klicks to the north and moving away from the spaceport instead of toward it, and none of the Lankies I see in the distance seem to be interested in coming any closer. Now the closest threats are the few Lankies remaining in the streets of Olympus City, but they're out of sight of Dmitry's team and moving away from the base as well. If there's a window for a large-scale landing, it's right now, while the neighborhood is freshly swept and the shock from the bombardment is still keeping the rest of the Lankies away from this place.

"Task Force Red, Tailpipe Red One," I send up to the units waiting in high orbit. "Red Beach is open. *I repeat, Red Beach is open.*"

———————

I can't see anything from my position in a dark control tower on a world with a low cloud ceiling, but I know that up in high orbit, my announcement has just kicked off Phase Three for the waiting ships of

Task Force Red. The battle plan has the cruisers use their rail guns and missile batteries to make holes in the Lanky minefield large enough for the drop ships to pass through unmolested, and then keep them open as the Lanky minefield tries to reconfigure and heal itself over time. And right now, the carriers are moving their drop ships into launch positions. I also know from experience that those first-wave drop ships are filled with scared and anxious troopers who want the trip down to the landing zone to be fast and take forever both at the same time.

The drop ships and the attack birds take a lot longer than kinetic rounds to make it down from orbit. Twenty minutes after I declare the drop zone safe, the first friendly air-support units show up overhead—not drop ships, but Shrike attack craft, wing pylons heavy with ordnance. Two pairs of Shrikes drop below the cloud ceiling and make a low pass along the runway of Olympus Spaceport, engines warbling the banshee wail that was probably partly responsible for the class name of the ship. It feels good to see close-air support overhead, to know that we have heavy ordnance on standby that doesn't require a trip down from orbit. The Shrikes split up into pairs when they reach the end of the runway, with one pair breaking to the east and one to the west. Their sensors and cameras immediately expand our TacLink awareness bubble by kilometers.

The first flight of drop ships shows up ten minutes after the Shrikes, and I use my radio to guide them in toward the undamaged VTOL landing pads on the southern end of the base. They are followed in short intervals by a second, third, fourth, then fifth flight, and more are coming in every minute. I pick deployment points in sensible locations for every four-ship flight and guide the pilots in by TacLink. A very busy half hour later, thirty-two drop ships have disgorged their infantry payloads, and Red Beach has an entire regiment of troops securing it in all directions. One flight of drop ships has landed near the foot of the little control-tower hill, and I see from the tactical markings that it has a company of combat engineers on board, precisely the people I need in this location right now. With the first wave on the ground and the drop ships starting to head back to pick up the next wave of troops, I upload the latest TacLink data to the fleet and run down the staircase to the bottom of the tower, taking four or five steps at once. Outside, the combat engineers are unloading their gear from their drop ships. Their company commander, a captain named Coonradt, comes forward to meet me as I approach the drop ships.

"A cold LZ," Captain Coonradt says after we exchange our brief introductions and courtesies. "I don't mind that at all."

"It wasn't so cold an hour ago," I say. "We dropped about a dozen. One of *Kirov*'s kinetics cracked the easternmost runway open, but the rest are whole. If I can suggest a priority list, let's get the power for the control tower and the refuelers online, and we can turn those birds around a lot more quickly."

"I have no issue with that list," the captain says. "But we'll have to bring in aux power for your consoles up there, 'cause that reactor over there ain't fusion-powering shit anymore."

Captain Coonradt summons his squad leaders and starts issuing orders. I trot up to the crew chief of the nearest drop ship.

"I lost my rifle in the orbital strike a little while back," I say. "Mind if I borrow some of the gear from your boat's armory?"

"Not at all, sir. Help yourself," the crew chief replies.

"Thank you, Sergeant."

I make my way up the ramp, through the cargo hold, and into the space between hold and cockpit, where the small armory of the ship is located. Every drop ship carries more than enough spare guns and ammunition to equip the embarked platoon with weapons and basic ammo loadouts all over again. To my dismay, this drop ship's armory has lots of fléchette rifles and MARS launchers, but very few anti-Lanky rifles, and the ones they do have on the racks are older models, M-80s and M-90s. I grab an M-90 because it uses the same magazines as the M-95 I lost, and I already carry three spare magazines on my armor that will fit the gun. Then I replace the magazine I expended earlier with a fresh one from the ammo locker. I have to resist the temptation to take one of the MARS launchers out of the vertical wall racks along with a few of the new silver bullets, the eighty-millimeter gas-filled anti-Lanky rockets. My job down here isn't to kill individual Lankies, as satisfying as it would be to one-shot them with those gas rounds.

Outside, the combat engineers have started to set up shop. Two of them are hauling a portable power pack to the base of the tower, where a third engineer is wrenching the cover off the universal connector panel on the outside of the building. I go back inside and climb the stairs to the control room again. Upstairs, Sergeant Dragomirova is looking out of the north-facing windows and talking in Russian on her radio while working on her admin deck, which is propped up on the windowsill. I clear off a space on a nearby console and set up my own admin deck. Because it's an NAC facility, I can connect my system to the computers in the control center once the power is back and run the show off the big holographic display on the center console instead of the small screen of my admin deck.

With every flight of drop ships that puts down in the landing zone, another company of troops is on the ground to reinforce the LZ and prepare to advance on our next objectives. My tactical screen, which was sparsely populated with friendly blue icons when we landed, is getting busier every minute, individual trooper icons organizing themselves into platoons, and then platoons into companies.

"We are go on power down here," Captain Coonradt sends from outside. "Say when, and we'll flick the switch."

"Go ahead on power," I say.

A few moments later, the overhead lights turn on, and all around me, I hear the hum of restarting electronics. Outside, not fifty meters from the west-facing windows of the control tower, the combat engineers' flight of drop ships takes off again one by one in five-second intervals, rattling the windows with the engine noise. I plug my admin deck into the main control console and fire up the systems. The Lankies smashed the radar and the fusion plant, but some of the auxiliary comms gear is still in one piece, and the data link works as well.

"Olympus Spaceport is back in business under new management," I tell the combat engineers. "Keep hooking up the lines, and I'll keep waving 'em in."

———

Sergeant Dragomirova and I spend the next hour directing units into the spaceport and keeping the airspace as organized as possible. The base has no active radar, so we have to keep everything tangle-free and direct dozens of drop ships and attack birds with nothing but data links and eyeballs while the cloud cover hangs a mere two thousand feet over the ground. In Combat Controller School, they called the ATC sections of the training "icon-pushing." I've learned over the years that pushing around icons on a screen can be just as stressful as being under fire if the spacecraft represented by those icons have forty or fifty people on them that will die a fiery death if you push one of those icons the wrong way at the wrong time.

"Tailpipe Red One, Red Beach C2. Come in."

When I get the call on the tactical channel, it's a distraction, but a welcome one from the high-stress monotony of directing air traffic.

"Red Beach C2, Tailpipe Red One. I read you; go ahead."

"There are two drop-ship flights on landing pad Charlie that are about to take off for civvie evac thirty klicks east of the LZ. They want a combat controller to ride shotgun in case they run into LHO presence out there."

"Copy that. You gonna send someone up to the control tower to take over ATC duties?"

"We will switch to local control for the time being. Can't have the only red hat in the LZ pushing tin all day. You are authorized to leave without relief by Ground Force Red Actual."

"Copy. Advise Actual I'll be at landing pad Charlie in five," I reply, glad at the thought of getting relieved of the important but tedious and boring air-traffic-control duty.

I let the local traffic know they're on their own until Fleet sends another ATC up here, and then tell Sergeant Dragomirova I've been called off for a different assignment. Just to make sure the translator didn't mangle my explanation beyond recognition, I also keep Dmitry in the loop.

"We have situation under control," Dmitry says. "Many Alliance gunships around. We get trouble, I can manage."

"See you when it's over," I reply. "Don't get killed."

"I will try," Dmitry replies. "But is not entirely up to me. Good luck."

I walk from the tower back along the hangar alley to the drop-ship landing pads on the south end of the base. Overhead, new drop-ship flights come in every few minutes. There are Shrike attack birds circling overhead above the cloud cover—I can't see them, but the banshee wail of their engines is unmistakable. All around me, platoons and companies gather in staging areas and move out toward their objectives. On the tactical screen of my suit, I can see that we are steadily expanding our bubble of control from the spaceport into the city and surrounding areas. The Lankies have not contested the beachhead since we plowed the ground north of the base with kinetic munitions. I am not unhappy about the rapid progress we're making, but something about this doesn't feel quite right. Our third wave is landing already, and we haven't run into any meaningful resistance yet, despite the presence of thousands of Lankies on the planet. If there's one thing I've learned from fighting them, it's that whenever we seem to get the upper hand against these things, there's a nasty surprise lurking just around the corner. I remember just how thoroughly a mere dozen Lankies managed to confound us on Greenland just by switching their tactics, and I wonder if they've been exchanging notes with their friends on Mars somehow. If this sudden knack for threat management is a species-wide development, then we're in deep shit.

Out on the Charlie pad, eight drop ships are standing in a staggered row with their engines idling and their tail ramps down. A bunch of SI troopers are busy loading modular equipment boxes into the cargo holds of the ships and strapping them down. I look for the brass in charge and see an SI captain and two lieutenants nearby. They see me trotting up in my bug suit and wave me over.

"You the combat controller?" the captain says.

"Affirmative, sir," I say. "What do we have?"

The captain—his name tag says "PARKER, M."—points over to the east of the spaceport.

"There's a science facility fifty klicks out, Tuttle 250. The Lankies wrecked the shit out of it like they did everything else, but their nuke shelter is still occupied. Four hundred personnel, military and civvies. We are going to go out there and fetch them."

"With eight Wasps," I say. "That'll be a tight squeeze."

"It's what we have, so it'll have to do. We need to go light because of all the weight we're about to add. No external ordnance on the hardpoints. Cannons only, and only one fire team per bird, 'cause we need as much space as possible for the civvies. I need you along in case we run into problems we can't fix with autocannons."

"Understood. What's the kit we're taking along?"

"FEPOS," Captain Parker says. "Tuttle 250 is low on oxygen, and their CO_2 scrubbers are shot. We're bringing five hundred FEPOS units with us so the civvies can make it to the drop ships without getting CO_2 poisoning."

The FEPOS units, fleet emergency personal oxygen supplies, are the successors to the NIFTI units that saved Halley and me when we had to evacuate the wreck of NACS *Versailles* over half a decade ago. They're little oxygen tanks connected to mouthpieces and computer-controlled rebreather elements. In an emergency, they provide enough breathing oxygen for maybe half an hour, and they work as CO_2-filtration units for bad air, like the atmosphere on Lanky planets.

The SI captain listens to a message coming on over a channel I'm not tied into. Then he looks at me and points his thumb over his shoulder toward the waiting drop ships.

"Hop in the lead bird, Lieutenant. You'll ride with me. Dustoff in two minutes."

"Aye, sir," I reply.

We lift off a few minutes later. The lead ship is first to take to the air, and the other ships follow in short intervals. I'm strapped into one of the jump seats at the front of the cargo hold next to the crew chief. I'm tied into the drop ship's camera system and watch as the landing pad falls away from us. Two hundred feet up in the air, the lead drop ship executes a sharp starboard turn around its dorsal axis and drops the nose to pick up speed. We cross the tarmac next to the spaceport's runways, which are packed with personnel and gear at this point. An entire brigade is using Red Beach as their jump-off point, more than we've ever put into one place away from Earth, and that's just an eighth of the forces we are landing on Mars right now. We have almost three thousand pairs of boots on the ground just on Red Beach, heavy weapons, air support, and plenty of ammo and fuel for resupply. But it still feels like the eerie calm before a bad storm, like a hard rain is about to fall. And all I can do is strap in and hold on and do what I can to keep dry.

CHAPTER 16

TUTTLE 250

The eight Wasps in our flight are thundering over the Martian landscape just a few hundred feet above the deck, to stay below the cover of thick gray clouds that are blanketing almost the entire hemisphere. We see Lankies on either side of the flight path, groups of five or ten or twenty, hundreds and thousands of meters away, but the drop ships hammer past those targets of opportunity at five hundred knots. With no ordnance on the pylons, the pilots don't want to waste cannon ammunition. I upload every target I spot to the TacLink network for any follow-up forces to engage or avoid. We're close enough for me to contact the bunker's command center on short-range comms.

"Tuttle 250 shelter, this is Lieutenant Grayson, NAC Defense Corps. Do you read?"

"We read you, Lieutenant. We read you loud and clear. This is the officer in charge, Colonel Mackay."

"Colonel, we are inbound with two flights of drop ships to evac your personnel. ETA five minutes. Make ready for a quick egress."

"Understood. We've been ready to get out of here since you showed up in orbit."

"I hear you, Colonel. You'll be on the way home soon."

"Two minutes out," the pilot calls out from the cockpit. I top off my suit's oxygen from the onboard system and make sure all my magazine pouches are full and ready to go. We are now forty kilometers behind the forward line of battle, far away from any ground support. I check the airspace for nearby units. Other than our eight drop ships, there's a flight of Shrikes twenty-five klicks to our north on a parallel heading, and three SRA attack birds about the same distance to our southwest.

Tuttle 250 is a research facility the size of a small college campus. Or rather, it was before the Lankies moved in and reduced every structure above ground level to piles of twisted steel and rubble. We swoop in over the facility, and the cloud ceiling is so low that we're practically on top of the first Lanky by the time we see it. Three of them are walking across the little plateau at a brisk pace, and all three turn their heads when they hear the noisy Wasps thundering over their heads.

"Tallyho," the pilot says. "Three LHOs in the open. All units, break right and weapons free."

We've shot past the Lankies already as soon as we've spotted them, and to me it seems like there's maybe a hundred feet of separation between our ship and the head of the lead Lanky. The pilot yanks the Wasp hard to starboard and pulls the nose up to slow the ship down as he swings it around. When we're through the turn, we've lost another fifty feet of altitude, and we're a hundred meters from the Lankies. The lead Lanky turns away from the drop ship and strides off in long, thundering steps. The other two move off in different directions, none of them attempting to come close to the drop ship.

"Where ya goin', pal?" the Wasp's gunner says, and opens up with the large-caliber autocannon mounted on the underside of the ship. The thirty-five-millimeter antivehicle cannons on the Wasp don't fire the new anti-Lanky silver bullets, the vicious gas-filled rounds we now use in our rifles, but they make up for it with sheer penetration power. The armor-piercing rounds can shoot through an up-armored mule from front to back, and not even Lanky hide is thick enough to stop the hyperdense penetrators in their tips. The pilot's burst catches the striding Lanky in the lower back and the legs, and it falls forward, carried by its own momentum. It crashes to the ground in a cloud of red dust. Behind us, the other ships of the flight swing around one by one and give the other two Lankies the same treatment, knocking them off their spindly legs with cannon shells and putting bursts into their prone forms just to be on the safe side. I scan for more threats in visual range and don't find any. The wind has picked up, and the visibility has dropped with the breeze to less than a kilometer, and I don't feel entirely sure about making the call, but Lankies don't show on thermal or radar, and I can't see further than the cameras in the nose of the drop ship.

"LZ is clear," I say on the tactical channel. "Propose we keep two birds in the air for overhead support while we load most of the civvies."

"We have to hustle," Captain Parker says. "Put 'em all down, but keep the nose guns hot, just in case, and watch your sectors. Fire teams, on the bounce."

We set down on the square in the middle of the facility, with the nearest dead Lanky just a few dozen meters to the right of the lead drop ship. With only eight fire teams and cases full of FEPOS rescue breathers to carry, there's no manpower for a security perimeter. The drop ships sit on a little hill among the ruins of the facility, so the optical sensors can see a few hundred meters, but if we get jumped by Lankies, the gunners have just a few seconds to bring their weapons into action. I keep the admin deck linked to the ship's systems, bring the feed up on my helmet display, and grab my own rifle to contribute to the rescue in progress.

The main bunker entrance is buried underneath the rubble of the research station. We dig chunks of heavy concrete out of the way for fifteen minutes with our entrenching tools and our bare hands until we've made a hole big enough to reach the door that's set five meters down in the vertical wall of the vestibule, and the piles of rubble look like they could shift and bury us at any time. Ideally, we'd have combat engineers and heavy equipment with us. But *ideally* went out the window the first time we made contact with the Lankies.

The bunker has an airlock system that's too small to support all the troops we brought with us. The SI troopers carry the boxes of emergency breathing devices into the airlock and then take up perimeter guard outside while Captain Parker and I stay in the lock until it cycles again. The air outside, with its almost 10 percent CO_2 content, would be fatal to anyone who isn't wearing a suit or a rebreather.

The air inside the bunker itself isn't much better. When the inner lock cycles and opens, the air-quality reading from my environmental monitor merely goes from "HAZARDOUS/LETHAL CO_2 ALERT" to "HAZARDOUS/POOR." Inside, the lights are on, and a handful of officers and civvies are waiting for us behind the airlock door. Behind them, there's a large entrance area with equipment racks and ATVs parked by the walls, and the place is packed with people, a few uniformed Defense Corps personnel and civilians, lots of civilians. There's a cheer going through the room when they see us.

Captain Parker and I salute the senior officer in the group, a female fleet colonel with the name tag "MACKAY, J." Her name triggers something in my memory. She looks tired and haggard, and everyone in the group is lean and looks like the shelter ran out of full-calorie rations quite a while ago, but Colonel Mackay's uniform is regulation clean and doesn't have a loose stitch anywhere. I check the patch on her shoulder: "NACS CALEDONIA CG-99."

"Colonel Mackay, Fleet," she introduces herself after returning our salutes. "I can't tell you how glad we are to see you. We are down to emergency chow and seven percent oxygen. The scrubbers quit over a month ago."

"What is your current personnel count, Colonel?" Captain Parker asks.

"Four hundred seventeen, myself included," Colonel Mackay replies. "Three hundred eighty-three civilians, sixty-nine of them children. Thirty-four military, mostly Fleet. And the nineteen bodies we left lined up outside. We didn't have space for a morgue."

"What bodies?" I ask. "We didn't see any when we pulled up."

Colonel Mackay looks puzzled, then concerned. "We had nineteen dead over the last year. Most were injured from the Lanky attack. Two suicides. We moved them outside months ago."

"There are no bodies outside," the captain reaffirms.

I try to imagine what may have happened to the corpses the colonists stashed outside the shelter entrance, and I decide that I don't like the ideas my brain is feeding me.

"Let's get these breathing units distributed, and then let's get the hell out of here," Captain Parker says. "This area is not secured yet, and we don't have the firepower to deal with anything more than stragglers."

"No argument," Colonel Mackay says. She waves over the military personnel nearby. "Tom and Adam, get these passed out as quickly as you can."

It takes ten minutes for all the breathing units to be distributed, and we barely brought enough for everyone in the shelter. I look around in the place, not much bigger than the flight deck of a cruiser, and shudder at the thought of spending a year in such a confined space with four hundred other people. But Colonel Mackay seems to have run a tight ship down here, because there is no pushing or complaining, as if they had all practiced their emergency and evacuation drills a lot while they were locked up down here.

"*Caledonia*," I say to the colonel after we've briefed her on the exfil plan. "Your ship was destroyed in orbit last year. I saw the marker on the tactical display when we flew by. I was on *Indianapolis* with Colonel Campbell. He said he went to the academy with you."

"I did," she says. "Is *Indy* with the task force?"

"*Indy* was destroyed last year when a seed ship broke through to Earth. I know you've been out of the loop."

"You can say that again." She looks at the patch on her sleeve. "We made it down in the escape pods. Some of us. Thirteen out of four hundred and fifty-nine. *Caledonia* took a hit to the fusion bottle and went up right as we were launching pods."

"I'm sorry, ma'am," I say. "But if it's any consolation, we just got 'em back. We killed twelve seed ships. Everything they had in orbit."

Colonel Mackay smiles, but the smile has a slightly hollow, haunted quality to it. "It's a good start," she says.

The civvies have been well drilled. They leave the shelter in a hurry, but very orderly, even though I know they've been confined to that bunker for the last year. Many of them stare at the dead Lankies in the dirt nearby, at the holes torn into their thick hides by dual-purpose cannon rounds. The crew chiefs are loading people up into the drop ships and filling up the seating rows quickly. A Wasp holds forty troops, and we only have eight of them, so we are short three ships if we want to get everyone out of here without violating weight limits and safety regulations. But the regs are the last thing on anyone's mind right now, and I'm glad the captain in charge sees it the same way.

"Fifty-two per bird!" Captain Parker shouts to the crew chiefs. The weight won't be far off from a regular infantry load because the civvies don't wear 150 pounds of armor and weapons each, but the space is definitely tight for almost twenty additional people.

Loading hundreds of people into military drop ships they've never been in takes some time. There's some shuffling and arguing as families want to stay together and go on the same ships, and the crew chiefs are visibly stressed out after a few minutes, but the ships are filling up faster than I would have predicted. I keep my TacLink screen up in one corner of my helmet display to scan for trouble, even though the information is limited to whatever the cameras on the drop ships and trooper helmets see.

I feel the incoming Lankies before I can spot them in the red haze. They weigh hundreds of tons each, and a group of them walking makes the ground below your feet alive with a multitude of impact vibrations. From the way the drumbeat of their footsteps feels under the soles of my boots, we are about to have a lot of uninvited twenty-five-meter guests at this party.

"Wind 'em up!" Captain Parker shouts. The civvies aren't trained in combat, but they can feel trouble when it's coming their way. They must have heard a lot of Lankies marching overhead when they were locked in their bunker for months on end after the Lanky takeover. The formerly neat and orderly boarding process degenerates as people rush ahead to get onto the ships. The crew chiefs have their hands full with the crowd, and one of them has to fire his sidearm into the air to restore a semblance of order on his loading ramp.

"Contact," one of the pilots calls out. "LHOs up ahead, coming in from the west, vector four-five. Distance nine hundred."

"All units, weapons free, weapons free. We have multiple targets in the open," I send to the drop-ship pilots.

"Multiple targets" seems like a slight understatement. Out of the dusty air to the northeast, dozens of Lankies appear, and they're not advancing cautiously. They know where we are, and they're striding with purpose. I know that at a brisk walk, a Lanky can cover those nine hundred meters in two minutes.

"Get those fucking ships off the ground," Captain Parker orders. "Take 'em up as they're loaded. We need to leave *now*."

The grunts don't try to board the ships with the civilians, and they don't need to be ordered into fighting positions. They run and deploy in the spaces between the drop ships, which are lined up on the plateau in a rough semicircle with the bows facing out and twenty meters of space between them.

I get on the local defense channel and boost my transmitting power to maximum. "All air units, all air units, this is Tailpipe Red One. We need priority close-air support at map grid Yankee Papa Five-Two. We have fifty-plus incoming LHOs and four hundred civvies in the way."

The drop ships open up first. Because they are on the ground, they can't use their heavy antiarmor cannons, which are rigidly mounted to the hull and need the whole ship to be aimed at the target. The ships with line of sight to the Lankies swivel their chin turrets around and open fire with their multibarreled autocannons. Hundreds, thousands of tracer rounds fly out across the distance and start tearing into the approaching Lankies. At eight hundred meters, more of the grenades ricochet off their thick hides than do any damage. The Lanky line starts getting thinned out, but not nearly fast enough. The stricken ones wail and flail around on the ground, but the others stream around them like river current around obstacles. Some of the SI troopers have MARS launchers, and at five hundred meters, the first rockets shoot out from our defensive line.

"Hold the MARS rounds!" I shout into the company channel. "Wait until they're two hundred meters out. And don't aim at their skulls. Center-mass shots."

With the heavy gunfire and the Lanky shrieks in the distance, all semblance of order on the loading ramps disappears as the civvies rush the drop ships to cram into the remaining space. I very much doubt anyone's bothering with seat belts right now. On my right, the first drop ship lifts off, closing its tail ramp as the skids leave the ground, and I can see that the room between the seat rows is packed with standing civvies that are going to get bounced around like loose shells in an ammo crate.

"Tailpipe Red One, this is Eagle One-Four," someone replies on the TacAir channel I just used for the emergency support call. "Copy your priority call. We are thirty kilometers to your north with air-to-ground." The pilot has a strong German accent, and I'm guessing this is a Eurocorps drop-ship or attack-bird flight.

"Eagle One-Four, expedite if you can. Stand by for TRP data."

I collate all the information from the gun cameras of the drop ships and the helmet cams of the troopers and draw a target rectangle on my PDP. The digital line of the western TRP border is practically in front of our drop ships' noses, but I know the Lankies will be on top of us in another minute. I put target markers on a dozen Lankies in the crowd surging toward us.

"We're going to drop right on top of you," the Eurocorps pilot says.

"I am aware of that. Just keep 'em in the TRP. Danger close, danger close."

"Roger that, Tailpipe Red One. Splash in fifteen seconds."

"Incoming friendly CAS from bearing three-five-five degrees!" I shout into the company channel. "Splash in ten seconds. Heads down, heads down. All drop ships, turn to starboard immediately at takeoff."

The first drop ship is in the air and clawing for altitude at full throttle. The second is just now leaving the ground, swinging the nose of his ship hard to starboard as instructed as soon as his skids are clear of the dirt. Nobody wants to be in the line of fire between a ground-attack flight and its targets.

The Lankies are now two hundred meters away and closing fast. I'm fifty meters behind the tail end of the drop-ship line in the entrance of the bunker, directing the close-air support and updating targets on my combat-controller deck for the pilots overhead, who are charging into the cloud cover to save our hides. To my left and right, MARS launchers pop and send their high-velocity rockets downrange. More Lankies crash into the Martian soil. One gets hit by two silver-bullet rounds at the same time and in the same general area of its chest, and the creature seems to blow apart from the inside, spraying bits of eggshell-colored skin and yellowish-white body fluid as it tumbles to the ground and kicks up a huge cloud of red dust.

I can only wait for the close-air-support ordnance to arrive, so I shoulder my own rifle and fire off a magazine into the charging group of Lankies. I know there are too many of them for us to stop them with hand weapons or even the rotary cannon turrets on the Wasps. Every time a Lanky falls, another steps over it and fills in the gap, and their line stretches a hundred meters or more. The third drop ship takes off, followed by the fourth, and now the lead Lankies are only a hundred meters from the remaining drop ships. There's no way the grunts will be able to make the ships in time, and I know that nobody would try even if they could. Every Lanky we kill is one less threat to the civvies on the remaining ships. I don't have time to get angry at Captain Parker for his call to put all drop ships on the ground at the same time and forego an aerial overwatch. I may have made the same call in his spot, and it doesn't matter in the end anyway. I am in the back because I want to update target data for the fighters until the last possible moment, but I can already see that I may not make that last drop ship if help doesn't arrive fast. The Lankies are surging on like a twenty-meter tsunami, slowly but unstoppably powerful. Like so many battles, this one turned on just a single decision made in a second.

The SI troopers on the ground are mostly green, young privates and corporals just out of training, led by sergeants without much combat experience, but they stand their ground and do as they were trained. Facing the relentless wave of Lankies coming toward them, they probably feel like infantry of the Middle Ages facing a massed cavalry charge. They keep their firing lines between the drop ships and reshuffle their formation whenever another drop ship takes off and leaves a gap in the line. But the line gets shorter the more gaps they have to fill, and the Lankies aren't dropping fast enough even though rifle rounds and silver bullets from the MARS launchers thin out their lines at the rate of one every few seconds.

This is what death looks like, I think. There's a bunker behind me, but I don't even consider ducking into it for shelter to avoid the flood of Lankies that is going to flatten us in thirty seconds, grind us into the Martian dust like pesky insects. There's no air left to breathe and wait out yet another rescue, and even if the oxygen tanks were full, my place is out here with the SI troopers. At least we'll go quickly under an open sky instead of getting buried in the dark.

Hope you make it, I think in Halley's direction. *At least we made them pay for it.*

"Shorten the line!" the captain shouts into his radio. "Fall back fifty meters by fire teams, bounding overwatch! Let's go, let's go!"

The ordnance from the Euro ships arrives in dramatic fashion before I can even see the launching units on my TacLink display. I hear the distinctive dull bursts of disintegrating cluster munitions containers high over our heads, and then many little explosions go off a thousand feet up in the air. A second or two later, the ground in front of our firing line is churned with impacts from many hundreds of kinetic penetrators. The effect on the attacking Lankies is immediate. Dozens of them crash to the ground, pierced by superdense, sharpened tungsten rods shooting from the sky, taking other Lankies with them as they fall, and many of the ones that are still advancing twitch and shriek their high-pitched wails as the submunitions injure them. But there are still too many left, and our rifle and rocket fire isn't thinning out the remaining line quickly enough. *So many Lankies.* We are like a formation of rabbits trying to stop a herd of charging bulls down here.

"On target!" I shout into the TacAir channel. "Do that again."

"Too close for cluster kinetics," Eagle One-Four replies in his German accent. "We have a visual on your TRP. Commencing strafing run."

The cannon rounds arrive before I can hear the reports from the ground-attack fighters that fire them. They're not the devil's ripsaw sound of the Shrike antiarmor cannon, but a higher-pitched bark at a slower rate of fire. The cannon bursts from two attack craft carve a swath of small explosions through the remaining Lankies, and more of them drop to the ground, screaming and flailing their limbs. The fifth and sixth drop ship are off the ground and roaring off to the south at top speed right above the deck, safe from the approaching Lankies but depriving the remaining grunts cover and the fire support of their chin turrets. The Eurocorps attack birds thunder across the leaden sky overhead, two hundred feet above the deck, sleek machines with gray paint jobs and Iron Crosses painted on their wings and fuselages.

"Bird Seven is away," Captain Parker calls out on the company channel. "Fall back by fire teams, cover and move. Go, go, *go!*"

At least ten Lankies are still alive and coming our way, and the closest one is less than fifty meters from our forward line of defense. None of the troopers in front of me make any attempt to fall back. All of them fire their rifles at the charging Lanky. I can see by the impacts on the Lanky's body that the riflemen are shooting regular ammo-piercing rounds, not silver bullets, and the Lanky absorbs half a dozen rounds before it stumbles and drops to one knee right in front of us. Amazingly, one of the SI troopers sprints up to the Lanky before it can recover, aims an M-95 rifle upward, and rips off four quick shots into the underside of the Lanky's jaw, the only part of their huge skulls that isn't armored like a fucking battlecruiser hull. The armor-piercing rounds don't have the penetration to exit the top of the Lanky's head, but they have enough punch to mess up whatever is inside. The Lanky flops to the ground instantly in a spray of red dirt. I can't tell whether the incredibly brave or crazy trooper got clear of the Lanky's body before it went down, but there are Lankies thundering past my position to my left and right, and my attention is now elsewhere. One of the Lankies swings a foot and sweeps aside the whole SI fire team in front of it, sending them flying through the air and into the billowing cloud of red dust that's now covering the plateau. I take aim and shoot the Lanky in the side, right underneath its arm. It shrieks and turns halfway in my direction, giving me a clear shot at its midsection. I cycle the bolt of my M-90 and shoot it in the chest, then cycle again, shoot again. My rounds are silver bullets, half-inch hypodermic needles with 1,000 cc explosive gas cylinders behind them, and they pierce the Lanky's thick hide and explode their payload inside the body. The Lanky is reaching out for me with a long, spindly arm when the gas rounds detonate. It wails and crashes onto its side. I don't stick around to see if it will recover enough to keep going after me. Instead, I turn and run toward the last remaining drop ship, which is just now goosing its engines and raising its cargo ramp.

The drop ship is fifty feet in the air and climbing quickly when one of the Lankies reaches up and slams an arm against the tail boom assembly. The ship jolts and spins around its dorsal axis violently. The pilot tries to recover, but the Wasp is way too low to the ground. The starboard horizontal stabilizer grinds into the rocky soil, and then the drop ship flips over and crashes into the ground, engines still running at full thrust. The Lanky doesn't let up. It stomps down on the tail end of the Wasp with its massive three-toed foot and pins the ship to the ground, crushing the entire aft end flat. I aim at the back of the Lanky and pull the trigger, but my weapon is empty. I scream a curse, eject the empty magazine, and pull a new one off my harness. Then I slam it into the rifle and chamber a new round.

The drop ship explodes with a cataclysmic bang. The shock wave from the detonation flings me backwards, and I smack hard into something solid. The red Mars dust is now so thick in the air that I can't see my own hands in front of me. On my heads-up display, multiple yellow and red warnings pop up to inform me of various damaged suit modules. Belatedly, I remember the polychrome camouflage feature of the bug suit. I activate the control for the camo and hope that it's not one of the suit systems that just took a hit. But my visor overlay dutifully changes color to let me know that I am now mostly invisible, and when I lift my hand in front of my helmet, all I can see is an outline.

The explosion slammed me into the remnants of a building's wall, a stub of ferroconcrete no more than a meter above the ground. I hoist myself over the obstacle and drop down behind it. Then I lie still and close my eyes to take stock of my appendages and their status. The armor caught most of the impact, but the bug suits aren't built for much protection, and my hip and back are badly bruised.

On the other side of the wall, the noise of the battle subsides. There are no more gunshots, no more Lanky wails, no more engine noise. *Seven ships made it off the ground at least*, I tell myself. I hear and feel the heavy footsteps of the remaining Lankies as they walk across the site. One of them slowly steps up to where I am hiding. I search for my rifle, but it's gone, ripped from my hands in the drop-ship explosion. I don't even try to go for my sidearm. I wouldn't be able to hurt the Lanky with it anyway, and I don't want to give myself away through movement, electronic camouflage or not.

The Lanky steps over the building ruin and puts a foot down on the other side of the wall, so close to me that I could reach across and touch the thing's leg. Then it crosses over me and strides off.

I stay motionless on my back until I hear no more Lanky footsteps in the distance. Then I decide to remain still just a little longer, for good measure. My TacLink screen shows the seven drop ships in the air, rushing west toward Olympus Spaceport and relative safety, with the

Eurocorps attack birds escorting them close behind. But on the ground, here at Tuttle 250, I am the only blue icon remaining.

I get up fifteen minutes later and peek over the edge of the wall remnant. The dust from the battle has mostly settled now. The drop ship that exploded is no longer in recognizable shape. Bits and pieces of the Wasp are strewn over a hundred meters of ground, and some of them are still burning. There are bodies scattered on the ground, some charred beyond recognition, and bits and pieces of human remains, the ugly debris aftermath of high-energy detonations.

I tap into the company channel and then the local TacAir, but there's only silence. I run a diagnostics check on my bug suit, and my suit computer informs me that my comms suite is off-line and that the internal oxygen feed has a slow leak the self-sealing lining can't plug completely. My oxygen is at 70 percent, but falling more quickly than normal—the computer predicts 10 percent per hour at low-exertion-level consumption. I'm fifty kilometers behind enemy lines, with no way to talk to my allies to let them know I'm still alive, and not enough air to make it back to friendly territory.

I look around for a weapon. There are plenty of rifles and MARS launchers strewn about. Some of the SI troopers must have tried to make that last bird and got caught up in the explosion, because I can only find eight bodies in battle armor. I collect an undamaged-looking M-95 rifle and have my suit check its function electronically. When it checks out, I remove the empty magazine and forage spares from the harnesses of my dead comrades.

Over by the body of one of the fallen Lankies, I see some movement, and I bring my newly acquired rifle around. But the source of the movement is an SI trooper, crawling out from the debris. It's the trooper who felled the Lanky by shooting it in the skull from directly below. I walk over to the trooper, who turns toward me at the sound of my footsteps in the rubble. The trooper looks up at me, and her face is about as exhausted looking as I feel.

"On your feet," I say, and hold out a hand.

She grabs it and lets me pull her upright.

"You in one piece?" I ask.

She nods and looks around on the ground. "Can't see my rifle."

"It's probably under that thing's head," I say, and nod at the dead Lanky. "That was the most inspired kill I've ever seen."

"You saw that?" She smiles weakly. The rank stripes on her armor are those of a sergeant first class, and her name tape says "CRAWFORD, K."

"Got it on visual record. If we make it back, I am putting you in for some tin."

Sergeant Crawford smiles weakly. "That and a twenty will get me a cup of coffee at the NCO club."

"Check your armor, and see if you have comms and air."

She pays attention to her visor display for a few seconds. "Got oxygen; comms and data are fucked."

"Same here, mostly. My near-field data link is still up."

"So what's the plan, Lieutenant?"

Sergeant Crawford takes a few steps, then stops and bends over slightly with a wince.

"You hurt, Sergeant?"

"Suit says I cracked a few ribs. The meds should kick in momentarily." She continues and walks the way I just came. After a few moments of searching, she picks a rifle off the ground and checks the loading status.

"Near-field data's got a twenty-klick range at best," I say. "The plan is we hoof it west until we get to within twenty kilometers of our forward line of battle. Hope someone sees us pop up on Tactical and comes to check things out."

"Through Lanky-controlled territory," Sergeant Crawford says. "With two rifles and two busted suits."

"Just another day in the infantry," I reply.

"I'm not infantry," she says. "Not usually. They assigned me to the infantry three months ago. Not enough grunts to go around."

"What's your primary MOS?"

"Oh-one-five-one. Administrative clerk. I run databases over at battalion S4."

"Logistics." I grin. "That Lanky got its clock cleaned by a *logistics clerk*."

Sergeant Crawford looks over at the dead Lanky she brained with four armor-piercing rounds from her rifle. "Uh, I guess so. It seemed like a good thing to do at the time, sir."

I laugh out loud. "Today, you're not a supply clerk. You are a pod-head now."

CHAPTER 17

— DANGEROUS GROUND —

We search the area for usable gear and supplies before we head out into open ground. None of the dead SI troopers have intact armor left, so I can't just change out of the bug suit and into standard battle armor. At least there's plenty of spare ammunition. Neither Sergeant Crawford nor I want to encumber ourselves with a MARS launcher, because the things weigh close to thirty pounds and are a bitch to carry around when you have to move quickly, and if we get jumped by ten Lankies, I doubt having an extra rocket or two would greatly influence the outcome. So we fill our magazine pouches and refill our water supplies from the suits of our dead comrades. I make sure I collect the dog tags of the dead out in the open, both the electronic ones and the physical metal ID disks each trooper wears around the neck. We don't bother sifting through all the bodies in the drop-ship wreckage because neither of us has the stomach to spend a few hours separating SI troopers from dead civilians. There were some kids in the crowd, and I don't want to find out whether some of them were on that last drop ship. The Lankies don't give a shit, of course—the difference between an adult and a child would be insignificant to them even if they could tell—but my earlier smidgen of empathy for the Lankies has melted away like an ice cube on a sunbaked armor plate.

"Let's check the bunker while we're at it," Sergeant Crawford suggests.

"Won't be much in there," I say. "They were running on fumes before we got there, remember?"

Then I recall a few details from when we opened the airlock and I got a look at the interior of the bunker earlier. "Hold on. Maybe we can save ourselves a whole lot of running, after all."

The comms unit in the bunker is toast. Whoever evacuated the station when we arrived did a by-the-book job and took out the hardware-encryption module and then gave the control console a few whacks with a fire axe. We can't use the station's radio to call for a ride. But there are four electric ATVs parked by the main airlock. They look dusty, but their charging umbilicals are still plugged in.

"I sincerely hope they kept these topped off for emergency use," Sergeant Crawford says.

"You and me both. I'm not a fan of long hikes through enemy territory."

Sergeant Crawford swings herself on top of one of the ATVs. Then she activates the vehicle's control screen.

"Hallelujah," she says. "Eighty-nine percent charge. Sixty klicks at sixty per."

"Outstanding," I reply. "Consider the day saved."

"No offense, sir, but the day ain't saved until I'm taking a nice hot shower back at the base," she replies.

We load up two of the ATVs with our weapons and spare ammunition. Sergeant Crawford is smaller than I am, so she has space for a

MARS launcher and two silver-bullet rockets, which she lashes to the seat behind her with elastic cords. The ATVs are made for two passengers, but we each take our own to have a backup in case one breaks in the middle of the Martian plains. I haven't driven an ATV in months, but Sergeant Crawford hasn't been on one in years, and she needs to take a few practice runs around the research compound to get familiar with the controls again.

"I think I got the hang of it," she proclaims when she pulls up next to my ATV a few laps around the block later.

"Is your map overlay still working?"

She checks her suit computer. "Yes, sir."

"Okay." I consult my own map. "The spaceport is fifty-one klicks away at two hundred sixty-nine degrees. We'll have to go a bit longer than that because of the topography. See that hill halfway and ten klicks to the south, the one labeled eighteen eighteen?"

"Affirmative."

"We'll go around the north slope, just high enough that we can keep an eye on the valley to the north. We go full throttle when we can, but don't flip that thing on a rock or into a ravine. And we keep each other in line of sight. Without radios, we won't know if the other breaks down or falls behind if we can't see each other. Standard infantry hand signals. Remember those?"

"Yes, sir," she says again.

"And if we get Lankies on our ass, point that thing downhill. The ATVs can outrun them, but only barely. If we get separated because of enemy contact, don't hang around for me. Head for the base, and have them send out some close-air support."

"Got it." She looks over the scene all around us, the wrecked drop ship, the bodies strewn everywhere. "I'm scared as hell, sir, to be honest."

"I am, too," I say. "Battle sucks. Don't let the grunts tell you otherwise. It's unnatural. Anyone who isn't scared of it is a fucking psychward candidate."

"I'll never bitch about my boring S4 job again, that's for sure."

I grin at her and nod over to the west. "Let's hit it. Your hot shower is waiting."

———————————

We set out from the science facility, leaving behind a small but bloody battlefield with dozens of dead Lankies and humans on it. The ATVs are made for Mars conditions, so they have big, knobby honeycomb tires and a bit more ground clearance than their terrestrial counterparts, but that makes them slightly more top heavy, and I almost end up flipping into a ditch before I get used to the handling.

We are going off-road, which on Mars means driving across a hilly, rocky landscape that looks like the places on Earth usually labeled "Badlands" or "Death Something-or-other." The ATVs can go eighty kilometers per hour at full throttle on a paved road, but out here, that speed would be suicidal. So we weave our way among rocks and across gravel fields going thirty, forty, sometimes fifty. I keep scanning the horizon for Lankies, but for a good while, I don't see anything except for rocks and dust devils. The ATVs spool off the kilometers dutifully, the battery status bars on our displays steadily depleting as the high-density cells discharge. Every few kilometers, we stop and compare map fixes, to make sure we're not following each other blindly off-course.

We see the first Lankies on this run when we're on the north slope of Hill 1818. They're moving across the plains to our north a kilometer in the distance, roughly away from the spaceport and toward the science outpost we just left half an hour ago. If the comms link in my bug suit worked, I could call in help from the air units we keep hearing above the cloud cover and rub the bastards off the map, but I'm as helpless as I've ever been on a recon run. Thirty klicks to our west, there's a base with dozens of drop ships and ground-attack birds, and they might as well be in orbit around Luna for all the good they're doing us right now.

As we come around the side of Hill 1818 and start to descend its western slope, we almost run into a group of Lankies that are coming up the hill in the opposite direction. We don't see them until we are around the bend of the slope and heading downhill, and we both hit our brakes and come to skidding stops. The Lankies, a hundred meters away and stomping up the slope, seem to sense us at the same time. There are six of them, and the two in the lead change their direction slightly to head straight for us.

"They can sense the electric engines!" I shout to Sergeant Crawford. "Go right, down the hill; hook left when you're at the bottom. I go left. We split them between us." I underscore the commands with hand signals that I hope to be unambiguous. *That way, double-time.* Sergeant Crawford looks terrified, but she nods and throws her ATV back into gear. Then she shoots off down the slope, and I shift my ride into drive and turn up the throttle to go left.

The ad hoc plan works—in a fashion. The Lankies split up to go after the radiation signatures from our vehicles. Two move to the left to intercept my ride. Four more angle to the right and go after Sergeant Crawford, who is kicking up long rooster tails of red dirt with the tires of her ATV as she's flooring it downhill. I correct my course to the left some more. We have the speed advantage because we're going downhill, and they're just now moving laterally on the slope. I don't need a ballistic computer to see that I'll outrace the Lankies on my way down the slope, but I can also see that it'll be close. Too late, I realize that doubling up on one ATV would have let one of us shoot while the other drives, but we also would have lost top speed and redundancy. Right now, all that's left for me to worry about is that window of space and time ahead of me, the invisible square I have to pass through with my ATV in the next ten seconds to make it out of the Lankies' reach. The two to my right quicken their pace, but they're not as fast as they're on level ground, because they're walking with the elevation lines on a twenty-five-degree slope. At their size, there are easily ten meters of height difference between their right and left feet, which gives an awkward, shambling quality to their gait.

The ATV shoots downhill much faster than I'd ever dare to drive without Lankies chasing me. One of my front wheels hits a cluster of rocks, and the bump makes me fishtail wildly for a few terrifying seconds. I bring the ATV back under control, keenly aware how close I just came to flipping over. If I do crash, I hope I break my neck instantly so I'm dead before a Lanky can stomp me flat or rip me in half.

I make it past the Lankies with very little leeway. The lead Lanky swings a giant arm at me to knock me off my ATV. It parts the air next to the vehicle, so close that I can feel the gust of changing air pressure. I straighten out the ATV and change course very slightly to my right, to make the angle unfavorable for them if they try to turn and follow me. I don't dare to check my mirrors. Like a pod launch through a minefield, I keep my focus on what's right in front of my nose so I won't know if death is about to catch up with me. Ten seconds pass, then twenty. The slope of Hill 1818 transitions into the plain beyond at a gentle angle, but there's a ravine at the very bottom of the slope, and I have to slow down if I don't want to make the ATV sail over the edge. I throttle back and turn the steering bar to cut across the edge of the ravine at an angle. When I take a second to look sideways, I see that the Lankies are still halfway up the hill. They've resumed their climb, apparently having decided that the bounty isn't worth the effort.

Sergeant Crawford's data link is off-line, so I can't see her blue icon on my tactical map, and as I drive down into the ravine, I have no eyeballs on anything except the rocky slope in front of me. I drive up the other side of the embankment and go full throttle again, in case the Lankies change their minds about my desirability as a chase target.

A kilometer from the ravine, the ground levels out again, enough for me to see more than a hundred meters ahead. I slow down and look to my right. Off in the distance, eight or nine hundred meters away, I see a lone ATV speeding across the rock-strewn plain, and I let out a small sigh of relief.

Out here, the surface is flat enough that I can see the outskirts of Olympus City on the horizon, fifteen kilometers away. I check my TacLink screen and determine that I should be in data range in another five kilometers. I mark the last-known location of the Lankies we ran into so the computer can upload the data to the tactical network the second I get a link.

Behind me, the Lankies I dodged continue their climb up the slope of Hill 1818, slowly and steadily, as if they have all the time in the world. I put the ATV back into gear and open up the throttle. Maybe I can make it back into data range quickly enough for some nearby air support to see those orange icons pop up on TacLink and ruin the Lankies' day.

———

I'm just a little over ten kilometers out from the spaceport when two bad things happen almost at once. I spot another troop of Lankies coming out of a ravine and walking across the plains toward Hill 1818, and my ATV lurches as the power output of the electric engine fluctuates. My full-throttle speed drops to thirty kilometers, then picks up again to fifty. When it drops again, I am rolling along at a mere twenty-five kilometers per hour, not enough to outrun a Lanky, and three of them just popped up on the plateau not two kilometers in front of me. I don't know if they've sensed my presence yet, but even if they haven't, their current course to Hill 1818 is going to take them right across the patch of ground where my ATV is currently starting to barf out its electric innards.

I know that Sergeant Crawford is a few kilometers to my northeast and going all out at fifty kilometers per hour, but there's a small crest cutting our line of sight, so she won't see me even if I make noise and wave like an idiot. I steer the ATV to my right to get out of the Lankies' line of advance, but I make it barely two hundred meters away from my original straight course before the electric engine simply quits without noise or drama. The sudden absence of electric drive whining is quite loud. The oversized tires crunch in the Martian gravel as the ATV comes to a stop.

My TacLink shows a lot of air traffic taking off and landing on the spaceport's runways and VTOL pads. With my comms online, I could call in close fire support from a drop ship or a flight of Shrikes and wipe the approaching Lankies off the map, but all I have is a data link, and TacLink transmissions only reach eight to ten kilometers in ideal conditions. I am just outside the maximum range for the near-field data link to connect to the nearest NAC units, and most of the air traffic is going out away from me, toward Orange Beach. I want to shout for help, but I don't have a voice that will reach far enough for anyone to hear me.

I get off the ATV and unlash my rifle from the backseat. Crawford had the good sense to take a MARS launcher, and I curse my judgment for not packing one myself. Just one silver-bullet rocket would help even the odds against the three Lankies ambling toward me across the plain, now a kilometer and a half away and closing in without hurry. But I only have the M-95 rifle and a few magazines of ammunition, and that will have to do the job.

I rest the rifle on the seat of the ATV and point it in the direction of the Lankies, towering over the ochre-colored gravel field even at this distance. Then I chamber a round. My radio is busted, and the data link is reduced to the near-field transmitter, but my suit's environmental controls still work, and the ballistics computer is online as well. I let the targeting software sort out the maximum effective range based on air pressure, gravity, temperature, and a dozen other factors.

"OUT OF RANGE," my computer display informs me.

"Not for long," I reply.

There's a small box of emergency gear mounted on the frame of the ATV underneath the saddle. I let the rifle rest on the seat and pop the emergency box open with some fumbling. Inside, there's a first aid kit, a thermal blanket, a two-liter bladder of water with a standard suit adapter, and a flare gun with five rounds of high-intensity pyrotechnic signal munitions.

"DISTANCE 1,258M," my helmet display reads, the rifle's targeting reticle firmly on the first of the approaching Lankies. They walk in their usual unhurried pace, heads swinging slowly from left to right, covering dozens of meters with each stride. They're not yet close enough for me to feel the vibrations from their steps, but I know it won't be long.

If I start shooting signal flares, it'll be like lighting a huge billboard over my head, a blinking arrow pointing straight at my location. But in a few minutes, they'll be close enough to spot the ATV anyway, and there aren't many terrain features out here to hide in.

I decide I won't be stomped flat while I'm running away from those bastards, and if the close-air units notice my flares, a drop-ship or attack-bird pilot may decide to give the area a closer look. I pluck the flare gun from the box, load it with one of the signal cartridges, and aim it roughly at the area between Sergeant Crawford's line of travel and the spaceport. Then I pull the trigger. The flare round arcs into the sky and explodes in a dazzling red burst of pyrotechnic wizardry. There's a sound component to the flare round as well, a sharp thunderclap that rolls over the Martian landscape like the report from a small artillery shell. I know that the flare also has components I can't see—an electronic signal flare that will pop up on every TacLink screen within a ten-klick radius and a radio noisemaker that's noticeable on comms gear even further away. I take the other four shells out of the emergency box and shoot them into the darkening Mars sky one by one. The cracks from the charges echo back from the nearby mountainsides.

The Lankies, now a kilometer away, react to the detonations of the emergency flares by swinging their heads toward the spot in the sky where the brilliant colors of the charges bloom, impossible to miss in a five-kilometer range unless you're blind and deaf. However they make sense of their environment without eyes, they can sense us and our mechanical and chemical toys just fine. They alter their strides, quickening their pace, and shift their course slightly over to my right. With the flare gun empty, I toss it aside and kneel behind my propped-up rifle again.

"DISTANCE 944M. OUT OF RANGE."

The anti-Lanky rounds have ballistic nose caps over the nasty-looking penetrator needles, but they are heavy and don't have a massive propellant load, so they can't reach further than about four hundred meters in direct fire if you still want to hit a Lanky, as big a target as they make. I keep my aim pointed on the lead Lanky and watch the skies for friendly air support that may have spotted the flares.

Come on, I think. *How could you miss those fireworks?*

The Lankies close to eight hundred, then seven hundred, then six hundred meters. I take the spare magazines out of the pouches to speed up the inevitable reloads I'll have to do. Nobody has ever stopped three Lankies in the field with just a rifle, as far as I know. The penetrative power of the anti-LHO rounds drops with range because of the physics involved, and once they're close enough for the rounds to have consistent effect, the Lankies are usually too close to make a solitary defense against more than one or two survivable. I scan the area around me again for cover. There's a shallow ditch starting thirty meters to my right and leading diagonally away from my position, and I resolve to burn through my ammo load in rapid fire and then duck into that ditch with my camouflage suit turned on. *Hopefully the ATV will distract them enough to stop looking for the occupant once they reach this spot.*

When my computer's distance readout shows "600M OUT OF RANGE" in my helmet display, I take a deep breath.

"Fuck it," I say, and take aim.

The Lankies stride on, more quickly but every bit as relentless and unconcerned as before. At maximum magnification, I can see their features in great detail—the massive cranial shields that are half again as wide as their skulls, the toothless mouths that look like something from a prehistoric stegosaurus, the tall and spindly bodies with the three-toed feet and four-fingered hands. They all look so similar to each other that I've never been able to tell any two apart, no variance in size or color or even behavior. It's like they were made in some gigantic biological three-dimensional printer to an exact and unchanging template. And you don't fully realize how enormous and powerful they are unless you are close to them and can see the amount of dust they kick up with each step, the deep impressions they leave on the soil, and the span of their arms when they stretch them out.

I put the target marker on the chest of the leading Lanky and override the "OUT OF RANGE" determination of my ballistic computer. Then I aim just a little higher to account for the extra two hundred meters of range and pull the trigger. The rifle barks its sharp, authoritative report, and the muzzle blast kicks up the dust around the ATV. I can see the first round hitting the dirt twenty meters in front of the Lanky with a puff just a few seconds later. I adjust my aim for the next shot—*Up a body height and a half*, I think—and pull the trigger again. The second round hits the Lanky in the hip midstride. It falters and stumbles a little when its foot comes down. With the range dialed in, I empty the rest of the magazine in quick succession, one round every two seconds, *one—two—three*. One round kicks up dirt right next to the Lanky's foot, but two more fly true and hit it in the upper body. For the first time, it shrieks its warbling wail as it stumbles again, but then it rights itself and keeps walking.

By now, the Lankies are four hundred meters away and have definitely located the source of the annoyance. They are purposefully striding toward the spot where I am huddled behind the little ATV I'm using as a rifle rest. I eject the empty magazine, insert a fresh one into my rifle, and work the charging handle to chamber a round. Finally, my computer concurs that I may have a faint chance of hitting stuff reliably and displays "RANGE 385—OPEN FIRE."

With the computer in the loop, I fire the next five rounds as quickly as the rifle will settle back down from the recoil, a second per shot. The computer actuates the servos in my armor to assist with the aim. All five rounds hit the Lanky square in the center of the chest, and this time they do more than just annoy it. At least three of the penetrators go through its hide and dispense their payload inside the Lanky's chest. Then three thousand cubic centimeters of aerosolized explosive gas ignite together and blow the Lanky's chest out from the inside. It lets out a tangled wail that is cut off when the thing crashes to the Mars floor, kicking up a billowing cloud of red dust.

The two other Lankies have closed to two hundred meters, and I have about ten seconds to figure out what to do next. I reload the rifle with my hands on autopilot, then jack a round into the chamber. At two hundred meters and closing, they are so imposingly large, so enormous in scale, that it feels like arrogant hubris to think you have a chance in battle against them.

Then I look past the arriving Lankies, and my heart sinks. Six more of them are coming the same way, five hundred meters behind the first group, heading for me like a twenty-meter wall of gray bio-matter. Even if I drop both Lankies in front of me, I won't have the ammo or the time to take on six more. But at this point, I can't run or hide, so I take aim and rip off five more rounds at the next Lanky.

This area has been secured for hours, I think. *Where the fuck do they keep coming from?*

The second Lanky goes to its knees when the salvo hits it, gas rounds spaced one second apart. One round hits the cranial shield and careens off. Two more hit the torso, one in the shoulder and one where the hip would be if they had human anatomy. One blows off the Lanky's lower right arm, and the fifth one misses altogether. I've hurt it badly— it stumbles and crashes to its knees with an earsplitting wail—but it isn't dead, and I won't have time to engage the last one, which is now less than a hundred meters away, four or five steps for a pissed-off Lanky. I eject the empty magazine and fumble for a new one, knowing full well that I won't be able to get the gun ready in time. I stumble backwards as I seat the magazine and grasp the charging handle, hoping that the Lanky will take an extra second or two to crush the ATV between us and give me just a little extra time.

Instead of stomping it flat, the Lanky kicks the ATV at full stride and catapults it through the air toward me. I flinch and duck away instinctively, and the vehicle flies past me and tumbles across the Mars soil in the distance. I can hear it breaking apart and spewing bits and pieces everywhere. I swing the rifle up at the Lanky, which is now mostly obscured by a big cloud of red dust, and I know that the next kick will have me as a target. But unlike in my dream, I know that the impact will not be painless.

Behind me and to my right, I hear the *pop-whoosh* of a MARS rocket launch. A very fast and angry firefly zooms past me and hits the Lanky high in the chest, near the vulnerable crook of the neck. The rocket can't be anything but a silver bullet, because the effects are instant and dramatic. The warhead pierces the Lanky's thick hide and explodes after a very short delay. A MARS rocket has a diameter of eighty millimeters, and the rocket's payload is almost ten times bigger than those of the rifle rounds. The dull explosion of the aerosolized and ignited gas inside the Lanky almost decapitates the creature, struck as it is in one of its vulnerable spots. Its momentum carries it forward, and it falls toward me without any semblance of control. I leap to my right, dropping my rifle in the process, and barely clear the bulk of the Lanky as it slams into the Martian ground. The impact lifts me off my feet and propels me ten or fifteen meters, and I crash to the ground myself in a graceless and uncontrolled manner.

When I get to my knees again and turn around, Sergeant Crawford has lowered her MARS launcher and is detaching the empty rocket cartridge. She has another round strapped to the back of the ATV that's parked twenty meters behind her, but I know how close that second group of Lankies must be by now, and there are six of them for just one more MARS round.

"Saw your flare!" she shouts at me. "I came as quickly as I could. Almost got stuck in a ravine."

"You did great!" I shout back. "Forget the reload. Six more coming our way. Let's get the fuck out of here, now."

We run to the ATV. She gets into the driver's seat, and with me having to take the backseat, there's no space for the MARS launcher or the spare round. She chucks the launcher tube into the dirt while I unlash the spare round and throw it away as well. Then I swing myself onto the ATV behind her and pat her on the back of her armor.

"Go northeast, and hook around to the west in three klicks!" I shout. "And don't let up on the throttle."

By now, the new group of Lankies is close enough for me to feel the ground bounce with their strides. I don't dare try to look past the corpse of the Lanky that Sergeant Crawford just dropped with a well-placed silver bullet from a MARS. Sergeant Crawford wastes no time. She throws the ATV into drive and guns it to the northeast, tires spinning in the red-brown gravel and dirt.

Overhead, a four-ship flight of Shrikes comes thundering out of the clouds. They make a low-level pass over the plateau and split up as they zoom overhead, two peeling off to the north and two to the south. Thirty seconds later, I hear the unmistakable roaring of the Shrikes' multibarreled, big antiarmor cannons ripping across the landscape, and the rapid firecracker sound of impact explosions follows a second or two later. In the distance behind us, the Lankies on the plateau shriek as they get pelted by heavy-caliber cannon shells, caught in a deadly rain with no protection or shelter. The cavalry has spotted my flares and arrived, and as usual they were a minute too late. Without Sergeant Crawford, those Lankies would still be dead, but I'd be a bloody smear on the Martian rock somewhere back there right now.

———————

We roll into the perimeter of Olympus Spaceport twenty minutes later, with a low-battery warning blinking in red on the ATV's control display and a "LOW OXYGEN-19%" alert on my helmet visor screen. The runways are a giant staging area for SI and SRA marines, hundreds of them. Overhead, the aerial ballet has not abated—drop ships of all nationalities coming in and depositing their human cargo on the airfield, then taking off again to repeat the trip into orbit and back. I don't know which wave we're currently dropping, but we're still landing troops, so the offensive must still be in full swing.

Sergeant Crawford steers the ATV over to the VTOL landing pad from where we started the rescue mission. A dozen drop ships are refueling simultaneously from the underground tanks. I hear portable power units humming everywhere. Nearby, a bunch of haggard-looking civvies are boarding a drop ship.

When the ATV comes to a stop, I climb off and stand on the tarmac for a moment on shaky knees. Sergeant Crawford gets off the ride as well and gives the saddle an affectionate pat.

"Good girl," she says.

"Thank you," I say to her. "I wasn't kidding when I said you're a podhead now. I don't know too many troopers who have two confirmed Lanky kills."

"I did what needed doing," she says. "But to be totally honest with you, I am looking forward to wrestling databases again. I don't know how you grunts do it. All the time, I mean."

"Be careful out there. I hope to see you back at Gateway when this is done, Sergeant."

"I hope to *be* back at Gateway when this is done. I've never been so scared in my life."

"Me, neither," I say. "Now go grab that hot shower."

We don't exchange salutes as would be proper considering our rank difference. Instead, we shake hands. I watch as she walks over to the staging area set up in a nearby hangar, hot food and ammo resupply stations set up along the walls, and wish we had about a thousand more like her.

I walk up the ramp of one of the refueling ships and commandeer spare battle armor from the ship's armory. Then I use the airlock between cockpit and crew compartment to depressurize my broken bug suit safely and change into the armor. It's not fitted to me, but each drop ship has half a dozen spare suits in predefined stock sizes, and a size 5 usually comes close enough to a proper fit whenever I don't carry extra garrison flab.

Once I'm in my new battle armor, I plug my battered admin deck into the suit and log into TacLink with my combat-controller access. "Red Beach C2, Tailpipe Red One, come in."

"Tailpipe Red One, this is Red Beach C2. We had you written off, Lieutenant."

"Not quite yet. Pass me on to Ground Force Red Actual."

"Stand by."

There's a pause on the command channel, and the C2 officer comes back on the line a few moments later. "Red Actual is tied up, but he says for you to get your ass over to the C2 post."

"Copy that," I reply, feeling mild irritation. "Be there in five."

C2, the brigade's command-and-control center, is in the back of a hardened spacecraft shelter halfway between the drop-ship pad and the control tower. On my way there, I roll the ATV past drop ships that are unloading mules, the SI's eight-wheeled armored fighting vehicles. We rarely ever take armor along on missions, because it's not weight efficient, but someone upstairs decided to throw the whole kitchen sink at Mars. The mules have modular weapons stations on top, and the ones rolling off the drop ships right now are fitted with what the armor guys call the Bastard, a large turret containing a thirty-five-millimeter automatic cannon and twin guided missile launchers. Nearby, several SI squads are geared and lined up to board their rides.

I drive the ATV right into the shelter and park it over to the side, out of the way of the troops rushing in and out of the place. The commanding officer on the ground is a brigadier general, quite a few pay grades higher than the field commanders I usually deal with on drops. The brigadier general has a bunch of staff and junior officers around him, there's a field-comms relay, and they even dragged out a portable holotable that's displaying the tactical situation in this section of the northern hemisphere.

I don't know the SI general in charge. The face behind the visor of his helmet is thin and haggard, but his eyes are sharp and alert as he looks me up and down. He has gray beard stubble, and on the whole, he looks to be about twenty years older than any brigadier general I've seen before. His name tag says "STERLING, P."

"Lieutenant Grayson reporting back from Tuttle 250, sir," I say, and salute. "I'm the red hat you sent along with the rescue birds."

The general returns the salute. "Those ships left for the carrier over an hour ago, as far as I know."

"All but one, sir. The Lankies got one bird on the ground when they overran the position."

"And you made it out? Holy hell, son."

I shake my head. "I was already out, calling in close air on the Lankies. The bird they took out had no survivors. Sixty KIA, mostly civvies. And Captain Parker. I got back here with another survivor. Sergeant First Class Crawford. Once we're done with this mess, I want you to put her in for a Silver Star at least. She took out two Lankies with hand weapons in close combat. Saved me from getting stomped into jelly."

"You and Sergeant Crawford hoofed it all the way back here on foot?"

"We took a pair of ATVs from the facility, sir. Had a close call or two along the way."

"I bet you did," the general says. "We've got Lankies crawling around on this rock in every direction. Well done, Lieutenant. I'd love to tell you to get some rest, but I'll have to send you back out. It's going to be a long day yet."

"Yes, sir. What's the situation outside of our LZ?"

"We're pushing the Lankies back wherever we meet them, but the low cloud cover is a bitch for proper close-air support. Our guys are in the weeds so much, we're using fuel at four times the projected rate. Thank the gods we got this spaceport intact. Without the fuel tanks down here, we'd have to send all those birds back into orbit and through the minefield to refuel. *Phalanx* is already down to less than half her missile load."

He steps back and waves me over to the holotable. Then he zooms into the display and spins it around so I can see the map sector he has magnified.

"We're expanding out from Red Beach pretty steadily, but the Lankies are pushing Orange Beach hard. We're going to use our armor and see if we can take the pressure off LZ Orange. There's a Lanky town right here"—he points to its marker roughly halfway between Red and Orange Beach—"and we'll push at it from the south to make them pull back their line to reply to the threat. You're going in with a forward-observer team. Insert will be here, and you'll set up shop on this hill. Once the armor gets close, you call in the thunder on whatever they manage to draw out of that settlement."

"I won't have much mobility up there," I say. "If the tactical situation changes, I won't be able to keep up with the flow of battle."

"The Euros have graciously provided us with one of their shiny new recon MAVs, Lieutenant. You are riding with their red hat and the one from the SRA. *Kirov* and *Westfalen* are repositioning themselves in orbit right now so they can support our push. Close air will be your job because most air assets at Red Beach are NAC, but orbital bombardment will be SRA and Euro bailiwick. Dustoff is in thirty-five minutes."

"Yes, sir," I say.

"Dismissed, Lieutenant, and good luck."

I salute and turn to leave but stop halfway through my heel turn. "Uh, sir?"

"Yes, Lieutenant?"

"Do we have word on the other LZs? My wife is flying a drop ship at Purple Beach."

The general looks at me for a moment. Then he turns back to the holotable and pans out the map until it's a large-scale hologram of the entire planet. He rotates it so that the southern hemisphere points up.

"The Lankies overran Green because the space control cruiser for Task Force Green hit a mine and couldn't keep the hole in the minefield open after the first wave. We've consolidated Blue and Purple and sent reinforcements through their joint beachhead. Last word I got, they're still holding the line, but the Lankies are pressing hard."

I think of Halley, ferrying wave after wave down to the beach and then flying close air for her troops, in a hotly contested LZ, and I try not to recall the images of the shattered wreckage of the Wasp back at Tuttle 250.

She's the best at what she does, I think. *She's fine. Probably having the time of her life, mowing down Lankies.*

"Thank you for the intel, sir," I say. Then I repeat my salute and walk off to leave the general to his strategic business.

One Lanky mine, and an entire landing zone is overrun. One brigade of troops, four battalions, almost three thousand men and women, wiped out because of a single proximity mine hitting the wrong ship in the wrong spot. Whoever planned this thing left the margins way too thin, and Halley and I are riding the edge of those margins. But three thousand more troops in LZ Orange are about to suffer the same fate if we don't relieve them, so there's no alternative but to saddle up and pick up the spears again.

CHAPTER 18

RED HAT EXPRESS

Dmitry is standing on the drop-ship landing pad with Lieutenant Stahl when I arrive on my ATV. Before all of this happened, I never thought I could be so glad to see an SRA marine's face. Just as I pull up on the pad, the battery of the ATV dies completely, and I roll to a stop. I disengage the electric motors from the drivetrain and roll the ATV off the landing pad so it's not in the way of the next drop ship.

"You are still alive, Andrew. This is good. What happened to insect armor?"

"It broke," I say. "Seventeen million Commonwealth dollars down the drain. Where's our ride?"

"Our ride will be here in two minutes," Lieutenant Stahl says. "We will not have much time for our mission briefing."

"The general gave me the idea," I say. "They drop us off in your MAV, we climb the hill, and we spot targets for the armor and the flyboys."

"That is the rough plan. You will both have to learn very quickly, though. The flight to the drop zone is only thirty minutes," Lieutenant Stahl says.

"Learn *what* quickly?" I ask.

"How to operate *that*," Lieutenant Stahl says, and points behind us, where an armored vehicle is rolling toward us across the tarmac in complete silence.

The Eurocorps scout vehicle is the coolest piece of military hardware I've ever seen, with the possible exception of the Blackfly drop ships we used for our commando raid on Arcadia two months ago. It's a four-wheeled, light-armored car, roughly similar in shape to the multipurpose assault vehicles used by the Spaceborne Infantry, but it looks somewhat bigger and much more imposing. In fact, it looks like a miniature version of the Blackfly put on all-terrain wheels. The armor is faceted everywhere, not a straight line in sight, and the windshield is so tiny that it looks like a pair of squinty eyes in the face of a predator about to jump. There's a weapons module on top and a sensor system on an extendable mast. As the vehicle pulls up to us and comes to a stop, the armor seems to ripple before our eyes, and the entire vehicle practically disappears, a vague outline that shows a slightly distorted view of the area behind the armored car.

"I will be in the command seat and drive," Lieutenant Stahl says. "You will be operating the weapons and the sensor array. Do not worry; it is very easy. But you will have to wear our helmets, because yours will not interface with the vehicle."

"Friggin' German engineering," I say. "This is a German design, right?"

"Yes," the lieutenant replies, with no small measure of pride in his voice. "It is called the LGS *Wiesel*."

"Weasel," I say. "What's LGS stand for?"

"*Leichter Gepanzerter Spähwagen*," Lieutenant Stahl says. "Light armored scout car."

"Very fancy," Dmitry says. He runs his hand over the side of the Weasel, and the polychromatic armor shimmers under his armor's glove, like he's putting his hand into an oil slick.

The driver turns the polychromatic armor off, and the vehicle becomes defined again. The hatch on the side of the Weasel opens, and the driver exits and salutes Lieutenant Stahl. They exchange a few sentences in German, and the driver salutes again and walks off.

"Please," Lieutenant Stahl says. He gestures toward the open hatch. Dmitry and I look at each other and file into the vehicle. The rooftop is lower than our heads, and we have to bend down to keep our helmets from knocking into the flanges of the steel hatch.

Inside, there are three chairs. One is up front and is obviously the driver's seat. The two seats in the back are arranged side by side. They have helmets sitting on them, which Lieutenant Stahl tells us to put on. He closes the hatch and climbs into the driver's seat. I wait until the air-quality display of my own helmet shows a green light before I pull it off my head and put on the Euro helmet instead.

"Where's the data-link jack?" I ask Lieutenant Stahl.

"There isn't one. It's a wireless system," he replies.

I don't know if the Weasel uses hydrogen or electric engines, but whatever is under the power-pack hatch, it's whisper quiet. When the German lieutenant hits the throttle, we roll off the landing pad with barely a sound. We cross over into a different part of the base, where a line of Euro drop ships is assembled.

"I have switched the control languages for the screens to English and Russian, respectively," Lieutenant Stahl says. "Please activate your screens and familiarize yourselves with the sensor system before we board the drop ship."

I turn on the control screen next to my armrest. The menu is different from the ones in NAC vehicles, but translated into English I have no problem finding my way to the sensor submenu. I turn on my helmet, and the view in my helmet's targeting monocle instantly changes.

"Whoa," I say. "It's a DAS array."

"What is DAS?" Lieutenant Stahl asks.

"Distributed aperture system. You have optical sensors all over the outer armor."

"That is correct. The monocle will ignore the vehicle around it so the operator can see the surroundings."

Wherever I look with the helmet monocle, it's like the armored car isn't even there, and I'm floating above the ground at fifteen klicks per hour. When I look down, I see the rough texture of the airfield concrete rolling past underneath the Weasel.

"You can switch to the feed from the sensor mast. It extends up to twenty-five meters and has two hundred magnification levels. You can read the name on a uniform from a kilometer away."

Dmitry looks around with his own Euro helmet, and from the little grin on his face, I know that he has tapped into the DAS feed as well.

"This is not so bad," he says. "Better than walking."

"Much better than walking," I agree.

Lieutenant Stahl does a few rounds on the tarmac in front of the Eurocorps ships. Then he rolls up to one of the drop ships and lets the crew chief guide him into the cargo hold, which has been cleared of seat slings. The hold is just wide enough for the Weasel, and it looks big enough to maybe hold two of them nose-to-butt. We watch with the DAS system as the Euro crew tie down the vehicle with remote quick-release clamps so we don't roll forward and crash through the bulkhead, or backward through the tail ramp, if the ship maneuvers hard.

We're in the air a minute later. The Euro drop ship doesn't have a DAS setup, so we can't make its hull disappear to our monocles as well. I turn the system off and familiarize myself with the recon setup of the Weasel. The Euros have a small military, but they love to use tech as a force multiplier, and their engineering is probably the best out there.

With one of these babies, we could do the job of an entire podhead recon team and cover the ground in a fifth of the time. Of course, the Weasel is much too big to fit into a bio-pod, so it wouldn't be of any use against Lankies at all unless we had air superiority, which has only happened twice in our history—in the Fomalhaut system during the joint rescue mission of the SRA colonists, and today.

The flight to the target area takes thirty minutes. The seat I'm sitting in is comfortable enough that I could take a nap if I wasn't wired with the anticipation of the upcoming drop, my third one today. I am bone tired, but the adrenaline keeps me afloat mentally, and I know that my life may depend on how well I know the systems of this battle taxi, so I learn what I can while I have time. The remote weapons turret can be operated from any of the three seat positions, although the driver would have to stop the Weasel to shoot the guns. The weapons pack in the turret contains a fifteen-millimeter machine gun, a much smaller bore than our autocannons, but more suitable for precise fire at long range. It also has a semiautomatic grenade launcher alongside the machine gun. I check the ammo load for both weapons. Twelve hundred rounds for the gun, one hundred twenty rounds for the launcher.

For a vehicle of its size, the little Weasel can put down a pretty good ass-beating on infantry, although the weapons load is not exactly optimized against Lankies. The gun rounds are dual-purpose rounds with tungsten cores and explosive payloads behind, and the grenades are an almost even mix of fragmentation and dual-purpose rounds, with ten thermobarics in the magazine as well. I would not feel underarmed taking this little death buggy into battle against the enemies Eurocorps usually face—belligerent smaller nations on Earth, or the occasional armed insurrectionists—but the invisibility of the Weasel will be much more valuable against the Lankies than its armament.

"Very German," Dmitry comments on the armament configuration.

"How so?"

"Small gun. Accurate. High rate of fire. Is made for precision. Russian guns are opposite. Not so accurate, but bigger shells. For bigger bang."

We put down in a narrow valley a few kilometers from our observation-post site. The Euro drop ship touches down and opens the tail ramp, and the crew chief remotely unlocks the safety clamps holding us to the deck. Lieutenant Stahl backs the Weasel out of the cargo hold smoothly and with obvious practice. The drop ship is back in the air before we're even fully turned around, and we're on our own in the semidarkness of the Martian evening.

"Whoa. This thing can really move," I say when Lieutenant Stahl takes us out into the fading light at full speed.

"Need to steal one," Dmitry agrees. "For taking home. Maksim would enjoy."

We drive out of the valley and onto the plateau at the foot of our target hill, and Dmitry and I turn on the DAS system to get all-round vision. The sensors automatically amplify the light outside, and the computer stabilizes the optical input to smooth out the bumps we hit. It's like I'm a disembodied 360-degree camera gliding above the ground at two meters of altitude. I scan the horizon for Lankies and don't see any, so I fire up the gun turret and get used to the targeting system in case we have need for the guns later. Lieutenant Stahl didn't lie—the systems are very easy to figure out, and the computer does most of the work anyway.

"This goes faster here on Mars," Lieutenant Stahl says jovially from the driver's seat. "Less gravity."

"Just make sure you remember that when you have to brake or make a sharp turn," I say.

The German lieutenant gives me a thumbs-up without taking his eyes off his heads-up display.

We climb the target hill at low throttle, carefully and with the poly-chromatic-camouflage mode engaged in case we stumble into a pack of Lankies on the hillcrest. But the top of the hill is empty, just a relatively flat peak two hundred meters above the surrounding surface. When we crest the hill, I can see our objective in the distance—the strange latticework structures of a Lanky settlement. They usually remind me of coral reefs a bit. I've always wondered whether "settlement" was an accurate assessment of their function. They are too airy to keep out wind and weather, but that's where the Lankies congregate, so that's what we called them when we first encountered them on colony planets.

I send a burst transmission to the forces that are now making their way to this map grid from Olympus Spaceport and waiting for our update.

"Ground Force Red, this is Tailpipe Red One. We are on station at OP Promontory. We have eyes on objective Lima."

"Tailpipe Red One, copy that," the reply comes. "Armor is rolling. ETA three hours, thirty minutes."

I relay the information to Dmitry and Lieutenant Stahl, who both mutter soft curses in their mother tongues.

"We will keep watch in shifts," Lieutenant Stahl suggests. "Thirty-minute watches. One of us can sleep while two are keeping the watch."

"Sounds lovely," I say.

"You go sleep first," Dmitry tells me. "I play with gun system and fancy computer. We wake you if trouble comes."

Lieutenant Stahl voices his assent—I must look much more tired than I thought—and I nod and recline my seat. Then I close my eyes. With the adrenaline from the drop subsiding, it takes me no time at all to fall asleep.

We each get in two shifts of thirty-minute naps by the time the armor arrives to the southeast of us. The fleet has managed to land a full armor company, three line platoons with four vehicles each, and the command platoon with two mules bringing up the rear. Overhead, we have close-air support as well, several flights of drop ships and attack birds from three different alliances. We hold the strings up here in our hilltop OP, and it's time to start yanking on them.

"Team Yankee coming up on your eight o'clock," the company commander sends. "Damn, you guys are well hidden. I can't even range you with the laser."

"That's the idea," I reply, still shaking off the sleep from the last nap I took. "Still got eyes on objective Lima, still no movement. Repeat, no LHOs in evidence."

"We will proceed to max firing range and start putting rounds into Lankyville. Get ready to call down the thunder."

"We've *been* ready," I reply. "Go ahead and advance. We have the overwatch."

The light tanks fan out into a long battle line with small gaps between each four-vehicle platoon. Fourteen mules advance across the plateau to our left toward the Lanky village. At this range, our near-field TacNet works, and I won't even have to call out targets for the tanks to be aware of them. They'll see what I see the moment I spot something.

The thirty-five-millimeter guns on the Bastard mounts have an effective range of five kilometers in direct fire. The battle line of mules rolls to within four and a half kilometers of the Lanky village. By now they are past our vantage point on the hill, and whatever is going to unfold now will happen in front of and below our elevated position. The mules all halt their advance and bring their gun mounts to bear.

"Engage enemy structure at twelve o'clock, twenty-round burst," the company commander sends. "Weapons free, weapons free."

Fourteen large-caliber autocannons start thundering. The muzzle blasts light up the valley floor, and hundreds of tracer rounds fly out and tear into the Lanky structure.

For a few long moments, nothing happens. Then there's movement in the structure, and a couple of seconds later, it's like someone hit a wasp nest with a broomstick. Dozens of Lankies come pouring out of the south side of the structure. Even from my elevated position, I have no real idea where they were hiding just a minute ago, in a structure so irregular and airy that you can see clear through it in places.

"Targets in the open," I call out. "Multiple LHOs at forty-five hundred meters and closing in fast."

The mules don't need any encouragement to open fire again. The automatic cannons that were firing twenty-round probing bursts just a moment ago switch to automatic control, with the computers all linked and the command vehicle's TacLink node calling the shots. It's a brutally effective method for coordinating fire—the computer shoots every single round, and no human gunner wastes ammo by engaging a target that's already under fire by another mule. Our firing line stretches for over half a kilometer, a mule every forty meters, and the guns fire in long, precisely calculated bursts. From up here, the streams of tracers cutting through the darkness and into the advancing Lankies look like laser beams from old Network movies. There are sparks whenever a round hits the ground or glances off the hard cranial shield of a Lanky, but most rounds find their mark, and the Bastard mounts are chopping them down one by one.

Overhead, I hear the wail of a drop ship's engines—not our Shrike, but an SRA attack bird. It starts firing its cannon even before it breaks through the cloud ceiling, and more Lankies drop to the hammer blows of armor-piercing cannon shells. Next to me, Dmitry is giving the pilot cool and precise-sounding instructions in Russian. Then I see the glowing fireflies of rocket motors from overhead, and dozens of unguided rockets pour from the sky and plow into the Lankies at a high angle.

All their size and strength, all their resilience isn't doing them any good against our ranged weapons and the fire we can rain on their heads from the sky. With their seed ships keeping our air and space units away, against infantry with hand weapons, they are terrifying and overpowering opponents. Without their protector ship in orbit, facing attack craft built to obliterate armor columns, they are hard-to-miss targets. I feel a deep sense of satisfaction as I watch the slaughter, and I'm sure almost everyone on the ground with me feels the same way. We have lost so much to them, suffered so many casualties, had our lives upended so often, that seeing them die by the dozens is a grimly joyful experience. The SRA attack bird pulls out of its run, and another follows it with the same attack pattern. The tide of Lankies coming from the village seems to stall, then reverse itself as the creatures try to retreat from the withering fire.

So they're not completely suicidal, I think. Whether by instinct or conscious decision, they aren't willing to run into effective gunfire.

"Team Yankee, advance as a company and engage on the move," the company commander orders.

Down on the plateau, the line of mules starts moving toward the village again, closing the distance meter by meter, their cannon mounts popping off bursts at retreating Lankies as the computers spot them. Gradually, the fire from the tank company slacks off until all guns are silent again, their targeting systems having run out of moving targets to shoot at. They close to three thousand, two thousand, then a thousand meters. A flight of four drop ships comes swooping from the sky, takes up formation above the tank column, and soars over the Lanky village. On the far side, five hundred meters from the southern edge, they drop cluster kinetics and fire their cannons. I hear the piercing wails of the stricken Lankies all the way at the top of our observation hill, five kilometers away. On the ground in front of the Lanky village, the mules' battle line gets untidy as individual mules have to swerve around the massive bulks of fallen Lankies.

"There's an opening wide enough for armor," I hear on the company channel. "Two hundred meters northeast."

I zoom into the spot with the magnified view from the Weasel's sensor mast. There's not a trace of movement beyond the opening in the latticework.

"It's clear from up here," I tell the company commander. "No activity."

"We're rolling in," the company commander replies. "Second Platoon, take the lead. Then First and Third. Go in pairs. And be ready to back out."

The platoon commanders toggle back their acknowledgments.

I spend a few pulse-pounding moments watching the first pairs of our armor column drive up to the opening and disappear inside the structure. From up here, I can see them turning on their infrared illuminators and targeting lasers. One of the lead mules turns on its external high-powered searchlight, and the others inside follow suit. I can see the light from the beams bleeding through the holes in the latticework and drawing dancing shadows onto the ground in front of the structure.

"It's empty," one of the platoon commanders sends. "Looks like they all cleared out the back. I repeat, the structure is empty. There's nobody home."

"That was little too easy," Dmitry says.

"I don't mind easy," I reply. "But yeah. I know what you mean."

I relay the information back to Ground Force Red Actual, the general who's calling the shots back at the spaceport a few hundred kilometers to our southeast. We have only a sliver of the available ground forces up here for this diversion, all the personnel that fit into the back of the mules, a hundred troops total. A full brigade has thirty times that manpower, but even three thousand troops stretch thin when you have to cover many square kilometers of ground with them. Our beachhead has expanded steadily, but now we're stretched to the limit, even with the reinforcements thrown in. If the line breaks anywhere, it'll be like someone sticking a needle into a balloon.

"Advance and recon in force; then swing northwest until you make contact with the Lankies pressing the attack on Orange Beach," the general orders. "But don't get in over your heads. Your job is to draw them back towards you and relieve the pressure on Ground Force Orange."

"Affirmative," our company commander replies.

"We are rolling," I add. There's not a Lanky in sight anymore, and the mules in the structure are advancing without resistance, but I feel reluctance when Lieutenant Stahl puts the Weasel into drive and turns off the polychromatic camouflage.

"Maybe now we use weapons a little," Dmitry says, and pats the handle of the fire-control system.

We catch up to the armor column just as the last tanks of the company roll through the gap in the Lanky structure. The experience of driving into one of their reef-like edifices is disconcertingly vivid through the many lenses of the Weasel's DAS sensors. I've gotten close to Lanky structures before, but I've never actually been inside one. The structure is much bigger on the inside than it looked from a few kilometers away, or maybe it just feels that way because of scale, because the armored vehicles look almost insignificantly small inside. Whatever the Lankies use for building material looks a lot like bone, but it's so airy and transparent that the searchlights from the mules shine through the structure and light it up from the inside. The scale reminds me of walking through a cathedral. There are many irregular arches and openings in the walls. It looks like a discarded carapace or the plaster cast of an organ more than a building, and the Lankies have never seemed more organic and biological to me than right now.

We roll through the structure slowly and carefully, weapons swiveling on their mounts as the gunners look for targets.

"I take gunner seat, we have nothing to shoot," Dmitry says with a tone of genuine disappointment in his voice.

The structure is several hundred meters across, and subdivided into smaller sections with those strange, semitransparent interior walls that look like they wouldn't keep much out or in. We should probably stop and take samples of the stuff, but I find that my curiosity has its limits. Any second, I expect the Lankies to spring some sort of unexpected trap or ambush, because that's what they seem to do whenever we feel like we have the upper hand for once. But we make it through the edifice and out of the other side without spotting a single Lanky.

There are dead Lankies on the other side of the structure where the drop ships strafed the retreating group. I count a dozen bodies, some still smoking from the bombardment. The armored column re-forms by platoons, and Lieutenant Stahl gooses the engine of the Weasel to take the lead. We're faster, and our sensors reach further, so we're playing eyes and ears again.

We're too far out, I think. On my TacLink screen, our column is a small cluster of blue icons halfway between Red and Orange Beach, and it's 150 kilometers to safety no matter which way we turn out here. Our air support is circling overhead and giving me some reassurance, but I'm very aware of just how far we're sticking our necks out right now, and I keep scanning the darkness outside with the green-tinged night vision of the Weasel for the blade that's sure to drop any minute now. But with every passing moment, we put more distance between us and the Lanky structure, and nothing is jumping out of the darkness at us.

Let's hope our good luck lasts for just a little while, I think, knowing good and well that it never does.

The ride through the nighttime Martian landscape has a surreal quality to it, and not just because of the green tinge from the low-light magnification. Lieutenant Stahl pulls ahead of the column until we are almost ten klicks in front of the pack, far enough out to provide ample warning to the tank company once we find trouble.

"Whatever you did, it worked," Brigade Command sends. "Orange Beach is reporting that the Lankies in their sector have stopped their push. They are moving southeast from LZ Orange and heading your way."

"Copy incoming from the direction of LZ Orange," I reply. "Do we have a head count?"

"They report several hundred individuals," C2 replies. "Be advised that Ground Force Orange is too depleted to pursue, and they have lost most of their close-air support. They're staying defensive for now, so it's all on you. Make contact, and give them something to chase south, but don't get into prolonged exchanges. You don't have the numbers to stem that tide."

"Copy that," I say. The tank-company commander sends back his curt acknowledgment as well.

"You're our tripwire," the company commander tells me. "You make contact, we'll get into blocking position, and you lead them back to us. No heroics."

"Not interested in any above-and-beyond shit today, sir," I send back, and he laughs.

"We're still looking good. Seventy percent ammo, sixty-five on fuel, and another half hour of close-air coverage. We may yet make it out of this in one piece."

CHAPTER 19

47 NORTHING

The terrain works in our favor. It's flat enough for the optics to pick up the first elements of the Lankies coming toward us from several kilometers away. They stride across the plains with purpose, but in no terrible hurry, kicking up puffs of Mars dust with every step.

"Incoming hostiles," I report on the company channel. The TacLink screen starts painting orange icons at the very edge of our visual detection range. "Bearing two-ninety degrees. Five thousand five hundred and closing in."

"All platoons, halt and assume defensive posture. Reload your magazines from the spares while you have time. We fire from max range and fall back two klicks. Shoot and scoot," the company commander orders.

The tank company halts and forms up in a long firing line. I see the icons of individual soldiers emerging from the vehicles as the troopers get out and set up firing positions in the spaces between the mules.

"Here we go," I say to the other two members of the Weasel's crew. "You'll finally get something to shoot at, Dmitry."

"Maybe this day will be some fun, after all," Dmitry replies. He grabs the control stick of the gun mount. I hear the mechanical ratcheting sound from the machine-gun mount on top of the vehicle as

Dmitry cycles the bolt remotely and readies the gun for action. He seems to need very little instruction when it comes to operating large-caliber weaponry.

"Two-thousand-meter range on the main armament," Lieutenant Stahl reminds him. "I will try not to get closer than fifteen hundred."

With the Weasel's polychrome camo, we could probably get much closer to the Lankies without being spotted, but this is about getting their attention, not staying hidden. Lieutenant Stahl aims the vehicle at the center of the advancing line of Lankies and goes full throttle again.

"Remember, Mars gravity!" I shout. "Don't flip this son of a bitch."

"Eurocorps has purchased comprehensive insurance on this vehicle," the lieutenant replies.

Dmitry laughs. "German humor," he says. "I did not think it exists."

The gap between us and the tank company opens as we race toward the approaching Lankies at top speed. We are thirteen kilometers in front of the mules and their guns, and we have to coax the Lankies to within five thousand meters. I keep my eyes glued to the distance readout. The gap between us and the Lankies shrinks too fast for my comfort. Three kilometers, two and a half, then two. When the distance readout shows 1,800 meters, Lieutenant Stahl hits the brakes and swings the Weasel around.

"Weapons free," he says.

Dmitry lets out a satisfied little grunt. He flexes his hand and flips up the safety cover on the control stick's trigger. Then he holds down the trigger, and the heavy machine gun on the roof mount hammers out a burst toward the Lankies in the front of the advancing pack.

The German gun is astoundingly accurate even without laser ranging, which doesn't work on Lanky hides anyway. The first burst from the gun hits a Lanky square in the upper chest, very close to the relatively vulnerable throat area. The gun has a smaller caliber than our autocannons, but the rounds have a much higher muzzle velocity and cover the range in a little over a second. The Lanky stumbles and drops to its knees. Dmitry follows up the first burst with a second one, which mostly hits the cranial shield of the now-crouching Lanky and sends ricochets everywhere. Dmitry shoots a few more short bursts along the Lanky line—not enough to drop one reliably with the smaller machine-gun rounds, but enough to inflict injury and hopefully piss them off. Then Lieutenant Stahl accelerates away from the Lankies.

We repeat the same process at every one-kilometer grid line. They are marked in northings on the TacLink map, a standard measuring unit for grid squares in the absence of other navigational references, and we started engaging the Lankies at the 60 northing line. We stop and shoot at 59 northing, then 58, 57, and 56, each time expending a hundred rounds of MG ammo and causing the occasional full-on casualties among the Lankies. The armor company has their battle line drawn up at 47 northing.

"You have them walking right into your guns," I tell the company commander.

"Keep doing what you're doing," he says. "When they make that little ridgeline between 54 and 53, we have them in the bag."

"Just mind your fire," I reply. "This thing can't take more than a stray hit or two."

In theory, the computer controls on the mule guns shouldn't allow the mules to fire at a positively identified friendly target blaring NAC or Eurocorps IFF ID, but at the ranges we're engaging, autocannons aren't exactly sniper rifles. As we speed toward the 54 northing ridge-line, I hope that the mule gunners are all experienced and alert, because one of those thirty-five-millimeter shells would wreck the Weasel comprehensively.

"TacAir, stand by to drop the hard stuff," I send to the drop ships overhead. "Dmitry, tell the SRA attack jock to stand by until they cross the ridge and we have them in the kill zone. Don't want to run them off before they can get into gun range."

"Remember: short, controlled bursts," the company commander says to the platoons. "We lay everything we have on them, then retreat to 45 northing. Repeat and leapfrog two northings until they stop coming."

Lieutenant Stahl seems to have the Mars gravity dialed in now. We shoot over the low ridgeline at 54 northing, and the Weasel momentarily catches air. We bounce back onto the dirt a moment later, the vehicle staying true on its track and absorbing the shock from the landing. It's definitely geared for recon, not hard combat, but for the job we're doing right now it's absolutely perfect—small, very agile, and with an outstanding sensor package. If I had a dozen of these for SOCOM, we could survey a planet the size of Arcadia or Mars completely within five days, and in air-conditioned comfort. I bet they even have the capability for a great sound system.

"Red Hat Express, we have you in sight," I hear on the company channel when we're across the ridgeline. The speed readout on my screen reads 110 kilometers per hour, the fastest I've ever gone off-world in anything that didn't have wings bolted to it.

Not quite a minute later, the Lankies come pouring over the low ridgeline, dozens of them in the leading group, and hundreds more right behind them. The tank platoon waits patiently until the bulk of the Lanky crowd is over the ridgeline and half a kilometer into the kill zone.

"Red Hat Express, break left to reading ninety and come around behind us."

"Understood," the German lieutenant replies. "Going around from bearing ninety degrees."

He corrects the course of the Weasel until we're almost parallel with the advancing front of Lankies a kilometer and a half behind us. Dmitry stows the gun again with a look of mild regret on his face behind the Euro helmet's visor.

"All units, switch fire control to autonomous. Weapons free, weapons free."

Just like back at the Lanky village, fourteen cannons open up with burst fire. The muzzle blasts from the thirty-five-millimeter cannons are enormous despite the flash dissipaters on their muzzle ends. From our perspective, over to the right side of their formation but still in front of the guns, the blasts from the guns look alarming. But the computers on the mules stay true to their programming, and the heavy shells streak over our low-slung ride and into the advancing Lankies.

For the next thirty seconds, the plateau is a shooting range with live targets. The cannons mow down Lanky after Lanky. The dual-purpose rounds from the thirty-five-millimeter guns are so powerful that Lanky limbs get torn off by direct hits on occasion, a very satisfying sight. Some of the Lankies assume their defensive postures, advancing at a crouch so their cranial shields cover most of their spindly bodies from the front, and I'm amazed to see that even the cannons from the Bastard mounts can't pierce those skull shields reliably. Lankies stumble and fall out of the group with fatal injuries right, left, and center, but the ones behind them simply climb over them and continue the advance into the murderous hail of fire coming from the mules.

I don't get it, I think. They retreated earlier at the village, showing self-preservation impulses, but these out here on the plateau aren't perturbed by clearly effective gunfire. We've already dropped over a dozen, but the others come surging forward, around or over their own dead, and advance on the mules. Then they're close enough to make the company commander concerned, and he blows the retreat signal.

"All units, cease fire. Load up the legs and fall back to 45 northing."

The mules stop shooting, let their infantry passengers board, and make quick 180-degree turns almost as one. Then they race away from the Lankies, back toward the 45 northing line two kilometers away. We shadow them in the Weasel on what is now their left flank, now that we're moving in the same direction as the Lankies. The cluster of orange icons behind the company has thinned out some, but not enough. We'll have to do this half a dozen times to take them all down, and the mules only have a limited supply of cannon ammo. The Weasel has a lot of rounds on board because the rounds are small in comparison to those fired from the Bastard mount jackhammers, but even with judicious burst fire, we've gone through half the ammo load on the machine gun just with our harassing fire earlier. When the company lines up at 45 northing again a few minutes later and repeats the process, I start to get the feeling that we are trying to put out a massive wildfire with handheld extinguishers.

"One or two more of these, and we'll have to disengage," the company commander says, echoing my thoughts.

"Not quite yet," I reply. "Bringing in close air on the next stop."

"Hallelujah," he replies.

"All air units, I am marking target reference point Alpha." I draw a big red box around the gaggle of orange icons on the plateau. "You are cleared hot. Everything north of 45 northing is hostile and a priority target. Weapons free, weapons free."

The drop ships come thundering out of the clouds somewhere over 44 northing. They line up in a four-abreast formation and ripple-fire all their remaining external ordnance at the approaching Lankies. A dozen missile trails streak out from the wings of the Wasps and scream into the Lanky formation. The Lankies that take direct hits to their bodies go down hard and tangle up the advance in their general vicinity. Some of the missiles hit the ground between the Lankies, and the explosive force is still enough to topple them over or make them stumble. The drop ships follow up the missile strike with long bursts from their cannons, which rake the Lanky lines and kill yet more of them. We are dropping them as they advance, and they are paying for each hundred-meter stretch of the plateau with half a dozen of their own. *But they keep coming.*

"Cadillac Flight is Winchester on missiles and close to bingo fuel," the pilot in charge of the drop-ship wing tells me on the TacAir channel. "We can give you one or two more gun runs, and then we have to RTB."

"Captain, we're going to get another strafing run at most," I tell the company commander. "I suggest we use it for cover fire while we haul ass out of the area."

"We've gotten our licks in," he sends back. "All platoons, cease fire and prepare to head south. Let's hope we pulled enough of these bastards away from LZ Orange."

The mules do their 180 again. The drop ships line up for one more attack run. This time, they come in from the northeast, perpendicular to the line of Lankies that is spread across several kilometers of the plateau and still surging toward us relentlessly and undeterred. The cannons drop a few more, maybe eight or ten, but there are too many left for those casualties to make much of a dent in their lines.

"We are bingo fuel, and Winchester on cannons. Cadillac Flight is RTB. Good luck down there," the leader of the attack-bird flight sends.

"That's it. We're out. All units, disengage," the armor-company commander says.

On the southern edge of the Weasel's sensor range, an orange icon shows up. It's joined by another, then a third. Within a minute, there's a line of orange icons to our south that's easily as long and dense as the one to our north.

"Enemy contacts, bearing one-four-five, distance eight kilometers. One hundred plus individuals," I inform the company channel, even though everyone has the same icons on their TacLink screen right now because my suit shared the data with the whole neighborhood.

"Where the fuck did they come from?" I say. "That area was cleared. We just went through there thirty fucking minutes ago."

"Ambush," Dmitry says. "They pull us away from village. Only pretend to flee so we go north right away. Then spring trap behind us."

We thought we were luring them into a trap, I think. *And all along, they were luring us into theirs. Threw away dozens of their own to get us out in the open like this. Just like Greenland all over again.*

The TacLink display is a tactical nightmare. Our line of mules is now sandwiched between two long battle lines of Lankies, and they are closing in on us like the pusher plates of a garbage compactor. We're hemmed in by a steep hill to the northeast, which leaves only the southwest end of this vise as an escape route, but the Lankies are already advancing their southern lines to close that gap, too.

It's a pincer movement. They know formation tactics.

The company commander has come to the same conclusion. He marks the shrinking gap between the Lankies' southern lines on the map.

"All platoons, make best speed for that map grid," he says. "Haul ass. Drive for your lives, people."

The whole column swings south, and the mules go full throttle. Our Weasel is up on the northern flank of our advance, by the foot of the hill hemming us in, and the rocky slope is run through with deep cracks and looks way too steep to climb with the recon car. So Lieutenant Stahl points the Weasel south and opens up the throttle to catch up with our mules, which are racing south for dear life.

With nothing else to do other than hang on and hope the lieutenant doesn't roll the vehicle, I train the sensor mast on the Lankies approaching us from the southeast. They're not moving at a leisurely pace. In fact, they are striding as fast as I've seen them go, ten yards per step, covering a kilometer in a minute. The group is as big as the one closing on us from the northwest, and they are coming up the very same path we took only half an hour ago to catch the other Lankies from behind. The area between the village was completely clear of Lankies, and I know that the mules moved faster than any Lanky can run.

Where the hell did they come from? It's like they popped out of the earth behind us.

Suddenly, I have a pretty good idea how they managed to spring this trap, and I hope I'm not right, because if I am, it means that this offensive is going to take it in the face hard, and not just in this sector.

The lead mules are rushing ahead with their engines at full throttle, but I can see that the southern pincer they're setting up will close on the escape route just before we get there.

"Don't let up," the captain orders on the company channel. "Don't stop to shoot. Drive right through them if you have to."

The first two mules reach the Lanky line just as they close ranks and march inward. The first mule makes it through the gap between two Lankies and shoots off into the darkness beyond. The second mule can't quite make the gap, and the driver decides at the last second that ramming speed is an adequate last fuck-you. He aims for the legs of one of the Lankies and plows right into them, twenty tons of wedge-shaped armored fighting vehicle against a creature that weighs hundreds of tons. The center of gravity difference favors the mule, but the laminate-composite armor on the nose of the vehicle isn't meant to survive that sort of high-speed impact against something so solid. The Lanky goes down, but the mule flips sideways, spewing armor panels everywhere, and rolls across the plateau violently around its longitudinal axis. I flinch at the sight—even if the grunts in the back were in sling seats, there's no way anyone's walking away from that under their own power.

The remaining mules have given up all semblance of coordinated formation driving. Everyone tries to find a gap in the wall of Lankies closing in on us. Some of the mules stop and open fire with their cannons, ignoring their commanders' order while trying to blast a hole into the ranks. Several Lankies fall, but others take their place almost instantly. I watch as a Lanky strides swiftly toward the firing vehicle from the side. Before the gunner can turn his turret mount around, the Lanky kicks the mule over, sending shards of armor flying. Then another steps on top of the overturned mule and starts crushing it methodically with its huge feet. Another mule opens fire from a different spot and hoses the Lanky off the wrecked mule with a long burst of cannon rounds.

The space between the Lanky battle lines turns into complete chaos. Each individual vehicle is maneuvering and fighting for its life separately. The Lankies simply kick the mules over or rip their weapons mounts off the tops of the vehicles. Lieutenant Stahl has engaged the polychrome camouflage again and is weaving between mules and Lankies at top speed. I decide that in some situations, the omnivision afforded by the DAS sensors is a little too much information. This is a nightmare run through a merciless close-range battle between machines and twenty-meter monsters.

"Day is turning less fun now," Dmitry says from the gunner seat. He has fired up the weapons mount again, and he's emptying the magazine in measured bursts, strafing Lankies as we shoot past them and pumping grenades from the automatic launcher into their midst.

We sideswipe a mule that appears next to us seemingly out of nowhere, and the impact makes the Weasel jolt and momentarily lifts the two right-side wheels off the ground. The Weasel fishtails for twenty or thirty meters and then almost runs right into the legs of an advancing Lanky. Lieutenant Stahl straightens out the fishtailing and immediately steers hard left, a turn so tight that it lifts the left-side wheels off the ground now. We bump over the tip of the Lanky's toe with one wheel just as the thing is starting another step. The left-side wheels hit the dirt again hard.

"Look forward, *durak*!" Dmitry shouts at Lieutenant Stahl.

"My name is not *durak*!" he shouts back. "It's Thorsten." He yanks the wheel left, then right, and we clear another Lanky by less than a meter as it swings for us. "And this is not easy driving, you know."

Amazingly, Dmitry laughs at this. "Is like driving car in Moscow on Saturday evening," he says. "Maybe little less dangerous."

"You Russians are all insane," Lieutenant Stahl growls back.

"Just fucking drive!" I shout.

I don't know how we make it through the gauntlet of Lankies and zigzagging mules, but a few moments later, we are out in the clear, away from the melee, and racing across the Martian plains. I swivel the optical mast backwards to see if we have Lankies in pursuit, but they're all pushing inward and pressing in on the mules that are still trapped in the pocket between them. I hate running away from the battle, but there is nothing we can do here.

Dmitry has been working the weapons mount for the whole mad dash, and now the magazines are empty except for a few thermobaric grenades for the automatic launcher, which aren't very effective in open spaces. We are out of ammo, down to hand weapons, and there's a disconcerting grinding noise coming from the right side of the Weasel. The TacLink screen is a total mess, orange and blue icons layered on top of each other, and more and more blue icons winking out of existence as the transmitters in the vehicles get crushed. Two more blue icons have made it out of the cluster of orange ones and are headed away from the battle at top speed as well, taking different headings. What was a full-strength light-armored-fighting-vehicle company just five minutes ago has been reduced to a handful of damaged survivors running for their lives. Our tactics were sound, our approach by the book, our execution flawless—and we got our asses kicked up to our ears. Too many Lankies on too big a planet, and too few of us to stem that tide, even after a whole year of cranking out new troops.

Lieutenant Stahl drives the Weasel south for ten minutes before we dare to stop on a small hill to take stock of what's left. The two surviving mules have been going roughly in the same direction, but they're several kilometers to our west. Both have SI squads in the back, led by staff sergeants, which means I am the senior surviving NAC member.

"Head south around that mountain; then make for Olympus Spaceport," I tell the commanders of the two mules. "Get your troops back to safety. There's Lankies all over the rock between here and there, so keep your eyes open, and don't take risks."

"Copy that, sir. See you back at the base. Good luck."

We get out of the Weasel and observe the exterior damage. The grinding sound is a piece of hull plating that is rubbing against one of the honeycomb tires. The side of the Weasel is dented and scraped all to shit from the collisions with the mule and the Lanky. The front-left wheel bearing is shot as well, but the recon car should get us back to the spaceport. Dmitry and I pull off the dangling piece of laminate armor and chuck it away.

"Which way do you want to go?" Lieutenant Stahl asks me when we're back in the vehicle.

"I want to go back north and come around the slope of that mountain the other way," I say. "High enough so we can use your superperiscope here and check out the plateau to the northeast of that Lanky village. I have some suspicions I want to lay to rest."

Lieutenant Stahl plots our course on the navigation screen. "We have the range," he says.

"Then let's head out. I'll try to get C2 at LZ Red along the way, once we're on that slope."

The news from C2 confirms my worst fears. I call in and inform command of the disastrous outcome of our mission, but it turns out that in the grand scheme of things, that's a minor problem right now. In the background of the transmission from C2, I hear heavy-weapons fire from airborne platforms.

"We have Lankies in our rear everywhere," Brigade Command says. "They started popping up behind the lines out of nowhere. Our perimeter around LZ Red is down to ten klicks around the base, and it's shrinking by the hour. LZ Orange is gone, and LZ Brown is in doubt. They're doing what they can with orbital support, but the cruisers are rapidly running out of missiles and kinetic warheads. Division is preparing for an emergency dustoff, so I suggest you double-time it back here if you want to be included."

"What about the southern hemisphere?"

"Second Division and the SRA are pulling out of there already. We're cutting our losses, Lieutenant. Get back to base, and Godspeed. C2 out."

We let the news sink in for a bit. Several LZs overrun, with a brigade lost in each of them. We gave them an ass-kicking in orbit, wiped out thousands on the ground, and then they punched right back. Maybe you can't effectively fight an enemy you haven't even begun to understand.

"Let's get going," I say. "I want to get eyes on the Lanky village again on the way back to base."

We make our way around the mountain, clinging to its side about halfway up the slope. I'm running the sensor mast, extended to its full height of twenty-five meters, and my field of view is a swath of Mars surface hundreds of kilometers wide. At one point, we get to within ten klicks of the site where the armor platoon got comprehensively folded up, and I train the mast sensors on the spot and crank them up to maximum magnification. It's still dark out, and the image intensifiers don't make for a very sharp picture from this far out, but I can see the wrecks of the vehicles scattered in the Mars dirt. Luckily, I am too far away to spot bodies if there are any.

A little while later, I see movement in the darkness on the plateau between the battle site and the Lanky village. We're five hundred meters above the plateau and six kilometers away, and even with the fuzzy, green-tinted imaging of the low-light sensors, I can see that a whole bunch of Lankies are converging on a spot out there.

"Stop the ride for a moment," I tell Lieutenant Stahl, who complies and lets the Weasel roll to a stop.

I focus on the spot out in the Martian desert. The plateau is pretty flat—I was able to see for several klicks while we were driving across it scouting for the mules earlier—but there are deep furrows and ravines from old erosion on either side of the plains, near the spots where the terrain starts to rise again. The Lankies out on the plateau, many dozens of them, are making their way into one of those ravines. I follow their movement until I find a spot where the familiar spindly silhouettes disappear in the darkness and out of sight. I had a suspicion earlier, about the way the Lankies managed to slam the trap door shut behind us so quickly even though we had just swept the plateau, and now I know how they pulled it off. I share the imagery with Dmitry and Lieutenant Stahl.

"It's a goddamn tunnel," I say. "They went underground. Into the rock. Just like they did on Greenland."

"That is why they can come up behind our lines," Lieutenant Stahl muses. "They hide in the tunnels and come back out when we are gone."

"We think we have a frontline, but they've been letting us push them on purpose. On the surface. So we'd overextend ourselves."

"I do not think this is battle we can win, Andrew," Dmitry contributes.

"No," I say. "Not on the ground."

We watch as the Lankies disappear in the tunnel mouth one by one. Unbidden, I remember the darkness in the tunnel on Greenland, my feelings of total fear and helplessness, and that same fear starts welling up again just at the thought of having to go after these things, down dark tunnels hundreds of meters below the surface. Just a dozen of them made themselves a nest and a small tunnel network on Greenland in one month. Mars has been in their hands for over a year, and there are probably tens of thousands of Lankies here. They had a lot of time to dig in and prepare. If these Lankies were half as busy and efficient as the ones on Greenland, there's a tunnel and cave network under the surface of Mars now that a hundred thousand SI troopers wouldn't be able to clear out in a year.

"What are they carrying?" Lieutenant Stahl asks.

"What?"

"The Lankies. It looks like they are carrying something. The ones that are going into the tunnel."

I zoom in at maximum. The image stabilization even at two-hundred-power magnification is a thing of marvel. The Germans really know how to do optics, but right now I wish they weren't quite as good as they are, because I can clearly see arms and legs dangling from the huge clawed hands of the Lankies. A sudden wave of nausea floods my brain.

"*Bozhe moy,*" Dmitry mutters when I freeze the image and share it on the Weasel's central screens.

"Bodies," I say. "Those are human bodies."

CHAPTER 20

— NO SUCH THING AS OVERKILL —

The sun comes up an hour later while we're still making our way around the slope of the mountain. I am busy scanning the plateau and the approaches to the Lanky village with the optical sensors. The area, which was empty when we breezed through it with our scout car and an armored company in tow, is now busy with Lanky activity again. They're not bunching up in the massive groups we saw during the night, but it's clear that they've gone back to business as usual. The village has Lankies going in and coming out of it. Some are dragging the bodies of their dead along with them. I see that even Lankies have physical limitations, because it takes two of them to move one body.

"What do they do with our dead?" Lieutenant Stahl muses. "Why do they collect the bodies? That is why there were almost no bodies in the city. They took them all."

"Food," Dmitry suggests. "Maybe they eat the dead."

"I don't know. Those things are thousands of times our body weight. There's not enough of us around. It would be like you trying to live off cockroaches."

Dmitry shrugs and opens his mouth, but I hold up a hand to make him hold in what he's about to say.

"If you actually have cockroach recipes from the Russian prisons," I say, "I am really not interested."

He grins and shrugs. "Is protein. Everything needs protein."

"Everything needs protein," I repeat.

"Could be for food," Lieutenant Stahl says. "Or could be for raw material. For building. I was an engineer before I became a soldier," he adds, almost apologetically.

"What the hell do you build with *protein*?" I ask.

"You do not build with it directly. But it is a component. It adds rigidity. Or flexibility, depending how you use it. Like in bones."

I look through the eyepiece of the sensor mast array and pan over to where the Lanky village stands, twenty kilometers away but very obvious on the red Mars dirt. Now that I see one closer up and in daylight, I am reminded of the skeletal remains of a long-dead animal.

"Like in bones," I say.

Underneath the Weasel, the ground shakes a little. Dmitry and I look at each other. Lieutenant Stahl slows the vehicle down and scans around for falling rocks or other signs of instability.

Then the ground shakes again, stronger than before. Small rocks and pebbles start bouncing down the slope in front of us.

"Volcano?" I offer.

"This part of Mars isn't volcanically active," Lieutenant Stahl says.

The shaking repeats, stronger still than the first two times.

"Helmets on," I suggest. "We need to get off the hillside before we end up in a rockslide."

A fourth tremor jolts the ground, and this one is so strong that it makes the Weasel move sideways a little. Then there's a deep, sonorous rumbling that starts in the valley somewhere and doesn't let up. It sounds like an earthquake, and it gets a little louder with every passing moment.

"Down there." Dmitry points. "Look."

A meter-wide crack has appeared in the plateau just to the south of the Lanky village. As we watch, it extends north, parting the ground like a world cut deeply with the world's largest and sharpest knife. We hear the sudden cracking and whiplash snapping of rock layers pulling apart. The surface crack races up to the Lanky village and disappears under the structure at its southernmost point. The sound that started out as a distant, rumbling cacophony is rising sharply in volume, and the tremors that accompany it get stronger by the second.

"Earthquake," I say. "A big-ass earthquake. Just what we needed right now."

"Not earthquake, I think," Dmitry says.

Over by the Lanky village, the ground has started to churn. The smaller rocks and the rubble are visibly bouncing on the ground with the vibrations of whatever is going on below the surface. The rumbling from below fills the whole valley and rolls across the plateau, a steady and energetic bass growl. It looks like two square kilometers of ground around the Lanky village have suddenly become semifluid. Then the crack bisecting the Lanky village widens. The earth on either side of it rises—five meters, ten, fifteen. The whole patch of ground around the Lanky structure heaves up, as if something huge is pushing through from below. Our vehicle, parked on a hill slope over ten kilometers away, shakes with the sonic energy of the low-frequency rumbling that increases with every second.

Then three kilometers of ground erupt upwards, and a gigantic oblong shape appears at the top of the new opening in the Martian soil. The top of it is rounded, and even though most of the object is still buried in the ground, I can tell just by looking at the curvature of the top part what it is that is bursting upwards through the rock and soil like the planet is giving birth. It's the sleek, deadly torpedo shape of a Lanky seed ship.

"Oh, fuck me running," I say.

Dmitry utters something at the same time in a low voice, probably the same sentiment expressed in Russian.

The Lanky village, the whole roughly dome-shaped structure, is connected to the top of the seed ship's hull. Now that the ship is breaking through the surface, soil and rock sliding off the hull like water off a surfacing submarine, the structure starts breaking apart. It looks like the seed ship is shedding itself of the latticework edifice, as if it's some component it no longer needs.

Maybe they aren't shelters after all, I think. The only logical conclusion is that every last one of the Lanky "settlements" is the surface component of a buried seed ship. Feelers, or roots maybe, but not Lanky housing. We still treat them as if they think the way we do, and they constantly show us that alien means *alien.*

"It's taking off," Lieutenant Stahl says with amazement. "How is it taking off? In atmosphere? It's *enormous.*"

"I have no idea," I say. "But if that thing makes orbit, it'll slice through the fleet like a sword through a soy block."

I fire up my combat-controller kit and dial in the direct link to *Phalanx* C2.

"Priority traffic. *Phalanx* C2, this is Tailpipe Red One, come in."

"Tailpipe Red One, copy four by five. Go ahead on priority traffic."

I send the video feed from the Weasel through the visual interface of my suit along with the next message.

"Request priority fire mission, nuclear release. There's a Lanky seed ship taking off from the surface eighty-three klicks northwest of LZ Red."

"Confirm your last, Tailpipe Red One. Did you say *a Lanky seed ship is taking off from the surface of Mars?*" The C2 officer's tone makes it clear that he thinks I've lost my marbles.

"Check the visual feed. He's halfway out of the ground right now. If he makes upper atmo and then orbit, nobody will go home today."

The C2 officer takes a few moments to check the feed and then breaks radio protocol by transmitting a very elaborate swear.

"Repeat, request priority fire mission, nuclear release. You have got to put some nukes on top of him before he's high enough. Do it right now. I am uploading TRP data."

"Tailpipe Red One, stand by."

I know that the C2 officer is making a panicked dash across CIC right now to tell the skipper, who is going to pick up the intership-comms handset in a few seconds to talk to the general in overall command of the task force. I predict that the answer won't take long, and my prediction proves correct. Twenty seconds later, I get a reply from *Phalanx*.

"Nuclear strike is authorized. The closest nuke-armed unit is *Kirov*, and she's repositioning right now. Shots out in seven minutes."

"Make it faster if they can," I reply. "Who knows how high this thing will be in four minutes."

"That impact will be an air burst for all intents and purposes," the C2 officer says. "You may not have enough time to get clear."

"There is no alternative, *Phalanx*. We need nukes on that ship now, or we all die today."

"Affirmative." The C2 controller pauses for a moment. "We passed the TRP data to *Kirov*. You have seven minutes to clear the area and get to cover."

"Copy that. Tailpipe Red One out."

I turn to Dmitry. "Talk to your pals on *Kirov*, and ask what kind of yield they're going to dial in for that nuke. Tell them to make it at least twenty kilotons. A hundred would be better."

Dmitry is on the radio for a quick and terse exchange. "Two megatons, single warhead," he says afterward.

"Shit," I say. "That's a big bang."

"Russian targeting systems are not so good as Commonwealth. We have to make up with bigger warhead."

"Get us out of here, Lieutenant," I say to Stahl, who is already spooling up the Weasel's engines.

"Where are we going?" Stahl asks.

He looks terrified, probably because he's never even been close to a nuclear warhead, never mind a detonation. The Euros declared themselves nuke-free seventy years ago, and to them an atomic warhead is some mystical angel of death. I've had enough shot into my general neighborhood to know their limitations well. They make a big bang, but the effects are predictable and avoidable if you know where to squat.

I check the topographic map and point to a spot on the other side of the hill from where we are parked right now.

"That ravine. Get us there in less than seven minutes, or our day is going to go to shit very quickly."

"Is already shit," Dmitry says.

As Lieutenant Stahl turns the car around and gooses it, I take one last look at the seed ship, which is now almost entirely out of the three-kilometer depression it left in the Martian soil. The latticework structure we dubbed the "village" has mostly fallen off the top of the hull, like withered roots that are no longer needed. There is something remarkably different about this seed ship—all the other ones I've ever seen have been obsidian black, but this one has the orange-red-ochre hue of the Mars soil that surrounds it.

"Shots out," *Phalanx* reports two minutes later. "Nuclear strike inbound to your TRP, splash in three minutes, forty-five seconds."

We are racing around the hill and down the slope at the same time, aiming for the shelter of the ravine that will be on the opposite side of the five-hundred-meter hill from the nuclear detonation. I know from experience that we will ride out the strike down there just fine unless the Russians misdial the yield selector and drop twenty-five megatons instead of two, but the German lieutenant is clearly scared shitless.

"I thought nukes don't work against a seed ship," he says, his eyes glued to his heads-up display again.

"They don't work in *space*," I reply. "Without an atmosphere, you don't have a shock wave, or thermal effects. And the Lanky ships have hulls that are twenty meters thick. They block out the hard gamma rays. Nukes aren't very effective in space. But down here in atmo, it's a different story."

Or so I hope anyway, I think. If our biggest stick can't even hurt them on the ground, then we are truly fucked, because we can't shoot Orions into planets and moons we intend to keep for ourselves.

Three minutes.

Lieutenant Stahl races the Weasel down the thirty-degree slope on the other side of the hill, as straight a line as possible without making us somersault at eighty klicks per hour. Even with the hillside between us, I can hear the humming roar of the seed ship slowly gaining altitude. I didn't see fusion-rocket nozzles, or anything resembling the systems we use to achieve atmospheric or space flight. Our capital ships can't even make atmo landings or takeoffs, and they have to be built in orbital fleet yards. And the Lankies seem to be growing theirs in the ground of whatever world they take over. There are dozens of recorded Lanky "settlements" on Mars, which means there are dozens of seed ships under the soil, waiting to burst forth and make orbit. I send a priority message to Ground Force Red C2 and apprise them of the situation as well, so they're not surprised when they see the mushroom cloud from a two-megaton nuclear explosion on the horizon in a few minutes.

Two minutes.

We reach the bottom of the hill. The ravine is narrow and has very steep walls, and Stahl almost flips the Weasel when we roll down into it, but he catches it just in time. I mark the best spot for us to ride out the nuke, and he navigates through the ravine around rocks the size of mules.

"Please tell me this vehicle is equipped with full nuclear-protection capabilities," I say to Lieutenant Stahl.

"Of course," he says. "It has overpressure systems and filtration, and an automatic decontamination system."

One minute.

"Stop here," I tell the German lieutenant. "Set the brakes. Park it tail-on to ground zero. Hurry, hurry."

Lieutenant Stahl does as he's told and then checks the tightness of his safety harness, as if that would make a difference if we got caught in the blast wave in a ten-ton scout car.

"Ready, Dmitry?" I ask. The Russian doesn't look a tenth as nervous as Lieutenant Stahl, but Dmitry rarely looks upset or agitated about anything.

"Is Russian artillery strike," he says.

"Hits mostly in the right spot," I finish for him, and he grins. We both know that if the warhead hits the wrong side of this hill, we'll be gone in a millisecond anyway, and there will be no time for pain or regrets.

The Russian warhead hits its target on the other side of the hill as promised, only four seconds after the predicted time-on-target. Two-megaton detonations pack a wallop. I've only ever ridden two out that were bigger, a five and a seven, but this doesn't seem much less powerful. We are shielded from the blast and heat waves behind millions of tons of Martian rock, but the sound is still world ending in its magnitude. There's nothing that sounds like a nuke exploding when you're close to ground zero. It sounds like the planet is rending itself in half. The shock wave transmits through the rock and bounces our little scout car around to the point where I'm glad for the excellent five-point harnesses on the Eurocorps vehicle. On the dash, a bunch of warning lights for the environmental system go ballistic as the vehicle's computer detects the alarmingly rapid changes in outside temperature, air pressure, and radiation.

I am used to riding out nuclear strikes in nothing but a bug suit, and I know that Dmitry is experienced in that field as well, but the German is very unnerved. For several minutes, there's nothing to see outside as the massive radioactive dust plume from the detonation makes debris ping off the hull of the scout car. The sound from the nuke rolls over the landscape and gets reflected back from the surrounding mountains, so it washes over us again and again.

When the effects have rolled over us, I tap Lieutenant Stahl on the shoulder. "Go back around and up to five hundred. I want to do a poststrike assessment to make sure we got the bastard."

"Shouldn't we wait a bit for everything to pass?"

"The worst is gone, and the radiation will be around for a while. Besides, you don't want to miss your first atomic-mushroom close-up."

We drive back around the hill to the spot we had occupied before. The valley and the plateau below us aren't visible to the naked eye because the air is thick with red-and-brown Mars dust bounced off the ground by the low-altitude detonation of the atomic warhead. I switch to alternate view modes until I have an infrared/thermal overlay. Lieutenant Stahl can't seem to stop gaping at the evil-looking black-and-red mushroom cloud that is roiling into the sky just seven or eight klicks in front of us.

Below, the seed ship is a shattered hull half its original size. Parts of it are still glowing white-hot with the energy from the point-blank nuclear fireball that evaporated the top half of the three-kilometer-long hull. The ship has crashed back to the ground and back into the depression from which it rose a few minutes ago.

"*Phalanx*, Tailpipe Red One. Poststrike assessment."

"Go ahead on poststrike."

"Direct hit, target destroyed. Pass it on to the gunnery department on *Kirov*. They just bagged themselves a seed ship."

"Copy that, Tailpipe Red One."

"And pass the word on to the task force. They need to put all the remaining nukes onto the settlements we've charted. I think they all have seed ships under the surface."

"Be advised that we already have that in the works."

"We are heading to LZ Red for dustoff. Tailpipe One out."

I kill the comms and nudge Lieutenant Stahl to draw his attention away from the mushroom cloud.

"Head for the spaceport," I say. "We need to get there before the last drop ship leaves."

"Two megatons," Lieutenant Stahl says, wonder and awe in his voice. "That's a bit of overkill, is it not?"

"Is no such thing as *overkill,*" Dmitry replies. "Anything worth breaking is worth breaking a lot."

CHAPTER 21

GETTING OFF THE BEACH AT HIGH TIDE

It takes us two hours to get back to Olympus Spaceport. The Weasel is very fast, but the area is lousy with big groups of Lankies moving in the same direction, and Lieutenant Stahl has his hands full weaving a course between them that keeps us at a safe distance.

"Well, that's gonna be a no-go," I say when I see the scene on the plateau in front of the spaceport.

The vista reminds me of the ancient western movies they used to play on the Networks in the shitty hours of the morning—natives circling the wagon trains of the intrepid settlers. There are many hundreds of Lankies on the perimeter of the spaceport, all pressing in and trying to overcome the defenses. There are drop ships in the air and attack birds making runs from higher altitudes, but our presence in the skies seems greatly diminished from when the fourth wave arrived and the base operations were in full swing. From ten klicks away, I see gun emplacements on the tarmac, autonomous SRA autocannon mounts next to crewed NAC autocannons, mules with twenty-five-millimeter gun turrets, and lots and lots of infantry in firing positions between the buildings and hangars. Inside the base, at the drop-ship pad, there are Wasps and Akulas taking off without engaging Lankies, and I am guessing they're loaded with civvies and troops for the evacuation that must have been ordered while we were busy with calling in the nuke on the seed ship and the long drive back to the base.

"We will not make it past the Lankies," Lieutenant Stahl says. "And if we do, we may run into friendly fire."

I get on the brigade channel and contact C2. The officer who answers the radio sounds very stressed.

"C2, this is Tailpipe Red One. I am ten klicks outside the wire with the Russian combat controller and our Eurocorps liaison, and there's about a thousand Lankies in our way. Any way you can send a drop ship to pick us up?"

"Uh, that's a negative, Tailpipe Red One. All our birds are committed to attack runs or evacs. You're going to have to run the gauntlet. But be quick about it. The evac window is only open for another sixty-five minutes, and *Phalanx* is out of missiles, so there won't be any more holes in the minefield."

"Well, fuck me." I decide not to argue with the C2 officer. It takes a drop ship forty minutes just to make it up into orbit, so we have twenty-five minutes to hitch a ride or be stranded on Mars until our air supplies quit. "On our way. Save us three seats."

"I have bad news for you, Lieutenant," I say. "No pickup from our side. How about yours?"

"Eurocorps has already evacuated," he says, a hint of dejection in his voice.

"Dmitry?"

The Russian just shakes his head.

"Okay, then. We have twenty-five minutes to make the landing pad if we want to get out of here alive."

"You take gun, and I drive vehicle," Dmitry suggests. "Is like busy traffic hour in Moscow, remember?"

"I cannot let you drive, because you have no official clearance on this vehicle type," Lieutenant Stahl says. Dmitry and I grin, and my grin turns into a short laugh when I realize that the German lieutenant isn't joking.

The air base has two access roads, one from the north and one from the south. We are coming in from the north, using the smooth pavement to bring the Weasel up to maximum speed. Three kilometers before the main gate, a group of Lankies block the road, but their attention is turned away from us.

"All units, all units!" I shout into the local defense channel. "You have a friendly MAV coming in on the north road, so check your fire."

Lieutenant Stahl swerves around the Lankies, who react too late to keep up with us. The Weasel has an honest-to-goodness warning horn, and the German lieutenant honks it as we zoom past the Lankies, emitting a loud and jaunty three-note warble from unseen amplified speakers. Dmitry just shakes his head and grins at me.

We could be running under stealth, but then our own troops won't see us and may mistakenly put cannon fire into us, so Lieutenant Stahl leaves the camo off and relies on his speed and agility to make it across the beaten zone in front of the airfield's runways. We are dodging groups of Lankies while tracers and cannon shells are coming our way from the direction of the hangars. I feel like I just drove into a live-fire range from the wrong end. Belatedly, I hope that the SRA cannon techs have added Eurocorps and NAC vehicles to the List of Things That Aren't Enemies to Be Shot to Ribbons in the targeting computers of their autonomous sentry guns.

A cannon burst streaks by our right side on the way to some unseen Lanky behind us, and more than once I hear rifle fire pinging off the lightly armored hull of the Weasel. To his credit, Lieutenant Stahl drives his vehicle like Halley flies a drop ship. He bobs, weaves, and anticipates the moves of the Lankies in front of us so he can thread the needle with the agile little scout car. With nothing to shoot at or spot, all Dmitry and I can do is to sit tight and hope we don't have cannon shells exploding in our laps before we've made it back to the ever-shrinking patch of friendly territory surrounding the hardened spacecraft shelters.

A kilometer before the outer edge of the defensive line, there's a loud explosion at the front of the scout car, and something blows up one of the Weasel's tires. The vehicle jolts violently and starts fishtailing, and Dmitry and I hold on to the grab handles above our seats, expecting the ride to tumble and flip any second. But Lieutenant Stahl manages to get the Weasel under control after a few terrifying seconds. When he opens the throttle again, there's a distinctly broken sound coming from the front-left quarter of the Weasel, a grinding scrape combined with a rhythmic thumping that tells of a shredded wheel at least, and probably a broken axle or suspension. Every time we hit a depression in the ground, the front end of the Weasel thumps hard enough to jar our teeth. With eight hundred meters to go to friendly lines, we may even make it at a run if we're forced to abandon the scout car, but the idea of climbing out into that much outgoing gunfire makes my stomach clench with fear.

Finally we are through the beaten zone and across both runways. Lieutenant Stahl lets off the throttle a bit. From my position in the right rear of the Weasel, I can see that his face is drenched in sweat. We're all breathing heavily. Dmitry reaches out and pats Lieutenant Stahl on the shoulder.

"Excellent driving. I take back the *durak*. For this, you can come drink with me on *Kiev* any time."

The infantry between the hangars gradually pulls back, letting the sentry guns and the few close-air-support units overhead do the work of holding back the surge of attacking Lankies. Hundreds of them are strewn across the beaten zone in front of the runways, but hundreds more are advancing. Evac window or not, this base will fall in the next thirty minutes unless we get relieved by a fresh regiment and a few dozen Shrikes.

We roll over to the drop-ship landing pad, where hundreds of people are trying to get into fewer than a dozen remaining drop ships. We get into the line for one of the ships, a Dragonfly, and the crew chief ushers us in. The seat rows are already packed with troops, most of them exhausted-looking SI troopers with thousand-yard stares. I take a spot on the floor and strap myself into the cargo eyelets set into the deck. I'll still get bounced around if it gets choppy, but at least I won't free-fall through the troop compartment and break my neck on the tail ramp. The Dragonfly, made for forty-odd troops and gear, has almost twice as many in it. Belatedly, I realize that I forgot my rifle inside the Eurocorps scout car, but it's not like it would do me any good in here. If we get shot down by a proximity mine, I'll be dead with or without a gun, and right now I am way too exhausted to care. Dmitry and Lieutenant Stahl are in different aisles, and I can't see them from where I am strapped down, but I know they're on board, so our fates will be intertwined for just a little while longer.

"Hey, Lieutenant," a familiar voice says from the row of seat slings to my right. I turn to see Sergeant First Class Crawford, the trooper who did the breakneck ride from Tuttle 250 back to the spaceport with me on the ATVs.

"Sergeant Crawford," I say. "Glad to see you made it to pickup."

"You, too, sir. You look like hammered shit, by the way. No offense."

"Rough day," I say. "Did you ever get your hot shower?"

"Not yet. Maybe up on the carrier."

"They have to run you through decon anyway."

"Well, there you go. First bright spot of the day."

"No, it ain't," I say. "You'll get to strip in front of the whole flight deck."

"At this point," she replies, "I'm so fucking tired that I wouldn't care if they broadcasted that live to the whole fleet."

We are the second-to-last drop ship to take off from Olympus Spaceport, the battered and tired remnants of First Brigade. Red Beach will be crawling with Lankies in a few minutes, but we left none behind except for our dead. I know we'll be passing through the hole in the minefield at the very end of its safe window, and if the Lanky mines have regrouped themselves a little ahead of their usual schedule, we'll all be frozen corpses in space in thirty minutes.

The scene outside is apocalyptic. I tap into the ship's cameras with tired fingers, using my combat-controller access one more time in regulation-skirting fashion, and almost wish I had remained ignorant about what's going on down on the surface. The Lankies are flooding into the spaceport on all sides, only held back in some spots by cannon fire from automatic sentry guns set up to cover the retreat of the last infantry troops. The Shrikes escorting us are making attack runs into the surging enemy crowd, dropping dozens with cannon shells and blowing more of them apart with wing-launched missiles, but already it's like trying to put out a bonfire with half a cup of water.

On the plains beyond the spaceport, where Sergeant Crawford and I battled the Lankies on our ride back from Tuttle 250, many more are coming out of holes in the ground that I know weren't there when we set out for the Tuttle 250 rescue. I never thought we'd be able to kill every last Lanky on Mars, but seeing more of them on the surface than we ever saw when we still had our full combat strength is disheartening and demoralizing. The cruisers don't have the nukes or the kinetic warheads to kill all of these new Lankies. And knowing how long it took just to train the troops we just lost, I know that we'd need twenty years of boot-camp cycles to get enough boots on the ground to stand a chance. Whatever the next phase of this fight will look like, we'll have to think of an entirely new angle to take.

In the distance, I can see the blinding spheres of nuclear detonations. The fleet got the word, and they are dropping all the nukes they have onto the Lanky "settlements." If every single one of them is a buried seed ship under construction—growing perhaps?—we can't afford to leave a single site untouched. But I take some grim satisfaction out of the knowledge that if we have to come up with new tactics, so do they, because they can't rely on the overwhelming advantage of those seed ships anymore.

I lie down on the rubber-lined deck of the Dragonfly between rows of strange SI troopers in filthy and dusty uniforms, and I find that I wasn't even aware of how tired my body is until I let all my muscles relax. And even with all the chaos thousands of feet below me, with the uncertainty of the orbital ascent and the nuclear strikes lighting up the surface of Mars, I find myself drifting off to exhausted sleep.

I don't wake up again until we're on the flight deck of NACS *Polaris* an hour later.

I spend the next half day wasting time on the carrier with decontamination, grabbing chow, and getting a fresh set of fatigues from the supply division. The flight deck is packed nose-to-ass with people and equipment, but unlike on the trip to Mars, nothing is neat or orderly. The emergency dustoff happened so quickly that the crews had no time for organization. The drop ships loaded us up and dumped us wherever they had space, and it takes the three of us six hours to catch a ride on a drop ship that's transporting *Phalanx* personnel back to their own ship. I look around in the cargo hold on the short trip over to *Phalanx*, but I don't see anyone else from the SOCOM detachment other than

Dmitry and Lieutenant Stahl, and my heart sinks a little. The MilNet is off-line, and TacLink is hopelessly overloaded and chaotic. I try to get a message through to Halley, but the network is so slow that even the failure notification takes thirty minutes to get back to me. Fighting against awful odds on the surface is one thing, but being stuck in orbit on a warship in near chaos, with no way to communicate with your wife or even check on her whereabouts, is a thousand times worse.

―――――――――

Back on *Phalanx*, I report in with the CO, even though there's nothing I want more right now than a private shower in my stateroom in Grunt Country and twenty-four straight hours of sleep. Colonel Yamin is in CIC with Major Masoud, who regards me with an expression that almost looks like paternalistic concern.

"We got our asses kicked," I conclude after I give my version of events.

"How do you figure, Lieutenant?" Major Masoud says.

"We'll never get them off Mars. They're underground now. They figured out how we fight, and they adopted countermeasures. It would take ten times the troops we had today, and we'd still lose half of them if we went down into the tunnels and flushed them out. Greenland was enough for me, sir."

"Tactically, we have a stalemate on Mars," Major Masoud agrees. "But we achieved almost all of our objectives. We rescued five thousand civilians, Lieutenant. Every holdout installation except for one. And we never needed to take all of Mars, just deny its use to the Lankies."

"If those underground seed ships make it into orbit, they'll have twice as many as before, sir. I'd bet that every settlement down there is really a seed ship. And I've seen other stuff . . ."

My voice trails off when I think of the Lankies carrying the dead bodies of our SI troopers back to their tunnels. Maybe some of them were even still alive. And we won't ever be able to go back and rescue them, or recover any bodies.

"We are leaving a garrison fleet in orbit," Major Masoud says. "The cruisers are taking on more ammunition as soon as the next wave of supply ships gets here. They are nuking all the Lanky sites they can find right now. I'm sure that in the next few days, they'll nuke them all a few times over. The fight isn't won yet, but by God, we haven't lost here. We made them *bleed*."

He looks at me and points to the CIC hatch.

"Go take care of yourself, Lieutenant Grayson. I don't want to see you out and about for another forty-eight hours. We will have plenty of time for a thorough debriefing on the way back to Earth. Clean up, eat, and get some sleep. We won a great victory today."

"Yes, sir," I say. This is the first order Major Masoud has ever given me where I don't feel like I'm being pulled around by marionette strings, and I don't utter a word of dissent.

There are things I have to take care of before I even fix myself. Back in Grunt Country, which is empty except for my Russian and Euro comrades who are already in their bunks, I go into my stateroom and turn on the neural-networks terminal. My personal message box is just the way I left it, with only two new messages on top of the read stack. One is from my mother's privileged-dependent account, and the other is from Gunny Philbrick. I check the time stamp of Philbrick's message and see that it's from today. I don't need to open it to know that he's okay, and if Humphrey or Nez got killed down on Mars, I don't want to know right now anyway. But there's no message from Halley, and I know she would have sent one if she had made it back from the surface already.

I fire off a message to her account to let her know that I'm okay, and tell her to reply the second she gets into network range again. We don't even have casualty lists out yet—everything is still in fresh postbattle chaos—and the pleasure of a hot shower and a clean bunk is tempered by my anxiety. I don't know if my wife is still alive, in the cockpit of a drop ship ferrying soldiers up to their carrier, or maybe holed up on the surface of Mars somewhere, waiting for a rescue that won't come. I don't want to contemplate her death, or the myriad ways in which she may have died down there, but my brain serves up a few of those anyway.

We won a great victory today, Major Masoud said to me in CIC. But I don't feel like we won a great victory. I feel like we went up in the ring against an evenly matched opponent, and we both took turns beating the living shit out of each other and left the ring without a clear winner.

I don't hear anything from Halley on the entire weeklong ride back from Mars to Gateway Station.

I log into my data terminal compulsively about fifty times every day, even though I have a PDP in my pocket that will relay the same messages to me, just so I don't have to wait for the wireless delay if a message does come in. But for a week straight, my inbox stays empty except for meaningless fleet bullshit and a few messages from my old friend Gunny Philbrick, who dropped into LZ Blue with Humphrey and Nez as his squad leaders. Humphrey is still alive but earned her third Purple Heart from friendly-fire shrapnel. Nez is gone, killed in action while trying to hold back a Lanky counteroffensive with a squad of green SI troopers, who all died to the last man and woman.

I know that Dmitry made one of the last flights out, because we were on the same Dragonfly. He took a shuttle over to the SRA carrier a few hours later, sparse with his good-byes in what I now know to be typical Russian brevity. I do wonder if Maksim survived the battle. As rock hard as Dmitry is, I feel that the loss of Maksim would wound him more than any Lanky ever could, and I hope the best for my new friend and his spouse.

In those cheesy military flicks on the Networks, things would have gone differently. I would have dropped with my wife in the cockpit of my drop ship and all my friends and comrades by my side, and we would have fought together. We would have taken some losses, friends dying in heroic last stands and giving profound last statements, and it would have all taught us something about duty and sacrifice and the futility of war. But this is real life. In a real war, you drop into battle with troops you've never met before, and your spouse is deployed thousands of kilometers away from you. In real battle, good people die fast and awful deaths, and terrible people make it out unscathed. Dozens of civilians die at the moment of their long-awaited rescue because an officer makes a bad split-second call, and then that officer dies with those civvies and never even gets a chance to regret his mistake.

In a real war, the enemy can take a savage beating and then turn the tables on you in an hour to force a bloody stalemate even though you've each killed thousands on the other side. Tires blow, batteries die, vital shots miss their target, and unlikely shots score almost-impossible bull's-eyes. When I was young and impressionable, I thought of war as a sort of romantic crucible, a test of one's manhood and mettle. In reality, it's merely a challenge to one's ability to stay sane.

But we will be back, again and again, as long as it takes until either we get wiped out or we annihilate them. Because just like the Lankies, we, too, are a species who just doesn't seem to know when it is beaten.

EPILOGUE

When the fleet returns to Gateway a week after Mars, the civilian fleet in Earth orbit repeats their earlier gesture for us. They line the approaches to the space station and blink their lights in synchronicity, to show their gratitude for what we did for the planet. I want to feel appreciation as I watch the honor salute on the external camera feed on the screen in my stateroom, but all I can think of is that Halley would have enjoyed seeing this, and that the last message I ever typed to her was right after seeing the same honor display when we departed Gateway. We all have shore leave now—technically for thirty days, but it's understood that no brass is going to jump anyone's shit for overstaying their leave this time around. I've never felt such a profound level of mental and physical fatigue before, a deep and aching tiredness that goes beyond a lack of sleep or a hard-fought battle.

I'd spent most of that week clutching my PDP and waiting for the incoming message signal to buzz. I sent Halley a message every day. At first, they were just requests, then pleas to get in touch with me. By the third day, I was writing her longer messages, detailing the stuff we're going to do together once we're back home, knowing full well that she may never read what I wrote.

Now that we are back, we have many after-battle briefings where everyone brings everyone else up to speed. The task force got off relatively light in space—we lost the priceless *Agincourt*, of course, but rescued most of her crew, and only one space control cruiser and an older frigate were lost to Lanky mines during the operation.

We only lost one member of our SOCOM team—the Spaceborne Rescueman, Lieutenant Paquette. He jumped into a drop-ship crash site and defended two wounded pilots and a dead crew chief against six Lankies and took down two before they overwhelmed the site. Word has it that Brigade is going to put him in for the Medal of Honor. All the Russians survived the battle and transferred to the carrier *Minsk* a day after our departure. I have grown fond of Dmitry, and I'm glad that he gets to go home and see his husband, Maksim, again, which makes the uncertainty about Halley's fate even more painful than it is already. There are a lot of dog tags to sort out, and there's a long list of names of troopers whose tags aren't officially collected but whose whereabouts are unknown. With so many brigades dispersed over so many ships, it'll take days to sort out everything—at least that's what I tell myself.

Twenty thousand SI troopers and SOCOM troops dropped onto Mars. Eleven thousand five hundred returned, and almost two thousand of those are wounded. Four thousand nine hundred are confirmed dead, and another three thousand six hundred are missing and presumed killed. On the opposing side, the Lankies got it much worse. We killed over ten thousand in direct combat, and God only knows how many when we nuked every single "settlement" seed-ship location from orbit at the end of the battle. They lost their entire fleet above Mars, and while there are suspected to be two or three stragglers out there patrolling the Alcubierre nodes, they haven't approached Mars or bothered the garrison fleet that's keeping an eye on things from above. We rescued eighteen different holdout shelters all over Mars and only failed to save the population of a single shelter.

Mars was a write-off from the beginning. The Lanky terraforming would have taken ten to fifteen years to reverse even if we had scraped all the Lankies off the planet. With the radiation from fifty high-yield nukes dropped on the seed-ship building sites, it will take much longer now for Mars to become suitable for life again. We can't use it anymore—but neither can the Lankies, and that was the objective all along: to take away their operating base in the solar system and remove the direct threat to Earth. They can't move against us with what they have left on Mars, with no seed ships to threaten Earth, and we have moved back into our respective corners with our noses bleeding and our eyes swollen shut. But I'm sure both our species will be back for the next round once we have caught our breath and nursed our wounds. We've pushed each other too far for this to have an indecisive ending. Either we walk away from this, or they do, but there is no room in this universe for both our species as long as they keep coming for what's ours.

I feel like I've left half of me behind on Mars, and I won't get that part of me back, if at all, until I know for sure where my wife is now and what happened to her. But my PDP is still silent when I gather my things and leave the ship for the lonely shuttle ride back to Earth.

I go down to Liberty Falls, because it's the only place I can think of being right now, even though Halley isn't with me. I leave my small kit bag in a locker at the transit station and go for a walk through the town. Winter has arrived, and there's a layer of snow on the lawns and the sidewalks. Outside the transit station, I step onto the lawn, brush the snow aside with one hand, and then touch the cold and frozen grass underneath, letting my fingers warm it up, remembering what it felt like in the spring and summer. I don't want to go to Chief Kopka's place just yet, because I don't want to see their faces when I walk in without my wife and they will know without me having to say a word. Instead, I walk through the town center and over to the little waterfall that gave the town its name. It's not overly impressive, just a six-foot cascade dropping over an artificial ledge prettied up with river stones, but it's a peaceful spot, and Halley liked it.

I stand on the little wooden bridge and look out over the river, the waterfall murmuring softly behind me, and I realize that I have no idea what I will do with the rest of my life if Halley is gone from it. I have a promise to keep to the Lazarus Brigades, to train their troops for a year and a half, and I'll have to resign my commission to keep that promise. But that's not something I have to do today, or tomorrow, or even next week. I take the military-issue PDP out of my pocket and turn it in my hands. It's the electronic leash that can summon me back to service any time, but I'm tired of heeding its call, and if that's all I have left in life, it's not much of a life at all.

With its smooth edges and its shopworn finish, the PDP itself looks like a river stone. I remember how many good and bad messages I got on that tiny little black-and-white screen, and I realize how many more of them were bad than good.

I want to pitch the PDP into the river. I want to be done with the life to which this device has me tied. And right now, with my wife missing and the tiredness in my bones seemingly permanent, I have to fight that urge more than usual. The military has given me a measure of self-determination, but also a lifetime of bad memories and an endless source for horrible dreams. But it has also brought Halley into my life, and I know that despite the sadness and exhaustion I feel right now, I'd do it all over again just because of that bunk assignment in boot-camp platoon 1066.

The buzz of an incoming message tickles my palm. I stare at the screen for a moment and consider pitching the thing into the drink anyway. Then I turn the device on and read the message on the screen.

>Still kicking.

It's not signed, and doesn't need to be.

The sudden joy and profound relief I feel makes the load I've been carrying for the last week roll off my shoulders in the span of a single long breath. I smile and slip the PDP back into my pocket. Then I close my eyes and breathe in the cold and clean winter air of Vermont. And just like that, it smells like home again.

ABOUT THE AUTHOR

Photo © 2016 by Rob Strong

Marko Kloos was born and raised in Germany, in and around the city of Münster. In the past, he has been a soldier, bookseller, freight dockworker, and corporate IT administrator before he decided that he wasn't cut out for anything other than making stuff up for a living.

Marko writes primarily science fiction and fantasy, his first genre love ever since his youth, when he spent his allowance mostly on SF pulp serials. He's the author of the bestselling Frontlines series of military science fiction and is a member of George R.R. Martin's Wild Cards writer consortium.

Marko resides at Castle Frostbite in New Hampshire with his wife, two children, and a roving pack of vicious dachshunds. His official website is at www.markokloos.com. He can be reached at frontlines@markokloos.com and found on Twitter (where he spends way too much time) @markokloos.